You and Me Against the World

A novel by

Lisa A. Nichols

PublishAmerica
Baltimore

First printing

ISBN: 1-59129-417-7
PUBLISHED BY PUBLISHAMERICA BOOK PUBLISHERS
www.publishamerica.com
Baltimore

Printed in the United States of America

This was written for my Lord and Savior, Jesus Christ

Acknowledgements

There are some people I need to acknowledge who ultimately contributed in some way to this project.

First of all and most importantly – My Lord – thank You for the talents You've given me and for allowing me to use them in a way that glorifies You. Thank You for keeping me confident about my writing when there seemed to be so many things about myself I wasn't confident or sure about. This project was something I believed in. Thanks for the inspiration.

To all the leaders at FCC – thank you for your leadership and dedication to the church body throughout the years. You have all acted as good friends and role models in the faith.

To my sisters – you guys (gals!) are ultimately the best friends I've ever had and you have supported and encouraged me in my writing from the very beginning. Thank you.

To Mom and Dad – thanks for being great parents and for always believing that I could accomplish anything, whether it was academics, drama, work, or some other activity. You have always supported me in all my decisions and have always had confidence in my abilities. You so often tell me how proud of me you are, and I would like to tell you that I have always been proud of you. You are truly the greatest parents anybody could ask for. Jesus loves you. I pray for both of you. Seek Him.

To Publish America – thank you for giving me this opportunity to have one of my dreams fulfilled and for giving me a step up.

And to everybody else out there who believed in me and prayed for me, I thank you.

Prologue

Glory belongs to God, whose power is at work in us. By this power he can do infinitely more than we can ask or imagine.
– Ephesians 3:20

October, 1997

The soft steering wheel that Lindsey clutched in her two hands felt icy, despite the fact that it was only October. However, on this particular October night, the air was chilly, and Lindsey finally reached over to switch the heater button on after driving for several minutes in the cold car. The car was warmed up after only five minutes, and the heat quickly aggregated itself inside the vehicle; but Lindsey's mind was too swirled with emotions and anxiety to concentrate on the temperature much.

The light peach-colored '88 Honda Accord drove smoothly and almost seemed to flow without the aid of Lindsey's foot lightly depressing the accelerator or her hands directing the steering wheel. In the state that Lindsey was in at that moment, the car might as well have been doing all the work on its own. Tears were streaming down her face uncontrollably as she tried all she could to keep them back and to concentrate on the road.

Surprisingly, many cars were on the four-lane highway this night. Traffic was slow, and every time Lindsey attempted to pass a vehicle, another was in the way, and then another. No matter how many times she tried, the vehicles just wouldn't let her pass. She was driving below the speed limit, so she found no harm in trying to get ahead of everyone else. Lindsey felt almost as if the drivers of these vehicles were trying to annoy her on purpose, and she quickly lost her patience. She took to her advantage the next exit that she could make her way to and began to drive on a back road that followed the highway.

Blackness projected the whole area around her, and as she drove out of town, the brightness of the many restaurant signs, vehicle headlights, and house lights quickly dimmed. Soon the only light available at all was the beam of brightness protruding from the front of Lindsey's car, and the distant spots of light provided by the highway's traffic many feet away. Close by, on the right side of the road, large trees illuminated and swayed in the cool October wind. The sight was eerie, and Lindsey felt a bit of fear climbing up inside her. She took her right hand from the steering wheel and turned up the radio, which had been playing quietly for the past twenty minutes. Recognizing a song she knew, Lindsey tried to sing and to fill her mind with the lyrics of the song. However, the song failed to drown out the feelings which were dominating her, feelings of anger, frustration, sadness, depression, helplessness, and, most of all, loneliness.

Lindsey had thought that this moment would bring her freedom and the feeling of joy in finally setting out to accomplish something. She was going to find her father. After so many years, she would be able to stare into his face and know she was part of someone. She could have someone to care for her and to take care of her. She could share her life with him and inform him on everything about herself that he'd missed over the years. Lindsey wanted her father to know how she grew up, how she had lived without him, and to reveal all of her beliefs, fears, strengths, and values to him. She wanted him to know who she was, and most of all she wanted him to care.

Without warning, a gripping instant seized Lindsey as she was wheeled back to the past ten years; to the moment at which her heartbreak began.

* * *

She could recall it clearly: the graying dusk; the one-story, pea-green house; the rusty-colored backyard lawn; the creaky swing-set; the mud-caked plastic pool void of any water; and the wail of her mother's moan as it drifted from inside the house to Lindsey's refuge outside.

Eight-year-old Lindsey pushed herself out of the small empty pool and rushed through the back door, carrying her cabbage-patch doll with her. Before she turned the corner into the living room to find her mother draped over the couch despairingly, she instantanty knew what was coming.

"Why isn't Daddy home yet?" she asked, the hopefulness empty in her voice.

Lindsey knew he wasn't coming back even as the words escaped her lips. It was that eerie, dark pit in the depths of her stomach as it churned with certain doubt that told her, no, he's not coming home. He's gone for good.

For the first few days of his absence, Lindsey's mother had told her that Dad was doing business. Her uncertain eyes and quivering voice defied her testament, though, and Lindsey knew something else was wrong. Yet, she kept pace with the world around her as if nothing was out of place in it.

After a week, it was becoming difficult to adhere to the gone-away-on-business tale, so her mother told Lindsey Daddy was staying with friends on a short trip because he needed some space – whatever that meant. The story did account for the loss of his clothing and belongings, but not every single one of them, save a plastic razor and black comb hidden under the bathroom sink.

When Dad was absent for two weeks, Lindsey had already witnessed her mother's desperate attempts to locate him. She frantically phoned neighbors, friends and relatives, all in unsuccessful progress. Wanting to preserve Lindsey, she justified his absence by telling her that he was probably staying with his parents in California. But by that time Lindsey could see through the façade.

Now, almost a month later, she stood innocent and helpless before her depressed mother, whose sobbing body indicated the worst. Next to her on a small table the telephone receiver hung limply by its cord over the edge, almost hitting the ground.

Jillian Milholland lifted her face from the retreat of her arms and stared at Lindsey with swollen eyes. After a sniff and a wipe of her face, she pushed herself off of her stomach and into a sitting position, patting her knee for Lindsey to come sit. Lindsey sat on the coffee table.

"That was Dad on the phone," she said.

Lindsey's face lit up, and her back straightened with anticipation. "It was? Can I talk to him?"

"Well, he's already gone."

"Where is he, anyway?"

Jillian's extended sigh told Lindsey that a story was coming – a sad and complicated story.

"Your daddy's in another state somewhere, honey, in Virginia, and he says he's not coming back."

The sting of the words struck Lindsey's heart like an arrow and diminished the miniscule amount of hope that was still present within. Although she was expecting this, she began to feel faint and weak, like she would tip over and crash to the ground any second.

"Lindsey, he wants a divorce."

A divorce. Lindsey knew what that was. One of her school friends had parents who were divorced. But that girl always seemed just fine, even if she didn't live with both her mom and her dad.

Lindsey began to cry then, but she wasn't sure why. She knew that this had been coming … waiting … perched nearby, contemplating its dark attack.

Jillian moved over to the coffee table and put her arms around Lindsey, pulling her in close to comfort her. "I know," she said soothingly, going on in cliche about how moms and dads don't always get along and sometimes can't live with each other.

Lindsey rolled her eyes at it, and the emotionless tears ceased. "Mom," she interrupted, pulling away to gaze into Jillian's face.

"Yes."

"Why are you so sad about Dad leaving? I mean, he was always hurting you, so why should you be sad?"

Jillian's eyes glazed over as she thought about that. She touched the scar on her lip where it had once been split open by her husband and really didn't know why she was sad.

* * *

Lindsey sighed as she brought her arm up to her face to wipe away the tears that were jumping out of the corners of her eyes. And just as the drops of saline that came from her eyes started to downpour, so also did the drops of water coming from that dark world above the treetops. The rain began to beat down hard, and as it mixed with the wind, it started lashing at Lindsey's car horizontally.

"Dang it, I can't see!" Lindsey groaned. She switched her wipers to their fastest setting, and yet, the sheet of water running down her windshield didn't seem to be swept away any better. "Why the heck is it raining here? In Montana?" she questioned. The sky was dark, the wind was whistling, and the new falling rain didn't help to relieve Lindsey's emotional state. It only assisted in making it worse. She switched her lights to bright and leaned forward to see better, but her vision was blurred from both her damp eyes and the rain-clad windshield. The road on which she was driving started to wind, and Lindsey couldn't see more than a few feet ahead of the front of her car. She intuitively stepped on the brake to slow the vehicle.

Soon the road came to a clearing, and Lindsey was no longer surrounded by hills and trees. As she glanced to her left, she could make out the headlights of the automobiles crowding the highway many feet away. Feeling a little more safe, but not quite sure why, Lindsey's nerves calmed a bit. But the thickly falling rain and the wind didn't calm down. As Lindsey's car traveled straight ahead at a speed of 45 mph, an unidentifiable animal scurried across the road. Lindsey's headlights caught it, and it froze in the middle of the pavement. Large, frightened eyes flashed like lightning in Lindsey's vision as the animal innocently stared into the beams of light that overtook its once secured sphere on the road. Lindsey gasped as her foot hit the brake and her hands pulled the steering wheel to the left. The tires of the Honda screeched as they were suddenly forced to turn, and just as quickly as an eye can blink, the car was lying on its side in a ditch.

In the seconds after the accident, the only sounds to be heard were the hiss of the steaming engine, the whiz of the rotating tires in the air, and the last traces of Lindsey's scream as it echoed over the landscape.

One

My heart is in turmoil.
The terrors of death have seized me.
Fear and trembling have overcome me.
Horror has overwhelmed me.
– Psalm 55:4-5

Two months earlier....

Wednesday, August 27, 1997

Here I am, sitting alone outside, with the sun so bright that I can hardly see what I'm writing because of the glare. The sun, that heap of orange fire burning in the galaxy, is beating down hard, and I feel I might as well be in hell. Why not? Hell would be no better than here, if not better. My body is burning, from the inside out. I feel dead, like my soul has left me, and the only thing remaining of myself is lifeless skin and bones. I don't want to live anymore, not now....

I have nobody. My mother was buried today. It was a nice funeral, with flowers everywhere. It was so colorful: pink and blue, green and red, violet and orange. I could hardly tell we were even in a cemetery. It could've been a big garden for all anyone knew, and the funeral itself could've been a wedding for that matter, except for all the black dresses and suits everyone was wearing.

I've always wondered, why wear black to a funeral, and why wear white to a wedding? Do black and white symbolize sad and happy, or dismal and bright? I didn't wear black to my mom's funeral; I wore a flowery dress. My grandparents almost wouldn't let me, but I told them that it didn't matter what they said, because they couldn't make me wear anything against my will.

So if I didn't wear black, then does that mean I wasn't sad? I haven't cried yet, not for four days. Not even during the funeral did I cry, and I saw people crying who weren't even family or close friends with my mother. I couldn't cry. I didn't know how. But I wanted to, because I didn't want people thinking I was okay about the whole thing. I'm not okay. I just haven't lapsed into reality yet, I guess. Moms aren't supposed to die.

I'm almost eighteen, and here I am, writing everything I know in a stupid journal. I suppose I write a lot, though, because it's my emotional outlet – my way to convince myself of reality by writing it all down....

"Lindsey, come inside, we're going to eat soon!" Lindsey glanced up from her writing to find her grandmother standing in the sliding-glass doorway to the house and staring at her.

"Okay, I'll be in in a second!" she replied, returning to her work. Chelsea Johns strode slowly toward her granddaughter, who was sitting in a lawn chair in the middle of the backyard, and stood in front of her.

"Oh, good, don't move," Lindsey said. "You're blocking the sun."

"What are you doing, Lindsey?" Chelsea asked with a touch of annoyance.

"Just writing." Lindsey closed her journal and looked up at her grandmother.

"You've been outside the whole time since we got back from the funeral, but everybody else is inside. Don't you think you should go in and visit a little?"

"Well, if they really wanted to see me, then they would come outside," Lindsey replied flatly, squinting up at her grandmother. Then, feigning cheerfulness, she proceeded, "It's so nice outside anyway. What is it with people staying inside on a nice sunny day like this? What's wrong with them all?" Lindsey turned her journal over in her hands and stared out past her grandmother at the stretch of beach beyond.

Chelsea had noted Lindsey's arrogant and nonchalant attitude toward the happenings of the day, and it caused her blood to boil with aggravation. Chelsea had found herself becoming aggravated at Lindsey almost every day lately. Her rudeness and seemingly unaware conscience toward anybody's feelings but her own had collided with Chelsea on a number of occasions, and she constantly found herself grappling with the disrespectful young lady.

Lindsey hadn't always been so cold around others. Of course there were times growing up when she would argue with her parents and grandparents, or ignore them if she was angry with them, but Chelsea had known that was typical behavior of a teenager. However, recently it had come to a climax with Jillian's death. Chelsea told herself Lindsey was just upset and shocked at her mother's sudden death, but nevertheless, she didn't feel it was right for Lindsey to isolate herself the way she had been lately and ignore the welfare of all the other people who had been shaken by Jillian's passing. At least she could show a little sensibility and thought toward Chelsea's friends and neighbors. For heaven's sake, Lindsey had deliberately worn a bright, flowered dress to the funeral! How unnecessary, not to mention it had embarrassed Chelsea. She wasn't unaware of the odd stares and pity-filled gazes the guests at the funeral had shot at Lindsey.

All at once, Chelsea leaned down toward Lindsey and grabbed Lindsey's chin in her hand. "What's wrong with you?" she asked firmly.

"They're not even family!" Lindsey growled, tossing her head back. "Why do I need to visit them? They're all just feeling sorry for me anyway!"

"You are feeling sorry for yourself!" Chelsea snapped.

"Oh, like hell I am!" Lindsey shouted, bolting up from her position on the lawn chair. "If I was feeling sorry for myself, then I'd be crying! You haven't seen me cry once yet, have you? I can't cry, because to me, this isn't happening! My mother isn't dead! She's just out of town somewhere, and dumped me here! So don't begin to tell me how I feel because you don't know!"

Chelsea stood silent for a second, bewildered by her granddaughter's fierce reaction, and started to back away towards the house. "Don't you ever talk to me like that again, Lindsey. How dare you! I deserve more respect than that, and these people deserve your company." Chelsea's words were accompanied by her twisted facial features as she fixed her stunned eyes on Lindsey's. "You'd better be in the house in five minutes," Chelsea finished. Lindsey thought she could see her grandmother's pursed lips quivering before Chelsea turned and walked rapidly towards the house.

Outside, Lindsey stood, furious, wondering if she should chance her next argument. "Or else what?" she finally shouted. Chelsea turned at the door.

"What?"

"What if I don't come in in five minutes, huh? Then what?" She fixed a dead stare into Chelsea's eyes, raising her eyebrows only slightly. It had become a sport of hers lately to challenge her grandmother. She wasn't sure why, but since her mother died she had unknowingly deemed her grandmother the enemy, her source of negative displacement. Chelsea didn't seem to respond to Lindsey's moods very understandingly, and it bothered Lindsey that Chelsea always had something to say to her, trying to direct how she should feel and act. It was true, the colorful young Lindsey full of surprises and the mild-tempered Chelsea, although oftentimes curt, had always clashed, throughout Lindsey's growing up. Overall, though, they had also always had a pretty good relationship. Next to her mother, her grandparents were the only real family Lindsey had ever known.

Chelsea sighed, and crossed her arms before responding. "Please, Lindsey, don't test me. Just come in soon, please." She then proceeded into the house and shut the door behind her. Lindsey dropped back into the lawn chair. She opened her journal to the spot where she left off and began to finish her entry.

My mother is dead; she is no longer on this earth. So where is she then? I know there's a place called Heaven, but who gets there, and how? Well, I suppose it will all hit me soon, and hopefully I'll be ready. I'm eighteen in a month and a half, so then I can leave and start my own life. I can deal with this. I've lived my whole life without a dad, so what's the difference in living without a mom?

Lindsey glanced up from her writing and stared out at the beach in front of her. The dark blue water was lapping against the shoreline gently, and the brightness of the sun was reflecting off of it.

I know the difference in living without a mom. I'll be alone. I won't have anybody. I don't have anybody, just myself. I'm not sure of anything right now, just that I'm Lindsey Milholland, I'm almost eighteen, I graduated this past June, I have no parents, and I'm alone.

The red-orange sun had set and was slipping slowly behind the horizon. The air had cooled, and the sky was gripping rays of pink in its background, an awesome backdrop to the mountainous islands that seemed to float on the waters of the Puget Sound. From the lawn chair in the backyard, Lindsey Milholland opened her eyes from her rest and sat up, yawning. She hadn't been aware of her falling into sleep and quickly brought her wrist up to check her watch. It was almost 9:00 p.m. The guests would all be gone, and everything inside cleaned up and put away, no thanks to her. Lindsey quickly jumped up and hurried toward the sliding glass door that would lead into her grandparents' kitchen. Once inside, Lindsey saw that she had been right. There were no traces that there had even been a huge get-together at the house in memory of Jillian Milholland. The dishes in the sink were few, and all the counters were wiped clean and spotless. The living room past the kitchen looked untouched and just as it had before the funeral. Lindsey felt that if there had been any good in coming to live with her maternal grandparents, it was the fact that she would rarely have chores to do, thanks to her grandmother's passion for cleaning.

Lindsey glanced around for a minute in the living room before calling, "Grandma?" There was no reply. "Grandma, Grandpa? Hello! Is anybody here?" Lindsey rushed up the stairs, only to find her grandparents' bedroom empty. She hurried back down the stairs and into the kitchen. "Hello, people!

Where did everybody go?" It was then that Lindsey discovered the small piece of paper awaiting her on the counter next to the stove. It read:

> *Lindsey, your grandpa and I decided to go home with the Wallaces and visit them for a little bit. I felt no need to wake you from your sleep. I know the past few days have been hard for you. I hope we can talk a little later tonight when Dan and I return. We should be back around 10:30.*
>
> *– Grandma*

Lindsey crumpled the note in her hands and threw it across the kitchen, making a perfect shot into the garbage can. "Okay then," she mumbled, heading toward the living room. "Since I have nothing to do…." Lindsey sighed and dropped into a plush chair as the memories of the day stirred inside her head. She could see the faces of all the friends of her mother who had been at the funeral. They were twisted in anguish, and faint red scarlet circled their eyes from the tears that wouldn't stop flowing. Lindsey could vividly remember every sob heard, every tear shed, and every word spoken as people comforted each other.

Lindsey shook her head and stood up. Retrieving her coat from the closet, she set out to take a walk along the beach, which was slowly disappearing with every sweep of sea that threatened to cover the shore. The breeze coming off the sea held a comfortable warmth as it drifted around Lindsey's round face, blowing her blond strands about. Lindsey approached the rocks that sat at the edge of the beach and began climbing them. Every night since her mother's death, Lindsey had sat on these rocks. They seemed powerful to her; they held a certain superiority. Climbing to the top, she then walked around to the front of the rocks, and back down toward the water. Resting at a destination only a few feet above the water, she sat and wrapped her coat closer around her body. Staring out at the familiar islands, and noting the sun hidden almost completely below the horizon, she couldn't help but think about the funeral.

Although the priest was talking, Lindsey wasn't paying attention to his words. She had heard the same words recited at other funerals and on TV. They didn't mean anything to her. Even if they did, she wasn't sure exactly what they meant, or why they were said. Her mother was dead, and no amount of preaching or praying could bring her back, so what was the point? Lindsey could recall all the roses, daisies, tulips, and other various flowers that were put on display at the occasion to make it brighter. The thought of that angered her. Why make a funeral bright? Why make a death a joyous occasion by covering every inch of casket with flowers? A person dying was a devastating thing, not a bright, colorful thing. But Lindsey knew why flowers were used. She herself had worn a flowery dress to the funeral, not wanting to convince herself that she was actually attending a devastating occasion. *It sure was a pretty service,* she thought.

The sun was gone, and the air turned chilly. The sky was crowded with dark clouds of every shape and size. Lindsey realized that the day had changed drastically, from warm, sunny, and bright, with white clouds that seemed to smile down on earth, to dark, bleak, and cold. *Just like my life.* And with the thought of that, and the realization of what had happened during the whole day, Lindsey started to cry.

A soft knock came at Lindsey's bedroom door, and before she could answer, Chelsea opened it and peeked through. "Is it all right if I come in?" she asked carefully, as if any second Lindsey might snap at her like before.

"Sure," Lindsey replied, sitting up from her reading position on her stomach. Chelsea walked over and sat on Lindsey's bed next to her.

"I thought maybe we could talk a little, about today," she suggested. Lindsey just nodded as she closed her book and tossed it aside. Not saying a word, she stared at her grandmother, waiting for her to say the next word.

"I was just wondering how you were. Did you really fall asleep, or did you just not want to come inside and visit? I could understand if you didn't ."

"I'm sorry, I really did fall asleep, but I was going to come inside."

"It's all right, I don't care about that anymore," Chelsea assured Lindsey. "I'm just concerned about you. I know the whole thing has been so hard for you, and I understand it's probably not natural for you to cry right away. Who says you even have to cry? People can express sadness without crying."

"I know that," Lindsey said.

"Well, I figured you did. I just don't want you to feel bad about not crying, because the way you said it to me, you...."

"I what?" Lindsey asked.

"You just sounded a little guilty for not crying; like maybe you felt like you should cry."

"I don't feel guilty," Lindsey quickly responded.

"I know, and it's okay." Chelsea reluctantly placed her hand over Lindsey's. "I just wanted to make sure, and I want you to know that you can talk to me about whatever's going on inside you. It's not healthy for you to keep all your feelings bottled in. You would feel much better if you told someone."

Lindsey eyed her grandmother, growing annoyed. She didn't have anything to tell, and certainly not to her grandmother. "I don't see the point in that," she replied. "Talking about your feelings isn't going to change the situation."

"It's not meant to change the situation. Nothing can bring your mother back. Talking about your feelings is just a way to share your emotions, and to discover that you're not alone in them."

Not alone. Those words hung in Lindsey's mind for a moment, and she couldn't move, couldn't say a word. She was alone.

"You would feel much better if you told how you were feeling. Then maybe I could understand and help you out. You said I can't tell you how to feel, and you were right. I don't know what you're feeling, but I would like to. It would really help me out if I knew. Then I could help you sort everything out."

"I don't need help with my feelings. I'm fine," Lindsey snapped.

Chelsea wondered if maybe she should back off. This obviously wasn't the right time to talk to her granddaughter. Yet, something held her there. She needed to settle this discussion now. "Fine? Just fine? Lindsey, fine isn't good enough."

"Well, maybe not for you, but it is for me."

"Lindsey!" Chelsea grabbed her granddaughter's arms with a tight grip and threatened to shake her. "You're not the only one who lost someone. I lost my daughter!" Realizing she was holding Lindsey in a grip, she loosened her hold, and continued. Lindsey's eyes were wide with bewilderment as she stared at her grandmother, confused as to what brought on her desperate outburst. "I want to help you," Chelsea continued softly, but firmly. "You can tell me if there's anything you want me to know."

"There isn't anything!" Lindsey shouted as she struggled from her grandmother's grip and stood up. "All you can do is argue, huh? Just leave me alone for once, will you? As long as you try to talk to me, we will always get into an argument. So why don't you just let me deal with this on my own?"

Chelsea stood up and walked toward Lindsey. "Because it's not healthy to deal with things like death on your own."

"What's healthy," Lindsey argued, "and what's not healthy? How can you determine that?"

Chelsea sighed, and shook her head in exhaustion. "There's no pleasing you, is there?"

"No, I'm fine! There's no pleasing you!" Lindsey stood straight, as if waiting for some enemy to come at her, ready for the attack.

"What do you have to help you deal, huh? Look at yourself. You go crazy anytime I try to talk to you." Chelsea waited for Lindsey's next argument, and when Lindsey said nothing, she went on. "What do you have, huh? Your journal? What's the good in writing things down? What help is it to you to talk to a few pages of paper!"

"Leave me alone!" Lindsey shouted. "Talking to paper, as you put it, is much more enlightening than talking to you!"

Chelsea's eyes flew wide, and her mouth opened in astonishment. Normally she would scold Lindsey, but thinking back on the afternoon, she decided otherwise. "Okay, then, if that's what you want, I'll leave." Chelsea turned and walked out the door, closing it behind her.

Lindsey covered her face with her hands, sighed, and fell down into a cross-legged sitting position on the floor. "What am I doing?" she silently asked herself. She sat with her head down, wondering how she would fix the situation with her grandmother. Looking up, she sighed and stood to her feet, knowing what she had to do. She walked hurriedly out the door, and headed to her grandparents' bedroom.

"Grandpa, where did Grandma go?" Lindsey asked quietly, stepping into her grandfather's study. Daniel Johns looked up from his work, and smiled at the sight of his granddaughter. The way she looked at that moment, timid and almost frightened, reminded him of when she was a child.

"Hey, I haven't seen you all day," he said, taking off his reading glasses.

Lindsey managed a smile and walked in toward the big leather chair next to his desk. "Yeah, I know, I've been outside." She sat down in the chair and crossed her legs.

"So what's up?" Daniel asked curiously.

"I was just wondering where Grandma went," she replied.

"I think she went out on a walk."

Lindsey nodded and gazed at the TV. There was a re-run of Home Improvement on, and Lindsey watched, laughing. After a few seconds, she turned back toward her grandfather. "I got into a fight with her, and I wanted to apologize."

"I know what happened. She told me. She tells me everything, you know."

"I know," Lindsey smiled.

"I don't want to be a nag or anything; trust me, I know what your grandmother can be like, but you don't have to tell anything that you are not comfortable talking about."

"I know that," she replied.

"Lindsey, I realize you're old enough to deal with things on your own, but everybody needs other people to lean on." Lindsey just stared at her grandfather, not saying a word. She didn't want to hear any more of this. "Just remember that you're not alone. You have Chelsea and me, and your uncle Adam."

Lindsey shook her head. It didn't matter to her how many people told her she wasn't alone, she felt alone. She wasn't close to her grandparents. They weren't the kind of people she felt comfortable talking to. And her uncle Adam didn't even live in the state.

"I appreciate that and all, but...." She stopped, not knowing how to explain herself. Instead of finishing what she wasn't sure she wanted to say, Lindsey stood up and headed out of the study. "I'm going to bed, 'k?"

"Sure, honey, good night."

"Night."

The next morning began with rays of sun streaming in through Lindsey's bedroom curtains and hitting her face, waking her. Lindsey groaned and finally rolled out of bed, noting that the clock read 11:43 a.m. She had plans for today. She was going out with a few friends, and nothing in the world was going to ruin this day for her. She was determined to make it like any normal day. She hadn't had a normal day in almost a week.

Almost an hour later, and ready to go, she bounced downstairs and found her grandparents in the kitchen. Daniel was reading a newspaper, sipping coffee, and Chelsea, hovered over the kitchen sink washing some fresh fruits, was working on lunch.

"There you are! I was beginning to think you would sleep forever," Chelsea laughed. Lindsey managed a weak smile and opened the refrigerator door.

"Hey there, sleepyhead!" Daniel exclaimed, looking up. "You missed breakfast."

"Yeah, I know," Lindsey replied. She grabbed an apple out of the refrigerator and closed the door, turning back to her grandparents. "By the way, I'm going out with some friends right now, so don't make too much lunch for me 'cuz I won't be here to eat it. Thanks anyway, but I thought you knew that I don't like hamburgers."

"'By the way?' Now you tell us?" Chelsea stopped her work and set one hand on the kitchen counter and another on her hip. "Please tell us beforehand if you have plans."

Lindsey widened her eyes, and innocence washed upon her face. She looked over at her grandfather, and he could do nothing but laugh.

"Daniel, don't you agree?" Chelsea asked her husband seriously.

"Sure," he chuckled. "But she's almost an adult, Chelsea. She's nearly eighteen. No doubt she's leaving the second she can." Lindsey smiled at him and, with a final wave of farewell, turned and ran out the front door.

"Daniel!" Chelsea slammed her hand on the counter. "She's not being respectful! You can't let her act like that toward us!"

"Act like what? She's a teenage girl, Chelsea, who just lost her mother. She's not going to be herself. I agree that she had no right to treat you the way she did yesterday, but there's nothing we can do about it."

Chelsea clenched her fists, knowing he was right. There was no controlling Lindsey.

"Lindsey's a good kid, Chelsea. She can handle herself," Daniel added as he took the last sip of his afternoon coffee. Chelsea just shook her head as she grabbed up a dishtowel and began running water into the sink. She hated for her husband to have the last word. He always seemed to get along with people better than she did. Although Chelsea didn't want to agree with Daniel, she did. She just didn't want to lose her granddaughter as quick as she had lost her daughter.

"Hey Lindsey!" shouted Marianne Pierce as she spotted her good friend strolling across the parking lot.

Lindsey glanced over to find Marianne walking toward her and proceeded to meet her halfway. A smile was stretched across Marianne's round face, and her strawberry hair shone brightly in the sun.

"Hey," Lindsey said as she approached Marianne. "What's up? Where's Janice? I thought she would come with you?"

"Nah, she decided to come along with Bill."

"Bill is coming?" Lindsey asked dryly, furrowing her eyebrows in distaste.

"Yep, 'ol Billy boy. Yippee, huh?" Marianne replied sarcastically.

Lindsey rolled her eyes as the two girls headed toward the restaurant door. "I guess he's not so bad, besides being a badly-dressed delinquent." Marianne tipped her head back and laughed.

"Not to mention extremely *inauspicious*."

"Ooh, good word," Lindsey chimed. "What's it mean?"

"Oh, you know … annoying, unpleasant, adverse.…"

"Ooh, *adverse*, another good word," Lindsey chuckled. "So are Janice and Billy going out now, or something?"

Marianne shook her head. "Nah, still friends, but not for long, I hope. They'd better go out soon."

Lindsey glanced at Marianne questioningly. "You don't like Bill, but you hope him and Janice go out soon?"

"Well, yeah, only because I'm getting so tired of hearing Janice's crush stories about him and her not doing anything about it."

Lindsey laughed. "Hmm, Bill and Janice, who knew?" she stated, with a smirk on her face.

The two girls entered the restaurant door and immediately spotted their friends. They waved as they strolled over to sit with them.

"Hmm, looks like we're late," Marianne commented as they approached the table. Joseph Norris, Janice Robertson, and Bill Colvin were all seated.

"Hey!" Joe Norris greeted. He scooted over in the booth to let Lindsey in, and Marianne got in from the other side. "So where's Nick?" he asked Lindsey. She shrugged her shoulders.

"I don't know, I haven't talked to him lately," she replied.

"So how are you?" Janice asked, casting sympathetic eyes on Lindsey.

Lindsey just shook her head before replying, "I'm fine." She looked out the window, and not one of the four other mouths said a word. Lindsey hadn't seen her friends since her mother died, and she knew they were probably tense around her, unsure of what to say.

"So...." Marianne started. "When are we all going camping together, huh? We're finally out of school, and summer's almost over. We need to go camping like we keep talking about." Lindsey was thankful for Marianne's company. She always had something to talk about. She glanced over at Marianne and smiled thankfully.

"Well, remember, I'm starting school in three weeks, so it'd better be soon," Janice replied.

"Hey, next weekend would be perfect 'cause it's the last weekend we could use my parents' beach cabin. They're selling it, you know," Joe commented.

"Oh, that'd be awesome," Marianne said.

The five teenagers continued to chat as the waitress came and took orders. For a couple of hours they sat eating and chatting. Lindsey felt normal for the first time in five days, and for those two hours she forgot all that had happened in her life in the past five days. Her face became reacquainted with smiles, and laughter found its place in her heart. Foolish talk and superficial chatter; this was Lindsey's world. Often it annoyed her; she would tire of the gossip and the crush-stories and the loss of anything intelligent to converse about, but she dealt with it. Her one exception was Marianne, and Lindsey had supposed more than once that Marianne was the only tie she held with these other people. Best friends since elementary school, Marianne and Lindsey grew up like sisters. From the sudden absence of her father ten years ago to the unexpected death of her mother, she always knew there would be Marianne to keep her head on straight.

Lindsey watched as Marianne stole everybody's attention with her social and bright personality. She was smart – the one who always had ideas and suggestions when everybody else was at a loss for creativity. In truth, Lindsey admired and adored Marianne; more than once she had wished she could have the carefree attitude that Marianne possessed. Wrinkling her forehead, she suddenly reasoned that she had always been Marianne's sidekick, her follower, and her shadow, in a way. She knew that's what made her put up with the social group she had been trapped with all throughout high school. It was only Marianne she really cared about.

"Well, let's leave now, we've been sitting for almost two hours," Janice complained. "Let's go see a movie or something."

The kids slowly rose out of their seats, and on their way out the door, Marianne leaned over to Lindsey. "Well, it doesn't look like your boyfriend is going to make it."

Lindsey shook her head and rolled her eyes. "Yeah, right. When does he ever make it?"

"When was the last time you talked to him, anyway?" Marianne asked.

Lindsey thought for a moment before replying. "A couple days before ... before my mom died." Speaking those words brought Lindsey back into her real world, and she wished she had never spoken them, as if keeping silent about her mother's death would make it fictional.

"He never called you to say anything?"

"No," Lindsey replied. She never expected Nick to call. Marianne, Janice, and Joe had called, but only once, and they hadn't after that.

"He wasn't at the funeral either, Lindsey."

"So what?" Lindsey snapped, keeping her voice low so she wouldn't create an audience. She stopped walking and turned towards Marianne. "I don't expect him to. Why should he come? My mom died, not his! He probably doesn't want to see me because he doesn't know what to say to me, just like you guys! He probably thinks I'm all crazy, and not myself, and maybe that I won't want to see him!"

"Hey, girls, are you coming?" Joe shouted, standing fifteen feet away from the two girls, right beside his '94 Nissan Sentra.

"Yeah, just a minute," Marianne shouted.

He continued. "We were going to see a movie. So how about we just meet you two at the theater, okay?"

"Okay," Marianne replied. She then turned towards Lindsey. Glancing around and sighing, she finally said, "Lindsey, I never told you this, but Nick told me once that he was thinking about breaking up with you."

"What?" Lindsey asked, confused at this sudden change of subject. "When did he tell you that?" Her heart picked up pace, and she quickly stuffed her hands in her coat pockets.

"It was sometime last week, right before your mom's accident."

"What did he say?"

Marianne shook her head. "Just something like, well, I can't exactly remember everything he said but…."

"Marianne," Lindsey pleaded. She was listening intently.

"He was talking about how he likes this other girl, and she really likes him, and stuff. He didn't want me to tell you though, but I thought I should."

Lindsey's head started to spin. *Nick wouldn't do this to me,* she thought. "What girl?" she demanded.

"I don't know her name, but she's younger than us. She's a sophomore."

"What? A sophomore?" Lindsey laughed, trying to hide her worry. "She still has two more years of school! What, is Nick just going to hold off college for two years and wait for her?"

"I don't know, I think it's pretty stupid too," Marianne replied. "But that's what I know. Sorry I didn't tell you sooner. I would have, but then the whole … situation happened." She stopped, and tipped her head down. "I really am sorry about the whole thing."

"What whole thing?" Lindsey asked.

"Just, both things, I guess. Your mom, and me not telling you sooner about Nick." Lindsey turned and started to walk away from Marianne. "I mean, who knows? Maybe it'll turn out he doesn't like this girl after all so…."

"So he'll just settle with me, huh?" Lindsey said. She pulled her keys out of her pocket and began to unlock the car door. "Why would I want someone who isn't fully devoted to me, huh? Every now and then he'll just decide he likes someone else, and once he gets sick of me he'll just dump me? Oh, but if he decides he doesn't like them, he'll stay with me? That's stupid! Why should I settle for that?"

"You shouldn't," Marianne explained.

Lindsey stopped and turned toward Marianne. "How will he decide if he likes this girl or not, huh? You know what I think? He wants to go out with her because she's young, and she'll sleep with him."

Marianne almost choked at Lindsey's bluntness. "Oh, well, that's interesting, Lindsey…."

"I know that's it," Lindsey continued, "because I wouldn't sleep with him, and he got all upset." Marianne just stood there, and her expression changed to sympathy.

"You never told me about that," she said sadly as her eyes shone with a glint of pity, and guilt penetrated her face.

Lindsey noticed the look and immediately became suspicious. "That's it, isn't it?" Lindsey asked. "Did he tell you that?" Marianne didn't say anything. "Marianne! Tell me! What did he say?"

"That might have been part of it. He did mention something about that," Marianne finally shared. Lindsey smirked, crossing her arms and leaning against the side of the car. She shook her head and glanced around. Her whole world seemed to be falling apart at this moment. She felt trapped. The summer was almost over, and when her mother died, Lindsey had dropped all her plans to start college that fall. She had no idea where she was headed in life, or where she would end up in the next year, or even the next month. And now, among all the chaos was another tragedy hurling itself at her. Now her boyfriend wanted to break up with her for a sophomore!

"You know, I would love to just drop everything I have at this point and leave."

"Leave? Like, where?"

The air was turning chilly, and Lindsey wrapped her coat closer around her as she stared out at the many automobiles passing by on the main road. No sooner had her eyes set their gaze on the road when an idea crept its way into Lindsey's head.

"I'm going home," she said as she opened her car door and got inside.

"But what about the movies?" Marianne asked, leaning over to speak to Lindsey through the window.

"I don't want to go. I have something I need to think out."

Two

But the path of righteous people is like the light of dawn that becomes brighter and brighter until it reaches midday.
– Proverbs 4:18

Lindsey's heart rate sped up rapidly as she peered outside from behind her bedroom window drapes and saw the sturdy figure of Nick Pruitt advancing up the driveway to the front door. Inhaling slowly, she sighed, blowing her long bangs in the air from her upward exhale. She backed away from the window and checked herself in the mirror, quickly playing over in her mind exactly what she intended on saying to Nick about their current relationship.

It was a bright Saturday afternoon, and since Thursday when Lindsey had found out the news about Nick, she had been determined to speak with him and break things off before he had the chance to hurt her anymore. She didn't feel she needed her heart filled with false love and acceptance just to have it all wrung out the very next second. Nerves bit her bones like an icy chill freezing water. She didn't have any proof that Nick had been seeing another girl, she had only her friend's word. Lindsey wasn't sure how predictable Nick's response to her accusations would be. *I won't accuse him of anything, I'll just ask him. Simply ask him.* Lindsey's thoughts halted as they began to travel down another road. *But he could lie. I mean, if he's the kind of guy who would even think about cheating on his girlfriend, then he could be a liar, too.*

The doorbell began to sing its cheerful tune, and Lindsey remained transfixed in front of her mirror, speaking to herself, deciding to let her grandmother answer the door. She hadn't seen Nick since last Saturday, the day before her mother had died. And the last time she had spoken to him was yesterday on the phone, only to quietly explain to him in two minutes her need to speak with him the next day. From downstairs she could hear Chelsea's hard steps as she walked across kitchen and into the living room toward the front door. Lindsey sighed again, trying to control her breathing. *Oh shoot, please don't have an asthma attack now, Lindsey. He's only Nick. You don't need to be nervous in front of him.* Her feeble attempt at self-comfort proved useless as her ears beheld the swooshing sound of the front door rubbing against the new carpet as it was opened. *Oh darn it all*! Lindsey made up her mind as she swung open her bedroom door and bounded down the steps into the living room.

"Hey," she greeted Nick as she swept her bangs out of her eyes. She looked at her grandmother, indicating that she wanted her to leave.

"Hey, Lindsey," Nick replied. He shoved his hands in the pockets of his cargo pants and leaned back on his heels. Chelsea turned abruptly and strode out of the living room, leaving Lindsey and Nick to their privacy. She knew the meeting would not be a positive one.

"So," Nick sputtered once Chelsea had exited the room, "how ya been? I haven't seen you since last week. Is everything okay?"

"Yeah," Lindsey sighed once again. "I've been okay. Not the best, you know. I mean, my mother *died* for heaven sake, so...." She purposely put emphasis on the word died, for reasons she wasn't sure of. In a way, she wanted Nick to feel guilty for not being there to comfort her and care for her in her time of distress when she had felt alone. He knew her mother had died, so why had he simply leaned back, unable to be of any comfort or care? Lindsey had justified him, though, hoping he had just been busy or unaware of the severity of her trials, but in spite of that, she believed that any human being who claimed to be a friend, or more, would come to the aid no matter what situation.

"I know. I'm sorry, Lindsey."

"Sorry for what?"

Nick clawed at the air for words, trying to grasp something with meaning. "I'm just sorry that she died, and that you've had to go through it. I can't even imagine what it would be like if my mother died."

"Yeah, well, maybe you should also be sorry for not being there for me. I can understand why you didn't come to the funeral, I mean, it was my mom, not yours. But you never even called me or came to visit to see how I was or anything. You probably wouldn't have even come by today if I hadn't have called you yesterday." Lindsey stopped and noted the distraught look gracing Nick's two blue eyes. Lindsey had always loved his eyes. Those were the part of him that had captured her in the first place. They were baby blue, with a glint of green in them, and they reminded Lindsey of a crystal clear lake, reflecting the hue of the sky while slivers of the sunlight's rays danced off the surface. As she gazed at his eyes, she almost felt herself drowning in that lake like she had so many times when she spent numerous amounts of time with Nick.

"I ... I know. I just didn't know what to say. It's weird, ya know, even for me. I didn't know how to act around you, I … I'm sorry, Lindsey. I'm sorry for not being there."

As Nick's words invaded her brain, Lindsey lowered her head, remembering the words Marianne had spoken to her about Nick's cheating. His empathetic words felt so sincere that Lindsey didn't know what to make of them, whether they were truthful sincerity or forced sincerity. She felt torn, as if Marianne was pulling one leg, begging Lindsey to follow her, while Nick grabbed tightly to an arm, swaying Lindsey his way. Not knowing what else to think or feel, Lindsey decided to be blunt and just tell Nick what had been the reason for his visit in the first place. She looked up.

"Marianne told me you have been seeing another girl." Her voice was quick and resolute, and she purposely stared right into Nick's face in order to catch any insecurity that might be hidden behind his boyish features.

Nicks' forehead creased as his eyebrows came together in astonishment. However, whether it was true astonishment or false, Lindsey couldn't tell.

"What? Why did she tell you that?" he asked, his voice a pitch higher.

"Well, I don't know, Nick, that's why I was asking you. I was hoping you could tell me whether it was true or not."

"Well, no…." his voice lowered, and his words were labored. "I mean, there is another girl that I've been kinda hanging out with, but we're not seeing each other. No, of course not." He stared at Lindsey's concerned features, which were tinged with a hint of anger. He knew she didn't believe him. He hadn't meant for anything to start with the sophomore girl, but it had. It had started at a party when things had gotten out of hand as a result of too much alcohol. He suddenly felt the hand of guilt slap him in the face and decided it was no use to keep anything hidden from Lindsey.

"We're going to two different colleges, Lindsey, I mean, this probably wouldn't have worked out anyway," he finally admitted, although college was just an excuse.

Lindsey's mouth suddenly down-turned as hurt and betrayal weighed upon her. However, she was determined not to start crying in front of Nick. It was too humiliating to have cared for someone so much knowing they had taken that for granted.

"College? Nick, I'm not going anymore. If you had been around the last week, then you would've figured that out."

"What? Why aren't you going?"

"I don't know, I just can't, not anymore. I was supposed to move onto campus next month, but I decided to wait another year or so, when things become a little more normal. So now that you don't have college as an excuse, what have you got to say for yourself?"

Nick shifted uncomfortably as he rolled his eyes. "Lindsey … this isn't going to work. I care about you, I do, but just not as much as I used to. It's faded, I guess."

"What's faded?"

"My feelings for you."

Lindsey's heart sank at the sound of those words. She closed her mouth and stared up into Nick's face, bewildered and confused. After a second, it was too much for her heart to bear to look up into the beautiful face that had kept her prisoner for two years. After two years, it had only taken a week for Nick's feelings to fade. Or perhaps, they had already faded long ago. Lindsey looked away as tears gathered in her eyes. She swallowed and held her eyes wide so that the tears wouldn't spill over and present themselves to Nick.

"Oh."

"I'm sorry, Lindsey."

"So would you have even told me this if I hadn't have mentioned the other girl? When were you planning on telling me about your feelings?"

"I don't know, soon. Sometime when I thought you'd be okay to talk."

"Well, wasn't that just generous of you to wait until I'd be okay." Sarcasm clung to her words, and it angered Nick.

"Look, I'm just being honest, okay. You asked, so I told you."

"I asked about that girl. She isn't just nobody, is she? You are seeing her, aren't you?"

Nick waited a couple of seconds before replying, "Yeah, I guess I am."

"Marianne told me you guys met at a party a few weeks ago, and it kinda flew off from there, huh?"

"Well, I didn't just meet her at the party, I mean, I've known who she was. But yeah, we kinda started things at the party. I guess I should have told you sooner." Although his words were forward and honest, there was no guilt or sympathy in them.

Lindsey bit her bottom lip and nodded her head in quick little movements. "Yeah, yeah, that would've been nice." Her head started to ache as she began swaying on her heels. "So, what is it about that girl that you like so much?"

Nick sighed, exasperated, and looked up at the ceiling for a moment. "I don't know, Lindsey … she's cute, I guess. She's fun."

"So you really, really like her then, huh?"

"I don't know … yeah, I suppose."

Lindsey laughed quietly. "You're giving me up for someone whom you don't even know how you feel about?"

"Lindsey, look, what's the big deal? This was gonna happen sooner or later."

"Did she sleep with you?"

Nick's eyes grew wide. "What?" He peered in the direction of the kitchen from which Chelsea had disappeared moments ago. "Keep your voice down, Lindsey."

Lindsey turned in the direction of his stare right before grabbing Nick's arm and pulling him out the front door and onto the porch.

"Did you? Please just tell me the truth, Nick. I need to know."

Nick hesitated and glanced around before replying, "It happened at the party, Lindsey. I don't even know how it started, but it did."

Unrestrained any longer, the tears which were brimming on the corners of Lindsey's eyes flew down her cheeks uncontrollably. Nick took a step backward and lowered his head.

"I thought you had said you weren't gonna drink anymore."

"It's hard, Lindsey. Have you ever just stopped doing something you had been doing for a long time? It's hard. But it wasn't just that, Lindsey. I wasn't so much drunk that I didn't have control over what I was doing. I mean, I wanted it to be you there with me, but I know how you feel about waiting until you're ready. And I guess she was just there, and I just couldn't wait, Lindsey. I couldn't wait for you."

Lindsey started sobbing, and she hid her face in her hands as she stood alone without any comfort coming from the young man standing next to her. *First Mom, now this*. Nick stood with his hands hidden within his pockets, unable to free them and give Lindsey a comforting touch or a sincere apology for causing her pain.

"I'll see you later, Nick," Lindsey finally said as she sniffed and turned to enter the house.

"See ya around." With those words tumbling through the air, Nick turned and slowly made his way back to his car and drove off. Lindsey listened as he drove off before entering the house and slowly climbing the stairs, feeling as though if she were lucky, she might fall backwards and rid herself of the pain that was tearing at her heart.

Two months later ... October 19, 1997

Caleb Lockwood drove downtown in his Ford, singing loudly to the lyrics of the song that was blasting through the speakers. The sun was bright on this Sunday in October, and Caleb had just gotten out of church, which always helped to lift his spirits, no matter what his mood was. He quickly took two minutes out of his singing to thank the Lord for this beautiful day, and headed home to finish some last-minute packing.

As he pulled up the driveway of his uncle's house, he was greeted by two

U-Haul drivers whom he was expecting. They were right on time. "Hey," he yelled as he exited his truck. "How are you guys today?"

A man in an old baseball cap and flannel shirt, who looked to be in his late 30s, turned around and greeted Caleb. "Hey, so are you the one whose stuff we're moving?" he asked.

"Yep, that would be me," Caleb replied. He wasted no time in showing the two men into the house and instructing them on the furniture that needed to be moved. "There's not much, mostly just the stuff in my bedroom, and I think my aunt and uncle are letting me take some of their things."

The men nodded as they listened to Caleb's instructions and followed him throughout the house. "So you're headed across country, right?" one of the men asked.

Caleb sighed, and a smile crossed his lips as he answered, "I'm going home, to North Carolina."

"Wow, North Carolina," one of the men commented. "All the way across the country. How come you're goin' back there?"

"Well, I just came over here a few years ago to stay with my aunt and uncle, and to go to college, but it didn't quite work out for me. So I've got other plans now, and I miss my parents, so I'm going home."

Caleb assisted the two men as they lifted up some bed rails to transfer to the U-Haul truck. "Well," one started, "I'm sorry it didn't work out for you here."

"Nah," Caleb stated, "in a way it did work out. Better things happened to me here then I would have ever thought could happen to me."

The U-Haul pulled out of the driveway that afternoon at 2:00. Caleb wouldn't depart for North Carolina until the next morning, however. He stood in the yard, and watched as part of his future disappeared down the road. He took a deep breath and slowly let it out as he allowed his eyes to close and titled his head backward to feel the warmth of the sun on his face. The wind blew lightly and lifted strands of his short light-blond hair upward.

He would miss Washington State and everybody he'd met here who had changed his life. It was true what he'd told the U-haul workers; better things had happened to him in the three years he'd lived in Washington than he could have imagined. Just a few months ago, Caleb had become a Christian, and with that new commitment, his life had changed.

"Caleb," called a voice. Caleb opened his eyes and turned to see his Aunt Elizabeth walking down the porch steps and heading toward him. "You look peaceful."

"Yeah, I am," he replied. "I was just watching that U-Haul go down the road, and I realized how much I'm going to miss it here. I feel like I've lived here a lot longer than three years."

Elizabeth reached out and gave her nephew a hug. He stood five inches taller than she did at six feet exactly. "Yeah, it does seem that way. I'm gonna miss you so much. You don't know how thankful I am to have spent these few years with you." She then pulled away and looked up at Caleb's face. "I'm so thankful to God for what he's done for you."

Caleb smiled and glanced at the grass beneath his feet. "Yeah, me too," he commented. He then looked at his aunt, her face smiling warmly, and something welled up inside him. He felt sadness tugging at his heart to be leaving his aunt and uncle who had cared for him, loved him, and helped change his life these past years. But at the same time he felt overcome with a happiness he couldn't quite define; a feeling of something complete, something finally filled in the deepest region of his soul. He knew it was Jesus, his newfound Lord and Savior who caused him to feel that unexplainable way.

He looked away from his aunt and back down the road. The U-Haul was out of sight, and from afar two children riding bicycles peddled down the road quickly, racing each other, and yelling back and forth at the same time. They were having fun, totally free from any restraints at that moment. They felt powerful, being able to out-race each other, accomplishing anything. Young, innocent, and free, Caleb felt just like one of them.

"Hey, Caleb!" shouted a big voice. Caleb's Uncle Chris, to whom everybody referred as "Bear," because of his size, walked up behind Caleb and Elizabeth. "So I can't believe you're leaving us tomorrow huh? Do you have everything packed, ready to go?"

"Almost, I still have a few more things to pack tonight, but besides that, I'm ready."

"Well then, if you're not doing anything right now, let's go out to eat!"

Chris held the door open wide for his wife to enter while proclaiming proudly in an exaggerated gentlemanly tone, "After you, my sweet." Caleb smiled as he held in a chuckle. It always amazed him to witness how much in love his aunt and uncle were, especially after so many years of marriage. He would have never thought it was possible for two people to hang on to each other for so long. But along with his new life in Christ, he had found out very recently that with God, everything was possible.

The three entered the Alfy's, and as they did, the strong scent of pepperoni, sausage, garlic bread, chili, and various other foods flooded Caleb's senses. He loved pizza, although it wasn't one of his favorite foods.

He would have preferred the Red Robin across the street, but his uncle had chosen Alfy's, and Caleb wasn't picky today. This was his last full day with these two people who had served as a shelter, refuge, and family for the last three years. Every time Caleb thought of this, a wave of emotion crashed over him, a feeling of loss and sadness, a feeling that dug into depths deeper than the ocean could ever reach. Caleb didn't believe there were any two other people whom he had loved more, not even his own parents. But he loved his parents, of course he did. It was the other Caleb who had had such troubles with them, but things were different now, and from now on. The feeling of sadness and loss was stitched in conjunction with the feeling of happiness that he would soon be with his parents again, and that was something he couldn't shake away.

As Chris and Elizabeth stood at the front counter deciding what to order, Caleb strolled across the tiled floor and searched out a place to sit. The dining room was very open, and long vertical windows on both sides of the restaurant faced each other, allowing light to cascade through and illuminate the dining area. As Caleb was walking down a row of booths, he quickly halted when he was suddenly interrupted..

"Hey, Caleb!" someone called. Caleb turned around to see a familiar face standing in the aisle. It was the skinny face of Rick Dawson, whom he had known from attending two years at Western Washington University.

"Hey, man, how are you?" Caleb asked as he walked up and outstretched his hand for Rick to shake. Rick took his hand and nodded, while replying, "I'm pretty good, what about you?"

"I'm fine. It's good to see you. What are you doing here?"

"I'm just here with Carrie and Phil," Rick replied. Then, as if lightning struck him, Rick thought of something to say and quickly added it. "Hey, you're not coming back to Western, are you?"

"Nah, I'm heading home tomorrow morning. Going back to North Carolina. I'm just having one last outing with my aunt and uncle right now before I leave."

"Oh, that's right, yeah. Hmmm, North Carolina, yeah, I remember, I knew that. Wow." Rick just nodded his head as he stared right into Caleb's face. "So you're leaving, huh? That's cool, man. I mean, for you. I'll miss ya at school. The whole team will miss you, you know."

"Yeah, yeah, I know. You don't know how many times I've heard that." He smiled. "So how's school so far anyway?"

"Ah, it's okay, you know, it's school," Rick replied.

"Yep, I know what you mean." Caleb just nodded as he searched for something else to say, all the while gazing at the long, shaggy figure that loomed in the middle of the isle. He had never really been more than acquaintances with Rick, so he didn't really know much about him. He had shared a few drunken times with him at parties, but besides that, Caleb really didn't hold much knowledge in his memory of this solemn-looking young man who stood before him inquiring of his well-being. Nevertheless, he thought the gesture of kindness was nice, and decided to inquire about Rick's well-being.

"So, Rick, do you still party a lot?" He didn't know why he asked that, he just felt like he should, just so he could know, just so he could give Rick one last warning, or at least something to think about.

"Ah, man, heck yeah," Rick answered as he took a step back, and glanced at the floor. He was a little reluctant in answering, knowing that Caleb had changed, and figuring he wouldn't like it.

Caleb cocked his eyebrows and shook his head left to right while saying, "You gotta get out of that stuff, Rick. It's your junior year, it'll kill ya, you know."

Rick just sniffed and replied, "Yeah, yeah, I know. Maybe someday." A pause followed in silence, lingering in the air, waiting to dissipate. Finally it did. "Well, I think that's cool that you're gettin' to go home. Are you going back to school when you get there?"

"Mmm, I'm not sure. I might, but if I do it won't be until next year, or something."

Rick nodded his head and glanced out the window. "Well, that's cool. Anyway, I hope you have a good trip tomorrow. Call me sometime, or email me, or whatever."

"All right, thanks, I will," Caleb replied.

October 20, 1997

The country road that Caleb had taken as an alternative to the busy freeway began to wind as it slithered and made its way around the bottom of hills. The shiny blue Ford F-150 rode smoothly, totally unaware of the many bumps and indents carved into the old pavement. The sun was showing off its radiance more than ever this day, and as its magnificent heat crawled inside the truck, Caleb quickly became aware of it and rolled down a window to rid of it. The heat helplessly flew away as the cool air overtook it, forcing its leave.

The ruts in the old country road soon smoothed out as the road leveled to a straightaway. On both sides of him the country looked beautiful: full fields of pure green, lush vegetation; in the distance stood some old country-style homes, a few owning barns which stood alone nearby the houses, along with cows scattered here and there about the fields. Large trees with thick stumps towered next to the houses, with the exception of a few apple, pear, and plum trees.

A half-smile formed on Caleb's face as he glanced about at his surroundings. He took a deep breath and exhaled slowly, letting go of that last breath of air as the last of his old life left him, staying behind as he set forward. He truly felt free, no restrictions held him, and no limitations hindered him. He felt new. As Caleb's mind whirled with anticipation, the words of 2 Corinthians 5:17 flashed before him: Therefore, if anyone is in Christ, he is a new creation; the old has gone, the new has come.

Caleb's smile broadened as his feelings of freedom, joy, and elation built up inside him, threatening to boil over at any second. Caleb rolled down the window the rest of the way and shouted as loud and as long as the air in his lungs permitted. He then turned the knob labeled "volume" up as far as it could rotate and began singing to the song, which was now filling every open space in the vehicle. His left arm hung out the open window with his hand tapping the side of his truck, while his right hand, which loosely rested on the top of the steering wheel, tapped in unison.

Three

A person may plan his own journey, but the LORD directs his steps.

– Proverbs 16:9

October 20, 1997

Well, I'm all packed and ready for departure across the country. That's right, I'm going cross-country. I can't believe it. It was just an idea back in September, I didn't even know that I'd actually go through with it, but things have become so hectic around here I feel I have nothing left to do but leave. I want to leave. I can't stay here any longer. I almost feel claustrophobic here at Grandma and Grandpa's ... well, in this whole town.

Nick and I split up a week after Mom's death. I guess I apparently wasn't as special to him as he always told me I was. I wonder what ever happened to his "I'll wait for you however long it takes" promise. That must've just been some cheap line out of a movie. How could I have ever even believed him? What is it with guys these days? Aren't there any real, sincere men out there anymore? Gosh, I'm beginning to think there's nobody I can trust, not even any of my friends. I feel so distant from them now, and I don't know if that's my fault or theirs. They were all really nice and sincere during the couple weeks after Mom's death, but I don't even know if they truly felt for me or not, and I don't know why I'm feeling that. Maybe it's just me. And in the last two months I haven't really been in much contact with them. They haven't really called me; but then again, I haven't been calling them much either. I haven't really left the house much 'cept to go get stuff I need from town. So I guess if anything, I'm the one who has secluded myself from everybody else.

I still feel so angry about my mom. I still haven't gotten over it. Things are so weird ... I don't feel normal ... I wonder if I ever will. It's a weird concept to think that my mother is no longer on this earth ... like, one second she was, and the next, gone. It's just weird. And I still wonder about where she might be, if she's anywhere now. What a terrible thought to think that after you die there's nothing. Is it like that? That really sucks. Death is such an odd thing. I don't know what to think about it. It scares me to think that there might not be anything after you die. But it also scares me to consider the possibility of a heaven. It seems so unrealistic, almost like a fairy tale. I asked Marianne what she thought about God, and she just said that she's never really wondered too much about it. She said that God to her had always just seemed like Santa Clause, or the Easter Bunny or something. I don't know.... Even if there was a God, or if there is, He seems like he'd be so much more developed and powerful than Santa Clause or the Easter Bunny. I mean, everybody knows that those are just made-up, but people still contemplate and wonder about God.

Anyway, I should probably get going now. I don't want to leave too late. I'm figuring I can make it to Spokane for today. I don't want to go too far. It'll be about five hours there, and I know that will tire me out enough. It's noon now, so I'll make it there in the early evening.

Lindsey closed her journal and stuffed it into her backpack. All her other luggage was already packed and waiting for her in the trunk of her Honda. Leaving her bedroom and trodding downstairs, she found her grandparents sitting in the living room, waiting for her departure.

"Well, I guess I'm all ready to go now," Lindsey quietly commented with a small smile on her face.

Chelsea and Daniel got up simultaneously and walked over to Lindsey to bid their farewells. "So you're sure you have everything packed then?"

"Yeah, Grandma, I do, thanks."

"You sure you're gonna be all right, Lindsey?"

Lindsey hugged her grandfather. "I'll be fine. You already asked me that a billion times. I know where I'm going, and I'll make sure I call you at every stop, okay?"

Chelsea and Daniel both looked at each other for a moment, silently expressing their worries to each other. "All right then," Chelsea finally chimed. She smiled, and after a moment, the two elderly people walked Lindsey outside to her car.

After final hugs and kisses and good-byes were given, Chelsea and Daniel stood transfixed in the middle of the driveway as they watched their only granddaughter drive away toward her unexpected future.

The dark clouds swam across the sky, moving together like a swarm of insects as if they were planning a rebellion against the earth, eerily concluding that rain would be the best attack. Caleb yawned as he pulled into a gas station right outside of Seattle to fill up for the next few hours of his trip eastward across Washington. He at least wanted to make it to Idaho before sundown. But with the unpredictable weather and the clouds quickly forming, he doubted he'd make it in that time.

Quickly filling up the gas tank, Caleb walked into the *Texaco* station and looked around for something to eat. He scanned the coolers lining the wall opposite the entrance and picked out a Mountain Dew before bounding into the candy aisle to choose something chocolatey. He felt like a child as he stood biting his lip with his concentrated gaze focused on the many selections lying before him on the rack. After a minute of contemplating, he chose a Butterfinger bar, suddenly realizing that as a child he had performed this same routine many times. He remembered one particular incident at a gas station in which he had just picked out his Butterfinger right before he heard the familiar shouting of his parents' voices mauling each other.

* * *

He had glanced out the small station window to witness his mother's angry exasperation as her husband had accidentally spilled some gas onto her pants and shoes while he was setting the gas nozzle back into its spot. Caleb remembered clearly the way the heat had abruptly risen into his blushed face as embarrassment overtook him. The women at the cash registers, as well as everyone inside and outside of the station, had stopped and stared at the fighting couple, some shaking their heads in disapproval, while others just chuckled and muttered under their breaths. Two teenage girls standing nearby Caleb had even rolled their eyes while one exclaimed how ridiculous the woman's temper had been.

Those are my parents, Caleb had thought, although he'd never let the girls know it, nor anybody else in and outside of the station. This was just one of the many times he had experienced his parents' brawling, and being in a public place only deepened the anger and hurt he was so use to feeling.

Caleb's mother began to cuss as she speedily threw off her shoes and hurled them in through the open window of the minivan. She opened the car door forcefully and tossed her body inside, slamming the vehicle door behind her, crossing her arms in annoyance. She held the appearance of a frustrated child, upset because she hadn't gotten her way. Caleb's body slumped as he slowly turned his head away from the incident between his parents, wishing he could disappear.

Although he had only been 12 years old when it had happened, he clearly recalled the words that he had spoken in his mind that afternoon: *She's so immature. Why can't she just hold her temper?*

* * *

"Oh, excuse me." A voice brought Caleb back into reality as he realized he had been staring vacantly at the rows of licorice and jelly beans that lined the rack while his mind had been wandering. Caleb moved forward to allow the young woman to pass by. She stepped by Caleb, stopped, and turned around to face him. Caleb sensed the eyes burning into his neck and tipped his head sideways to see the girl focused upon him. Her large eyes reflected innocence as her contradicting mouth was twisted in a sly grin.

"Having trouble deciding?" she asked, although it was obvious she wasn't interested in Caleb's choice of candy.

"Oh, uh, nah," Caleb answered, straightening up and moving to pass her. "I was just thinking I guess." He stopped and smiled, looking into her young face, waiting for her to move so he could pass her.

"So how old are you anyway?" she asked, placing her hands on her hips and tipping her head sideways as if to examine Caleb. He was taken off-guard by the question, and his brows came together in confusion. This girl was cute, but he didn't know her and wasn't interested in anyone so young. He smiled and laughed a little.

"That's kinda out-of-the-blue, isn't it?" he asked.

"It's just a question," the girl answered confidently as she shrugged her shoulders. Caleb glanced to his left to see two other girls of about the same age in the next aisle with their eyes peering over their lowered heads. One started to quietly laugh.

"Hmmm," Caleb muttered. He didn't want to play games with any little girls. "Well, how old are you?" he finally asked.

"Seventeen," the girl replied. He heard more laughs coming from the girls in the next aisle.

Caleb shook his head. "How old are you really?"

The girl waited a moment before replying, "Fourteen, but a lot of people say I look older.

"Ah, I see," Caleb answered, nodding his head. He smiled as he stepped forward to leave the aisle. The girl walked backwards, keeping at his pace, still facing him.

"So are you gonna tell me how old you are then?" she pried, not willing to give up her search so easily.

"Too old for you," he answered as he walked past her smiling, giving her one last glance with raised eyebrows.

The girl stood in the aisle and watched as Caleb paid for his gas and candy bar and slipped out the door of the small *Texaco* station, glancing back one last time to shrug his shoulders at the young girl still in the aisle who was eyeing him menacingly.

As the engine of the pickup began to roar, Caleb laughed as he departed from the gas station and back onto the road. There was one incident he wouldn't be able to match from his childhood, and it sure lightened up the memory of his fighting parents.

Caleb turned onto I-90 at 3:25 that dreary Monday afternoon. The next four or five hours toward Idaho didn't look promising, and as he drove on, his body began to feel wearisome and his head began to ache. He quickly decided he wouldn't travel the whole way to Idaho but instead stop and spend the night at a motel in any town east of the Columbia River.

Caleb rolled up his window the rest of the way, and as he did, a small gush of fresh, damp air squeezed its way inside before the window could permanently trap it outside for the rest of the night. The air, which held a familiar aroma, swirled eerily around Caleb's face and soon invaded his nostrils, sending a response through his nerves that tackled his whole mind. Caleb shuddered at the smell as it opened a door which had been locked safely in the cellar of his memory. However, this memory was not new to Caleb; he had replayed it in his mind several times, but not as vividly until now, when that unidentifiable aroma had stirred the memory in his head.

Tirelessly, Caleb allowed the familiar scene to unfold like a blanket inside his brain. His eyes were focused on the winding road stretched ahead, but the scene in his mind overtook his whole vision.

* * *

A slurring of voices hoarded the small, cramped living room of Apartment #18, while outside neighbors cautiously contemplated whether to intervene on the battle going on inside or not.

What a life to live, thought a tall, slender neighbor woman. How can they live with each other? That boy has got problems.

Cramped and musty-smelling from a carpet overdue on vacuuming and furniture in need of washing, Caleb violently thrashed his head back and forth as he tried to explain his feelings to the two human beings standing helplessly before him. They were lost, searching for a solution to their son's awkward and sudden behavior. Kathryn Lockwood's tiny fingers gripped the back of a wooden chair as it served as a shield for her body. Her wide blue eyes held fear as they set their focus on the tall young man who was crying out in emotional anguish.

"Caleb, what do you want us to do? Please, whatever you want, we can help you, we will help you, just please calm down." Her voice was shaking as it desperately attempted to control the frightened tone it held. Kathryn Lockwood felt as if she was on the edge of a mountain, trying to hold herself up and keep herself from falling down and sobbing.

"No," Caleb wailed, "you don't understand! You just don't get it!" His harsh voice cut through the space between him and his parents as his words forcefully shoved aside his mothers'. "You don't know what's wrong with me. You say you do, you say you understand, but you can't because you're not living it!" Caleb stopped and cast swollen, red eyes upon the faces of his bewildered parents. His muscular body surged with anger, and the hopeless look on his parents' pity-held faces only worsened it. How could they understand anything he was living through? They thought they had it made, these two creatures now overtaken with confusion thought they held the world steady in their hands. Jon Lockwood was a college professor of psychology, but Caleb didn't believe his father's brain contained the capacity for such an amount of knowledge, nor the intellect to separate, analyze, and truly understand what it all meant. If it had, he should have been able to figure Caleb out a long time ago and help him then.

"Caleb, we know you're depressed, we know you need help. You just have to be willing to let us help. I'm a psychologist, I know what you're going through." His father's sturdy voice attempted to surface above the uncertainty painted across his face.

"No!" Caleb screamed out in exasperation. "You're not a psychologist, you just teach psychology. You don't know what I'm going through, you've only studied it, never felt it."

Jon Lockwood nodded, inching closer to his troubled son, trying not to worsen his behavior. "You're right, that's true, son. I guess I can't say that I truly know what you're going through, but from studying it, I do understand what goes on in the minds of depressed teenagers." Caleb winced as his father said the word 'depressed'. He was restless, tottering back and forth and left to right on his feet, feeling as though he would collapse any second. Jon Lockwood hadn't even been the one who noticed Caleb's symptoms in the first place. It had been his mother, Kathryn, who had first noticed Caleb's depression and decided to discuss the matter with her husband one afternoon.

"Jon, I think something's wrong with Caleb. I really think he could have some kind of disorder or something. Maybe he's depressed. I noticed the other day how he...."

"Kathryn," Jon had interrupted as he looked up from grading student papers at his desk, "you've been paranoid like this about Caleb since he was a child. How many times do we have to talk about this? You always bring up some sort of worry, and nothing ever comes of it. I'm sure Caleb's just fine."

"No, but this is different, Jon. You can expect little kids to naturally withdraw or get angry at little things, or to behave oddly, but Caleb's almost 18. I've noticed for a long time how he's always been different from other kids his age. He's not normal, there's something wrong with him, I know it. I even went and talked to Dr. Phillip and he said that…."

"You talked to the doctor?" Jon questioned.

"Well, yes, I did, I was concerned, and I knew from previous experience that you wouldn't listen to me. You'd just try to brush it off as nothing because you don't want to face that your son could possibly have a serious problem or something."

"Don't tell me how I feel, Kathryn. I'm a psychologist, I would notice if there was any strange behavior in Caleb, and I would be able to diagnose it."

Kathryn sighed heavily. Her husband always seemed to use his psychologist mask as a defense against his insecurity. She shook her head as she walked up to her husband's desk and tore the papers from under his nose. "You may be a psychologist and know about this kind of stuff, but even if you could notice a disorder in somebody, you wouldn't notice it in Caleb because you hardly acknowledge that he exists."

The words fumbling from Kathryn's lips had slapped Jon Lockwood in the face that afternoon as he realized the truth in them. But not willing to back down from any defiance, he stood up and attempted to deny what he knew was plainly shining through him.

"How can you say that about our son? How can you stand here and tell me I've never noticed him, never cared about him? He's my only son, for heaven's sake."

"Jon, I didn't mean that you've never cared about him or noticed him at all." Kathryn's voice became soft. "It's just been the last few years, when you've gotten so caught up in everything else that you haven't had proper time for him. And this is the worst time in his life, with being a teenager and all. Don't you remember your teenage years? Don't you remember what it was like thinking your father didn't care about you or love you?"

"Is that what Caleb thinks?" Jon stood erect, his hands glued firmly to his desktop, anticipating what information was to be thrown at him next.

Kathryn hopelessly shook her head and cast her eyes to the floor. "I don't know," she replied. "I don't know anything for sure, that's why I wanted to talk to you about it. That's why I went to see Dr. Phillip." She sat in a corner chair and put her head in her hands.

Throughout the whole conversation, the one thing that the two

Lockwoods weren't aware of was the presence standing ten feet away from the office door. Caleb ears had drunk up every word the adults had poured out, and his features had drained from any emotion shown on them as he realized how his mother had indeed figured him out, and figured his father out. He praised his mother for that afternoon and loved her even more for it.

* * *

Caleb tried to shake the intertwining memories from his head. Those were remembrances he didn't want swimming around his head his whole life, always surfacing to haunt him. He knew that in time, the memories would fade – the hurt already had, and he had forgiven his parents, but he also knew that even though the memories would fade, they could never be erased from his mind. He knew that trying to forget about his past life and repressing it would solve nothing but instead cause the memories to soak up all the emotion they could before squeezing it out negatively when he least expected it. And those were grudges he couldn't afford to hold. He would just have to learn to live with his past, since it couldn't be changed, accept it, and get on with his future.

Lindsey held her breath as the Honda sailed across the bridge of the Columbia River. Normally, Lindsey would have been feeling fine crossing any bridge, but this one was different. This wasn't a bridge built high above the water; it was lowered so much that it looked as if it floated on the river itself. If an earthquake or hurricane or some other monstrous natural disaster occurred, the bridge would crumble as easily as a cracker between two hands. That idea, along with the bleak cloudy sky, created an uneasy feeling in Lindsey that she couldn't shake away.

It was definitely nerves, but not from the bridge and weather itself.

She was anxious about how she could possibly drive all the way to Virginia on her own ... battling inconstant weather, fighting ruthless bridges, and overcoming the soul-pervading loneliness that swamped her being a little more with each infinite hour that passed.

Finally arriving safely on the other side of the bridge, and cursing it behind her with a forced laugh, she followed the near-empty highway up a small hill, turning into a lookout point at the top. From there, the whole Columbia River – and that detestable bridge – was in view.

Lindsey turned off her Honda and gazed around the small lot area. There were two other vehicles there, one of which was just pulling out. Lindsey cocked her head to the side and rubbed the back of her neck before stepping out of the Honda and slowly making her way across the narrow pavement paths to the actual look-out. She was alone there, as she hoped.

What a forlorn scene, she thought. The Columbia River was not a pretty picture, at least not on this damp afternoon. Cutting out a small canyon in the rocks, it was trapped on both sides, and its waters clutched an ugly brownish black pigment, most likely from the reflection of the sky. Lindsey shook her head in disgust, leaning on her arms, which were draped over the information plaque.

She closed her eyes, allowing her ears to enfold the melody of wind, and of swishing waters … and car engines as they zoomed by on the highway. And then Lindsey sighed, again gazing out at her dismal surroundings. Although she wanted to leave, to flee this place, which seemed to be using some force to pull her in, she couldn't bring herself to budge. Maybe it was fatigue, or laziness, or the sense that she was making a huge mistake.

What am I doing? she caught herself thinking. *Why am I even considering this trek across the country? For heaven's sake, I don't even know exactly how I'll get to Virginia. I have a map, but what if I take the wrong roads?* Her hands started to shake, and she suddenly felt as if her legs would give way. *Why did I think I could actually do this? I'm so crazy; I'm so crazy. This isn't going to work; this isn't going to work! I'm alone, I'm alone, I'm alone….*

A tear rolled down her round cheek, and she quickly swiped it away with a trembling hand. No more crying, she told herself, but it was too late.

"May I ask what's wrong," a woman's voice sounded behind her.

Lindsey swung around to find a tall, skinny girl with thick, wavy hair staring at her with concern in her eyes. Lindsey wiped at her eyes again, mumbling "no" as she offered a short, quick shake of her head and walked right past the girl.

Turning and following Lindsey with her eyes, the girl called out, "Are you sure? You just looked a little sad and shaken up."

Lindsey lowered her head. She wasn't in the mood to be bothered by a stranger, but she didn't wish to be rude, either, especially to a kind, lovely girl who had mysteriously deep eyes and a genuine touch in her voice. Lindsey turned.

"I am shaken up," she said slowly, nodding her head slightly. "I just … I don't know … well, I…." She stopped, putting her hands over her face.

The girl walked toward her. "You don't have to explain," she said. "So there's things going on in your life right now, huh?"

Lindsey nodded, wrinkling her nose. "Yeah, lots of things."

"Yeah, I know what that feels like," the girl agreed. A moment of silence passed. Who was this girl? And why was she talking to Lindsey like this?

Sensing Lindsey's discomfort, the girl straightened and stepped back a little. "Oh, I'm sorry if I'm being too nosy," she apologized. "I don't even know you, but I saw you standing there looking distressed, and I just couldn't ignore that. I don't know why, I just have a soft spot for wanting to help people, I guess."

"Don't worry about it," Lindsey assured her. "It was very nice of you to even be concerned about a stranger."

"Yeah, well, I'm no anti-social personality, I guess." The girl smiled, exposing almost perfectly white, straight teeth, save for an upper tooth at the side which was twisted and stuck out a little bit.

"I guess so," Lindsey said.

"So, how can I help you?" the girl asked sincerely.

Lindsey huffed. "Geez, I don't think you can. It's just something that I need to work out, I guess."

At that response, the girl furrowed her brows and wrinkled her nose a little. "Oh, well you can't always deal with tough stuff on your own, you know."

"Yeah, I know, but right now I don't have anybody to help deal with it."

Sure you do, the girl thought, but she didn't voice it. Instead she replied, "If it's my place, Lindsey, I would like to tell you that there is always somebody out there who cares about you and wants to help. You just have to let Him."

Lindsey nodded, and glanced at her feet, again feeling awkward. She supposed the girl was right, though, that there was somebody who would always care. There were her grandparents, of course, and Marianne; they cared about her more than anybody else she knew, certainly more than Nick did. Yeah, they cared about her and loved her, but then why hadn't she felt like she should stay for them? They weren't enough for her. All she knew in the weeks following her mother's death was that she was going crazy and needed to get away fast.

Suddenly a wave of apprehension flooded over her and she felt the same way. She needed to get away fast. This stranger with her odd, puzzling comfort was beginning to make Lindsey nervous. *This is weird. Who is this girl?*

"Uh, I really need to get going now," Lindsey said quickly.

The girl nodded. "Yeah, me too. I haven't even taken a look at the river yet."

Lindsey grumbled. "Don't, it's not pretty."

"All God's works are pretty. They're just affected by change. In this case, it's the weather. I'm sure the river looks more promising on a hot, sunny day where brightness is just radiating off of it."

"Uh, yeah, you're probably right." *Gotta get out of here!* "Thanks for chatting with me a bit."

"No problem, Lindsey."

It was the second time she said her name. Had Lindsey given the girl her name?

Lindsey wasted no time in pulling out of the lot as quickly as she could, neglecting her seat belt, nor even checking her mirrors. There were no other cars in the parking lot anyway, and no other people.

No other cars....

Lindsey frowned. No other cars in the parking lot. There was nothing on this side of the bridge from where she could have come. Had the girl just walked across the bridge from the other side?

Yeah, Lindsey concluded. *She must've walked from the little diner on the other side of the river. But then how did she know my name?*

Caleb turned into a *Motel 6* in Spokane early that evening. Parking and exiting the truck, he made his way toward the front entrance of the motel. He stepped into the lobby and peered around. A big round desk was placed in the center of the lobby, and he slowly walked over toward it to ask for a room.

"Hello, sir," the woman behind the desk greeted Caleb in exaggerated friendliness. Caleb could see the weariness encasing her features, and her eyes drooped slightly from long working hours. "I suppose you need a room, huh?"

"Gee, how'd ya know?"

"Hmm, I guess I'm just psychic, I guess." Caleb chuckled at the repetition in her sarcastic sentence and glanced around. The room had another section to it that was littered with a few couches, tables, a television, and coffee tables with newspapers scattered about them. As the woman behind the counter continued asking Caleb questions, a flash of blond hair lying on top of one of the couches caught Caleb's eye.

"So what floor would you like?"

Caleb turned around. "Oh, it doesn't matter. Three, I guess, if you have anything up there."

"Yep, we do, or else I wouldn't have asked."

Caleb just nodded as he watched the woman who looked to be in her late twenties type away at a keyboard, entering information. "Looks like you could use a room too," he sputtered.

The woman looked up, her tiresome gaze peering directly at Caleb's flustered face. He wondered if maybe he shouldn't have said anything at all. She just slowly smiled and resumed her work while declaring, "I think you're right. I'm working too long, that's all. But you're right." She looked up again. "You wanna switch spots? You come back here and work for me while I take your room and get some sleep?"

Caleb smiled and laughed out loud. "I feel for you, I really do," he stated teasingly, putting a hand across his heart to emphasis his 'sincerity', "but I need to be getting sleep myself."

"Well, Mr. ... whatever your name is ... I appreciate that, I really do."

"My name's Caleb. And you're welcome." Taking his key from the woman, he smiled one last time as he turned to leave and seek out his room. As he was nearing the elevator, he glanced to his right to find a pair of eyes peering at him from over the top of the couch where the blond hair had been. Once Caleb spotted her watching him, the girl quickly turned around and continued her television watching. Caleb's eyebrows raised as he caught a glimpse of the pretty face outlined by the long, blond hair. Nevertheless, he shrugged it off as he tossed his room key in the air, caught it, and entered the elevator that would take him to the third floor of the *Motel 6*.

The hum of the television was drowned out as Lindsey focused her attention on the young man in the lobby nearing the elevator. He had caught her staring at him from over the couch, and so she dared not glance back again. She just focused her ears on his shuffling steps to the elevator but kept her body turned forward on the couch.

The elevator chimed, and Lindsey heard the sound of its doors sliding open. The boy entered, and then Lindsey peered behind her again, slowly, cautiously. She hadn't gotten a good look at him before, but he appeared to be good-looking.

When she was successfully turned so that she could see him, the elevator's doors had just closed. *Oh well, he's just a dumb guy and it's not like I'm gonna hook up with him.* Lindsey swung herself back to her normal sitting position on the couch and continued enjoying her television show.

Four

Don't forget to do good things for others and to share what you have with them. These are the kinds of sacrifices that please God.

– Hebrews 13:16

The automatic sliding doors of the supermarket opened for Nick Pruitt as he approached them, quickly entering the store. He walked fast-paced, not wanting Vanessa to be waiting long in the car for him. As he turned a corner to enter an aisle, he flinched when a figure walked right into him.

"Ouch!" Marianne exclaimed as the few items she was carrying flew out of her hand. "Thanks a lot," she said sarcastically, glancing down at her foot that Nick had just stepped onto.

"Geez … oh hey there," Nick said as he recognized Marianne. "Sorry about that."

Marianne looked up to see Nick standing, his face apologetic. "Oh Nick, I'm sorry, I didn't even know it was you," she said. "If I did, I wouldn't have been so rude. Whatcha up to?" she asked as she bent over to pick up her scattered grocery items.

Nick bent over to help Marianne. "Oh I'm just getting a few things for tonight. Some friends are coming over to hang out," he replied, standing up.

Marianne stood up and raised an eyebrow. "Oh, like Vanessa?"

"Uh, yeah, but not just her. She's waiting in the car now, so I don't want to be long."

Marianne nodded her head and peered up at Nick with a sympathetic look on her face. "What a nuisance huh?"

Nick ignored her comment and instead brought up a new subject of conversation. "So how's Lindsey doing? Have you talked to her lately?"

"Oh, yeah, yeah I have, I talked to her the other day actually. She's fine I guess," Marianne replied as she slipped a loose strand of her thick red hair behind her ears.

"That's good."

"Yeah, She's gone, you know. She's probably in Idaho about now."

Nick's eyebrows raised in curiosity. "What? What do you mean?" he exclaimed, confused. "I didn't know she was gone. Where's she going? Is she on vacation with her grandparents or something?"

Marianne's face broke into a grin, and she chuckled. "Nick, Nick, Nick...." she said slowly as she shook her head. "Why are you so interested in Lindsey's life all of a sudden? And what makes you think you even deserve to know where she is and why she went? What business is it of yours?"

Nick sighed, growing annoyed. "What do you mean? I'm still her friend. I just want to know, that's all. What, did she move or something?"

Marinanne chuckled again, gazing at the floor with amusement lighting her face. "You call yourself her friend? Have you even talked to her since you guys broke up? And yeah, I guess you could say she moved. Or she's in the process of moving."

"Where? Why did she move?"

"Well, if you were her friend, then I'd think you'd already know that."

"Will you just get off my back about that, Marianne? What do you want me to say or do? It didn't work out with us, okay? But I still care about her."

Marianne thought for a second, deciding whether or not she should tell Nick about Lindsey's trek across the country. "Okay then. I guess if you didn't care about her, you wouldn't be asking, huh? She left to go across the country. She's gonna find her dad in Virginia and live with him."

Nick's eyes grew wide in astonishment. "Are you serious? She's driving all the way across the country by herself?"

"Yep."

"Why? Why is she moving?"

"Well, geez, Nick, let me think," Marianne stated sarcastically. "Her mom is no longer alive, she's not going to college anymore, I doubt she wants to live with her grandparents, and you kinda added a damper to everything because of the jerk that you were to her."

"Shut up, Marianne, you don't know anything about what happened between us."

"Oh I know enough. But it doesn't matter anymore because it's already done with, right? She's gone and I doubt she's ever coming back." Marianne sighed and lowered her head. Her voice changed its tone from sarcasm to sadness. "Basically, I'd say she probably felt she didn't really have anything here to hold on to. She'd kinda be wasting away here, ya know?"

"What about you and the other girls? Aren't you guys even important enough for her to stay?"

"Apparently not."

Silence trailed behind that last comment as the two teenagers stood in the middle of the aisle facing each other but not looking at each other. Nick closed his eyes for a moment and rubbed his forehead. He knew he hadn't treated Lindsey right, and all of a sudden he felt totally responsible for Lindsey's leaving.

Lindsey sat up in bed that morning with her head pounding as if a large hand was knocking on it, and after a few moments of unconsciousness she woke up and realized that someone was knocking on the door of her motel room. She groaned and crawled out of the large bed, her right hand rubbing her temple. She wondered who would be looking for her in Spokane.

"Housekeeping!" came the sound of a woman's voice from outside the door. Lindsey slowly opened the door a crack and peered out to find a small, tired-looking woman standing with one hand on her hip and her mouth pursed in annoyance. "Housekeeping," the woman said again, then added, "Checkout time was ten minutes ago, you need to be out of the room unless you're staying another night."

"Oh shoot," Lindsey cursed as she swung her head around to check the digital clock on the nightstand that read 11:12 a.m. "I'm sorry, I slept in. Just give me an hour, okay? I'll be out by then."

The woman rolled her eyes and tilted her head. "I'll give you 'till twelve, all right? I don't have all day you know, I'm on a schedule."

"I know, I'm sorry," Lindsey apologized, closing the door with a slam. "Some people...."

As noon approached, Lindsey was already showered, packed, and checked out of the *Motel 6* before the housekeeper could even knock at the room that had been occupied by her.

The waitress tilted her head back and laughed as a fellow waitress charmed her and a few other workers at the *Denny's* with an amusing anecdote. She was still chuckling when she brought the bill to the young man waiting silently and patiently at table 31, sipping his orange juice.

She smiled warmly at Caleb as she set the bill down on the tabletop. "Would you like another orange juice? They're free re-fills, you know."

"Nah, that's okay. I'm fine, thanks."

"All right then," she said, but she didn't go. Instead, she sat down in the chair opposite Caleb and folded her hands on the table. She had an oblong face, outlined by dark hair and garnished with large brown eyes and a small nose. Caleb thought she had a unique look. After a couple of seconds, she spoke. "I'm not really supposed to take a break, but I was just wondering ...

why is it that a good-looking young boy like yourself is eating breakfast all alone? I mean … if you don't mind me asking."

"Oh I don't mind," Caleb replied, then went on. "I'm actually not from here. I'm just passing through. I'm working my way to North Carolina."

The waitress's eyes grew wide as she re-clipped her course brown hair back into a ponytail near the top of her head. "Are you serious? You're going across the country?"

"Uh huh."

"Are you driving?"

"Yep."

"Alone?"

Caleb laughed at her child-like curiosity. "Yeah."

"Wow, so you're just passing through, huh? Where are you coming from?"

"Bellingham, Washington."

"Oh, I know where that is. So you haven't been on the road long then, huh?"

"No, I just left yesterday. I spent the night in Spokane."

"So how do you like Coeur d'Alene?" the waitress asked, glancing to her left to make sure she wasn't needed amongst the other workers.

"Oh, well, I just got here, actually. I stopped to eat, but I don't think I'll be taking any time to do anything. I'm gonna head out in a few minutes."

"You driving into Montana?"

"Yep."

The waitress sighed and leaned back in the chair. "Well, you have a long trip ahead of you. I think that's great, though. It's good to do stuff like that when you're still young. I mean, I've lived in this town my whole life. I haven't been around much, you know." She stopped, gazing out the window. Caleb's eyebrows came together in confusion. He noted that her eyes held something solemn within them, almost like a longing of some sort. He realized that this woman hadn't had a very promising or happy life, and he suddenly felt for her.

"Well I'm not going for fun or anything," Caleb stated, not exactly sure what to say to her changing mood. "My parents live in North Carolina, so I was just going back home to live with them."

"Yeah? So why were you living in Washington?"

"My aunt and uncle live there, and I went there for college."

The waitress nodded. "Really? That's great. I never went to college. Most of the girls that are working here now are in college, and this is just a part-time job for them. This is a full-time job for me though. So I think that's good that you went to college and everything."

Caleb sat silently, nodding his head but not knowing how to reply.

"I'm sorry," the waitress said, noticing that she had made Caleb uncomfortable. "You don't even know me, I shouldn't be dumping out all this stuff on you."

"No, no, it's okay," Caleb replied, sensing that this woman just needed somebody to talk to. "I mean, you can still always go back. If you have an idea of what kind of job you would like, you can go to a community college and take a few classes that could help you."

She shook her head. "Well, I don't have the money for that. I mean, I suppose I could save it up, but you don't make much waitressing, and I have a daughter that I need to support anyway."

"You're not married?"

"No. I was, but we got divorced. It didn't work out."

"I'm sorry about that." There was a moment of silence before Caleb went on. He suddenly wanted so badly to share his faith with this woman, but he was reluctant in doing so. He didn't know if it was something she would want to hear. "You know, happiness isn't really found in jobs anyway. I mean, even if you did have a job that you liked better than this, and that you made more money in, that doesn't guarantee that you'd be any happier or more content. I mean, you probably would be for a while, but not for long."

"You think so?" The waitress lowered her head and placed her hands in her lap. "I don't know about that."

"Well then, what do you think you need out of life to be happy?"

She shrugged her shoulders. "Oh I don't know. Besides a good job and making good money? A husband, I suppose." She stopped and eyed Caleb curiously, almost suspiciously. "How would you know whether I was happy or not anyway?"

Caleb shifted in his seat. "I just thought you might not be. Your eyes … they don't look very happy."

"Well, it's on and off, you know," she said. She smiled and continued talking. "I'd like a nice marriage, a nice home, a small family. I don't know. Can people ever really be happy all the time, or content in their lives? It seems like nowadays there's always something wrong going on in everybody's life."

"Well, I don't agree with that," Caleb stated almost defensively. "I mean, of course nothing's ever going to be perfect. People are always going to run into troubles and trials, but I think people can still be happy in spite of them, as long as they can deal with them."

The waitress stared at Caleb, amazed that such a positive outlook could come from such a young man. But she didn't take to heart what Caleb said, because she knew that he probably hadn't been through what she had been through. However, there was a hope inside of him that attracted her. It was almost as if a light was shining through him, and she wanted to jump in front of him and be part of it. She wanted that hope and that young, positive outlook on life.

"You do, huh?" she said as a small grin spread across her face. "Maybe, but I don't see how."

"Maybe you're just looking for happiness in all the wrong places."

"Mary! What are you doing? We need you back here. Stop socializing with the customers, please!"

Mary turned her head to find one of the other waitresses summoning her. She quickly stood up, and Caleb followed her lead, clutching the bill in his hand. "I'm sorry, I have to go. Sorry to have kept you waiting," Mary apologized.

"No, it's okay. It's nice to have met you, Mary. I'm Caleb." Caleb outstretched his hand for Mary to shake it. She took his hand and smiled into his face.

"It was nice to meet you." She stood for a long time shaking his hand, not wanting to end the conversation so abruptly. Finally, she said, "Can I ask you something?"

"Sure."

"What makes you seem so happy and positive? Where do you find happiness?"

Caleb was stunned at her question, but knew that this opened a door of opportunity to share his faith with this stranger. His heart started to beat more rapidly, but he silently prayed that God would give him the right words.

"Well, I believe that happiness comes from God."

"God?"

"Yeah."

"Mary! Please, Tim isn't gonna be happy if he knows you've taken a break."

"I'm sorry, I really have to go. Thanks for your company. Maybe I'll run into you again sometime if you come back to Coeur d'Alene."

"Sure, I'll see you then."

"Bye." Mary ran off toward the kitchen, and Caleb watched her, feeling disappointed that he didn't get to speak with her more about God. Nevertheless, he knew that whether she found what she needed or not, that would be God's doing, and not his own. With that in mind, Caleb walked to the cash register, paid his bill, and headed out of Idaho toward Montana.

The Johns' telephone rang almost incessantly until Chelsea Johns finally picked herself up off the couch with a grunt and walked toward the office to retrieve it. She shot a look toward her husband who was lounging in his desk, reading a book, and shook her head in disapproval before picking up the receiver. "Hello, Johns residence."

"Hi, Grandma, it's me."

A smile instantly took over Chelsea's downturned grin. "Lindsey, hi, honey."

Daniel glanced up from his reading with raised eyebrows at the sound of Lindsey's name.

"Where are you?" Chelsea asked.

"I'm in Missoula, Montana. I just got here."

"Oh good, good. But I figured you'd be further by now." Chelsea stood straight up, wrapping the spiral phone cord around her fingers. Daniel laughed at his wife's display of child-like enthusiasm. That had always been one of his favorite qualities.

"Well, we jumped ahead an hour already, and I'm taking my time anyway."

"Are you going to stay there tonight?" Chelsea asked Lindsey.

"Uh, I don't think so. I think I'm gonna drive a little further." Lindsey replied.

"Well, that sounds good, but don't go too much further if you can't. How are you feeling?"

Lindsey held the pay-phone receiver to her right hear, covering her left ear with her hand in order to hear her grandmother better. She turned and stared out of the booth, squinting at the harsh orange sun descending to its sleep. Glancing up at the sky, she noticed the dark rain clouds gathering, giving the town a dismal appearance in spite of the sunset. "I'm fine; kinda exhausted I guess. Driving gets pretty boring and lonely. There aren't many clear radio stations out here."

Chelsea chuckled and her eyes shone with laughter. "Well, I'm just glad you're all right. I hope you're being a careful driver."

"Oh, Chelsea, don't bug her about that, she'll hate it," Daniel warned, dropping his book to his lap. Chelsea ignored him and turned her back to him.

"Yeah, I'm fine, Grandma. You know I drive safe."

"I know, I know."

The television set in the Johns' office was mumbling something, and Chelsea cast her eyes on the program covering the screen. Her unsettled heart calmed down as she was able to hear her granddaughter's voice and know she was all right. At that moment, she felt she could smile forever, but as that feeling matured inside her, words invaded her ears that killed it instantly.

"Besides, Grandma, whether I was driving safe or not, there would be nothing you could do about it now anyway," Lindsey shot out, smiling.

Chelsea's smile dropped to the floor and her mouth opened in shock. "Lindsey," she said quietly, offended. "Why did you say that?"

Silence permeated the phone lines, and suddenly the only sound present was a buzzing from the line before Lindsey answered, "I don't know, I'm sorry, Grandma. I didn't mean that. It just came out. I didn't mean to be rude."

"I should hope not. That hurt my feelings, Lindsey."

"I'm sorry, Grandma."

"Do you think that fixes it all, Lindsey? Just saying sorry?"

Lindsey rolled her eyes and tipped her head back as she predicted what was coming – another pointless argument with her grandmother which had caught on fire over small embers. "Well, what do you want me to do, Grandma? What else is there besides sorry?"

"Well, how do I know you mean it?"

"Oh my gosh, Grandma, you're being ridiculous."

Chelsea spun around to face her husband, staring at him incredulously. "How dare you call me ridiculous, Lindsey. That's not very respectful."

Lindsey was a fraction away from slamming the phone down, but she restrained herself. All her grandmother could do to her now was talk, and Lindsey wasn't going to let it affect her. She was gone from all the chaos at her grandparents' place, and she wasn't going to let Chelsea forget that.

"This is one of the reasons I left, Grandma, so that I wouldn't have to put up with all your crap. What do you want me to do … sacrifice myself so you know how sorry I am? Why can't you just leave me alone? I'm calling like you want me to, and you're still treating me like I'm there."

Chelsea swallowed a sob and held the phone out to her husband to grab it from her. Daniel stood up and took the phone from Chelsea. "Hi, it's Grandpa."

"Hi."

"What's going on?"

"Ask Grandma," Lindsey replied quietly. "Besides, it doesn't really matter what I say."

"Yes, it does. Anything you have to say is important."

Lindsey rolled her eyes once again. "Maybe to you. I can't seem to say any of the right things to Grandma."

"She's just stubborn and old-fashioned, Lindsey, you know not to take everything she says so personally." Chelsea gasped at Daniel's reply and quickly stomped out of the office. Daniel smiled as he watched her leave in a huff. *Silly woman*, he thought.

"Well, I don't know what to do, I said sorry to her."

"She knows you're sorry, Lindsey, she just misses you."

"I really didn't mean to be rude. It was meant to be a joke."

"What was?"

Lindsey sighed. "I just basically told her that it didn't matter what I did because there's nothing she can do about it now that I'm gone."

"Oh, declaring your independence, huh?"

"Well, every time I seem to do that it gets me on bad terms with her."

The old clock hanging in the green wallpapered office ticked loudly. Daniel didn't reply right away, and Lindsey thought she could hear the ticking of the clock over the phone.

"I can hear your clock ticking."

"Really?"

"Yeah," she replied. "It reminds me of the first time I stayed overnight at your house when I was little. I don't remember how old I was, but it was late at night and I came downstairs to get something to drink. I remember I wanted a Hi-C. And that clock was the only thing I heard, and it scared me because it was such a creepy sound to hear all alone in the dark."

A half smile lit Daniel's face as he recalled the memory. "Yeah, I remember that. And I remember how afterward you came and jumped in bed with me and Grandma because you were scared."

Lindsey laughed and leaned against the side of the phone booth. "Yeah, I told you that the clock was scary, and you both looked at me really weird before you started laughing."

"I laughed at you?" Daniel asked. "I don't remember laughing at you. For goodness' sake, you were terrified."

Lindsey straightened up and wiped the amusement from her face. "No, *you* didn't laugh, Grandma laughed at me. I remember, just Grandma."

Lindsey's head dropped as she listened to the silence speaking to her from the other side of the phone line. Finally, Daniel spoke up.

"Chelsea really loves you, you know. She gets too concerned sometimes."

"I know."

"I'm always the peacemaker, aren't I?"

"What's that?"

"I'm always trying to work things out between your grandmother and you, trying not to choose sides. It's always been like that. I don't understand why it's so hard for you two to talk."

"I don't either. Maybe someday."

"Maybe. Hopefully."

"I'm sorry, Grandpa. I never meant to put you in the middle of things."

"No, no, don't worry about me. I know you have good intentions. I trust you."

Lindsey was relieved to hear those words out loud, coming from a family member. When she had left the previous morning, she felt she had nothing to hold on to anymore, not even her own family. But with her grandfather's true and honest words, she slowly started to realize how wrong she might have been.

"I love you, Grandpa. Tell Grandma I'm sorry, and that I love her too."

"I will. I love you too, honey. Have a safe trip."

"I will, thanks. See ya later."

"Bye."

The sound of the rain against his truck reminded Caleb of thousands of miniature drums all beating concurrently, stirring up an eerie tune. As his eyes focused on the stretch of highway ahead of him, his ears inhaled the rain's melody. But as he listened, his ears got tired when he realized that there was no organization to the beating of the rain. There really was no tune, no melody.

The sun had kneeled below the horizon, and only dimness penetrated the sky, allowing easy sight, but not for long. Caleb switched his headlights on and kept driving. His last stop had been outside of Missoula, and from the weariness creeping into his body, and the sleepiness overtaking his eyes, he knew he probably should have stopped there to stay the night. Common sense convinced him that he needed to stop soon to search out a motel.

The next exit caught his eye right away, and he carefully checked his mirrors to change lanes to catch the exit. He was surprised that there were so many cars on the road this time of night and in this almost barren land called Montana. The road off the exit was curvy and led in between two large hills, clothed by a thickness of trees. He felt reluctant to take that road, but the sign on the side of the road had promised a motel at the end of it. Caleb continued on his way.

The rain eased a bit, and Caleb finally turned on his radio to find some interesting music to fill his ears. As he drove on, he saw a small light ahead on the side of the road. He dismissed it and went along singing quietly to the radio as he concentrated on not slipping on the wet road. But as he drove even closer, the light became bigger, and curiosity made its mark on Caleb. He slowed down and leaned forward, squinting in the dark to view the thing on the side of the road. After a couple seconds of squinting, a shape of a car leaped out of the darkness, and Caleb soon realized that the light he saw was the headlight of the car.

"Oh my gosh," he slowly exclaimed to himself as he suddenly realized that the car was turned on its side in a ditch. He slammed on his brakes right next to the vehicle and jumped out of his truck without turning the engine off. He approached the vehicle, the engine of which was still steaming freshly from the recent crash, and he suddenly stopped two feet away from it. Caleb's heart was racing, and his legs grew weak. He felt he could faint as he recognized his helplessness of what to do next.

"Uh, hello." Caleb's voice was weak and shaky. He took a step forward. "Is somebody in there?" There were no major dents on the Honda, but the hood was popped open with a thin cloud of steam rising from the engine. Caleb looked behind him and noticed the fresh skid marks on the road.

A groan rose from inside the Honda.

Released from his panic, Caleb took the final steps to the vehicle and grasped the door handle to open the door. It wouldn't open. He couldn't open the other door handle because the car was lying on its left side. He peered inside the window and saw the figure of a person leaning against the driver's seat with their head down. Caleb noticed the long hair cascading down covering the face and realized it was a woman trapped inside.

"Oh, God, please help me. What do I do?" As he uttered those words, he looked around and his vision beheld a large rock near the tire of the car. Without hesitation he grabbed it and smashed it against the window, shattering the glass. He reached his arm inside and fumbled to find the door lock.

The girl groaned again and tossed her head back. Caleb opened the door quickly, almost knocking it off its hinges, and crawled inside the vehicle, taking a quick glance in the backseat to see if there was anybody else in the car. There was nobody else but the girl. Her eyes were closed and she was unconscious, but Caleb could see her chest rising from her breathing. It seemed pretty steady, so Caleb just focused on pulling her out of the car. Once he did, he picked her up under his strong arms, and she immediately put her arms around his neck to hold on. He set her inside his truck in the passenger seat, and before speeding off to a hospital, he paused a moment and grabbed her purse from the front seat.

Five

Pray in the Spirit in every situation. Use every kind of prayer and request there is. For the same reason be alert. Use every kind of effort and make every kind of request for all of God's people.

– Ephesians 6:18

The blackness seemed alive, almost as if it were its own entity, hovering in vast nothingness, but it was alive. Although it was only blackness and looked as if it was never changing, it moved, it crawled, it was deep and endless. It was only blackness, but it pervaded her whole mind. Blackness was all Lindsey could see, although, since her emerald eyes weren't actually open, she wasn't physically seeing blackness, only perceiving and envisioning it. But it was there, and she was consciously aware of it.

Her body rocked back and forth, and she smiled at the feeling of being totally limp against the soft, cushioned seat while it moved as the truck bumped along the road. Lindsey's head softly fell to the right and her eyes slid open. The blackness now took on another form as it began to whiz past her outside, and small dots of light began to pass through it. Lindsey groaned as she regained consciousness and realized that what she was staring at were the stars in the dark night sky. And before her mind could register anything otherwise, it began to pound and throb as if some large being was trapped inside it, knocking on her head, trying desperately to free itself from all the pain and confusion wrestling inside. She groaned again and shut her eyes tight.

Caleb's nervous heart had ceased no less as he drove at a desperate speed through the windy road to find the nearest hospital. His sweaty palms gripped the steering wheel tightly, and at the sound of Lindsey groaning, his right foot pressed down the accelerator once more to gain speed. He glanced over at her and noticed that her head was moving. She was awake most likely. Suddenly she rolled her head to the left side and her tightly shut eyes slowly opened. Caleb turned his head back to the road. Lindsey's vision was blurred, and she continued shutting and opening her eyes to re-focus her vision. Her head pounded painfully, and within a few seconds, her body also started to ache. First her neck, then her shoulders and back, and before she knew it the pain had sunk its way to her legs. She leaned against the seat in total surrender. She could barely hold her head up. At first all she saw as she opened her eyes once more was one of the seat belt buckles on the seat. Then her eyes moved upward and she saw a body. Someone driving. Her gaze continued upward; she saw hands, and a steering wheel occupied by those hands….

Caleb's body sat rigid, unmoving, except for his arms that guided the direction of the steering wheel. He was aware of Lindsey's gaze on him, and he was reluctant to turn his head once again to look at her. What if she got scared? What if she didn't know what had happened to her or where she was or why? She wouldn't know who he was, although somehow he had found her unmistakably familiar. As her throat cast out another groaning noise and it entered Caleb's ears, reflex caused him to look over at her against his will. His eyes caught hers. She was staring at him. His breath caught in his throat, and he turned his head once again to the road. Her eyes had looked large and frightened, and he couldn't bear to look at her for long. *Oh no, she's gonna have a heart attack and start freaking out.*

Caleb cleared his throat and was about to introduce himself, when at once Lindsey made a remark that surprised him and her both. "Uhhh, my neck and back hurt."

Caleb looked at her in astonishment. Her eyes were still large, and her face beheld the innocence and concern of a child. He smiled, suddenly relieved that she was conscious and sane, and that her brain hadn't turned to mush in the car wreck.

"Uh, yeah, you got into a pretty serious car wreck, you know," Caleb replied.

"Oh I did?" she asked slowly as she closed her eyes for a moment and brought her hand up to rub her forehead. "Yeah, I think you're right, I did, didn't I?"

Caleb almost laughed. "Yeah, but it looks now like you might be okay. I'm taking you to a hospital though."

Lindsey groaned again, although this time not from physical pain. "Oh I don't like hospitals. I don't know why, I just don't. I think it's cuz of my mom…." her voice trailed off and she took a deep breath. Caleb could tell she was falling back into sleep. She could hardly keep her head up straight, and her eyes were falling closed again.

"Just hang on, okay, we're gonna be there soon. You'll be okay."

"Mmmm, okay." She turned her head back to her other side to stare out the window, then turned it back again to face Caleb. "What's your name?"

"Caleb," he answered. "My name's Caleb."

"Okay." Her head dropped slightly, and she turned it back towards the window. Her eyes closed one last time that night, and before her body drifted into a relaxing and painless sleep, she uttered a few last words, "You're my hero, Caleb."

Caleb smiled, and all he could think of to do was pray, *Lord, please let me get there in time. Don't let her fall asleep forever.*

Chelsea awoke to the soft pounding of rain on the bedroom windows and on the skylight in the ceiling. As her eyes opened, she stared up at the black sky peeking through the skylight, the rain quickly blurring the dull image. Chelsea turned her head, still heavy on her pillow, to read the time. Her digital alarm clock read 1:06 a.m. She turned in the bed and sighed heavily. She and Dan had just gotten to bed two hours ago, and the only sleep Chelsea could catch were little 20 minute-intervals of unconsciousness. She was still shocked and disillusioned with the phone call earlier from her granddaughter.

Even more than the pattering of the rain droplets from outside and the spark of hurt from the phone conversation that had been keeping her up, something else suddenly intruded upon her sleep. She didn't feel right about something. All of a sudden she felt concerned and burdened, as if a heavy weight were tied around her ankles and she couldn't get it off. It was that feeling of knowing something was left undone or unfinished in the house right after taking off on vacation – something wasn't right, and Chelsea could feel it. It bothered her.

"Dan, Dan, are you awake?"

Dan turned over in bed to face his wife and smiled graciously. "Of course not. How about you?"

"Oh yeah, I'm sound asleep." Chelsea joked. "How come you can't sleep?"

"Uh, I don't know. I guess I was never really all that tired. What about you? I keep feeling you moving around in bed, that's probably why I can't get to sleep, gosh darn it." Dan watched his wife's face contentedly. In the darkness, with the only light being that from the distant moon hovering in the immense sky, Chelsea's face, lit with a tiny smile pursing her lips, looked as young and beautiful as ever. The moonlight peeking through the skylight cast a shadow on one side of her face, which successfully concealed any signs of age that had once before taken shelter within the last thirty years of their marriage. But despite age, Dan always believed that his wife looked the same as when he'd met her forty years ago.

Chelsea laughed, and for a second she had laughed away that distraught feeling clutching her. "I don't know. I'm still a little upset about that phone conversation. And all of a sudden I got this really bad feeling, like something's happened. Something's not right."

"Something, huh? Like what?" Dan couldn't help but frown a little from the look on Chelsea's face.

"I don't know, maybe something with Lindsey. I'm concerned about her."

"Chelsea, you've been concerned about her since she left the other night. That's not anything new."

"I know, I know, it's just, well, I can't explain it."

"You're just feeling extra emotion because of that phone conversation, that's all," Dan replied, grabbing his wife's hand from under the covers. "I know Lindsey really upset you, she knows that too, but don't worry. She's not totally ignorant of the way she treats you."

"Gee, thanks," Chelsea retorted sarcastically. "How come it's me and not you? Why are you always the peacemaker? Why is it me who always gets on her bad side?"

"Because you're the only person who will voice your concerns about her," Dan said. "She knows already, Chelsea; she knows you care about her and get worried. You just don't need to remind her all the time, you know? She doesn't want to hear that."

"I know, but I just worry so much."

"Well, yeah, so do I. But what can worry really do for us anyway? She's already gone, and for us to sit around worrying about her so much isn't going to change anything she's done or will do. It's kind of out of our hands now, you know?"

Chelsea closed her eyes and squeezed her husband's hand. She felt so lost and empty at that moment, but she knew Dan was right. "Dan, do you really think there's a God? I mean, have you ever actually thought it through and considered that possibility?"

"Well, I don't know. Yes, sure, I think there might be. I can't say I really ever have considered it much, though. Why?" He stared into Chelsea's face as it held a twinge of curiosity and concern at the same time. He was slightly curious himself.

"Well, if there is, do you suppose He's watching over Lindsey right now?"

* * *

Caleb darted out the door and down the porch steps of the apartment building, dodging an eavesdropping neighbor as he rounded the corner, almost knocking the neighbor to the floor. He flew through the apartment complex to the parking lot, where his truck was waiting for him. Jumping in the vehicle, he turned on the engine and sped away with the last sound being the squeaking of tires.

"Caleb!" shouted Kathryn and Jon simultaneously, racing after their son. They had reached the parking lot in time to witness the blue Ford screeching its way down the block. Jon quickly headed for his vehicle in order to go after Caleb, but Kathryn stopped him.

"No, Jon, don't follow him," Kathryn pleaded, grabbing Jon's arm and pulling him back. "That's not what he wants. It will only upset him more."

Jon viciously pulled his arm away from Kathryn's gentle grip and stared at his wife with anger crossing his eyes. Kathryn backed up, confused by her husband's violent reaction. She shook her head and continued backing up slowly, her face drained of all color, and her eyes filling with tears. "Don't you start it, now, Jon. Don't you get angry on me like your son did." She turned and ran back into the apartment, and Jon was unable to do anything but stand alone in the parking lot, perplexed, drained of all energy and emotion.

Caleb sped down the road at 15 miles over the speed limit. He was angry, upset, bitter and depressed. He felt as if his heart had been torn open, breaking all emotional bonds from their security, and he wasn't sure why it was happening to him. He was depressed, and his parents weren't any help. They didn't love him, not like he wanted them to. They were just extra burdens in his life, always harassing him and complaining about him. Caleb couldn't understand so many aspects of his life. Everything he ever did seemed so pointless. Where was he headed, and for what reason?

Caleb kept up his pace in the Ford, not paying attention to the speedometer, and not even caring. He was hoping maybe if he was lucky, he would get into some kind of wreck and end his miserable existence. Why do I feel this way? Why can't I just be happy?

* * *

It was the voice of one of the two hospital receptionists that finally awoke Caleb from his memory. He twitched his head, realizing he had once again been gazing into his past, staring vacantly at the floor without seeing it.

"Are you okay?" the woman asked, noticing Caleb's empty stare.

"Yeah, I'm fine; just tired, I guess."

"Well, okay then, I just wanted to make sure you weren't gonna fall over or something."

Caleb nodded, and the two receptionists began conversing again, leaving Caleb to himself. He checked his watch. It was 1:30 in the morning. He yawned and lay down on the couch he was occupying in the main lobby of Powell County Memorial Hospital in Deer Lodge, Montana. He began to pray. *Lord, I just hope that this girl is all right. God, whatever Your reason was for me to find her and bring her here, I hope it all turns out according to Your will. I don't know why I'm here or why I'm still even in this waiting room, but I am, and it's got to be for a reason, right?*

It was at that moment that a doctor came to the lobby and noticed Caleb sprawled out on the couch with his hands covering his face as he prayed. Doctor Jones drifted across the lobby quickly and leaned over Caleb.

"Excuse me, are you the young man who brought in the woman from the car crash?"

Caleb abruptly stood up and placed his hands in the pockets of his jeans. He was taken aback by the doctor's young appearance. "Uh, yeah, that was me. She had long, blond hair, and I...."

"Yes, well, I just wanted to let you know that she's all right. She's mostly in a state of shock, but there were no signs of concussion or anything like that."

"Oh, good, good," Caleb replied, silently thanking God for her safety. "Uh, can I see her? Is she okay to have company?"

"Well, yes, but first I have to ask you some questions."

"Okay," Caleb said. He waited for the doctor to respond. Doctor Jones stayed silent and instead made a nodding gesture with his head signaling for Caleb to sit down. Caleb caught on and took a seat on the couch he had been lounging on, waiting impatiently for the doctor's next words.

"Do you know who this girl is that you saved? Is she a friend or a relative?"

Caleb straightened in his seat. "Oh, no, I just found her car on the side of the road and pulled her out of it. I don't think I've ever seen her before in my life."

"Okay. Well, her name is Lindsey Milholland, as indicated by her driver's license and other identification. She's 18 years old, and she comes from out of state."

Caleb nodded his head, taking in all the information.

"We talked to her and she said she didn't know who you were either, so I just wanted to check that out. She also said she wanted to talk to you if you were still here."

"Do you have any idea where she was headed, or why she crashed?"

"She said she swerved to avoid hitting an animal on the road."

"Oh, okay. Well, can I go see her now, then?"

"Yes, you can. Let me show you where she is."

The two men stood up, and the doctor led Caleb down a few halls to where Lindsey occupied a room. Caleb took a deep breath before entering, glancing at the doctor, who only smiled in reply before taking off down the hall to another assignment. Caleb entered slowly, peering around the curtain-divider to find Lindsey propped up in the hospital bed, staring out the window. Upon hearing footsteps, she turned her head to find Caleb approaching her cautiously. She smiled.

"Hi. Caleb, right?"

Caleb suddenly loosened up and allowed a smile to cross his face. "Yeah, that's right. You remember?"

"Yeah, yeah, of course I do. I remember taking a nice little ride in your truck, too. I wasn't dead in there, you know."

Caleb laughed. "Well, I'm glad you're okay. The doctor told me your name was Lindsey."

"Yep, that's me. Thanks for saving me, Caleb. I saw an animal in the road and just swerved automatically, you know, like reflex. Normally I know you're not supposed to endanger your life for an animal."

"Yeah, well I was just gonna tell you that so I'm glad you read my mind," Caleb replied. He walked over near the window and sat down in one of the chairs. "So you're definitely okay then, right?" he asked as he leaned forward and rested his elbows on his knees.

"Oh yeah, I'm fine. My head still hurts a little, but no big deal. I don't even know why I have to be in this bed. I'm not crippled or injured. Sometimes hospitals go to too great of lengths. It's really unnecessary."

Caleb just laughed a little and outstretched his arm for Lindsey to shake his hand. "Well, it's nice to meet you, Lindsey."

"You too, Caleb. And you really are my hero."

Before Caleb could reply, a nurse walked in the room, holding Lindsey's purse with her identification in it. "The police went and checked out your car and they retrieved all your luggage and things that were found inside. But the car's gonna need some repair, they said, and that might take a day or so. It was towed away to an impounding lot, and so they just need your say-so to take it to a repair shop."

"Okay, then I give you my say-so," Lindsey stated, shooting a smile in Caleb's direction.

"Do you have insurance?" the nurse asked.

"Of course," Lindsey replied. "You should find everything you need in my purse and in the car."

The nurse went on. "We were just about to call the number listed in your checkbook. Is that okay?"

Lindsey suddenly seemed adamant. "Oh, no, you don't have to call it. It's just where I live ... by myself ... so nobody's gonna answer anyway. I'm kinda on a little vacation right now, that's all," she lied.

"Well, is there anybody else that I can call for you? Any other family or relatives?"

"No, no," Lindsey replied a little agitated. "There's nobody you need to call. I'm fine. I'm an adult, I can take care of myself."

"All right then," the nurse replied slowly, turning abruptly and walking away. Lindsey rolled her eyes and tilted her head back.

"You don't have any other family or anything?" Caleb asked, curious. He could sense that there was something wrong in Lindsey's voice when she had answered the nurse.

Lindsey looked at him, contemplating whether she should answer his nosiness or not. "I didn't say that. There's just none of my family that is important enough for them to call."

Caleb creased his forehead, shocked by her answer. "Well, how come they're not important enough? I'm sure they'd want to know how you are, especially if you got in an accident."

"I'm fine!" Lindsey retorted. "Besides, the only family I've got is my grandparents, and I *would* let them know what happened except that they'd freak out, especially my grandmother, and I can't stand her when she gets all concerned."

A beeping noise from outside the room distracted Caleb as his thoughts sorted through what Lindsey had told him. Her grandparents were her only family? What about her mother or father? He wondered whether he should pry and ask her these questions, but he didn't want to be too overanxious or curious. He was still a stranger to her.

"Why should I even bother telling my family I got into an accident when I'm fine anyway, you know?"

"So that's not true that you live by yourself then, right?" Caleb asked, delving into a different subject.

Lindsey sighed. "No, I lived with my grandparents; the address and the phone number in my checkbook is my grandparents' place. Not mine."

Caleb nodded. "Okay." He wasn't sure what to say next. He thought he would have had so much to talk to this girl about, but in the discomfort and oddness of the situation he felt at a loss for words.

"Can I ask you something else that's kinda personal?"

Oh here it comes, Lindsey thought, figuring that Caleb would drill her on her history, and why she didn't have a mother or father.

"They said you're from out of state. So where are you from?"

Lindsey felt relieved. She smiled again. "That's not a personal question. Yeah, I'm from Washington."

"Really? I am too."

"No way, you are, really?" Lindsey exclaimed, leaning forward.

"Yeah," Caleb beamed, his face lit. "I mean, I'm not *from* Washington, but I've lived there the past few years with my aunt and uncle. Wow, what a coincidence, huh?"

"I guess so. So what are you doing over here, then?"

"Oh, well I'm on my way back home, to North Carolina. My mom and dad live there."

"Really?" Lindsey asked, enthused.

"Mm hmm."

"You're driving all across the country, huh?"

"Yep."

Lindsey shook her head as in disbelief, before replying, "So am I."

"You're joking!"

"No, I'm serious," Lindsey said, nodding her head, her eyes wide. "That whole thing about me taking a little vacation ... it's all bull. I'm moving across the country. It's more like a permanent vacation."

"Really," Caleb asked. "What for?"

"My dad lives in Virginia, so I'm going over there to live with him."

So she does have a dad, then, Caleb thought. "Well, that's cool," he voiced.

"Lindsey, a few police officers just arrived and they wanted to ask you a few questions about your accident," Doctor Jones interrupted.

Lindsey groaned. "Oh geez. Okay, whatever."

"Caleb, would you step out, please, while the police officers come in?" Doctor Jones asked. "They have some personal things to ask Lindsey."

"Oh yeah, sure," Caleb replied as he swiftly stood out of his chair. The doctor left the room, and Lindsey leaned in toward Caleb.

"As annoying as that man is, I don't ever think I've seen a better-looking doctor than him. It kinda makes the visit here worthwhile, you know," she whispered.

"No, I wouldn't know," Caleb laughed before exiting the room. "I'm not really attracted to handsome, young doctors, you know? I don't know why, it must be a guy thing."

Almost an hour had passed, and the police officers – two robust-looking middle-aged women clad in blue uniform – were still chatting endlessly with Lindsey. Caleb rubbed his strained neck and walked over to the coffee machine in the lobby to re-fill his Styrofoam cup with yet another bit of wake-me-up. His eyes were beginning to droop, and his whole body felt heavy. *What am I doing here? What am I doing here? I should just go, she's fine, and I'm running late.* But Caleb wasn't really on any time schedule. He just hated to be immobile. Becoming impatient, he made his way out of the lobby, around the corner, and down two different halls right outside Lindsey's room to see if he could come in yet.

During his small walk, he noticed that hospitals definitely do have a particular smell about them. Maybe it was the sickness, or all the medication in the air. He didn't know and could never figure it out. But every hospital he'd ever been in, the smell had been there. In almost every room he passed, the doors were open, and the sounds of quiet television shows murmuring and nurses whispering dominated the area. In one room, however, a small child was yelling and crying, and out of another room came a sort of groaning noise. Caleb instantly knew it belonged to an old man. Caleb frowned at the hospital noises and sounds and was relieved when he finally reached Lindsey's room.

She was still busy with the officers. Caleb was about to turn away when he realized that the setting in which the three women were engaged seemed oddly informal and personal. Lindsey sat up straight in bed with her arms wrapped around her pulled-up knees, and the two officer women sat in the nearby chairs, listening very intently to what Lindsey was telling them. Their faces were etched in curiosity and empathy. Instead of walking away, Caleb stood near the door, leaning on the inside of the doorway.

"I was just, really … well, it's hard to explain. I mean, I know you shouldn't drive when you're emotionally unstable or overwhelmed, and I know if I hadn't been so upset I wouldn't have gotten into that accident. I didn't see that animal right away because I had been crying so hard, and so I just all of a sudden panicked and swerved without thinking."

One of the officers with dark brown hair pulled up in to a messy bun nodded her head sympathetically. "That must've been frightening," she responded.

"I would think the whole idea of just driving across the country alone would be frightening, especially in your condition," the other officer added.

Caleb turned away and left the scene, feeling like he had been eavesdropping. *She is confiding in them, I shouldn't be listening.* Not only that, but Lindsey's words had gravely imitated an incident which had happened in his life back when he was 18. It gave Caleb and eerie feeling, and he knew he didn't want to hear anything else she had to say.

He returned to the lobby and attempted to get some sleep on the couch, but he couldn't get comfortable, and the fact that he was in a hospital added to the discomfort. Not only was his body heavy from fatigue, another unseen burden had thrust itself upon him at the sound and application of Lindsey's words. He felt restless and distracted. Only five minutes had passed when Caleb thrust himself off the couch, snatched up his coat and car keys from the nearby table, and hurried out of the hospital, not leaving any word of his return for Lindsey.

Six

God is the one for whom and through whom everything exists.

– Hebrews 2:10

Lindsey awoke that morning with cramps invading her body and stiffness darting up her neck. As she became consciously alert, she moved her fingers to find that her right hand was asleep. "Aw, wake up," she moaned to her hand as her eyes rolled open. The first object her sight caught focus on was the handsome young face of Dr. Jones staring down at her.

"How do you feel?" he asked, with a smile spread across his lips.

"Uh, okay, I guess," Lindsey replied, caught unawares. "My head is hurting, though."

"Well, I'll get the nurse to give you something for that."

Why can't you give me something for it, why does the nurse have to do it? Lindsey thought. She mentally slapped herself in the head for thinking such a ridiculous thought. *But he's so good-looking; I can't help myself.*

"So do I get to be released today?" she asked.

"Yes. As you know, you're all right and very healthy. There's no big concern that you need to worry about." The doctor walked over to Lindsey and helped her sit up in bed, propping a pillow up behind her.

"Where's Caleb?" Lindsey asked suddenly, looking around the room as if she expected him to be close by.

"Who?"

"Caleb. You know, the guy who brought me in here yesterday, or, earlier today, whenever it was."

"Oh yeah, him. I haven't seen him since last night. One of the receptionists earlier said that she saw him run out of here. She said he seemed in a hurry. I suppose he had somewhere to go."

Lindsey body slumped as her spirits abruptly dropped. "Yeah, I suppose he must've," she stated sadly.

Dr. Jones began to check Lindsey's vital signs – her pulse, her forehead, etc. "What? Didn't he let you know he was leaving?"

Lindsey shook her head. "No, he didn't even come in to say bye. All I remember was that the officers were talking to me, and after they left I fell asleep. Caleb never told me he was going to leave."

Dr. Jones noted the regretful tone in her voice. "I'm sorry, Lindsey," he said sympathetically. "I guess it must've meant a lot to you how he helped pull you out of the car."

"Yeah, it did. And not only that, but we're both heading in the same direction. I mean, we're both traveling across the country, and I just thought that … well, I kind of don't want to finish the trip by myself."

"You don't even know this guy, Lindsey," said the doctor as he took a seat in one of the soft chairs.

"Well, I know, but I don't know you either and I'm telling you all of this."

"Well you have a point there," Dr. Jones laughed.

"How old are you, Dr. Jones?"

"Why do you want to know that?"

"You just seem awfully young to be a doctor."

The doctor cocked his head to the side. "Well, I guess I am pretty young to be a doctor. I'm twenty-seven. And by the way, you can call me Matt."

"Matt. Okay, Matt, thanks." *Oh he's such a cutie!* Lindsey couldn't hide the bright smile on her face.

"And I know you're 18," Matt said.

"Yes, I am. My birthday was just this month, on the 10th of October."

"Oh! Well, happy belated birthday, Lindsey."

"Thanks, but I hate the word 'belated.' It sounds so stupid."

Matt chuckled as he turned his back for a moment and replied, "Well then, happy *late* birthday, Lindsey."

Just then a nurse interrupted the two, bringing in some painkiller for Lindsey's headache. "When you're feeling better, you can get dressed anytime, and we'll make hotel arrangements for you to stay in Deer Lodge while you're waiting until your car is repaired."

"What kind of repairs are needed?"

"A few new parts, I think, and some dents in the body. Unless of course you don't care about the outside appearance of the car and you could just keep the dents; save yourself some money."

"I have full coverage," Lindsey announced proudly. Thank goodness money wouldn't be a problem. But as for the time length, it sounded as if it would take more than a day or two for her car to be fixed. She wondered if she could spare that much time. She was eager to get going, eager to put her unappealing past behind her.

Lindsey and Matt continued conversing, but during the whole morning, Lindsey couldn't push Caleb from the back of her mind. She felt so distraught that he hadn't come back last night to talk with her once the officers left, and that he wasn't at the hospital that morning. Would he ever come back to say good-bye? Or had he just run out of time and did he have to leave suddenly last night without any departing words to Lindsey? She felt like she had so much to tell him. There was something about him that had struck Lindsey as odd. He was so gentle and sweet. She hadn't known too many guys in her lifetime that could fit that description, aside from Dr. Jones here, whose job required him to be gentle and sweet to every patient.

Although Lindsey's outside features hid it well, she was inexpressibly depressed that whole morning, and into the afternoon.

The sun streaming in through the curtains of the small motel room dove into Caleb's closed eyes, and he groaned as he turned over in bed. His eyes opened slowly and he glanced up at the ceiling. The small fan rotated quickly, creating a cool breeze that drifted down and blew across Caleb's face. *Oh no, I can't believe I left Lindsey last night at the hospital without saying anything. She must be thinking I just took off. I have to go see her.* With that thought Caleb wasted no time in throwing himself out of the small bed and into his clothes.

It was 12:30 p.m. that chilly, sunny afternoon. Lindsey sat on the dull green lobby couch with one of her legs folded up under her other leg, which dangled over the edge of the couch. Clad in a fuzzy blue cardigan and dark blue jeans, she sipped the spicy apple cider, thankful for its comforting warmth. She closed her eyes and inhaled deeply. *What am I going to do now?* As the thought entered her brain, her eyes flooded with tears and she allowed them to run down freely. She felt so overwhelmed and without hope. Her car repair would keep her in town for a few days, but then what? Did she even dare getting back on the road again with her world still crumbling around her and her emotions running wild? What a terrible start to her trek across country! *Maybe I should just go back home to Grandma and Grandpa.* Although that thought should have provided Lindsey with a reassuring alternative, it instead caused her dispirited mood to deepen. She didn't want to go back home where she'd only be reminded of her past life; the life that was suddenly altered with her mother's death. Jillian Milholland had been Lindsey's whole world – her best friend. Lindsey knew that most of her friends hadn't maintained good relationships with their parents, so Lindsey had always felt lucky to get along so well with her own mother. She knew it must have been partly due to her father's absence throughout the years. Lindsey never had anybody else to lean on besides her mother. She didn't understand why Jillian was taken away from her all of a sudden.

Setting down her cup of apple cider, she wiped her eyes with the sleeve of her cardigan, and grabbed the remote control to find something interesting to watch on TV. Lindsey was grateful that no other patients occupied the lobby that afternoon.

A small, young, thin receptionist walking back from a bathroom break spotted Lindsey and walked toward her, taking a seat on the couch across from Lindsey's. "How are you doing?"

Lindsey sniffed. "I'm okay, I guess."

"I like your sweater, it's really cute."

Lindsey smiled. "Thanks. It was a birthday present."

"Oh, when was your birthday?"

"October 10th. But please don't tell me, 'Happy belated birthday.'"

The woman laughed as she pulled her long, straight brown hair into a ponytail. "All right, whatever you say. It's a nice morning, don't you think?"

"Yeah, after all that rain, I'm extremely glad to have the sun come out."

"Definitely. There are cloudless skies too."

"Oh, good. Did you see a rainbow yet?" Lindsey asked.

"Nah, not yet. I love rainbows; they're so beautiful. I've never been able to understand how those colors form in a rainbow, though. I mean, it's a wonder to think how a rainbow must work."

"I know, I've wondered that myself. I didn't even know it rained very much in Montana."

"Well, it doesn't rain too bad. Once you get to the eastern side of Montana, the mountains flatten out and there's not as much vegetation. It's a lot more barren and sparse, but still pretty in its own right."

"It's like that in Washington, too."

"Oh, you're from Washington huh?"

"Yeah. I live, I mean, I *lived* about an hour north of Seattle," Lindsey replied. "It's a really nice place, right in the San Juan Islands."

"Oh, I don't know where the San Juan Islands are, but I have been to Seattle a few times. I have a relative who lives there. I like Seattle, it's a very pretty city."

"It's okay," Lindsey said as she flipped through channels, stopping on the Disney channel.

"Well, I can't stay and chat," the woman said as she checked her watch. "I have to get back to work. It was nice talking to you." She stood up to leave.

"Yeah, thanks," Lindsey replied, watching her walk away. She was nice.

Caleb parked his Ford in the hospital parking lot and jumped out, speedily making his way toward the entrance. In his left hand he gripped a paper bag which held a few breakfast pastries that he thought he could share with Lindsey. Entering the building, he checked at the receptionist desk to find out whether he could go in and see Lindsey.

The same woman who had been talking with Lindsey set down the phone receiver and turned to Caleb. "Hello, I suppose you want to see Lindsey."

"Yeah, is it all right if I go visit her?"

"Of course it is, but she's checked out of her room, already."

Caleb, half-turned and ready to head down the hall, stopped in his tracks and looked at the woman with a confused face. "What? What do you mean? Is she still here?"

The receptionist laughed. "Yes, she's still here, don't worry. She's in the lounge around the corner."

"Thanks," Caleb replied as he took off down the hallway.

Lindsey lay down on the couch, with her head on the armrest, still flipping through channels to find something good to spend her time watching. She sighed heavily, still disappointed from the morning. Upon hearing footsteps in the hallway she turned her head to look toward the entrance of the lobby. The tall, blond-haired, masculine figure of a young man entered, stopping at the edge of the room. Lindsey's eyes widened, and she flung herself off the couch and ran toward Caleb.

"Caleb!" she shouted as she ran and hugged him.

"Whoa," he exclaimed as he stepped back, almost falling backward from Lindsey's embrace. He smiled to himself and put his free arm around her waist to hug her back. "Uh, long time no see, I guess...." he joked, then, "I thought you'd be madder at me than this."

Lindsey stepped back. "Oh my gosh! I thought you had left. I woke up this morning and you weren't here, and I thought you were gone for good. I'm so glad you're still here."

Caleb blushed at Lindsey's enthusiasm. Stunned, and not knowing what to say, he offered Lindsey some breakfast. She agreed, and together the two sat back down on the couch. Lindsey slouched down and propped her feet on the coffee table.

"I'm glad you're still here," Caleb said.

"Well, they're making hotel arrangements for me to stay here in Deer Lodge until my car is repaired."

"And you have the money for all of that?"

"It's all good, don't worry about it." She smiled.

Caleb also smiled. "I'm sorry I left last night," he apologized. "I just got really overwhelmed all of a sudden and had to get out of here. I'm not too excited about hospitals. I've had a few bad experiences with them, myself."

"Really?" Lindsey asked, curious. "Me too." She thought of her mother. "So what kind of bad experiences are you talking about?"

Caleb squirmed, hesitating whether he wanted to get into it or not.

"You don't have to tell me if you don't want to," Lindsey assured, taking a bite of her apple turnover.

"No, it's okay." As Caleb said that, a picture flashed into his mind. It had been there last night too, and had caused him to flee the hospital.

* * *

Caleb was still picking up speed in his truck and contemplating his pointless life when he noted a sharp curve in the road up ahead. His heart began to thump louder, and his breathing became heavy. At the last second, Caleb slammed his foot onto the brake, and as the vehicle stopped suddenly, Caleb lost control of the steering wheel and the Ford skidded off the road. It flew into the deep ditch, and Caleb was thrust out of his seat, his head hitting the windshield in front of him.

* * *

Caleb shivered as the memory invaded him. He had been so careless that night, so full of hate and anger and confusion, that he wished his life would end. It almost had.

"I heard you talking last night, with the two officers," he began. "I didn't mean to eavesdrop, but I heard you talk about how you were really emotional when you got into the wreck. I've gone through a situation like that too." He stopped, glancing at Lindsey. She said nothing. "I got into a car crash a few years ago, when I was your age," Caleb finally breathed. "I was almost killed. I barely lived. God really kept me safe that night, in spite of my carelessness."

Lindsey watched him, wide-eyed. She couldn't believe it. He looked so calm and serene and that moment, but she wasn't quite sure that the same story was going on inside of him. She knew it must have been a terrible memory and felt bad for bringing it up.

"Oh, gosh, really?" she asked incredulously. Caleb nodded. Lindsey went on. "What do you mean 'in spite of your carelessness'?" Lindsey knew there was something else to this story.

Caleb hesitated for a second, keeping his eyes ahead of him. "I just, well,

I was a totally different person then than I am now. I mean, I was pretty depressed. I left the house really upset and emotional, and I took off in my truck. I was driving fast on purpose. I almost wanted to die."

Lindsey's eyes widened more at that statement. There was something about Caleb that really drew her towards him, and it actually relieved her that he had gone through such a terrible situation like she had just gone through, with her mother's death and her car crash. "I'm sorry, Caleb."

"Don't worry about it."

Lindsey stopped eating her turnover, and set it down on the coffee table. She took a deep breath and stared at her hands. "My mother died a couple months ago," she said. Caleb looked at her. "That's why I don't like hospitals. I feel like I've spent a lot of time in them." She stopped, biting her bottom lip. She glanced at Caleb, noting the sensitive gleam in his eyes. She almost began to cry.

"That must've been terrible."

Lindsey chuckled. "Yeah, it was."

"So that's why you're going to Virginia to live with your dad, huh?"

"You got it."

"And you used to live with your grandparents?"

"Yeah, when my mom died I started to live with them."

"Why didn't you just go to your dad's right away?" Caleb wondered.

This time it was Lindsey's turn to hesitate. Caleb had found her other soft spot. She sat up and looked at him. "Because … I haven't seen him or spoken to him since I was eight."

"You haven't?"

"No, he – uh," she swallowed. "He took off when I was eight, leaving my mom and me alone. So he's gone, been in Virginia ever since."

"Oh, wow," Caleb expressed. "I don't mean to be rude or anything, but if you haven't talked to him or seen him since then, why do you want to go live with him? I mean, does he know you're coming, and do you know if he will even want you to stay?"

"Well, I'm not sure," Lindsey replied, her face saddening. "I'm just hoping, I guess. I know where he lives because he's sent my mom child-support over the years, so I have an address. And they got a divorce, too, a couple months after he left. So it's not like he's been totally anonymous or out-of-touch. I've just never wanted to see him, though."

Silence ensued after that last comment, and together the two sat staring ahead of themselves, occasionally taking small bites of their breakfast. Lindsey began flipping through channels again – more out of the oddness of the moment rather than trying to find something to watch. Her palms became damp with every passing second as she sat wondering whether she should have told Caleb any of this information about herself. It was one of the first times she had opened herself up after her mother's death. She hadn't even talked to any of her friends back home this way after her mother had died. *Oh well, whatever he thinks, it was nice to get it all out, and it's not like I'm ever gonna see him again after today. He's going to North Carolina, for gosh sakes, and I'm going to ... Virginia.*

Suddenly the temptation was almost too strong to bear. It was true what she'd told Dr. Jones. She didn't want to travel the rest of the way to Virginia alone. And Virginia and North Carolina were so close! In fact, they were neighboring states. What could be more perfect?

Mary Jenkins got off work early that evening and took only a few eager seconds to gather together her coat and purse and book it out of the *Denny's.* Relieved to be off for the night – she had worked five nights in a row – she began her long walk back to her small house, a couple of miles away from work. She thought about taking the bus home but decided that the money used for bus fare could be better spent on more important things for her daughter, six-year old Andrea. Besides, she didn't mind the walk, especially at this time of evening when the sun wasn't so bright, but instead dim and orange, casting a fiery hue on the hills around Coeur d'Alene. Not to mention that the walk helped improve her health and shape her legs. *At least I can work off those pounds I put on during the weekend with my constant eating.* She giggled to herself.

Coeur d'Alene was busy tonight, with vehicles of all shapes and sizes traveling this way and that, honking, skidding, breaking down, engines failing, and the like. Mary was convinced that she made it home faster by walking than she would stuck in traffic had she a car to drive.

Stepping off the curb to cross the street, Mary suddenly began to think of the young man whom she had crossed paths with yesterday morning. What was his name? Caleb, that was it. It was such a nice name, and he had been a nice boy. Most of the young men that Mary had known – especially those Caleb's age – had been cocky, irritating, and oftentimes arrogant men. Caleb had given Mary a whole new perspective on the male species and had actually brightened her day, too. She wished she could have told him that, but now she'd probably never see him again.

Another thing that struck Mary as strange about Caleb was how he spoke of God. God? Sure, she had grown up hearing God's name many times being from a traditional Protestant background, but she had never actually adopted Christianity personally. Since her parents had both been strict Protestants, she had been made to attend church when she was a little girl. For most of her childhood years she had found church dull and unexciting, and she never really subscribed to the whole God thing. After she grew old enough to have a mind of her own, she used it to her full extent, battling her parents for the right to choose her beliefs and to have her own say on whether she should go to church or not. Knowing they couldn't force Mary to believe in something she didn't want to believe in, and not aware of any other way to control their rebellious teenager, Mary's parents had given her her own way. She had stopped going to church when she was fourteen. Her parents gave her hell about it, never ceasing to remind her of how her behavior "was unpleasing to God," or how she was incessantly "making the devil a happy camper," with her defiance of God. And of course there was the classic, "Sinners go to Hell!" which she heard not only from her parents but also from some of her Christian friends at school. Needless to say, they weren't her friends for very long.

As far as Mary could recall, Christians seemed kind of self-righteous with their air of betterment and their noses sticking up in the air. The Christians in Mary's life had always known just where to push her buttons, never failing to let her know what she was doing wrong "in the eyes of God." Mary always managed to shrug them off, though, telling them, "How would you know how God sees me?" In the long run, all the heat she had been given about being a rebellious teenager and a disappointment to God had only given her a greater passion to rebel, not to mention it drew her away from the church all the more. She became angry with many people, including her parents.

While Mary grew up, there had only been one or two people she could remember who had been gentle to her regarding Christian issues, and one of them was her granny. Granny Deedee had been a Christian just like her parents, but also a lot different than her parents. The only things Mary could remember Granny Deedee telling her was that Jesus loved her no matter what, and that He would always be waiting for her if she ever wanted to believe in Him.

Although Mary hadn't really understood too much about it, nor even cared, Granny's gentleness and love had always made her feel better, like maybe she wasn't a disappointment to God after all. But then again, she was never sure if she even believed in God, so what did it matter whether she was good or bad?

Yes, in all her life, Mary couldn't recall encountering a person who spoke of God as if he was a normal, natural person and part of life as Granny had. And as her focus left her past and returned back to Caleb, she suddenly got the feeling that he was one of those people, just like her granny. He had spoken so easily about God, not in a condemning or judging manner, but in an honest, inviting way. *Well, I believe that happiness comes from God.* It was such a small statement, but it had tackled Mary's brain most of the day. Besides that, their whole conversation had given her the idea that this young man was probably the way he was because of his belief in God. Did many people have the same positive outlook on life and on God as Caleb had?

There were many churches in Coeur D'Alene, but Mary didn't personally know many people who attended church besides some of her family, and she knew she didn't want to get involved with all of that again. It had been too many years since those days, and for the most part she had put all of that behind her, never really giving any thought to returning to church again. Even though she had a small past with church, she had never actually thought about or understood the significance of it and why people went. *Maybe there's something more to it,* she now wondered as she thought about Caleb and about her granny.

Halfway home, Mary's thoughts diverged as she began to dread returning home. She would have to call her parents to bring Andrea home, and then clean the house, and then make dinner if her parents hadn't already fed Andrea. Then, tomorrow would come quickly and would be like any other day in Mary Jenkins' tedious life. *I'm doing it all for Andrea,* she assured herself, trying to build up her spirits. But even with that thought, she wondered how much longer she could do it. At least her parents were willing to take in Andrea while she was at work without any cost to Mary. She was incredibly thankful for that. As was her custom almost every night, Mary whispered silently, *Ted, why did you have to divorce me? Why did you have to make things so hard for us*? But she knew regrets wouldn't get her anywhere except deeper in pain.

Passing by the Christian Community Church, which she did every night when walking home, Mary abruptly stopped. Normally she would have kept on walking, but today it was different. The short conversation she had had with Caleb and his mentioning of God just kept coming back to her. She couldn't brush it aside very easily. It had meant something to her. If God had worked some kind of happiness into that boy's life, then maybe He could do something for her too. She wasn't sure what, she wasn't sure how, and she wasn't even sure if she believed in God or not. At this point in her life – a life that seemed to be headed nowhere with no promising outlook – Mary wouldn't mind trying anything. Once again, her mind began to whirl as thoughts flowed through her brain. *I don't even know anybody who goes to church. Why would I just all of a sudden up and go? Everybody in the congregation would think I'm weird. They wouldn't know who I am. I wouldn't belong there. Maybe church is only for people who have got it together in their lives*. With that, Mary resolved that she would stick it out a little bit longer… without church.

Settled into her small room at the *Super 8 Motel* – the exact same motel that Caleb was staying at – Lindsey walked outside to the patio and took a seat at the edge of the empty pool, where Caleb was dangling his legs over the side.

"Thanks for suggesting to the nurses this motel," she quietly stated.

"No problem. I thought you might feel more comfortable staying where I'm staying, just for the fact that I'm the only person you know in this town, and you're the only person I know."

"How long were you planning on staying, anyway?" Lindsey asked. "I mean, you have no reason to stay. You took me to the hospital, you stayed until I was out, you helped me get a motel room, and now I'm all fine and dandy. You don't have to stay. Don't you have somewhere to get to?"

"Well yeah, but it's not like I'm on any time limit. I was thinking maybe I'd leave tomorrow, or stay until your car is repaired." He looked over at Lindsey. She was shivering from the coolness of the early evening. He would have offered her his coat or sweatshirt if he had one with him at the moment, but he didn't.

"You don't have to wait for me," Lindsey explained. "It would suck up too much of your expenses staying here."

"Well then, I'll just drive extra long one night to make up for it."

"Yeah, but then you'd be wasting gas money."

Caleb chuckled at her remark. "Well, I guess you can't win then, huh?"

"Guess not."

The two were quiet for a few seconds, looking up at the bare mountains that encircled the town.

"You were at the hotel in Spokane, weren't you?" Lindsey asked suddenly.

"What?"

"The *Motel 6* in Spokane? You were there, weren't you?"

Confused, Caleb nodded, wondering how Lindsey would know that. Since he had pulled her out of the car wreck, he had thought she looked vaguely familiar, but couldn't put his finger on it. All at once, it hit him: the blonde-haired girl whom he had seen peeking over the couch at him in the lobby of the *Motel 6*. That was Lindsey! That was where he'd seen her before!

"Oh my gosh!" he exclaimed, turning to face Lindsey more. "I remember now. You're that girl I saw in the lobby, right?"

"So you did see me, huh?"

"Yeah, peeking up over the couch or something?"

"Yep, that was me. I knew you looked familiar, and I just realized why a few hours ago."

"Weird," Caleb said. He shook his head in disbelief.

"Yeah, it's weird," Lindsey agreed. *Maybe it means something.*

What does this mean, Lord? Caleb questioned. *I don't know why, but since I took Lindsey to the hospital, I've felt a need to stay here for her. Why haven't I left yet*?

"What day did you leave Washington, to go across the country?" Lindsey asked, breaking into Caleb's thoughts.

"Oh, uh, two days ago, on Monday."

"Yep, me too. I drove straight to Spokane to stay there for the night."

"Wow, me too. Gee, that's a coincidence."

Yeah it is, thought Lindsey. She hadn't talked to Caleb yet about her feelings on crossing the country alone, and she wasn't sure whether she should. She didn't want to be a burden to him, and she didn't want to appear dependent and scared.

Caleb just stared across the pool, thinking. Or rather, praying. *Oh Lord, please reveal to me what this all means! Why have I had such a burden to stay and watch over Lindsey until she departs? I hardly even know her. But I feel for her so much, especially after hearing about her mother and father. Lord, we're both traveling in the same direction....*

"I was thinking," Lindsey began. Caleb looked at her. "I, uh, well," she stumbled, not sure how to bring it up. Her hands began to tremble, and she quickly put them under her legs, which were dangling over the side of the empty pool. "I guess I was just thinking, that, well, this is so much of a coincidence. I mean, we're both going to virtually the same places, at least in the same direction, and if you were planning on waiting for me anyway, I just thought that...." She stopped and looked up at Caleb. His eyebrows were raised, and she could tell he knew what she was trying to say. She blurted it out. "Why don't we just travel across the country together?"

Caleb was stunned. He hesitated for a moment before replying. "Well, I've thought about that too," he confessed.

"Really?"

"Yeah, I mean, I guess it doesn't make any sense for me to wait for you until you leave here, because if I did, then we'd both be like, driving next to each other on the freeway most of the trip." He smiled. Lindsey laughed.

"I'm just really glad that you've actually stuck this out with me this past day, and you're not gone yet. This accident has made me wonder whether I should travel to Virginia alone or not. I don't know if I'm even fit to travel alone, and besides that, I don't think I want to travel alone anymore." Lindsey gazed up at Caleb, with large, pleading eyes. "I'm just scared, I guess, and really shaken up. Back at the hospital I was wondering if I should just go back home instead of going to Virginia anymore. I was so upset. I felt, I don't know, hopeless, or something."

"You don't ever have to be hopeless," Caleb stated silently. "There's always something to be hopeful for."

"I guess so," Lindsey commented. "I mean, you came back, didn't you?"

Caleb nodded. *Maybe we should go together. It would be nice to have company to North Carolina, and this girl seems so sad. It might be good for her. She doesn't seem to know You, Lord. Perhaps You could reveal Yourself to her.*

Noting Caleb's silence, and the confounded look embracing his features, Lindsey's heart sank. *He doesn't like the idea.* She began to stand up. "I'm sorry, I shouldn't have put you in this situation. I hardly know you, and you hardly know me, and you must be thinking I'm weird or something."

Caleb stood up and followed Lindsey, who was quickly retreating back to her room. "No," he stifled.

"I don't want you to feel sorry for me; that's not what I was intending to do. I'm sorry. I'll be fine on my own. Thanks for all your help." She still had her back to him. Caleb swung around and stepped in front on Lindsey. She halted.

"No," he said. Lindsey looked up at him, her arms crossed. He could see she had tears in her eyes. "No," he said again. "I think it's a good idea."

Seven

Help carry each other's burdens. In this way you will follow Christ's teachings.
– Galatians 6:2

Terry Milholland and his wife, Jenna, had just arrived home from a business weekend that had called them out of state. Bursting through the door, Jenna exclaimed her feelings over getting home.

"Oh, thank heavens!" she gleamed. She rushed inside the house, through the large, clean foyer and into the spacious living room, making haste for the soft maroon leather couch. She threw herself into it. "I'm so glad to be home, you don't even know, Terry!"

Terry, almost forty-five years old, set down his suitcase and other belongings in the middle of the foyer before joining his wife in the living room. "Jenna, don't forget to take your shoes off, the carpets were cleaned while we were gone, remember?"

"Picky, picky," Jenna scowled. She lazily slid off her dress shoes and threw them into the foyer. They barely missed Terry.

"Watch it," he said, slipping off his own shoes. He then proceeded into the large living area, blanketed by a beautiful white carpet and furnished with two large plants, two couches, a plush leather chair, a 52 inch television set complete with a stereo system, and an elegant coffee table. The ceiling rose high above their heads, sloping upward and meeting at a point where the skylights provided a view of the musty October sky. Terry joined Jenna on the couch. She was sprawled across it, drained of all energy from the long week, and Terry wasted no time in invading her space.

"Hey," she laughed, "get off of me, you're invading my area. Go find your own couch."

Terry smiled and gathered his wife up in his arms. She smiled. He had always been a romantic. But before anything else could happen, Terry stood up, still holding his wife, carried her over to the other couch, and dropped her onto it. "Hey," she scolded, beginning to laugh. Terry then slid back to the other couch and plopped himself onto it.

"Hehehe," he snickered. Jenna sat staring at her husband. He was her second husband. She had been married before, but it didn't work out. Then, eight years ago, she had met Terry, and they had started a life together. He seemed like a simple man. He had come from Washington State and had been married once, too. Then, divorcing his wife, he had traveled across the country to start a new life. That was all Jenna had really known of his past, and Terry had informed her that it was all she needed to know; there was nothing else important to be known. She fell in love with him a few months after they met, and a short while after that, they were married.

"Ah," she sighed, remembering the romantic days of the old when she and Terry had just begun dating. "I think I'm going to check the messages on the machine." She jumped off the couch and headed toward the kitchen. Terry remained on the couch. The first thing Jenna always did after coming home from anywhere – whether a business trip or a trip to the supermarket – was check the answering machine. Terry listened from his spot on the couch as she pushed the "play" button, and numerous voices swam out of the machine.

"So who called?" he shouted from the living room.

"Well, so far just Jim and Randy," Jenna called back. "They said something about a barbecue next week."

Terry nodded his head. He sat up and grabbed the newspaper lying on the coffee table and began to go over some old news.

From inside the kitchen, the various messages had been playing one by one, but none of them had caught Jenna's attention like the second last message had. It was a young girl's voice, quiet and disturbing.

"Hi, Dad, this is your daughter, Lindsey. I uh … Mom died and … uh…." The girl on the answering machine sniffed as if she had been crying. "I don't even know if you still remember me or even care about me, but I didn't know what else to do. I was thinking about driving over there to Virginia to find you and be with you." Jenna's heart stopped. From up until the point the girl had mentioned Virginia, Jenna had thought that the caller must have made a mistake and called the wrong number. But now her ears were open. "I wish you were there so I could talk to you, but … I'm sorry for these past years when we haven't spoken. I've just disregarded the fact that I had a father, and I'm sure you've done the same for me. It was you and Mom who had the disagreement, not you and me, so I don't see why we haven't kept in touch over the years. But I suppose I never really wanted to. I was so angry for what you did to Mom and me, just leaving us like that. But besides all that, Mom's dead now, like I said." The words came out bluntly, void of emotion. "So I wanted to come over to find you. Is that okay?" Silence followed for a few moments. "Even if it's not okay, I'm coming over anyway, because I feel like I don't have a life here anymore. I can't stay here, and I'll go crazy living with Grandma and Grandpa. I graduated this June, did you know that? Yeah, I was supposed to go to college but then cancelled at the last moment after Mom died. It really sucks. My whole life is altered. Anyway, I'm coming over. I hope you still remember me, and I hope you still love me. Bye ... Dad."

"Who was that, honey?" Terry called from the living room, noticing the distinct sound of a young woman's unfamiliar voice.

Jenna didn't answer him, nor did she pay attention to the last message playing on the machine. All she could do was stare at the answering machine in disbelief, as if it had just lied to her. She pressed her finger on the "rewind" button and began to rewind the tape to listen to Lindsey's recording again. As she did, she hoped it would reassure her that the call was just a mistake, but she was proved otherwise. On the answering machine, Jenna and Terry had always clearly stated who they were: *Hello, this is the Milholland residence, but Terry and Jenna aren't able to come to the phone right now. Please leave a message and we will return your call as soon is possible. Thanks!* The girl would have hung up if she had dialed the wrong number. But, perhaps she was seeking another Terry Milholland ... but another in Virginia? Jenna became panicked. What was going on?

Terry's eyebrows raised, and his curiosity was fixed as he heard the same message being played again. He stood up, tossing the old newspaper to the couch, and strode to the kitchen. As he approached the entranceway, he noticed his pale wife, standing dumbfounded, staring into the answering machine. His stride slowed dramatically. Recognizing the voice on the machine, his heart sped up, and he leaned against the wall to keep his weak knees from collapsing on him.

"I'm sorry for these past years when we haven't spoken," Lindsey's voice played.

Lindsey, Terry's heart breathed.

"I just disregarded the fact that I had a father, and I'm sure you've done the same for me."

No, never, how could I? It had been ten years, but every now and then he had sent a birthday or holiday card. Those had eventually ceased once he stopped hearing from his ex-wife and daughter, but he had kept track. All through the ten years, he had kept track of his daughter's growth. He knew she would have graduated this June – supposing she was never kept back a grade. In his own heart, deep in the place where he buried the memory of his former life, he was proud of her.

Jenna turned and found her husband standing at the entrance to the kitchen. Her mouth was agape, and she found herself with nothing to say.

Terry had an odd look about his face. She knew he had heard the message, and behind his eyes there hid a sort of shame almost.

"What was that?" she finally stumbled out. Terry stood motionless for a moment, unable to answer. He had kept Lindsey a secret from his present wife since he had known her, although he didn't have a logical reason why.

"That was Lindsey," he said weakly, forcing a smile.

"Who's Lindsey!" Jenna demanded. Terry drew a long breath.

"She's my daughter, honey."

Jenna Milholland's world began to spin. She had no idea how to respond to her husband's comment. Terry had a daughter, a teenage daughter? Jenna shook her head in disbelief, confusion scattering her mind. How can this be? *Terry would've told me, he would've ... why would he keep such a secret?* Unable to force any words out of her mouth, she blindly walked past Terry, out of the kitchen and into the living room. Tears starting brimming on the edges of her eyes and she sat down in the large leather chair and stared at the wall in front of her.

Terry followed his wife silently. He could tell she was at a loss for words. She was stunned, confused, and bewildered. Her face clearly showed it. Terry thought she looked as if she would suddenly choke and have a heart attack. He knew he needed to say something. He would have a lot of explaining to do. *My marriage could now be at stake here*, he thought, but in truth, he very much wanted to see Lindsey again, and possibly start a new relationship with her, even if it meant risking his marriage. It had been ridiculous that they hadn't kept in touch over the years. But like Lindsey had said in her message, she had disregarded the fact that she had a father, and Terry had nearly done the same to her. The memories of his young daughter growing up – at least the good ones before he had gotten abusive – were always too painful for Terry to remember and live with, so he had felt it would be better if he just tried to forget her altogether. It was hard for him, however. All he knew to do was stop all contact with Lindsey, hoping it would help him forget her and all the pain that came with the memories. One of the reasons he had started a life with Jenna was to start over, start anew. Now, with the truth of Lindsey coming out, he feared he might lose Jenna as well.

Terry walked over and kneeled on the floor directly in front of Jenna's gaze and looked straight at her. She kept her eyes glued to the wall.

"Jenna, honey," he whispered. A tear fell down her cheek. Terry swallowed hard. "Jenna, I know what you must be thinking, but I want you to know that I do love you with all my heart. I love you so much. I don't want to lose you. But I haven't been honest with you."

"Why haven't you ever told me?" she burst out angrily, casting hurt eyes into his face. Her stare tore Terry's heart in two. "Why? What does this mean? You have a daughter? I ... I ... I don't understand, and...." She stopped and covered her face with her hands while sobs overtook her body. There were so many things she wanted to say and ask, but it wouldn't come out at once, and she wasn't sure how to say it all. So she just cried out of confusion and exhaustion.

Terry grabbed his wife's hands and gently pulled them away from Jenna's face. He took the sleeve of his shirt and wiped her eyes dry and held Jenna's hands in his.

"I'd like to be honest with you now. I would like to tell you everything and answer any questions you have. Can I do that now?"

Jenna sniffed and nodded her head.

"I do have a daughter. Her name is Lindsey Rose Milholland, and she was 18 this month. I've been keeping up to date on her life all these years. I tried to forget about her, but it hasn't been easy for me. A parent can never really get over their children."

"Was your previous wife, Jillian, Lindsey's mother?" Jenna asked weakly.

"Yes, she was. You know all about my marriage to Jillian; I've told you all about her," Terry explained while Jenna nodded. "Well, I haven't told you all about my marriage."

"Yeah, you didn't tell me you had a kid with her."

"I know, I know, and I should've."

"Why didn't you?" she asked, staring into Terry's eyes. Terry took a deep breath. *Here goes*, he thought.

"Jenna, I wasn't a very good husband to Jillian, and I wasn't a very good father to Lindsey. When she was eight years old, I left her and her mother. Jillian and I didn't get divorced until a couple months after I had been gone. I didn't keep in touch much over the next few years, and a short while after that, I stopped all contact whatsoever. I just started to believe that it would be less painful for me if I could try and forget about her and Jillian; about that life."

Jenna was silent a moment. She took her hands out of Terry's, and wiped her face with her sleeve. "Why did you leave them, Terry?"

"I was abusive, Jenna," Terry stated regretfully, and Jenna's eyes instantly became teary again. "It started one day when I lost my job, and then all of a sudden a bunch of other things in my life seemed to go wrong all at once. My drinking became excessive, and I became very abusive. Although I wasn't always physically abusive to Jillian, I had always been verbally and mentally abusive to her, almost from the start of our marriage. I never touched

Lindsey, though; never hit her, never hurt her. At least I don't think I did. Alcohol can mess up your mind. I just always hurt Jillian. I didn't mean to most of the time, I just couldn't help it. My temper was very bad, and I lost all self-control. Finally one day I came to my senses and knew that this wasn't how a marriage was supposed to work. You weren't supposed to hurt the people you loved. I had tried getting help, but I was never willing to make it work. So I knew the only thing I could do was get away; leave my wife and child so that they wouldn't be hurt anymore. It was the only way I knew how to save them."

Terry stopped, and Jenna, eyes large and wide, put her head down and began crying again. Terry stood up and pulled her out of the chair and into his arms. "I'm so sorry, Jenna," he whispered. After a few minutes, she stopped, and the two sat back down on the couch. "After that, Jillian and I got divorced, and she made it clear to me that she didn't want to see me again, or have me in contact with Lindsey. I think she was still really afraid, and I suppose she didn't want Lindsey to grow up with any bad memories of her father. I only visited them a few times after that, and all the times I did Lindsey was gone. I never got a chance to see her. I think Jillian made sure of that. So then I moved out here to start a new life. I got help, I stopped drinking, and I changed my life. Only, I've never really been able to forget about Lindsey, and I think keeping her locked up in the corner of my mind has only made the pain worse, not better."

"Why didn't you ever tell me, Terry? Why? Do you think I would've thought something different of you if I had known you had a child?"

"It's not so much the fact that I had a kid that I was worried about. Like I said, I came here to start a new life – a life free of any past memories and mistakes. I didn't want to remember them, so I've never told anybody about them. And I definitely didn't want to tell you about my drinking and my abuse. I didn't think it mattered anyway, because it was in the past, and I was all better."

"That's still no excuse not to tell me."

"I know it's not. You're right, Jenna. I had no right to keep anything from you. I should've trusted you more."

Jenna nodded. She sat up straight suddenly, and sighed. "I don't know what to do, now," she said.

"What do you mean?"

"I just," she put her head down, and began twisting the edge of her shirt. "I don't know what to think anymore. I know you're still the same, good man I've always known and loved, but the fact that you hid something from me, it...."

"It what?"

Jenna looked up into his face. "It just makes you seem so different all of a sudden. I don't know what to think about you anymore, you know?"

Terry just nodded. "I still love you, Jenna. This is not going to affect my love for you. I just hope it won't affect your love for me."

Jenna stayed quiet.

The Johns spent the evening with their good friends the Lindbergs, and the time had passed swiftly until they found themselves in the car driving home. It was Wednesday, October 22nd, and they hadn't gotten a phone call from Lindsey that whole day. The last they had heard from her was yesterday, when she had called from Missoula and gotten into an argument with Chelsea.

"I don't know why I'm bringing this up now, but did Lindsey absolutely call her father before she left?"

"Of course she did, Chelsea, why wouldn't she?"

"Oh, I don't know. I just keep thinking that maybe we shouldn't have let her go."

Daniel glared at her. "Let's not get into this, again," he stated firmly.

"No, no, I'm not talking about generally," she explained. "I just mean that she hasn't kept in touch with her father for all these years. It just seems odd that we let her go live with a complete stranger, unless of course he hasn't changed from the man he used to be, you know?"

"I know that, Chelsea. Don't you think I've thought of that?" They were approaching the house now, and when Daniel parked, he turned to talk to his wife face to face. "I've personally received a few letters from Terry myself in the past few years. In them he's asked about Jillian and Lindsey. He's been afraid to talk to her. But I believe he's gotten a lot better." Chelsea stayed silent. "Chelsea, I believe he's a better man than he was. When he left Jillian and Lindsey, it was for their own good. He knew he wouldn't be able to stop his abuse, so he took action and left to save them any more pain. I know that seems like the actions of an uncaring, unsympathetic man, but he knew he had a problem. He knew the only way out was to get himself away from the girls before he hurt them any more."

"I know," Chelsea said silently. She and Dan had been through this conversation before, but it had never satisfied Chelsea.

"I don't know about you, but I call that love. He was always a good man on the inside. He just had a really bad alcohol problem, and he didn't know how to control his anger."

"You don't think he's still that way, do you?"

"No, I don't. And even if he was, there's nothing we can do about it. Lindsey's a grown girl. She's 18 now, she's an adult. We wouldn't have been able to stop her from going anyway, because there's no way we could have legally kept her here. There was no reason we should have, anyway."

"I know, Daniel. You're absolutely right, but...."

"He's kept the child-support payments rolling most every month for these past 10 years because he loves Lindsey. He loves his child."

"But how come he has never bothered to write to Lindsey personally or keep in touch with her? Why?" This was the first time that Chelsea was expressing her concerns over Terry Milholland's lack of communication to his daughter. She had stressed over it many times in the years but had never voiced them much. Nobody had ever voiced anything about Terry Milholland much. Not Dan, not Jillian, not Lindsey, and so neither had Chelsea. He had left ten years ago, and with him had left the terrible memories of years of abuse and hardship. Despite his good or bad intentions for leaving, everyone just wanted to forget it, most of all Jillian. Lindsey, who had never been close to her father growing up anyway, had numbed herself to the pain and pushed it way back until she was convinced that her father hadn't even existed. She didn't care, and she didn't want to care, and basically the whole family had felt that way. So with Terry's leaving, a new life for Lindsey and Jillian had begun.

"He has tried to keep in touch, Chelsea," Dan commented, staring straight into her eyes. "It was Lindsey who didn't bother with him."

That night in bed, the wind kept Chelsea up. It wasn't raining like the night before, but nature still took its toll on Chelsea. The moaning of the wind increased Chelsea's melancholy state, and she couldn't stop thinking about Lindsey or Terry Milholland all night.

Thursday, October 23, 1997

I must be the luckiest girl in the world! Okay, maybe not the luckiest, since I've had a few pretty crappy experiences in my life. Like Tuesday night/Wednesday morning I spent the night in a hospital because I was in an accident. I don't feel like getting into details, but I can't believe I'm all right. It must be some sort of miracle. Or maybe I am just lucky??? Anyway, right now I'm the luckiest girl in the world because Caleb and I are going to go across country together! I can't believe it. I was released from the hospital yesterday, and Caleb set me up at this small motel that he's staying at, and last night we talked and agreed to travel together the rest of the trip. I'm so excited, and relieved. Gosh, I can't tell you how relieved I am. I was so scared, but now I think everything's going to be fine. I've already made a friend, not to mention a pretty cute one at that.

Also, there's something about Caleb that I can't put my finger on. He's so ... so ... nice. All I can say is that he's nice. There's no other way to describe him, although he is much more than nice. He's ... unexplainable I guess. I've never met any guy like him. He's very tenderhearted. He's not like any guy, at all. Or maybe I've just had misconceptions about guys over the years. My dad was definitely not a tenderhearted guy. And Nick ... well, Nick is just a jerk and I don't even want to mention him again. Maybe not all guys are like Nick, or maybe I'm just being naive. I suppose I should watch out for Caleb; he might get jerky on me any moment. Anyway, the point of the matter is that I'm not going to be alone for this trip. I have Caleb now, and hopefully soon, I'll have my father. I don't know what's possessing me to suddenly get back in touch with my dad, but I'll just feel empty without him. He's still my family. And it's been ten years, so he could've changed. I hope so.

A soft knock came at Lindsey's motel room door, and she shut her journal and stood up to let Caleb in. "You know what, Lindsey," he spoke as soon as he entered.

"What?"

"I think you and I will actually save some money traveling together."

"Really?"

"Yeah, I was doing semi-calculations in my head. With one vehicle we'll definitely save gas money."

"Yeah? That's good."

The two had done a great deal of talking the night before – making plans about traveling the country together and getting things into order. Lindsey had called the garage where her car had been taken and found out that they had already begun the repairs and were almost finished with them. Lindsey quickly let the man on the phone know that she wanted to sell the car to a car dealership for anything she could get for it.

"Are you sure?" one of the men at the garage had asked. "It's such a nice car, and the damage isn't that bad. I don't think you'd want to give it up."

"Please don't ask many questions. I just want to get rid of it as soon as I can."

"Well," the man began to think, "I know some places that would be willing to take the car and give you a good price for it."

"All right," Lindsey had agreed.

"Lindsey, are you sure you don't want to keep your car and just follow me or something? You don't have to get rid of it. You can pick it up later somehow. I still think that seems a little drastic," Caleb now insisted.

Lindsey's thoughts jumped back into the present. "Oh, yeah, I'm sure. Don't worry about it. I don't think I want to drive anymore, anyway."

Caleb raised his eyebrows. "All right, then," he said slowly.

That afternoon, Caleb and Lindsey went out to lunch and pondered over a road atlas, determining the route they wanted to take to the East Coast.

"Since we're taking my truck, I'll probably just drop you off at your dad's house in Virginia, and then make my way right down to North Carolina. So why don't we just take your route to Virginia."

"All right," Lindsey nodded, picking up her small glass of orange juice and taking a sip. She was staring at the large map of the United States covering two pages of the Atlas.

"So which way were you planning on going?" Caleb proceeded to ask.

"Well," Lindsey began as she set her juice glass down and leaned forward in her seat to study the map. "I was mainly just going to follow I-90 all the way past Billings, and down here into Wyoming." She traced with her finger as she went along. Caleb nodded. "So we'd go through Sheridan at the top of Wyoming, and that's probably where we could spend the night."

"That'll be a long drive tomorrow," Caleb said.

"It won't be so bad," Lindsey commented. "Besides, I've never really been much of a travel-planner so all my ideas of distance and things are just estimates. If we get too tired, we can stop before Sheridan."

"Sounds good to me," Caleb assured.

Lindsey went on. "So from Sheridan we'd just keep following I-90 south, get off on I-25 and follow it all the way to highway 26, which will take us into Nebraska. We could probably stop for the night there in Scottsbluff."

Lindsey continued to trace the way, flipping the pages of the atlas to each individual state that they would cross. From the opposite side of the table, Caleb turned his body and tilted his head in order to see the map better. He noticed that she had highlighted the route in bright yellow, circling the cities she had guessed she'd stay for the night. Caleb nodded his head slightly in approval; Lindsey had obviously planned well.

"This is where my dad lives, in Marion," Lindsey stated once she had arrived at the page of Virginia. She placed her index finger on the city name and held it there, staring for a few moments at it. Caleb noticed the hesitation and frowned, but before he could think anything of it Lindsey went on, sweeping her fingers down into her lap.

"It's in the south-eastern part of the state. I've never been there before, I wonder what it's like."

"Well, I've been to southern Virginia a few times and it's actually pretty nice," Caleb informed.

Lindsey was ecstatic, and a smile quickly crossed her face. "All right then. So do you think the route's okay? Or would you rather we worked something else out?"

"I think the route's just fine. I was pretty much going to go in the same direction, except I would've been traveling a little farther south. But I can just hop on 77 here and head on home," Caleb said, pointing to the freeway on the map.

Lindsey nodded as she grabbed a piece of her whole-wheat toast smothered in strawberry jelly and took a bite.

"How's your brunch?" Caleb asked, changing the subject.

Lindsey made a face. "Uh, it's okay. The eggs are fine, but the hashbrowns are a little too soft. I like mine nice and crunchy."

"Me too," Caleb agreed. "With lots of salt."

"Oh yeah," Lindsey said. She smiled, and together the two finished their breakfasts and headed back to the hotel, making last-minute plans in order to be ready to leave early the next morning.

Eight

Be ready to spread the word whether or not the time is right. Point out errors, warn people, and encourage them. Be very patient when you teach.

– 2 Timothy 4:2

The engine of the Ford F-150 seemed to roar especially loud the next morning as Caleb drove it down Interstate 90. Lindsey was asleep in the passenger seat with her head facing the window, and her damp blonde hair spread over her face. Caleb smiled as he looked over at her. She looked sweet and peaceful, just the way Caleb was feeling. It was a new, fresh morning, and Jesus was heavy in Caleb's heart. He knew he had a job to do, and he knew Lindsey was the target. Still being fairly new to his faith, he prayed that God would help him do and say the right things to Lindsey. *Lord, already I care for this girl so much. I know You love her, Lord, and I just pray that You reveal to me what You want me to do here. I'm a little scared because I've only become a Christian a few months ago, and I still seem to struggle over lots of things. Hopefully, sharing Your truth with Lindsey will help strengthen my faith as well. Help speak through me, and maybe by the end of this trip, Lindsey will have gotten a glimpse of You, or more.* Caleb stopped praying, staring straight ahead of him on the dry, cracked road ahead, and turned up the music a little louder.

About a half hour passed as Caleb drove on, periodically checking in the rearview mirror to make sure that all of their bags and luggage that were tossed in the back of the truck weren't flying away anywhere. Lindsey and Caleb had decided to leave early that morning and stop for breakfast somewhere between 10:00 and 11:00 a.m. It was 9:30 in the morning, and Caleb wasn't becoming any more awake as the morning wore on. He would occasionally catch himself becoming droopy-eyed and scold himself to take more care and stay awake. *We're gonna have to stop for breakfast sooner than 10:00 so that I can get some coffee and wake up*!

The Ford went over a pothole in the road, and the disturbance brought Lindsey awake. She turned her head over and groaned, bringing her hands up to her face to rub her eyes. Caleb's light brown eyes met her green ones, and Lindsey just smiled at him. A few moments passed before either one said something.

"It's only 9:30 in the morning," Caleb informed Lindsey. "Do you mind stopping for breakfast early?"

"No way," Lindsey exclaimed, sitting up and stretching. "I'm hungry. The sooner we can eat breakfast, then the sooner we can eat lunch."

Caleb laughed. "Well, I know what your favorite part of this trip is going to be."

"The eating!"

Almost a half hour later, Caleb was heading off I-90 onto Interstate 115, heading toward Butte. Entering the city, Caleb headed for the nearest *Denny's* restaurant.

"Do you want to eat at *Denny's*?"

"Sure, I love *Denny's*."

"Me too, I always eat there."

"That's because they have breakfast all day," Lindsey said enthusiastically.

"Oh yeah, you can't beat that 24-hour breakfast."

"I know; fried eggs and hashbrowns!"

"Definitely hashbrowns," Caleb agreed.

About ten minutes passed until Caleb was pulling into the parking lot of the *Denny's*

"Have you ever been here?" he questioned Lindsey as they walked toward the restaurant entrance.

"Where? To *Denny's*?"

"No, Butte."

"Oh." Lindsey felt embarrassed. Of course he hadn't been talking about the *Denny's*.

"No, there aren't many places I've been besides Washington's neighboring states, and Canada. Have you ever been here?"

"Yeah, a few years ago, when I drove over to Washington from North Carolina, I came this way and stopped here."

"Let me guess, you ate at this *Denny's*, right?"

"You know it."

The two were seated in a matter of minutes, and Lindsey had ordered orange juice, while Caleb eagerly anticipated his coffee.

"So how long did you live in Washington?" Lindsey questioned.

"Three years. I came over in the summer of '94 to live with my aunt and uncle in Bellingham, and to go to college there at Western."

"Oh. How come you decided to go to college there and not somewhere closer to home?"

Caleb hesitated for a moment before replying. "Well, college wasn't the reason I actually moved to Washington. In fact, at that point I wasn't really planning on ever coming home."

Lindsey was confused. She could tell by the look on Caleb's face that they were about to enter a subject that was sensitive for Caleb, and she wondered whether she should push the issue any further. She suddenly got a feeling of déjà vu as she recognized that look on Caleb's face. She had seen it at the hospital while they had been talking about his car crash. Nevertheless, as always, curiosity had gotten the best of her, and she pushed the subject anyway. If Caleb didn't want to talk about it, then he wouldn't, she assumed.

"Why not?"

"Well, like I told you at the hospital, I was a different person then. I wasn't happy; I was depressed, and I had a lot of problems with my parents."

"Well, all kids have problems with their parents."

"Of course they do, but I always took my problems to too high of a level, as if I was the only one who experienced them. I was a sad kid; into drugs and alcohol, so that didn't help my problems very much. I was selfish, always feeling sorry for myself."

Lindsey's eyes widened. "You told me back at the hospital that you wanted to die," she mentioned.

"Yeah, that's true."

"I can't picture you being like that."

"Well, I was," Caleb said regretfully.

"I think I know what you were feeling, though; not so much about the parent problems, but about feeling sorry for yourself and wanting to die."

Caleb stared at Lindsey. When his eyes met hers, she looked down at her menu and tried to concentrate on it. Like before, she regarded whether she should have mentioned anything or not.

All Caleb was thinking was, *oh no*! Lindsey was going through the same thing he had gone through. Before he could say anything, the waitress came and took their orders. After she left, the two young people sat staring out the window and occasionally picking up their beverages to take small drinks of them.

Finally Lindsey broke the uncomfortable silence. "So how old are you anyway, Caleb? Twenty or something?"

"Twenty-one. I just turned it this summer."

"Ooh, big man, huh?"

"Not really, I still feel like a kid most times."

"Yeah, me too."

Caleb laughed at that. "Well, you kind of still are a kid."

"What? I'm eighteen! That's legally an adult, you know."

"Maybe legally, but not necessarily mentally."

"Hey now," Lindsey smiled.

"Besides, eighteen is still a teenager, and a teenager is still a kid."

"That's not true," Lindsey argued.

From then on the conversation lightened, but only for the next hour as they sat in the restaurant. When they would hit the road again, with the bright sun disguising the chill in the air, they would still have much more to learn about each other's lives.

Cold air burst its way into the small foyer of the restaurant as Lindsey pushed the glass door open and walked outside, Caleb trailing close behind.

"Thanks for paying for breakfast, but I would've paid my own bill, you know," Lindsey said as they were walking across the parking lot.

"I know you would've. If you want you can pay the bill next time."

"The whole bill? Even your half?"

"Heck yeah, it only makes sense!" Caleb exclaimed.

"Gee, you're such a gentleman," Lindsey stated sarcastically, punching Caleb in the arm.

"Hey now, don't get violent with me, woman!"

"Why don't you just let me drive the rest of the day, too, please!" Lindsey joked. As she walked around the truck to get into the passenger side, she caught a glimpse of the phone booths standing near the restaurant doors that they had just walked out of. Caleb noticed Lindsey's creased eyebrows and knew she was thinking of something. He turned his head to follow the direction of her gaze.

"What are you looking at?" he asked.

"I think I want to call Marianne."

"Who?"

"Marianne. She's my best friend," Lindsey explained. "I haven't called her since Monday." She began crossing the parking lot while Caleb followed her.

"Are you sure you don't want to wait until tonight when we stop somewhere for the night?"

"Yeah, I kind of want to call her now. You know how it is when you get a hankering to do something and you just have to get it done then?"

"A *hankering*, huh? Yeah, I guess so."

"Well, this is one of those times." Lindsey slipped into the phone booth and picked up the receiver, using her free hand to search her coat pocket for change.

Marianne Pierce flew down the hall and into her bedroom at the sound of her phone ringing. She flung herself on her bed and picked up the receiver. "Hello?"

"Hey, Marianne, it's Lindsey."

"Lindsey!" Marianne screeched excitedly, bouncing up and down on her bed, while her thick red curls flung around her face. "I miss you! You haven't even been gone a week and I already miss you!"

"I miss you too," Lindsey said softly as her eyes brimmed with tears. She hadn't expected to miss her best friend so much, and it was nice to hear Marianne's enthusiastic voice again.

"Gosh, I didn't even expect to hear from you until another week or something. So how are you?"

Lindsey swallowed hard, attempting to keep the emotion out of her voice. "I'm pretty good, I guess."

"Lindsey," Marianne caught on. "Are you sure? What's wrong?"

"Oh, not much," Lindsey sighed heavily. She peered out through the phone booth at Caleb and found him watching her. He could tell she was upset. It showed in her emerald green eyes. They looked very disturbed all of a sudden.

"I just don't know how I actually thought I could do this. I mean, I don't know how I thought I could get through it all."

"You mean the whole trip to Virginia? You've got guts, Lindsey. I would've never taken up an idea like that."

"Well, it's not just that, Marianne."

"What is it? Did something happen to you? You don't sound too good."

"It's just hard dealing with everything right now. I guess I hoped running away from home would help me start over and deal with my mom's death, but it doesn't really. I'm reminded every day of her, and so far the pain isn't any less than it was two months ago." Lindsey stopped, afraid she would get emotional. "It's just so hard. It's really … hard … unexplainable. Maybe I'm not being realistic about this all. Maybe my whole reason for leaving was just to hide so that I wouldn't have to face the fact that my mom really isn't alive anymore. It's so … unreal."

Marianne wasn't sure how to reply to Lindsey's statement. She had never lost anybody special in her life, so she wasn't familiar with Lindsey's pain. She was especially at a loss for how to console Lindsey. Also, it wasn't the first time that Lindsey had this conversation with Marianne, and every time Marianne had felt that Lindsey was putting her on the spot. Did she want Marianne to say something to make her feel better, or did she just want somebody to listen? Marianne didn't know how to help Lindsey, and frankly, the subject was beginning to aggravate her. She dropped her shoulders and sighed, tipping her head upward to gaze helplessly at the ceiling.

"I don't know what to tell you, Lindsey. I mean, it can only get better, right?"

"I guess," Lindsey breathed, regretting calling Marianne, or at least in bringing up the subject of her mother. More than a few times Lindsey had gotten the impression that Marianne didn't really want to hear about her problems. It had always been hard maintaining a friendship with Marianne, and Lindsey had always felt that she was forced to give more than she received. She never knew whether that was a good thing or not, but she did know that it exhausted her.

"Well, I suppose it already has gotten a little better, sort of," Lindsey remarked.

"Yeah? What do you mean?"

"Well, I won't tell you about the car wreck I was in, but I will tell you about the nice guy who I'm now traveling to Virginia with."

"What? What are you talking about? A car wreck?"

"Well, not really, I just swerved off the road, and this guy named Caleb came and saved me because I was knocked unconscious." Lindsey again peered at Caleb with a huge smile painting her face. "He's my hero," she added. Caleb was smiling also, but shaking his head left to right as he rolled his eyes jokingly and walked away.

"Whatever, Lindsey! You are lying so bad!" Marianne insisted. "Like that would happen!"

"Well, why wouldn't it?"

"It just seems a little fairy-taleish, that's all."

"Well, it's true. Besides, if it weren't true, why would I still only be in Montana? It's the fifth day already, so I should be farther, but I was stuck in Deer Lodge for a couple days."

"Okay, so maybe you got in the car wreck, but I don't think I believe you about that guy. Besides, how would I know you're in Montana? You could still be here, for all I know, calling from Nick's house or something."

Lindsey's smile faded. "Why would I be at Nick's house?" she asked. Caleb was pacing the parking lot, and as he glanced back over at Lindsey, he saw that the smile and laughter was gone from her face. Out of concern and curiosity he walked back toward the booth.

"I saw Nick the day you left. He was in the supermarket."

"So what?" Lindsey said dryly.

"So he was asking about you."

"And I'm supposed to care?"

"Well, I don't know. I still think it's a shame that you two broke up."

Lindsey was almost outraged. "I can't believe you, Marianne! That was two months ago. How come I didn't know you felt this way?"

"Would it have mattered?"

Lindsey changed the subject. "What did you tell him about me?"

"I just told him where you were going. He had no idea. I can't believe you never told him."

"Well, why should I have told him? He's a big jerk, he deserves the worst in life."

"Well, that's a little harsh, don't you think?"

"Not as harsh as what he did to me!"

Caleb was standing nearby, but he could hear Lindsey's side of the conversation clearly, wondering who the "him" was to whom Lindsey was referring. He scolded himself for eavesdropping and quickly crossed the parking lot to get into his truck.

"Lindsey, I only told him because he looked genuinely curious and concerned. I know he still has feelings for you. He did look upset. I mean, he was asking about you, Lindsey. What does that tell you?"

"That it's not working out with that other stupid little girl he's been seeing, so he needs a back-up person."

"It means that he cares about you," Marianne explained, ignoring Lindsey's comment. Lindsey stayed quiet. She was seconds away from slamming the receiver down. "I think he really misses you, Lindsey. And I know he's sorry for what he's done to you."

"Well, that's his problem now."

On the other end of the phone line, sitting against her bed backboard, Marianne shook her head in disbelief. "I can't believe you, Lindsey."

"Well, I'm sorry," Lindsey answered, on the verge of tears.

"Lindsey, I'm really concerned for you. Will you please tell me what's really wrong?"

"I told you already. It's just everything."

"Maybe you really should find yourself some company to travel with. It's going to be a long trip across the country."

"I told you, I already have company!" Lindsey barked, angry that Marianne didn't believe her about Caleb. "His name is Caleb, and he's going to North Carolina!"

"Well, isn't that convenient," Marianne stated flatly.

Lindsey slammed the phone down, and thrust her forehead against the windowpane of the booth. From inside his truck, Caleb had been watching the whole scene. He wondered whether he should intervene, but he wasn't sure that Lindsey wanted sympathy, so he decided against it. A few moments later, Lindsey was striding quickly across the parking lot and jumped into the truck.

Caleb forced a smile. "Is everything all right?"

"Sure," Lindsey answered. Her eyes were angry, but Caleb could tell that she was just trying to be tough. She had been crying, and the redness circling her eyes and nose revealed it. Caleb just nodded his head and started the engine. He knew he needed to hold off on all his questions about her phone conversation for later when she was feeling better. She may not even want to tell him, but Caleb felt that if they were going to be traveling together for a number of days, it would only be fair if they could be open with each other. There seemed to be so much hurt in Lindsey's life aside from her mother's death, and Caleb knew she didn't know how to deal with it. Right now, she was just acting, holding in all her fear and pain and sadness, trying to disguise it in a tough exterior. But Caleb knew better. He had done the same thing himself, but in the end he didn't win. His emotions had gotten the better of him, and he had almost lost his life. It was only by the care and mercy of his Lord Jesus Christ that his life was saved, physically and spiritually. For that Caleb would be forever grateful. It was amazing to him how a life could be changed so drastically because of Jesus. Right now, all Caleb wanted was for Lindsey to understand that fact, also.

"This is pretty cool," Lindsey remarked a couple of hours later, referring to the song and lyrics streaming through the speakers as the two resumed their trek on Interstate 90, heading toward Billings. She sat up and stretched. "Who is it?"

Caleb said the name of a band that Lindsey didn't recognize, and she frowned.

"I've never heard of them."

"Well, that's probably because they're a Christian band."

"A what band?" Lindsey asked.

"A Christian band."

"Christian?"

Caleb glanced over at Lindsey and raised his eyebrows. "Yeah, Christian ... like the religion."

Lindsey lifted her chin to nod. "Oh, okay. I see," she said. "Well, they're pretty good. I've never heard of a Christian band before."

Caleb snickered. "Well, they're just a normal band like all other mainstream bands, except that they sing about God, and about their faith."

"They do?"

"Yeah. If you listen to the words, then you'll notice what they're singing about."

Lindsey stared at Caleb as he kept his eyes fixed to the road, driving carefully. Curiosity began to obtrude her mind, and she questioned Caleb again. "So are you like, a religious person?"

"I guess you could say that," Caleb answered proudly as a smile crossed his face. "But I prefer the term 'person of faith' or 'believer.'"

"Do you go to church?"

"Why, yes, I do."

"Do you like it?"

"Yeah, actually I do. The church I go to, or, the church I *went* to, was really cool. It was fun, and I learned a lot."

"You learned a lot? About what? God?"

"Well, yeah, and about Jesus Christ and the Bible, and what the Bible says about certain issues, all that good stuff."

"Oh, so you believe in God, huh?" Lindsey asked.

"Well, yeah. Why? Don't you?"

She shrugged. "I don't know, it seems kind of far-out, you know, the whole concept of a God, or some higher being or whatever."

"Well, not really," Caleb stated as nerves began to hit him. He silently reminded himself to just stay comfortable and let God speak through him. "It's not so far-out if you know more about God, and consider the way that he is."

"What do you mean?"

"Well, God is personal. Try and picture God as a person just like of one of us; someone who is kind and loving and approachable, almost like your ideal best friend who you can talk to about anything, except that He's invisible and much more powerful than any person on earth. That's Him, that's God."

"Really?" Lindsey commented. Her brows had come together in thought, but her eyes reflected a small bit of sarcasm.

"Mmm hmm," Caleb answered.

"Well, I don't know, I suppose there could be a God, who knows?"

"Well, look around you, Lindsey," Caleb invited. "How could there be so much beauty and order in the world and in the way things work if there wasn't some quote-unquote 'higher being' to have put it all together?"

"Oh, I don't know," Lindsey said, glancing out her passenger window. The only sights she saw were dry grass, some depressing-looking brown hills, and a few scattered animals grazing the lonely fields. There didn't seem to be much beauty and order there.

"I've been to church a couple of times," Lindsey said, starting a new subject.

"Yeah?"

"Yeah, when I was younger, but I don't really remember anything about it. I just remember that it wasn't much fun. I thought it was kind of boring, actually."

"Well, I can't argue with you there," Caleb answered. "Little kids don't really find it stimulating to sit in a pew for two hours and listen to a bunch of talking that they don't really care about or understand."

"Yep," Lindsey nodded, her eyes drifting as if she were re-living the church experience in her mind.

"Well, at least as older people we know that there's more to church than just sitting in pews listening to a pastor speak. At least, you can make it more than that."

"How?"

"Well, you can actually, really listen and take in the words that the pastor is speaking, and apply them to your life."

That response made Lindsey think. What kinds of things did a pastor talk about? What kinds of things did someone apply to their life? However, Lindsey wasn't curious enough to continue asking about that. She also didn't want Caleb to think she was really interested in this religion stuff, because she wasn't....

Instead, another thought came into her mind. It was about her mother. Despite her efforts to keep quiet in order not to encourage Caleb, she asked what had been on her mind for quite some time.

"Do you believe in a heaven?"

"Yes, I do."

"So, who gets there?"

Oh no, Caleb thought. He knew where Lindsey was headed. She was thinking about her mother, and it probably wasn't the first time she had questioned a heaven. Caleb suddenly panicked, not wanting to tell Lindsey anything that might hurt her or scare her. The truth was, as far as Caleb knew, that Jillian Milholland had not been a saved Christian, and God's kingdom was only for those who have been saved by Jesus Christ and committed their lives to Him. Caleb's throat closed a little, and for a long time he remained silent, not knowing what to say to Lindsey. However, he knew that he couldn't just dismiss the subject; Lindsey had asked honestly, and he knew he must answer honestly. Also, keeping quiet about God's truth, especially when somebody was asking about it, was not right.

"What is it?" Lindsey asked, noting Caleb's panicked look.

Caleb shook his head. "Well, the Bible makes it clear to us that God's Kingdom – Heaven – is only for Christians; believers and followers of Christ."

A moment of silence followed as Lindsey's face contorted into a confused mask, and she stared at Caleb.

Oh Lord, help her to understand, help her to not get upset and dismiss You because of this.

"Why?" she finally asked.

"Why what?"

"Why do only *Christians* get to go to heaven?" She said the word "Christians" with such spite that it was as if an arrow had been shot right through Caleb's heart. Lindsey's voice and questioning had been so child-like, and it filled Caleb with a deep compassion. He knew this girl had been through a lot, and she was confused and lonely.

"Lindsey," he said.

"Yeah."

"If you don't know if you believe in God, then why are you even worrying about a Heaven?" Caleb wasn't sure it was the right thing to say, and he was hoping he wasn't saying it as a way out of the conversation. But it was the first thing that came to him, so he had voiced it.

"I don't know," Lindsey answered, realizing she wasn't being very discreet about her curiosity. She didn't doubt there was a God, it was just an idea that was hard for her to grasp all at once because it wasn't something she had grown up with. Caleb here, on the other hand, probably had been a Christian his whole life, so he was probably God's number one fan. Also, Lindsey was most interested in the idea of a Heaven because everybody she knew, whether Christian or not, had some idea or belief in a beautiful place that souls go to live after death. It was a nice idea to think that after a person dies, they have afterlife. Lindsey hadn't thought about death much throughout her life, but her mother's passing had forced her to, and it hit her hard. Lindsey had become very depressed and confused, wondering where her mother was and if she was still somehow "alive" and watching over her. She didn't know for sure, but she didn't like the idea that after death there was just nothing forever. She always thought that it would make living life so pointless if there was nothing at the end of it. Who knew what life was about? It seemed so pointless anyway every time Lindsey had really sat down and thought about it.

"Are you okay?" Caleb asked, pointing concerned eyes in Lindsey's direction. Her body had slumped, and she was leaning her head against the back of the seat, staring blankly at the cassette player.

"Yeah, I'm fine," she said flatly. Her voice scratched a little, almost as if she was holding back a sob.

"Are you sure?"

She just nodded.

"Are you thinking about your mom?"

Again she nodded.

Caleb didn't know what to say then. He suddenly realized that this whole venture was going to be tougher than he imagined. But he also realized that God was in ultimate control, and only He could change Lindsey and heal the pain that she was feeling. After a couple of minutes had passed by in silence, all Caleb could muster was a quiet, "It'll be alright." He knew it would because God was there, but Lindsey wasn't quite so sure.

Nine

How can a young person keep his life pure?
He can do it by holding on to your word.

– Psalm 119: 9

It was Friday afternoon, and Mary Jenkins was already nervously anticipating Sunday morning. She had resolved to take herself and Andrea to the Sunday Morning service at the Christian Community Church. A couple days ago, she had been telling herself that church wasn't for her, and that she could stick it out without God, but today she wasn't so sure. The phone call from Ted had only made things worse.

"I'm not going to be able to pick up Andrea for the weekend," he had explained.

"Ted, why not?" Mary complained. "I need you to take her. I have to work a late shift tonight, and nobody's going to be able to be home with Andrea. I need you to take her, Ted. If not for the whole weekend, then just for tonight, please."

"I'm sorry, I can't do it. I'm going to be too busy."

"With what, Ted?" Mary asked nervously as she lowered herself into one of the yellow-cushioned kitchen chairs and laid a shaking right elbow onto the kitchen table, resting her forehead in her hand. "I thought you were on vacation from work."

"That's the thing, Mary. I only get until the middle of next week for vacation, and I just made plans last night to fly to San Diego. After I get back, I'll spend as much time with Andrea as I can, but I just can't this week."

"But she's your daughter, Ted," Mary explained angrily, although her voice was weak and teary. "You would actually choose to go to San Diego instead of spending time with your daughter?"

"You know I love spending time with Andrea, but if I don't take this vacation time, then I won't get a vacation for the rest of the year."

"It's October, Ted," Mary stated strictly. "It's almost the end of the year anyway. Once 1998 rolls around, you can take your vacation early in the spring or something."

"I don't want to wait, I need this time, Mary."

"Why do you *need* this time, Ted? It just sounds like you *want* this time you selfish bas...."

"Hey now!" Ted stopped her. "Don't get like that, Mary. I can't stand it when you get all whiny and complainy on me. You're so immature, did you know that?"

"If I'm so immature, then why am I the one taking care of Andrea and working full time in order to do it? You hardly ever see her! Do you think your child-support helps make up for anything you've done to us?"

"What are you talking about? What have I done to you?"

"You left us, Ted. It's too hard for me to take care of her by myself." Mary's voice lowered at the end of her statement as she stifled out a sob unintentionally.

"I didn't leave you and Andrea. You and I got a divorce, Mary. I can't believe you actually think I left you. Are you crazy? What are those late nights doing to you?"

Mary set the phone receiver down for a minute and tried to compose herself before she broke down and started crying uncontrollably. She was still in love with Ted, and she didn't know how much longer she could survive without him. He knew how she felt, and he did all he could to make her understand that it was over between them.

Ted noticed the silence and resumed his talk. "Maybe you should get a hobby, Mary. You're depressed. I don't think it's healthy for Andrea to grow up in that kind of environment."

"Like you give a crap about Andrea!" Mary screamed. From down the hall the sound of a cry began to ensue, and Mary turned to find Andrea standing at the entrance to the kitchen, crying as she watched her mother, listening to every word she spoke. Etched into a canvas of confusion, the six-year-old's features tore Mary's heart. She spoke silently into the receiver, keeping her eyes on Andrea. "Take your precious vacation. Andrea and I will be fine without you." But that wasn't the truth.

"I'll come by and see Andrea right after vacation."

"No, Ted, don't even bother," Mary insisted, lowering her voice to a harsh whisper, and turning her face away from Andrea's glare. "I don't ever want to see you around Andrea again. She has a right to know that her father cares more about his own life than about hers." Mary slammed down the receiver and quickly made her way across the kitchen and to her daughter. The small girl had her hands around her face as she sobbed for her father.

"What's wrong with daddy? Isn't he coming tonight?" she cried.

Mary picked up her daughter and cradled her like a baby. "Shh, it's okay," she soothed. "Daddy's got something he needs to do this weekend, so he won't be seeing you for a while, okay?"

"No!" Andrea screamed as she wriggled her way out of her mother's arms and took off down the hallway into her bedroom. She slammed the door behind her. In the kitchen Mary sank down into one of the worn dining room chairs and sighed. She didn't know what to do. Dealing with her still fresh divorce and trying to raise her daughter right was something Mary felt unfit to do. She began to cry silently as she replayed her and Ted's conversation in her mind. *Why don't you get a hobby, Mary*, Ted had suggested. She knew he wasn't being serious when he said it, but all of a sudden the idea of attending church flooded her mind. Mary decided that it couldn't be such a bad idea. Right now, all she knew was that she needed something to do, something to take her mind off of her troubles. Maybe church could do that. Maybe Mary could meet some new people at church who would become new friends. Mary was doubtful, but at the moment she felt desperate. *If this God thing is real, then only something good can come of it, right?*

Vanessa's high-pitched voice was beginning to annoy Nick by the minute. As she sat in the passenger seat of his new Mustang, chatting about her last shopping trip and gossiping about the latest news, Nick just pretended to listen as he rolled his eyes in irritation. *What was I thinking giving up Lindsey*? It wasn't the first time he had regretted getting together with Vanessa. She was a small, cute sophomore with beautiful large eyes and a playful personality, but after a while, it had gotten really old. He couldn't handle her talkativity and her endless whining when something didn't go her way.

"I tried it on in like, four different sizes and it still didn't fit. So I went to another store," she explained, suddenly changing the radio station without Nick's permission. "Oh, do you know who I saw there? Oh my gosh, you wouldn't believe it."

Nick really didn't care. He just raised his eyebrows and kept his gaze focused on the road. Outside, the street was lined on both sides by tall trees whose leaves were quickly shedding from the autumn season. The colors were beautiful, backed up by the orange-red sun, dimming in the distant horizon. A few stray leaves of various yellows and greens were held in suspension by the blowing wind and flew across the front of the Mustang's windshield. Nick always loved nature and appreciated how much a pretty sunset could lift his spirits.

"Nick, are you listening to me?" Vanessa asked, although it was more of a complaint than a question. Once again Nick didn't understand how he could have gotten mixed up with such a young and immature girl.

"Not really," he answered honestly. Vanessa face contorted into a look of offense, and she quickly reached over and shut off the radio. "Well, maybe now you'll listen."

Irritation flooded Nick as he sharply turned his steering wheel to the right to pull over. He stopped the car next to the sidewalk. "And maybe now you'll stop touching my radio or walk the rest of the way to the party."

Stunned and hurt, Vanessa glared up at Nick's irritated features before turning her head around toward the window. "You don't have to be so insensitive, you know."

"And you don't have to be so annoying."

"You are so rude!" Vanessa whined as she opened the car door and jumped out. "I would rather walk than ride the rest of the way with a jerk!"

By the time she finished her sentence, Nick was already pulling away from the curb, his tires screeching in the distance.

"Hey Nick!" Marianne called when she saw him enter the small living room. She began to make her way through the crowd of teenagers standing in small clusters and sitting on every piece of furniture available. From across the room, she could see Nick wave his arm at her. Finally they found each other.

"Hey, I'm glad you made it. I didn't know if you'd be here or not."

"Yeah, well, I wasn't going to come. This partying is becoming a little old."

"I know what you mean," Marianne agreed as the two began to squeeze their way into the kitchen where there weren't quite as many people. "There wasn't supposed to be any alcohol at this party, but someone managed to sneak some in. Oh well, what else is new, huh?"

"Well, at least these people have good, well-minded friends like you to stay sober and be the designated driver," Nick laughed, although he was totally serious. Marianne had done him a world of good more than one night when he wasn't fit to drive home.

"Gee, I feel so loved," Marianne replied sarcastically. "So where's Vanessa? Wasn't she coming along?"

Nick was averse in answering. "I sort of dropped her off on the side of the road a few blocks down."

Marianne's eyes grew wide. "Are you serious?" Nick just nodded, trying to hide a smile. Marianne laughed. "I knew you'd become irked at her some day."

"Irked?"

"It means annoyed, Nick."

"That's a funny word."

"So what are you doing here, then, if you don't really want to be here?" Marianne asked as she opened the refrigerator door and pulled out two Pepsis. Nick loved Marianne's casual and nonchalant attitude towards everything, and appreciated her company, especially after spending the day with Vanessa. Marianne, although very upbeat most of the time, had always seemed to be in control and knew what she wanted with her life. Although he would never admit it to her, Nick thought very highly of Marianne and looked up to her.

"It's Friday night and there's nothing else for me to do."

Marianne tipped her head to the side. "There's plenty of things to do on Friday nights, Nick, besides going to parties. But I suppose a big partier like you wouldn't really know about that."

"Like what?"

"Well," Marianne began to explain while handing a Pepsi to Nick, who accepted it without hesitation. "There's the ever-popular going out to see a movie. Or you could have a movie night with some friends and just rent a bunch and stay home watching them. There's roller skating and iceskating rinks that are always open nearby, or dancing clubs for teenagers which are smoke and alcohol-free." Nick nodded his head as he listened. Marianne went on. "I love just going out with a few friends for dinner, the mall, and a movie. Sometimes we stop at the big bookstore in Bellingham – *Barnes and Noble* – and just hang out there. Or some nights I like taking walks or going on a jog right before the sun sets. There's lots of things to do that don't involve getting sick while partying."

"You've never really invited me to any of your non-party nights," Nick said.

"You're right. You and I are going to have to do a lot of hanging out then, to make up for it all." Marianne smiled.

"The real reason I came here was because I wanted to talk to you," Nick explained, changing the subject, "about Lindsey."

Marianne nodded and pulled herself up onto a counter to sit. "What about Lindsey?"

"Have you talked to her lately?"

"Yeah, actually I talked to her earlier this afternoon."

Nick's eyes seemed to light up. "Really? Where is she?"

"Well, she was in Montana, but by now she's probably a little farther. I would guess she's out of Montana by now."

"Wow, I still can't believe she's actually driving all the way across the country by herself."

"Yeah," Marianne agreed. She tipped her gaze downward, and stared at the Pepsi can in her hand.

Nick noticed her sudden change of attitude. He could tell there was something else that she wasn't telling him. "Is something wrong?" he asked genuinely.

"Nah, I mean, I don't think Lindsey's doing too good."

"What do you mean?"

"We got into a fight over the phone, and she hung up on me."

"She did?" Nick seemed appalled.

"Yeah, I didn't know she had it in her. She was pretty upset."

"About what?"

"Well, there's the infamous incident with her mother. I guess she is having a hard time dealing with that. But also because I didn't believe her about something she told me."

"What's that?" Nick urged.

Marianne sighed. "She claims she was in a car wreck the other day, and this guy came and saved her, or something, and now the two of them are traveling together across the country because he just happens to be going to North Carolina, which is right next to Virginia."

"Gee, that seems a little coincidental."

"Yeah, I told her a little sarcastically that it was pretty convenient, and she hung up on me."

"Oh man, she must really be upset about something if she did that to you."

"Yeah, I don't know if she really was in a car wreck or not, but I don't know if I even believe her about that. I think maybe she's just gone a little wacko because of everything that's happened. It probably wasn't the right time for her to leave. She should've waited until she was a little more ready, or something."

"Do you really think she's that bad?" Nick asked, the concern obvious in his voice.

Marianne nodded. "I can't imagine how it feels to have your mom die on you, but I know it has to be worse than I could ever conceive. I don't believe Lindsey's doing very well dealing with it, and I don't think it's going to get any better on her trip. I'm afraid that in her condition she won't even make it to Virginia."

"How do you know she was lying about that wreck, and about that guy?"

"It just doesn't make sense, that's all. It's too perfect, I guess. I just think Lindsey made it up because she's going a little crazy, and she wants attention or something."

All at once Nick became very worried for Lindsey. Marianne hadn't given a very good report, and he started reasoning Lindsey's chances of making it all by herself to Virginia. It didn't appear good.

"Did you say anything to her about me," he asked quietly and hopefully.

"Yeah," was Marianne's indefinite reply.

"What did you say?"

"Well," Marianne began, lingering for a moment. "It wasn't good. I mean, I just told her that I saw you at the supermarket and that you asked about her. I told her about our little conversation, and she didn't seem to give a rip about any of it."

"Really?"

"Yeah," Marianne confirmed. "She was kind of being a little rude about it; it wasn't a very nice scene. She's been hurt, you know? Really bad."

Nick lowered his head and closed his eyes. "I know I hurt her. I can't believe what a jerk I was to her, but I'm different now, and I still care about her."

"I told her that, but she didn't care. She figured that since it wasn't working out with you and Vanessa you were just trying to crawl back to her in order to be with someone. She doesn't feel special to you anymore."

"I know," Nick admitted.

"Nick, even I don't know if I could trust you to be with her again. You did a big injustice toward Lindsey, and she's deeply hurt. Who's to say it wouldn't happen again?"

"I don't know so much whether I'd want to be with Lindsey again in a relationship. I just know that I care about her, and I wish that she at least wanted to be my friend."

"Well, that's going to be kind of hard considering that she's gone now."

"I know," Nick agreed. "She left at the worst possible time, do you know that?"

"Yes, I do," Marianne exclaimed. "She just ran away from it all, you know? That was so unhealthy of her to do."

"Nick!" came a shrill voice from the kitchen entranceway. Marianne and Nick turned their heads in unison to find Vanessa standing with murder in her eyes.

"Hey there, Vanessa," Marianne greeted her cheerfully.

"I can't believe you did that to me, Nick," she whined, stepping into the kitchen.

"Well, I'm sorry, Vanessa, but I haven't really been in the peachiest of moods, if you know what I mean."

"No, I don't know what you mean, but I wish you would apologize to me for dumping me on the street."

"I just did apologize, Vanessa, and I didn't dump you on the street. You got out of the car, remember?"

"That's because you were being rude to me," she explained, pointing her finger in Nick's face. "Besides, you told me to get out of the car before I actually did."

From the side, Marianne covered her mouth with her hand to hide a chuckle. Vanessa glared at her.

"Vanessa," Nick said calmly and slowly. "I'm sorry for being rude to you and dumping you out on the street, okay?"

"Fine," Vanessa replied.

"Also, I think I should tell you now that it's over between us, okay? I really don't think this is working out."

Vanessa's features abruptly transposed from anger to confusion. "What do you mean?"

"Must I explain?" Nick breathed. "Sometimes, Vanessa, you just seem more like a little sister to me than a girlfriend. I find myself getting annoyed at you and upset at you, and it's just not working, okay?"

Instead of saying a word, Vanessa turned her back and walked away toward the party.

"Well, Nick, you're just a regular heart-breaker, aren't you?" Marianne stated whimsically.

Nick had to agree with her. He didn't know why he was wasting his time.

It was only early evening, and Caleb and Lindsey could have driven much further into Wyoming, but they decided to stop and spend the night in Sheridan. Lindsey had already been exhausted from spending almost seven hours on the road. Caleb stopped the truck in the parking lot of a Days Inn. The two young adults stepped out of the truck and quietly made their way to the lobby entrance.

"We need two rooms," Caleb informed the man at the counter. He began to type at the keyboard.

"No, wait," Lindsey stopped. She turned to Caleb. "Why don't we get one room with two beds? It would save us money than if we got two separate rooms." Caleb hesitated a moment. He had thought of that, but didn't know whether Lindsey would be comfortable with it or not. He stared at her as she raised her eyebrows to confirm Caleb's thoughts. "What do you think?"

"Well, I suppose that makes sense." He turned to the man. "Just give us one room."

"All right then," the man said as he began to register them in.

A few minutes later, Lindsey and Caleb were transferring their luggage down a hallway and into their room.

"Are you sure you don't mind sharing a room," Lindsey asked. "You're not just doing it for me, are you?"

"No, no, I don't mind," Caleb assured her. "You're right, we could save money like this."

"Next time I'll pay for the room, k?"

"That's fine with me," Caleb beamed, throwing his things onto his bed. "So every time we stop, do you want to share a room?"

"Of course," Lindsey said. "Besides, it will be more fun this way because then we can stay up late at night and watch movies together and order ice cream and all that good stuff."

Caleb laughed. "You're going to be very entertaining on this trip, I can tell."

"Why, thank you," Lindsey said.

"So where should we eat tonight?" Caleb asked, walking toward the window and gazing out of it.

"Let's just do fast-food tonight, k?"

"*Burger King*?"

"Sounds good to me."

"And is Miss Lindsey going to pay?"

Lindsey chuckled. "I suppose, since you paid for breakfast and lunch!"

"Don't forget the room!"

"Hey, I would've paid for lunch but you just wouldn't let me," Lindsey contended. "And I bet tomorrow night when I offer to pay for the room, you probably won't let me then, either, will you?"

"You never know," Caleb teased.

"Well I'm going to, whether you want me to or not!" Lindsey demanded as she walked by Caleb and pushed him in the shoulder. He toppled over a bit.

"Hey! There you go getting violent again," he clamored as he followed after Lindsey to push her back. She screamed and jumped over the bed to get away. Caleb followed close after her. She leaped onto the other bed, the one occupied by Caleb's things, and began jumping on it.

"Hey!" he cried. "That's my bed, woman! Get off of it!" he teased. Lindsey began laughing.

"Woman? You're calling me 'woman'? What's that supposed to mean, you, you, man!"

Caleb jumped on the bed and tackled Lindsey. She fell on her back and began laughing hysterically. Caleb stood up and acted like he was going to body slam Lindsey. She screamed again and turned over to get out of the way, falling onto the hard floor.

"You're too much fun, Caleb," she said, standing up.

"I know," Caleb replied in conceit, smiling. Lindsey quickly moved forward and grabbed one of his legs, pulling it, causing Caleb to fall over onto his back.

"Oh that's it," he cried, moving off the bed. Lindsey shot for the door and opened it quickly, practically falling onto the floor of the hallway outside, giggling the whole way.

The sun finally descended, and it wasn't long afterward that the moon replaced its beauty, hovering powerfully in the universe above. The sky was a dark blue hue, almost black, and Caleb finally moved off his bed toward the window to close the shades.

Lindsey was sitting against her backboard with her legs crossed, very engrossed in the television show that they were watching.

The day was catching up with Caleb, and he was becoming tired very quickly. It was amazing to him how much he had already enjoyed Lindsey's company. She wasn't a bad person, she was funny and silly and bright and sensitive and … lonely. Caleb could tell in more than one instance that she was lonely. He knew right then that she must really appreciate his company as much as he appreciated hers. But even Caleb knew that he wasn't enough for her. Caleb knew what she needed, whom she needed.

"How did your mom die, Lindsey?" he asked suddenly.

Lindsey glanced over at him, turned the volume to the TV down, and answered instantly, "A plane crash."

"Really?"

"Yeah," she replied softly.

"I'm sorry," Caleb said.

Lindsey grinned. "Don't be," she said. "People always say that, but I don't understand why. They don't have anything to be sorry for. Their mom didn't die."

Caleb was almost hurt. "They say they're sorry because they empathize for you, Lindsey. They feel bad for your loss, that's all. It's just the polite thing to say, I suppose."

"Well, I would rather not hear it." Caleb noticed that her voice had become defensive and harsh. He stayed silent. "I'm sorry," Lindsey apologized when she realized what she had said. "I know you're just trying to be nice, and I'm probably not making it any easier."

"It's okay," he said. "It's got to be hard for you to talk about your mother."

"Yeah, sometimes it is."

"I heard what you were saying to your friend Marianne on the phone; about how you're reminded of your mom every day, and how it's hard dealing with everything right now." Lindsey just nodded and tipped her head down. "I didn't mean to be eavesdropping, I'm sorry," Caleb apologized.

"No, no, it's fine, Lindsey assured him. "You didn't know that when I called her I wasn't just going to ask about how she's doing and all that jazz." Caleb nodded, and Lindsey went on. "One of my mom's friends owns a small plane, and so he was going to take her on a short ride. I guess something got screwed up in the engine, or whatever, and the plane went out of control. I don't know all the details. I didn't really want to know. My mom was killed instantly, though, when the plane hit."

"Wow," Caleb breathed. "What about her friend? Did he live?"

"Yeah, he lived. He barely survived, but he did."

Caleb nodded slowly, feeling terrible for this young woman. "Does that make you mad sometimes?" he asked quietly.

"What? That he lived and she didn't?"

"Yeah."

"Sometimes," she answered honestly. "But I know I shouldn't be mad at him. It's just something that happened. Lots of bad things happen, but I don't think it helps to put blame on people. That's just like taking out your anger on someone. It doesn't do any good."

"Have you done that to anybody you know? I mean, take your anger out on them?"

Lindsey was quiet for a moment as she thought about Caleb's question. "Yeah," she answered slowly. "I know I have."

"Do you think that's what you did to Marianne today on the phone?"

Lindsey looked over at Caleb and wrinkled her nose. "You sound like a psychologist or a counselor or something."

Caleb grinned. "I'm just trying to help out, that's all."

Lindsey smiled. "Yeah, I hung up on her. I've never done anything like that before. I've never gotten really angry."

"What were you so mad about?"

Lindsey almost started to laugh. "Because she didn't believe me about you."

"Aw, that makes me feel special," Caleb said in an exaggerated child's voice.

"I was also mad because she brought up my ex-boyfriend."

"Yeah?"

"Yeah, his name's Nick, and I just have this big...." She paused, trying to think of a word that would describe her feelings toward Nick. "This big ... maliciousness for him, I guess."

"I take it something good didn't happen between you two."

"Well, it wasn't something good that caused us to break up, I can tell you that."

"Do you want to talk about it?"

"I don't know if you really want to know."

"Well, I just thought that maybe it might help," Caleb said slowly and unsurely, "but if you don't feel like talking about it, then you don't have to." His remark surprised Lindsey. She knew Caleb was a nice guy, but this was just too much. All Lindsey ever wanted was someone honest and genuine in her life whom she could share anything with. Even her friends back in Washington hadn't ever amounted to that. Even her best friend Marianne had missed the mark at times.

"I just don't know if you want to hear about all my problems. Nobody else ever seems to want to."

"Well, I'm not like everybody else."

"What makes you so different?" Lindsey asked curiously.

Caleb's mouth twisted into a sly grin. "Jesus," he answered confidently. Lindsey didn't quite understand what he meant – it was a Christian thing, she supposed. But nevertheless, she liked Caleb and how he was so different. Gazing at him now, Lindsey noticed how soft his light brown eyes were. They were nice eyes, not as nice as Nick's, but more honest and sincere. He looked like his age: a clean-cut, confident young man of the age of twenty-one, with well-defined, sharp features, especially his chin, but a slightly narrow face. When he smiled and laughed, however, his cheeks showed off dimples, and Lindsey could see the child inside of him. His hair, cut in a short style, but not necessarily styled at all, was blond, which added to the child-effect; small and innocent and blameless, holding the world in his hands. But Lindsey knew that wasn't true. He had told her himself about his past problems of drinking and drugs, and about his contorted relationship with his parents. Although Caleb hadn't told her the details, the sound in his voice at the time had given her enough clues to assume that it wasn't good. She knew Caleb was trustworthy, and she knew he was somebody she could talk to right now. So far he hadn't let her down or made her feel uncomfortable or unwanted.

"Are you awake?" Caleb asked, diving into Lindsey's thoughts. She had been studying him, and her eyes, which had become still and glassy, suddenly blinked.

"Nick and I broke up because he cheated on me."

"Oh, that must've hurt."

"Yeah, a whole lot. And we're not just talking about a kiss or a date, or something like that. Nick slept with another girl."

Caught off-guard, Caleb's voice halted in his throat, and he was unable to comment for a few moments. "Are you serious?" he finally managed.

Lindsey just nodded her head.

"Hmm," was all Caleb could muster. He wasn't sure how to reply to her comment, but he took the chance to ask her a personal question in the next few moments. Narrowing his eyes at her, he asked, "Were you and Nick ever, uh … you know?"

"Oh no," Lindsey quickly answered. Deep down Caleb sighed with relief. "No, it wasn't like that between us. I'm still a virgin. So was Nick. He knew that I wanted to wait until I was ready, and even though I probably wouldn't have been ready for a while, I was positive that it was going to be him." Lindsey gave a little chuckle. "Guess I was wrong, huh? He said he just couldn't wait for me. He was drunk at a party when it happened."

Again Caleb didn't know how to respond. He knew what it felt like to be wasted at a party, and he also knew what kinds of things intoxication led a person to do. Caleb himself had many times regretted his behavior while under the influence of alcohol. However, he knew that he was forgiven by his Savior, and that he was washed clean of all his past mistakes. It was still hard for him not to think about them, though.

"He was never worth it, Lindsey," Caleb quietly stated.

"I know that." Silence followed before Lindsey commented again. "So how do I know when somebody is worth it, huh? I've thought a lot about that since Nick, especially since he was the only guy I've had such an involving relationship with. I mean, we were close; we were practically best friends. Is finding the right guy just too good to be true, or am I missing something?"

Caleb ran his fingers through his hair, taking a breath, and moved to sit on the edge of his bed, facing Lindsey. "You know what's a good way to tell whether a guy is worth it or not?"

"How?" Lindsey asked, forming a smile at the way Caleb was obviously trying to make her feel better. She appreciated his effort.

"If they say they'll wait for you, they're worth it; and I don't mean just wait for you until you're ready, but wait for you until you're both married. Then you know that he's worth it because he's willing to hold off until you're both married and committed."

"It's the abstinence thing, right?"

"Sort of, but it's a little different. Abstinence is more about holding off until marriage in order to keep safe from unwanted pregnancy or STDs and that kind of stuff. What I'm talking about involves real love, and saving yourself for the sake of each other. Who wants to get married to someone knowing that person has been with somebody else? It just doesn't make it very special, does it? Sex is a gift, and you wouldn't want to know that your partner has given that gift away to other people."

"I guess I've never really thought of it that way," Lindsey admitted, thinking about what Caleb was telling her.

"Sex isn't an obligation to a relationship," Caleb continued as the words came to him. "Just because you're going out with somebody doesn't mean you have to sleep with them. That doesn't prove anything. If somebody really loved you, they wouldn't say 'Sleep with me,' they'd say, 'I want us to save ourselves just for each other,' which means waiting for sex until marriage. If that person can follow through with that promise, then they're definitely worth it, don't you think?"

"Yeah, that makes sense," Lindsey agreed, a little stunned at how openly Caleb could talk about the subject. He definitely wasn't like any guy she had ever known. "But what if you both know you're in love, and you're even engaged, or close to it? If two people are in love, why not then?"

"Because it's dangerous. Somebody could just tell their partner that they love them just so that they'll sleep with them. I don't care how trustworthy a person is. Waiting is the only sure way. Even if your partner does truly love you, and you love them, then *why not* wait until marriage just to confirm that? Why would it be so difficult for two people to do that?"

"It probably wouldn't be if the temptation wasn't so bad," Lindsey stated. "I'm sure a lot of unmarried couples feel the way you do, and they do plan on waiting until marriage, but when a situation arises where they're being very intimate or something, then it can just happen without warning."

"Well, that's why it's safe to stay away as much as you possibly can from intimacy before you get married to that person."

"That wouldn't be any fun," Lindsey smiled.

"It wouldn't be any fun if you base your relationship solely on the physical aspects," Caleb replied. Lindsey raised her eyebrows. He had a point there. What was the point of relationships if it wasn't for the physical?

"I think a relationship is about getting to know somebody on a more personal level. Although that does involve physical aspects to a degree – especially if the people really care about each other – a couple can still be a couple and stay safe. I would hope a person doesn't base their relationship fully on the physical aspects, because if that's so, then they're just using you." Caleb was using the term "you" generally, speaking about any person, but Lindsey felt like he was speaking to her personally. She suddenly realized how much sense it all made to her, and she began to analyze her and Nick's relationship. It had been very physical, but Nick and Lindsey had always had something more. At least Lindsey always thought they had. Now she wasn't quite so sure.

"Does any of this have to do with your Christian beliefs?" Lindsey asked suddenly. Caleb smiled.

"Yeah," he replied honestly. "I don't know if a person who wasn't a Christian could ever believe in any of this, do you?"

"I don't know."

"Well, at least I never thought this way before I was a Christian, but in the Bible, God clearly defines that sex is a gift, like I said, and that He intends it to be shared between a man and woman in marriage." Lindsey nodded, and Caleb continued. "It really does make sense. God doesn't ask us to do things just for the heck of it, He always has a purpose behind it. I believe waiting for sex until marriage is the only logical, sane, and 100% safe way to go, not to mention it pleases God."

"So what if you don't wait until marriage for some reason? What does God do then?"

Caleb was hesitant for a moment, but he was glad Lindsey was asking. It showed that she had a curiosity in his beliefs, and in God. "Well, we have a very loving and forgiving God, and if you're thinking he's just gonna drop you in a ditch or something for doing what he doesn't want you to do, then you're wrong. He always offers forgiveness if you need it and want it. All you have to do is recognize your sin and ask for his forgiveness."

Lindsey just stared at him before slowly nodding her head in understanding. "Yeah, I know I've heard that before," she said. "Like I said, I've been to church before, when I was little."

"Yep, you told me," Caleb smiled.

Lindsey sighed hugely and stretched her arms out on her side, nearly reaching Caleb's head with her left arm. "Well, hombre, I'm tired, what do you think?"

"Ice-cream," Caleb replied instantly.

"What?"

"Ice-cream sounds darn good."

"Room service," they both said in unison.

That night, while the wind blew loudly against the window pane outside, Caleb was thanking God that his and Lindsey's conversation had gone so well, and he asked God to put a continued curiosity and longing in Lindsey's heart so that she would seek Him.

Ten

The Messenger of the LORD appeared to Gideon and said, "The LORD is with you, brave man."

Gideon responded, "Excuse me, sir! But if the LORD is with us, why has all this happened to us? Where are all the miracles our ancestors have told us about?"

– Judges 6:12-13

As the pickup bounced along the highway, Lindsey leaned in toward the passenger side window and stared outside at the passing hills and shrubs, with a cloudy gray sky visible right above. The scene made for a very depressing mood, and in seconds, Lindsey wasn't feeling at her best. Caleb sat by her side, silent, with his music playing very quietly on the radio. As Lindsey gazed up at the sky, the soft sound of an airplane engine buzzed above the truck, and within seconds, the plane itself was within ocular distance. Lindsey stared at it as it cascaded across the sky – it was a small plane, just like the one her mother was killed in.

* * *

That day Lindsey had spent the whole afternoon and evening out with her friends, and they had all been down in Seattle, occupied with a concert and various other activities. Nobody had any way of reaching Lindsey because none of the teenagers owned cell phones. When the day was over, and Nick had just dropped off Lindsey on her front porch, giving her a long goodnight kiss, she entered the house smiling and laughing. Jillian wasn't home. Lindsey remembered how her mother went on an airplane ride with one of her close friends that afternoon, and so she wasn't worried or suspicious right away. As she walked into the kitchen to open the refrigerator door, her eyes caught sight of the clock hanging above the stove, and she was reminded of how late it was. It was past midnight. Her mom should have been home from her plane ride long ago. However, Lindsey just shrugged it off, reasoning that her mother had just decided to stay out with her friends. Instantly Lindsey made her way to the answering machine to check messages to see if her mother had left anything for her. The message she got wasn't what she was expecting. Instead of her mother's playful and hearty voice, another one, soft, scared, and weak, was coming through the machine speakers. It was her grandmother's voice, nervously indicating to Lindsey that she and Grandpa were at the hospital, and that her mother had been in an accident. Chelsea told Lindsey on the answering machine to get to the hospital as soon as possible. When the message was over, the automatic voice on the machine indicated that the message was left at 3:30 in the afternoon. Two more messages were left, both Chelsea, both asking why Lindsey wasn't home yet, and pleading for her to get to the hospital. Each new message sounded more desperate. Lindsey's thoughts halted, and suddenly she had become very confused and light-headed. Her mother had been in an accident. An airplane accident? Her grandmother hadn't specified. Nonetheless, Lindsey couldn't feel her body working as she forced herself to move from her spot in the kitchen and grab her car keys to make her way to the hospital.

When she arrived, and she wasn't sure how she did, nor could she remember the trip there, her mind was in a whirl as she entered the building. *What do I do?* she thought. *Where do I go? What if I heard wrong?* Before she could figure out answers to those questions, a voice grabbed her from behind. She spun around to find her grandfather standing in the waiting room entrance with a poignant look etched about his face. Lindsey knew it wasn't good. She slowly walked toward him. "I got your messages," she sputtered.

"Yeah," Dan replied, his voice catching in his throat. Lindsey stopped walking toward him. She noted his fatigue, and the somber way he was presenting himself. His head was slightly downcast, and his eyes, instead of focusing on Lindsey, were watching his feet. Lindsey had never witnessed her grandfather so … not in control.

"What's wrong?" Lindsey asked, not wanting to waste any time. Chelsea walked out from the waiting room and stood by Dan. She had been crying.

"Jillian has been in an accident," she quietly said, speaking for Dan.

"I know that!" Lindsey growled, disgusted that her grandmother was beating around the bush, trying to spare her. "You told me that three times on the answering machine. What's wrong!?"

"She's dead," Dan stated.

Lindsey blinked in disbelief as the room began to spin, and the two figures standing in front of her became blurry. Dead? That was a weird concept. Her mother, dead? Not alive? No longer on the earth? "What do you mean?" Lindsey asked softly.

"You know what we mean, Lindsey," Dan said. He understood Lindsey was just shocked for the moment, but she knew perfectly well what they were talking about.

"What do you mean?" she asked again, not knowing that she was saying it. Her mom was her best friend, the closest person she had in the world; the only person she had in the world.

"Lindsey," Chelsea said soothingly, walking toward her granddaughter and putting her arms around her. Lindsey backed away, shaking her head left to right before taking off down the hall and out of the building. The only sound she could hear from behind her was the distant call of her name as she fled from the hospital. Jumping in her car, she pulled out of the parking lot and down the street, heading for home. *This isn't happening ... this isn't happening ... it's all a joke. My mom's not dead. Dead? What does that mean anyway?* But Lindsey knew what it meant, and for days it was hard for her to comprehend the fact that her mother was never going to come home at the end of the day again.

Lindsey closed her eyes, forcing herself not to cry as the memory played in her mind.

* * *

Caleb saw the airplane also, and as he glanced at Lindsey, he knew she was thinking about her mother. He wanted to say something, but he wasn't sure what, so he kept quiet. If she wanted to talk about something, she would. In a matter of minutes, Lindsey was the one who finally began the conversation.

"So how long till we get to Nebraska, Caleb?" she asked quietly, working to make her voice sound as strong and normal as possible.

"Well, we'll definitely get there today, before 6 p.m.," he answered.

Lindsey nodded. "Good," she said. "Wyoming is beginning to depress me."

"I know," Caleb agreed. "I'm not used to all these rolling hills either."

"I need water, and green, and snow, and all that West Coast stuff."

"Yeah, I know what you mean. Even when I lived in North Carolina I lived on the coast, so I'm not used to barren hills and mountains either."

Lindsey turned and sat up straight in her seat, facing the front window. "Can we stop soon for breakfast?"

"Sure," Caleb said. That morning they hadn't left as early as they had the day before, but Caleb was still tired.

"Ugh," Lindsey moaned, dipping into Caleb's thoughts. "All this driving is wearing me out already, and I'm not even the one driving."

Caleb laughed. "Well, at any time if you want to take over, then be my guest."

Lindsey glanced down at his clutch stick. "I don't know how to drive a clutch."

"Are you serious?" he asked.

"Yeah. Why does that seem so hard to believe? Lots of people don't know how to drive clutches."

"Well, woman, I'd say you were spoiled then."

"Thanks a lot," Lindsey answered non-enthusiastically, "and stop calling me 'woman.'"

"I'm joking, Lindsey," Caleb reassured her. He glanced over at her and found her slumped in her seat with her arms crossed, staring straight ahead. He knew she wasn't feeling in a very hearty mood, so he decided he should take it easy on her.

"I'll teach you, okay," he offered.

"Teach me what?" Lindsey asked rudely.

"To drive a stick, of course."

Lindsey shrugged her shoulders. "Okay, whatever."

About fifteen minutes later, Caleb was pulling into the driveway of a *McDonald's*, and Lindsey was suddenly in a brighter disposition.

"Mmm, sausage McMuffin," she sang out. "Yum yum, I just love those things."

"You're weird," Caleb informed her. She smiled at him.

"Yes, I am, but that's not a bad thing."

"Nope, it's not. So I take it you want a sausage McMuffin."

"Aw, yeah," she said, taking off her seat belt and folding her legs up Indian-style on the seat. Caleb shook his head. He thought she was too silly and adorable.

"Don't you have any other music?" Lindsey asked honestly, noting the fact that everything they were listening to was not without a "God" or "Jesus" in their lyrics.

Caleb glanced over at her, almost offended. "Yeah I do, but not much, why?"

"Oh, I don't know," Lindsey said playfully, tipping her head to the side. "This is all just too godly for me, I think."

"Yeah, I used to think that too."

"Well, it's good music, I mean ... I like the music, but I'd rather listen to something I know and that I could sing along with."

"That's understandable," Caleb agreed as he popped out his tape of various Christian artists. The blurry scratch of the radio became audible, and Caleb quickly began changing the station to find something clear.

"It all sounds like country-ish stuff to me," he noted.

"Yeah," Lindsey agreed, dissatisfied. "Oh well, I don't care what we listen to, it's not important."

"We could just turn off all music whatsoever, and sing ourselves," Caleb offered. He raised an eyebrow at Lindsey, and she couldn't help but grin back.

"I don't know if I could do that."

"Let's try it." Caleb switched off the radio, and for a few minutes, the two young people sat in silence, periodically glancing over at one another and grinning.

"I thought you were going to sing," Lindsey asked after five minutes had passed.

"I'm not going to sing by myself," Caleb said. "Besides, if I did it would be something 'godly,' as you call it."

"Why?"

"Because I don't listen to a lot of other things."

"Well, that's boring," Lindsey insisted.

"Not to me," Caleb said, defensively. Her comment had offended Caleb, and he could have had so much to say to Lindsey about it to defend Christian music, but he didn't want to get into an argument. One of the hardest things for Caleb as a new Christian was to try and stay out of pointless arguments. One of his favorite bible passages was second Timothy 2:23, which simply stated, "Don't have anything to do with foolish and stupid arguments. You know they cause quarrels." As an unbeliever, Caleb always tried his best to win an argument, no matter what it was about. He always wanted people to see his point on issues, but he didn't care much about what the other person thought. It was hard for him when his aunt and uncle finally told him about Jesus. At first Caleb didn't want to listen, but in time he broke down, and he knew he couldn't resist the Truth any longer.

"So how did you became a Christian," Lindsey unexpectedly questioned, as if reading Caleb's thoughts. Caleb was taken off-guard. Nobody had asked him that, yet. Nevertheless, he was glad she was asking and showing interest.

"By my aunt and uncle, about three months ago, in July."

Lindsey was stunned. So he hadn't been a Christian all his life like she had thought. "What did they do?"

"They just told me about God and who He is, and introduced me to Christ. They explained to me about how God sent Jesus to the earth, and about His life, death, and resurrection."

"Resurrection?" Lindsey was confused by what Caleb meant.

"Yeah, Jesus Christ was killed, but He rose from the dead on the third day," Caleb explained. He noticed how Lindsey's eyebrows rose a little. "By doing that, He defeated death. He died, but He didn't really die. He came alive again, and He's alive today."

"Like he's wandering the earth somewhere now?"

"No, He's with God, in His kingdom."

"Heaven?"

Caleb nodded.

Lindsey frowned a little. She didn't understand how somebody could be 'resurrected' from the dead. "How did Jesus just rise from the dead?" she asked.

"By God," Caleb answered enthusiastically, but inside his heart he was praying for God to give him the right words to say, and to be calm and as inoffensive about it as he could be. "God is really, really powerful you know. I mean, He's ... God."

"Well, why did he do it? Why did God bring Jesus back to life?" Lindsey asked, her matter-of-fact tone of voice inciting a challenge rather than a genuine curiosity.

"To show that Jesus Christ really is God's Son and the world's Savior. If He had just died and stayed dead, then He would've been just like any other human being; He would've been a normal man who just knew a heck of a lot about God."

"Hmm."

"By Jesus' resurrection we are shown God's power and his faithfulness to us in fulfilling his promises."

"Resurrection, huh?" Lindsey stated, somewhat skeptical. "That just seems, I don't know, a little incomprehensible. Actually, it seems rather impossible."

Caleb panicked. *Oh Lord, help her to understand. I felt the same way she did at one time. I know You can change her heart, Lord, because You changed mine. Help me to be patient and trusting.* "Well," he began, addressing Lindsey, but keeping his eyes focused on his driving. "A lot of things in today's generation are incomprehensible. People don't have faith in anything anymore. It's actually kinda sad. But just because something seems incomprehensible, it doesn't mean that it's impossible." He glanced over at Lindsey, who wasn't looking at him, but rather down at the seat as though she was assessing what he was saying. She still looked confused. He went on. "Did you know that back in the old biblical days, before Christ came, God actually spoke to his people, physically?"

"What do you mean? Like they had tea parties or something and just chatted?"

Caleb almost laughed. He couldn't tell if she was being serious or sarcastic. "No, God would just speak to them, from Heaven. The people still never saw Him, but they heard His voice. I'm sure the closest anybody ever got to physically seeing Him was when He appeared to Moses as a burning bush."

"Is that so?" Lindsey stated.

"Yeah, before Jesus came, that is," Caleb answered, feeling like he wanted to stop the truck and whip out his bible to give Lindsey all the facts on why it was trustworthy, and to prove to her that God really did exist. He restrained himself, however. He knew it wasn't his job to save Lindsey. Only Jesus could do that.

"Well, that is still hard to believe," she admitted.

"Would you like to believe in it?" Caleb asked.

Lindsey shrugged. "I don't know; it's not so much a matter of whether I want to believe in it or not, it's just a matter of how hard it is to believe in something like that."

"Well, it just takes faith."

"Faith," Lindsey repeated quietly. "What is faith, anyway?" Lindsey asked. She had heard about faith many times, but all the faith she had ever had in anybody or anything had always diminished. Her mother died, Nick let her down, even her friends and her grandparents weren't what she wanted or needed. There was no such thing as faith.

"'Faith assures us of things we expect and convinces us of the existence of things we cannot see,'" Caleb quoted from Hebrews 11:1.

"Did you make that up?"

"No, it's straight from the Bible."

"Where?"

"I don't know, somewhere in the New Testament."

"Oh, so little Christian boy doesn't know where he's quoting from?" Lindsey stated sarcastically.

"Hey now," Caleb warned calmly. "God doesn't give us brownie points on how much Scripture we've memorized." Lindsey just grunted. He could tell she was losing interest, or she was just trying to hide her curiosity. Caleb wasn't sure, but he decided he better not push the issue. "The next major town we hit, do you want to stop at the mall or something," he asked quietly, changing the subject.

Lindsey glanced up at him without answering, thankful for the change of subject.

"We could go out to eat and then maybe see a movie or something fun like that."

"Why don't we just wait 'till we get to Nebraska? You said we'd make it before six o'clock," Lindsey suggested.

"Okay, that makes more sense."

The rest of the trip to Nebraska was made in near-silence, except for a few choice moments when Lindsey and Caleb played some highway games. Most of the time Lindsey kept her gaze focused out the passenger side window, and Caleb kept his on the road ahead. They were nearly out of the Rockies. The high elevation wasn't pleasing to his ears.

For the last two hours of the trip, Lindsey had gotten out a book from one of her suitcases and begun reading it. She didn't get past one chapter the whole two hours, however, because all she could think about was the young man sitting next to her. She didn't understand him at all. It wasn't just his belief in God; he was so sensitive and caring. She knew she shouldn't have been so sarcastic about their God conversation, and she felt bad for it. But instead of getting angry or defensive, Caleb had taken a hint and changed the subject for her. Lindsey didn't have any reason to not want to talk about God. She found Caleb's beliefs and viewpoints rather interesting. She recalled how he told her earlier about his drinking and drug habit. He had only become a Christian a few months ago, so she knew that his Christianity was the reason he wasn't into that stuff anymore. It was a good thing, and she thought it was wonderful that he was such a changed person, yet she didn't understand how a belief in some God could be what changed him. Lindsey knew that lots of people sought out to change their lives. Some people went on diets, some went to therapists and counselors, some turned to medication, and some followed after other religions or practices. It was all the same, right? So Caleb's belief and faith in God was just another one of those things, right? Even as Lindsey questioned it, she wasn't sure if she believed it. God, whoever and whatever he was, just didn't seem to fit in with therapists and counselors. She knew of people who had tried all those things and who had never ended up happy, or totally changed in the end.

All Lindsey could figure was that there was nothing wrong with Caleb, or anyone else for that matter, to believe in God. Even Lindsey couldn't say that she felt God didn't exist. She just never really thought about it much until her mother died. So far, all she knew was that Caleb was a good person. If it was God who was making him that way, then she had no objections to that. She just didn't know how it worked.

Then, without thinking, she just blurted out the question. "Caleb, do you think that if Nick believed in God, then he wouldn't have treated me the way he did?"

Caleb turned down the music. "I think that if Nick knew Jesus, then no, he wouldn't have done what he did. He should've known better."

Lindsey almost began to cry. It still hurt so much to think of Nick. She felt like she wanted to talk to him, but she wasn't sure why, or what she would say to him. She figured he wouldn't want to talk to her anyway. She was still very angry.

"Would you ever do anything like that to a girl?"

Caleb shook his head. "Never. I would die before I hurt somebody like that."

Lindsey swallowed hard, and had to force hard to keep her tears to herself. Caleb was too good to be true. She knew he would make his future wife a very happy woman. Lindsey wanted that. She wanted somebody just like him.

Caleb spoke again. "Before I became a Christian, I might've done something like that if I had the chance, but thank God I never did."

"What do you mean?"

"I didn't really go out with many girls throughout high school and college."

"Why's that?"

"Oh, I don't know, I don't think many girls liked me." As he spoke, a half-smile formed on his face. "I remember it was such a bummer then, but now I look back and realize that God was sparing me for now, when I would become a Christian. I'm glad I don't have any mistakes that I've made with women to be accountable for."

"So you're still a virgin, right?"

"Yep, and I'm really, really proud of it."

"That's neat," Lindsey smiled. "I'm glad I am, too."

Caleb glanced over at her and smiled, feeling as though he wanted to put his arms around Lindsey and give her a big hug. But instead all he said was "That's good to hear."

Lindsey's hands shook as she reached out for the telephone receiver. She didn't know why she was so nervous about calling Marianne. Their conversation the day before hadn't gone well at all, but Lindsey wanted to make amends. It usually wasn't her custom to hold grudges against her friends. Besides, something about Caleb's warm spirit and loving heart encouraged her to want to be a better person. She thought that sounded corny, but it was true.

It was almost 8:00 p.m., and Lindsey and Caleb were settled in their motel room in Scottsbluff, Nebraska. They had decided to hold off on the mall and movie until the next night. They were planning on driving straight through Nebraska, most likely right outside of Lincoln.

Lindsey cursed herself for being so nervous about calling Marianne, and she quickly grabbed up the phone receiver and dialed the number. Her heart was pounding, and warmth crept up her face. *Oh, be normal, Lindsey*! She was afraid Marianne would be angry with her, but she was hopeful. *Oh please, God,* she said unintentionally, not realizing she said it. Before she could, Marianne picked up.

"Hello," she said, sounding tired.

"Hi," Lindsey's soft voice managed. "It's me."

"Lindsey," Marianne exclaimed. "How are you?"

"Better than before," she admitted. She decided not to waste any time in her apology. "I called because I wanted to apologize for before, when I hung up on you, and for getting so angry."

Marianne was relieved. The last thing she wanted was another fight with Lindsey. "Oh, I'm so glad you called," Marianne said cheerfully. "Thanks for your apology."

Lindsey nodded, grateful that her friend was so understanding and forgiving. "I'm glad you're not mad at me."

"I'm your best friend, Lindsey. I couldn't ever stay mad at you, no matter how hard I tried." Lindsey almost laughed. "Besides," Marianne went on. "I know you've been having a hard time with everything, and I'm sure you were just over-emotional yesterday. I should've been easier on you."

Lindsey creased her eyebrows. Did Marianne think she was a nut or something? No, Lindsey figured she was probably right – Lindsey was emotional over all that had happened, and that's why she had treated Marianne so strangely.

"Well, thank you," Lindsey said honestly.

"So where are you?"

"Nebraska."

"Oh good, I'm glad you're making it. Nick and I were getting worried about you last night."

"You were?"

"Yeah, we were afraid that in your condition you might not make it very far."

"Well, right after my wreck I was seriously considering going back home."

Marianne hesitated for a moment. *There she goes with that car wreck stuff, again.* "Lindsey?" she quietly stated.

"Yeah?"

"Were you really in that car wreck?"

"Of course, why would I just lie to you?"

Marianne kept silent. She wasn't about to tell Lindsey that she thought she was delirious and desperate for attention. But she believed Lindsey now.

"I don't know," Marianne lied. "I guess I just thought that … I don't know, it just seems kind of incomprehensible."

Lindsey smiled. "Just because something's incomprehensible doesn't mean it's impossible."

"Well, I suppose," Marianne stated flatly.

"So Nick was actually concerned about me?" Lindsey asked quietly.

From the opposite side of the room, trying to work on the heater, Caleb's ears perked at the sound of the work "Nick." Caleb was instantly attached. For some reason he felt anger toward this Nick that he didn't even know. He knew he shouldn't be feeling it, but at the same time it was as if a spark of jealousy hit him when Lindsey mentioned him. Did she still like him? *Noooo*! He cried to Lindsey in his mind. *He's not worth it, he'll only hurt you again.* All at once Caleb realized he wasn't having a very Godly attitude and he immediately stopped himself. *Stop trying to save Lindsey, Caleb*, he told himself. *You can't keep her from other people, or from other beliefs. Just stop trying to be her Knight-in-shining-armor. Stop trying to do God's work.*

Before he knew it, Lindsey had hung up the phone. She didn't move but sat staring at it for a few minutes before turning toward Caleb. He was watching her.

"How'd it go?" he asked.

"It was fine, she's not mad at me," she answered. "We couldn't talk long because she had to go eat dinner or something. I gave her the number here so she could call back."

Caleb nodded. "That's fine," he said.

"Yeah, anyway," Lindsey said quietly, "I think I'm going to go work out in the fitness room, okay?"

"All right."

"Yeah, so if she calls back before I'm back, will you please come get me? The fitness room's only down the hall."

"No problem," Caleb agreed.

Within ten minutes, Lindsey was changed and down the hall, her mind occupied with Nick.

The clock read 8:15 p.m. when the phone on the desk in the motel room rang. Caleb glanced over at it from his TV program, wondering why Marianne was calling back so soon. It hadn't even been a half an hour since Lindsey got off the phone with her.

"Hello," he answered as he picked up the receiver.

"Hi," came a deep male voice from the other end. "Uh, is Lindsey there?"

Caleb knew at once that this must be Nick. He became irate all of a sudden and did not want Lindsey communicating with this guy at all. *Lord, help me not to give this guy a lecture right over the phone, please.*

"Hi," was Caleb's irritated reply. "Who is this?"

"It's Nick," he answered timidly. "Do I have the right number? I'm looking for Lindsey Milholland."

"Oh yeah," Caleb said, using all his drive not to say "no."

"Who's this?" Nick asked, a bit confused by the male voice answering Lindsey's motel room phone.

"Oh, this is Caleb. I think Lindsey told Marianne about me yesterday."

A light clicked on in Nick's head. So Lindsey had been telling the truth about Caleb. Marianne was sure going to feel stupid about thinking Lindsey was just a nut.

"Oh yeah, she did, but we really didn't believe it."

Caleb grinned. "Well, now you know. Let me go get Lindsey, all right?" he said in an exaggerated friendly tone.

Nick caught on to his irritation, and uttered a short, "Okay."

Less than two minutes had passed by when Lindsey hesitatingly picked up the telephone receiver. "Nick?"

"Yeah, it's me, Marianne called me and gave me your number."

"Why'd she do that?"

"Because she knew I wanted to talk to you."

"Oh," Lindsey said, unable for other words. She glanced at Caleb who just rolled his eyes and walked out the door. She felt bad for him all of a sudden.

"I'm sorry for what I did to you, Lindsey. I really am," Nick apologized.

"I believe you," she said honestly. She twisted the phone cord around her fingers. "Just don't make that mistake with another girl again, okay?"

"I won't, believe me."

"So how's Vanessa?"

"Out of the picture," Nick answered.

Lindsey threw her head back in exasperation and sighed deeply. Here it comes, she thought. *Oh Lindsey, please take me back, I really do love you,* la di da di da.

"Lindsey?" Nick asked, noting her silence.

"Yeah,"

"I wish you didn't leave."

"Why? So that you could get back together with me?"

Nick slumped his shoulders. "Maybe. I don't know. It'd be nice I suppose, for you to give me a second try."

Against Lindsey's will, she began to feel sorry for Nick and for the way she had spoken to Marianne about him so badly on the phone. Nick had never been a bad guy. He was just ... misled and misunderstood sometimes. After all, he had been the only guy Lindsey had ever felt that she loved. She had been with him longer than she had been with any other boyfriend of hers.

Lindsey leaned her free elbow on the table as she sat in a chair and turned toward the doorway. Caleb had left, and he was probably sitting in the lounge somewhere all by himself. She could tell he wasn't happy about Nick's call. *He cares about me*, she thought. *He probably hates Nick right now with the way I've talked about him.* Confused and bewildered, Lindsey sighed.

"Are you all right?" Nick asked.

"No," she choked.

"What's wrong?"

"It's you, and Caleb, and everything else."

"Do you and him have something going?"

"Of course not, Nick," Lindsey answered harshly. "I haven't even known him a week, but...." She stopped. It was true, she had only known Caleb for four days, but everything about him was beginning to attract her.

"But what?"

"But he's so perfect. I mean, he's the nicest guy I've ever met, you wouldn't ever believe it, Nick."

Nick didn't think he cared. He only wanted Lindsey back.

"I'm sorry, Nick," she stated quietly and regretfully when Nick didn't answer. "It wouldn't work out with us again anyway, because I'm gone now, and I don't think I'm coming back."

Nick nodded, casting his head downward. He knew she was right. "Thanks for talking to me," he said. "And I hope you really do understand how sorry I am."

"I do," she said.

The TV in the motel lounge was buzzing with Caleb's program when Lindsey entered the room a few minutes later and threw herself in one of the comfy-looking armchairs. Caleb turned to look at her. He wasn't smiling. She was.

"So what did Nick have to say?"

"Ooh, such spite," Lindsey said playfully. Caleb still didn't smile. "Caleb," Lindsey said, sitting up and facing him. She took the remote from his hands and turned off the TV set. "Please smile. I'm not used to you looking like this, and being so angry."

"I'm not angry," he said. "I'm just…."

"Trying to protect me?"

"Yeah, I guess that's what you could call it."

"How could you care about me so much in so little time that we've known each other?" she asked, leaning forward and resting her elbows on her knees.

Caleb shook his head. He didn't know what he felt for Lindsey. He just knew that the girl sitting in front of him seemed so lost and lonely, and whether she realized it or not, she was searching for something, anything, to grasp and hold on to; something that would last. Wasn't that what everybody wanted? It was certainly what Caleb wanted before he found Jesus. He didn't know how to tell her that, though.

"I just do," he said quietly. It was hard for him to admit that he cared about her. Before coming to Christ, Caleb hadn't been much of a sap – he never revealed his feelings to anyone. He held most of what he felt deep inside him until it hurt. All those locked-up feelings had come out in the unhealthiest ways, including excessive drinking, some drug use, depression, and bad behavior toward his parents. Thinking about it all now made him squirm. He didn't understand how he could have been that way.

Noting Caleb's downcast spirits, Lindsey got out of her chair and reached out, putting her arms around Caleb, hugging him closely. Caleb wasn't expecting the gesture, and he returned her hug. For a while the two sat there, embracing and comforting each other. Warm tears began to spill from Lindsey's eyes, and Caleb did all he could to keep from crying. Everything was silent, except for the sound of a few passing cars outside the motel. Only a few lights were on in the lounge, dimly lighting the room. Caleb breathed in deeply, and finally let go of Lindsey. She sat back and wiped her eyes.

"Besides my mom, I don't feel like anybody's cared about me like you have," Lindsey told Caleb.

"I'm sure you're wrong," he said softly.

"Nick apologized," she said suddenly.

"That's good," Caleb replied, and he meant it.

"Yeah," Lindsey said, turning her head toward the blank TV screen. "He said he's sorry for what he did to me, and if it was possible he'd want to get back together with me."

"What did you tell him?"

Lindsey looked back at Caleb and smiled. "I didn't want that."

"You weren't rude to him, were you?"

"No, not at all. Before he called I was kinda hoping to talk to him soon."

Caleb just nodded. "I was rude to him," he admitted.

"Really?" Lindsey's eyes grew wide.

"Yeah, I should probably apologize."

Lindsey chuckled. "That is so funny, I just can't imagine you getting mad and trying to stick up for me."

"I can tell you, I was seconds away from lecturing him on what he did to you."

Lindsey laughed harder. "Gee, I have my own personal bodyguard now, don't I?"

"Yeah, I guess so. Against my will."

Lindsey huffed. "Oh, c'mon, you know you love me."

"You know it," Caleb joked. Then, "Hey, I was thinking."

"About what?"

"About teaching you how to drive a clutch tomorrow."

Lindsey creased her forehead. "Uh, I don't know...."

"If you don't let me teach you to drive my truck, then I won't love you anymore!" Caleb argued childishly.

"Oh, please, don't torture me like that!"

At the request of the motel desk clerk to lower their voices, Caleb and Lindsey began laughing even louder, and finally raced back to their room, Lindsey taking the elevator while Caleb took the stairs. Caleb won.

Eleven

God's family is the church of the living God, the pillar and foundation of the truth.
– 1 Timothy 3:15

Volkswagen Jettas, Toyota Tacomas, Oldsmobiles, and various other vehicles found themselves in the parking lot of the First Christian Church in Coeur d'Alene on Sunday morning. Mary Jenkins, nervously fidgeting in the front seat of her '88 Chevrolet Cavalier, also found herself in the parking lot of the church. She had been sitting there for almost fifteen minutes now, and the parking lot was nearly full. *There's not going to be any more seats left for me.* In a way, she was hoping to use that as a justification for not getting out of the car and advancing toward the building. She knew, however, that to make a difference, she would need to make that extra step, and at least get out of her car. Sighing heavily, and checking her hair in her rearview mirror, she opened the driver's side door and stepped out into the warm breeze. Holding her floral-print skirt down so that the wind wouldn't blow it upward, she advanced toward the church building, giving herself a pep talk the whole way. *Don't worry, there's nothing to worry about. Just take a seat in the back and don't worry about people staring at you. This is a church, people are supposed to be nice. Some might even say "hi."*

A gust of October air flew into the church foyer as Mary opened one of the glass double doors. Entering, she stood a few moments in front of the door looking around. The church smelled nice. She wasn't sure what the aroma was, but it was something unique. Ahead of her was the entryway into the sanctuary, and inside she could see what looked like a myriad of people filling the pews. Even the foyer was bustling with people walking to and fro, greeting eachother and chatting up the latest church news. Mary's thumping heart gave way to a flustered face, and in response she swung around to leave the building. She was stopped before she had even touched the door handles.

"Good morning," a gentle voice greeted her. Surprised, and not sure whether the man was talking to her or not, she turned her head to see a man in his late 30's approach her. He was stunningly attractive, with short, dark hair and a dark goatee lining a strong, square jaw.

She stopped and turned around. "Hi," she said, forcing a smile, and stuffing her cold hands into her coat pockets.

"I don't think I've seen you here before," the man observed before offering his hand for Mary to shake it. "I'm Bryan," he said.

"Mary," she replied as she took his hand, reluctant to say anything more. All at once she became very aware of her appearance and desperately wished she could run to the bathroom to check herself. She unconsciously lifted her free hand to remove a strand of thick hair out of her eyes, lowering her head nervously.

"So are you new to the congregation?" Bryan asked in a very friendly tone.

Mary looked around as her mind searched for some reasonably decent answer to give the man. "I uh, no, have never been here before. I was just –" She pointed her hand to the door to indicate that she was just leaving, but before she could say another word, Bryan interrupted.

"You don't have to leave," he insisted. "I noticed that you seemed a little nervous or something."

"Oh, just a little," Mary replied sarcastically, attempting a chuckle.

"There's a lot of room left in there to sit. Would you like me to help you find a seat?"

Mary glanced into the big room and noticed that the service was beginning.

"We're late," she said.

"No, they're just getting started. C'mon. Since you're here, you might as well give it a shot, right?"

Mary managed a weak smile and shrugged her shoulders. "All right," she submitted.

"Mmm, Chelsea, what smells so good?" Dan asked anxiously as he caught a sniff of the strong, pleasant aroma of roasted chicken wafting down the hallway.

"What do you think?" Chelsea laughed. It was their anniversary, and like every year when the two weren't going out to eat at a nice restaurant, Chelsea would make Daniel's favorite meal – roasted chicken with real mashed potatoes and thick gravy. It was a simple meal, but one that the two had enjoyed for many years. For Dan's part of the deal, he would make sure the kitchen table was furnished with the fancy silverware and china glasses they kept in a case, only to be used on certain occasions. He would also bring out the long, brass candlesticks and set white candles in them, to eat in a dimly lighted, traditional, romantic setting with no music, just the placid melody of the ocean and her waves.

Chelsea smiled as she closed the oven door and made her way toward the living room to join her husband. It was Sunday, and the two of them hadn't heard from Lindsey in days. Nevertheless, Chelsea was learning to deal with the lack of communication between her and her granddaughter. Dan had convinced Chelsea that Lindsey needed her space and her own time to work out her problems the way she felt best. He had assured her that if anything negative happened to Lindsey, then they would hear about it.

So Chelsea had let it go, and she had forced herself not to worry about why Lindsey hadn't called since Tuesday afternoon.

She waltzed into the living room, light on her feet, but she had barely made it to the couch when the phone rang. She grumbled, and Dan picked up the phone on the side table before she could reach it.

"Hello," he uttered.

"Daniel?" came a reluctant and weary male voice.

Dan recognized the voice at once. He sat upright on the couch. "Terry, is that you?"

Chelsea gasped slightly, and covered her mouth with her hand in shock. "It's Terry?" she whispered.

"Yeah, Dan, it's me," Terry replied.

"Terry!" Dan exclaimed excitedly, with a strong, male resonance that invaded the room. "It's good to hear from you. Has Lindsey arrived yet?"

"Uh, no, actually, that's what I wanted to talk about."

"Has something happened?"

"No, nothing like that. I just wanted to ask about a few things."

Chelsea watched the expressions on Dan's face in awe as she took a seat in the armchair opposite the couch. She tried whispering questions to Dan, but he held up his hand to quiet her.

"How's Jenna?" Dan asked.

"Oh, she's really good." Terry became silent.

"Terry? Are you there?"

"Actually, she's not good," Terry explained, lowering his voice. "Lindsey called and left a message on my machine the other day, explaining how she was coming over...."

"Yeah, Chelsea and I made sure that she called you."

"It was so odd, Dan. I ... I never thought I'd hear from her or see her again." Terry choked up, and Dan's features etched into concern. He sincerely felt bad for the man who had been deprived of his daughter's love for so many years.

"It's okay, Terry, take as much time as you need," Dan comforted.

Finally, Terry spoke up again. "It was so unexpected, and you see, I never told Jenna about Lindsey, before. I never told her I had a daughter."

"Terry, you didn't?" Dan exclaimed.

"No, I don't know why, I just … was scared." He stopped for a moment. By his choppy conversation, Dan could tell that he was just as confused and bewildered as he was. "I guess there's no excuse, but the fact is, I never told her. So when Lindsey left that message, Jenna found out about her, and she's not doing well. I don't think she trusts me anymore."

"Well, Terry, I would say that Jenna might be validated for feeling that way."

"I know, I know," Terry admitted. "I just love her too much, I don't want to lose her the way I lost Lindsey and Jillian."

"Terry, you heard that we … lost Jillian, right?"

"Yeah, I know. I am truly sorry," Terry replied regretfully.

"A plane accident," Dan confirmed.

"Yeah."

Silence followed for seconds before Terry spoke. "So Lindsey's really coming over, huh?"

"Yeah, pretty sudden, huh?"

"Yeah, it's tough to believe."

"Chelsea and I actually tried to prevent her from going. It all seems really crazy."

"It does. Why would she just all of sudden decide to up and drive across the country?"

Dan shook his head. "There was no reasoning with her. She's changed since her mother died, and I think her biggest motive for leaving was just because she didn't know what else to do. Her whole life was shattered, and so she just left in one big puff of emotion."

"So it was a spur of the moment type of thing?"

"Yeah, except that she actually planned it out pretty nicely. She made sure she waited until after her eighteenth birthday."

"I can't believe she's eighteen already."

"I know how you feel," Dan agreed.

Chelsea stood up and walked into the kitchen while Terry and Daniel continued to talk. Checking the boiling potatoes and turning down the heat, she proceeded out through the sliding glass door and onto the beach where she let the cool breeze blanket her. She looked to the sky, feeling as though her heart would burst because it was so full of emotion that she couldn't define it. She didn't know what to do. All their worlds had changed – Lindsey's, Terry's, Jenna's, Daniel's, and hers. Chelsea didn't know how much longer she could take it. She wanted Lindsey home; she wanted Jillian home, and she wanted things back to normal.

Oh, God, why? She uttered in her mind as she dropped herself onto the beach. In a matter of seconds she was sobbing, confused, bewildered, and angry. The afternoon was just rolling around, but the ominous dark sky hovered and reflected itself off the water. The waves lapped on the shore and seagulls cried above her head, and Chelsea lay on the sand crying.

Waking up late, Caleb and Lindsey had only gotten on the road by noon, and doubted whether they would make it to Lincoln by the end of the day. Only a few miles down the country road and stopped at a rest area, Caleb and Lindsey had switched seats so that Caleb could teach Lindsey how to drive a clutch. With Lindsey driving, Caleb was almost positive that they'd still be miles away from Lincoln in the six hours they planned to travel that day.

Reaching over from the passenger side, Caleb leaned forward to turn down the radio.

"Hey, that was a good song," Lindsey objected as the noise faded until the only audible sound was the loud engine of the Ford.

"Well, you need to concentrate and just focus on your driving and worry about the music later, okay?" Caleb enforced jokingly, with a stern, paternal look on his face.

"Yes, Dad," Lindsey replied.

"So are we going? We're still in the parking lot wasting gas."

"Gee, you're authoritative all of a sudden," Lindsey complained.

"That's because I'm the teacher, so you have to listen to me."

"Well, don't bite my head off please!"

"Okay, enough talk," Caleb silenced her, putting up a hand in mock imitation. Lindsey laughed. "So, Lindsey, what you need to do is slowly lift your foot off the clutch pedal and at the same time start pressing the accelerator...."

"I'm not dumb, you know. It's not like I'm totally ignorant on how to drive a clutch."

"Okay, missy, let's see what you've got."

Lindsey swung her head around to look behind her – the parking lot was clear. She slowly attempted to back up out of the parking space. The Chevy smoothly inched its way backward before Lindsey let up on the clutch pedal too much and it lurched forward, coming to a stop.

"You killed it," Caleb exclaimed, acting astonished.

"It happens," Lindsey replied nonchalantly.

"Well, at least you're out of the parking space. We've gotten this far...."

"Shut up," Lindsey said, punching Caleb in the shoulder.

"Ouch," he said childishly as he brought up a hand to rub his shoulder. "That hurt, you know."

"You wanna take this outside!" Lindsey challenged.

"Hey, let's not get feisty, woman...."

"Stop calling me woman!" Lindsey brawled.

"Why should I?"

"Because I'm not your woman."

"Yes, you are," Caleb insisted whimsically. "You're my woman, so I can call you woman."

A chuckle escaped Lindsey's throat before she could utter a word in protest. "Let's just drive," Lindsey said, restarting the engine and cautiously moving the truck out of the parking area.

"Okay, but remember to be careful; I replaced my clutch right before I left." This time Caleb was serious.

"Okee dokee artichokee," Lindsey sang out.

"You're weird."

The minutes passed by quickly as Lindsey drove down the two-lane state highway following the North Platte River southeast; slowly catching on to shifting the gears. She reached over and turned on the radio when Caleb wasn't looking.

"Hey, what did I say about music?"

"Hey! I'm doing good now, aren't I? You haven't even had to say hardly two words to me since I started driving."

"Yeah, what's up with that?" Caleb asked, amazed at how naturally Lindsey learned. "I thought you said you couldn't drive a clutch."

"Well, I've driven one before; my mom had a stick shift and she taught me, but I was always freaked out about driving it, so I never did. I only drove it like, once or twice before I got my license, and then my grandparents bought me the Honda, so I never had to think about stick shifts again."

"So you're grandparents bought you that nice Honda you left behind in Wyoming?"

"Yeah, right after I got my license, right after I turned sixteen."

Caleb's eyebrows raised. "Geez, I'd say you have pretty cool grandparents."

Splitting through the air unannounced, Caleb's words slapped Lindsey in the face in a moment of realization. "Yeah," she stated quietly, suddenly conceiving how true it was. Lindsey had great grandparents, loving grandparents. She had grandparents who had literally given her anything she wanted or needed. It was Dan and Chelsea who had convinced Jillian to allow Lindsey to drive her own vehicle when she earned her license; it was Dan and Chelsea who had offered to pay for all of Lindsey's college tuition no matter what the price was. They had always supported her in her good and bad times, and they would have let Lindsey live with them for as long as she wanted had she not suddenly up and left to go across the country, and for what? To find her father? Lindsey wondered if that was really the reason for her departure, or was she just merely running away from an honest and loving home?

"We still have to go to the mall, remember," Caleb remarked, oblivious to Lindsey's solemn-stricken eyes.

"Oh yeah, of course I do," Lindsey replied, regaining herself as she downshifted to fourth gear. The small truck chugged forward sharply before picking up speed again and sailing along the road smoothly.

"I don't know if we'll make it into Lincoln tonight, but we could wait until tomorrow morning and then hang out in Lincoln and do fun stuff, just for a road break, okay?"

"Sounds good to me," Lindsey breathed.

"Well let's stop soon," Caleb suggested, "and when we do I need to call my parents and let them know how I am. I haven't called them once since being on this trip. The last they heard of me was right before I left."

I don't even know if my own father knows I'm coming. Lindsey thought. *He might not have gotten that message. Maybe he's gone on a trip or something.*

"Yeah, I should probably call grandma and grandpa. I haven't talked to them since Montana."

"What, when you called them to tell them about your accident?" Caleb asked, leaning forward to strip off his jacket. "Geez, how did they take that, anyway?"

Lindsey's heart thumped in her chest and she could feel her face flush with shame. She had never called her grandparents to let them know she had been in an accident. They didn't even know she was with Caleb. What would Caleb do when he learned that? He wouldn't be happy, no doubt.

"Uh, yeah," Lindsey mumbled before unexpectedly pulling the Ford over to the side of the road, intending to tell him the truth. She turned off the engine.

"What are you doing?" Caleb asked. "Are you done driving?"

Lindsey took a breath as her thoughts tried to compose themselves into some meaningful arrangement with which they could present themselves to Caleb.

"Oh, yeah, I'm done driving," Lindsey stated instead. Caleb's brows furrowed as he caught the uncertainty in her voice.

"Okay," he said suspiciously as he opened the door and walked around to the driver's side to get in. Lindsey followed suit, and soon they were back in the truck. Caleb pulled his seatbelt on, started the engine, and waited. Confused by Lindsey's odd reaction, he turned to her.

"So you did call your grandparents then, right?"

"Oh yeah, of course I did. They're cool with everything," Lindsey lied.

"Okay," Caleb said, taking to the road again. He gazed up at the bright sky ahead, teeming with frosty-white clouds against a light blue hue, and realized to his dismay that the actual temperature outside was much less than its environment depicted it.

"Hey, we could go iceskating," he suddenly announced, "when we get to Lincoln."

"Sure," Lindsey answered placidly, her face intent on studying the shedding vegetation and dampened pastures beyond the highway.

"Did you want to drive later sometime?" Caleb asked reluctantly, unsure of Lindsey's waning good mood.

"Sure," she answered again while her mind set to work, knitting up some clever response with which she would reveal to Caleb that she had just lied to him.

It was almost 12:30, and the church service was coming to a finish. The congregation stood up at the pastor's invitation and, with the band playing a wonderful tune, began to sing and move about excitedly. The pastor had called it "worship and praise" at the beginning of the service, and Mary was awed by it. Although Mary knew that singing was something churchgoers did, she had always thought as a child that Christians sang because they were supposed to; it was in the agenda; it came with the package. But watching the congregation now, Mary could see that their singing was more than just an action of obligation; they were sincerely and joyously pouring their hearts out to … God? Singing to God? It was an odd thought to Mary.

Numerous odd thoughts were swimming in Mary's brain. During the service, the pastor had spoken of God and His love for humans. It was hard for Mary to conceive of a powerful, imperceptible being who actually had love for humans. Why? Even if she was totally sure that God was real, why would it be that He would have such love for humans, and was it the same kind of love that humans themselves felt toward eachother? Pastor Hall had mentioned that God loved humans because they are His creations and His children, and He wants to be in a relationship with His children. He had said that God loved His children so much that He sacrificed His own son Jesus to show people how much He loved them. When Pastor Hall mentioned Jesus' death, Mary hadn't understood exactly what it meant to have our sins paid for by His sacrifice, but she could understand the offer of love it demonstrated. Mary pictured her own child being killed that day on Golgotha, and it had captured her breath. It was a terrible thought. She knew that she could never give up Andrea to or for anyone, no matter what the cost was. She concluded that God must truly love humans if He actually allowed His own son to die for them.

Mary had scrutinized the pastor's words; they were nothing she had ever expected to hear. As a child and young teenager she had sat in her family's church bored and uninterested. She barely paid attention to what the pastor spoke about, and when she did pay attention, she only heard what was said, but she never listened. She had heard about God, known about God, but she didn't realize how much there actually was to Him. Now, although she had heard about Jesus, she was suddenly listening and absorbing all that she could about God's son, about Jesus, who was presumably very important in the Christian faith. All the information was astonishing and incredibly interesting to Mary, but also very overwhelming.

The music continued. Mary kept her body facing forward but let her eyes search the room. A number of people had raised their hands in the air. Mary had seen this kind of stuff before, but being in the room herself, she suddenly realized how real it all was. The praising was honest, the celebration authentic, and the people filled with an energy and joy that Mary didn't understand. It was just singing, after all. It looked nice, though. Mary couldn't remember the last time she had felt utterly joyous and excited. Mentally tracing back, she concluded that it must have been the day she married Ted. Where had all those feeling gone, she now wondered. How many years had it been that she hadn't felt complete, even with Ted in her life?

Mary had always loved to sing and dance, but this seemed a little different to her, and when she realized that she was one of the few people not singing, she suddenly felt uncomfortable. She wished she could be a part of whatever these people were feeling, because it looked wonderful. But as despondency tugged at her heart, a fleeting thought crossed her mind. *I really don't fit in here.*

Bryan glanced over at the woman standing three inches below him to his right side. She looked very solemn all of a sudden. She had looked terrified when he met her in the foyer at the beginning of the service, but during it she had eased up a little. As Pastor Hall had eloquently and passionately spilled out his words of God's love and grace, reminding the congregation of the sacrifice God made by allowing His son Jesus to die for the world, Bryan had noticed that Mary's body had leaned forward in curiosity. However, throughout the entire service, her face had been etched with confusion, attempting understanding. Bryan had figured out instantly that she was not a normal churchgoer. He wondered what it was that would have led her to attend church in the first place. He doubted that someone had invited her, since she had perceivably come alone to the service. Nevertheless, he suddenly felt a need to make her comfortable and knew right away what he needed to do.

Placing his left hand on her shoulder, he leaned down toward her and spoke in her ear. "Can I talk to you in the foyer for a few minutes after the service?"

"Sure," Mary replied, glancing up at his smiling lips.

A few moments later, the singing ebbed and the pastor began to pray. Mary tried concentrating on his words, but as thoughtful and loving as she knew they were, she just didn't understand them, and she definitely felt that they didn't apply to her. When the final "Amen" was spoken, people began bustling about all at once. Bryan put his hand on Mary's shoulder to guide her along as she attempted to weave her way around through blobs of people trying to leave at the same time. Some were stopped in the aisle, chatting and shaking hands, with big laughs, great hugs, and smiles. Mary was beginning to believe she'd never make it to the foyer when Bryan lightly grasped her arm.

"This way," he urged, finding a clear route through a path of dispersing people. Mary followed behind. Instead of occupying space in the foyer, however, Bryan kept walking through the foyer and out the front doors where the bright sun and cold weather greeted him.

Mary buttoned up her black wool peacoat and stuffed her hands in her pockets. She glanced up at Bryan. "Thanks for finding me a place to sit," she said graciously.

"No problem," he announced. "I thought you looked like you needed a little direction."

Isn't that the truth, Mary thought. "Well, I've never actually been to church before, except when I was a kid, so I wasn't quite sure about it."

"Yeah, I could tell," Bryan replied. "What brought you here?"

My ex-husband told me I needed a hobby. "Uh, just checking it out, I guess," she mustered. Bryan suspected that there was something more personal than "just checking it out" that she wasn't mentioning, but he wasn't going to pry.

"Oh, well, I'm glad you came, Mary. And you're always welcome back."

Mary grimaced at his words. "Uh, I don't know," she said uncertainly, feeling as though another visit would complicate her swarming thoughts even more.

"Is there something you didn't like about the service?"

"Well, no, it was wonderful, really," Mary replied. "It's just, I don't know...." she stopped, raising a hand to rub her eyebrow; an action she performed when she was unsure or nervous.

"I don't mean to pry," Bryan interrupted, taking note of her reluctance. "If there's something you don't want to tell me, then don't mind me. I just want you to know that you're always welcome here, and if there's anything you want to know, or if you have any questions, then you can call me." The words flowed out so gently and honestly that Mary was stunned. Here was a perfect stranger whom she'd just met this morning, and already he had offered her a seat in church and reassuring encouragement. Mary sighed, knowing that if she was going to learn anything, she should accept his encouragement and offer of help.

"Bryan, that was your name, right?"

"Yeah," he replied with a chuckle.

"I liked the service; really I did. I just didn't understand it all, and I felt a little out of place."

"Oh, well, that's to be expected, Mary, don't feel bad about that."

"I don't feel bad, I just feel a little, confused. I've never ... thought about God before. I mean, I've thought about Him, but never really cared to make it a big thing in my life, like my family. Like I said, I went to church when I was a kid, but it was sheer force of will. I stopped going as soon as I could, and I haven't really given God a second thought. I just feel like ... is it wrong that I came to church and I don't know God?"

"Of course not."

"I mean, I don't even know if I believe God exists. I know that it looks like a wonderful thing to believe, but I don't know if I do."

Like a broom had swept away his thoughts, Bryan had no idea what to say. There could have been so many things to say, but nothing would come out. This was a woman who desperately needed to know Christ, and he wanted to be there for her. Instead he nodded, prompting Mary to go on.

Mary shook her head as jumbling thoughts ravaged her brain, and confusion flooded her mind. "I don't know what to think. I have never even known anything about Jesus at all, so everything I heard today was new and a little ... inconceivable. I don't know what to think," she said again, casting her eyes to the ground and furrowing her brows in thought. "This has been an odd experience, and so it's hard for me to decide right away if I want to come back."

"Well, there's no pressure, Mary, and like I said, you can always call me if you need help clearing something up."

She nodded, thankful for his kindness.

"Can I walk you to your car?" Bryan offered suddenly.

"Oh, yes, that'd be nice, thank you." The two walked across the parking lot, weaving through the tangle of vehicles, finally approaching Mary's Cavalier. She turned to face Bryan. "I'd like to come again, Bryan," she said, "but I honestly felt like I didn't belong, like I shouldn't have been here. Do you know what I mean?"

"I can't say that I do," he admitted. "I've grown up my whole life being a Christian and believing in the Lord, so anything apart from that would be where my discomfort lay."

Mary nodded and stared at the ground again. Bryan could see that emotions were at war inside of her.

"Here's my number," Bryan said, stretching a hand toward Mary's face. She looked up and took the small piece of paper clutched in his fingers, thanking him. "Let me know if there's anything you ever need, okay? Even if it's not God-related, I'll be here. I don't get out much."

Mary chuckled. "Neither do I."

Twelve

Jesus said to him, "Why do you call me good? No one is good except God alone."
– Mark 10:18

Caleb stepped into the littered phone booth at 2:00 in the afternoon and dialed his North Carolina phone number.

"Hey, Mom, it's me!" he exclaimed when his mother's soft voice greeted him over the telephone.

"Caleb! Honey, how are you?" she asked excitedly, turning around to call to her husband that their son was on the phone.

"I'm good."

"Oh, I'm so glad you called," Kathryn went on quickly. Jon stepped into the house from the garage after hearing Kathryn's call to find her motioning with her hand to have him come stand by her. "We were wondering when you were going to get here," she stated enthusiastically.

"Well, I'm only in Nebraska right now."

"Nebraska? I thought you'd be farther by now. Is driving wearing you out?"

"Yeah, but that's not the reason I'm behind," he answered honestly, totally prepared to tell his parents about Lindsey.

"Well, I hope nothing serious happened," Kathryn's concerned voice asked.

"No, nothing like that," Caleb said. "I've got a traveling partner now." Caleb glanced over at Lindsey and winked. She laughed. Caleb decided he liked it much better when she was smiling. She wasn't an extremely attractive girl, but she was cute and had a remarkable smile when she was in the smiling mood. He decided he could grow fond of it.

"Oh really? How's that?" Kathryn asked, interested.

"Yeah, her name's Lindsey, and...."

"Oh, it's a girl," Kathryn interrupted, raising her eyebrows at her husband. Jon Lockwood leaned in closer to catch what pieces of the conversation he could listen in on.

"Yeah, Mom, it's a girl," Caleb replied slowly, glancing at Lindsey and making a face. Lindsey laughed again and turned to walk away. She ran out to the middle of the near-empty parking lot of the *I-Hop* and started performing cartwheels on the pavement.

"So go on," Kathryn urged.

"I pulled her out of a wreck when I was driving through Montana."

"Oh no," Kathryn gasped. "She was okay, though?"

"Oh yeah, she only had to stay in the hospital one night. So I hung out for the night to make sure she was fine, and then the next day we talked and I found out that she's going to Virginia."

"Really?"

"Yeah, she's going to find her dad and live with him. Anyway, we talked and decided to travel together since we're both heading in the same direction." Caleb stopped and watched Lindsey in the parking lot dancing and acting crazy, trying her best to get a laugh out of Caleb. He remembered the concern he felt for her that day in the hospital when they'd talked, and she'd told him about her mother. "But besides that, Mom," he went on, "she wasn't in any condition to travel alone."

Kathryn caught the concern in his voice. "Why not, Caleb?"

Caleb was sure Lindsey was out of hearing distance, but he lowered his voice and turned around just in case. "She lost her mother," he said quietly, hearing his mother's gasp on the other end of the line. "I guess she died in a plane accident a few months back, so Lindsey has been pretty upset. I can tell she hasn't taken it well."

"Oh no, that's terrible."

"I know. It was weird at first when she suggested that we travel together, because we hardly knew eachother, but I just had this … feeling. I just … I don't know,"

"It's called compassion, Caleb," Kathryn informed him.

"Yeah, I know, but it's more than that. I felt bad for her … yeah, but that's not why I let her come along. I just, knew that … that I had to do this for her, like God was speaking to me, or something. I hardly knew her, but I didn't want her to be alone, and I didn't want her to be sad anymore, you know? It's so weird, I can't explain it."

"You were always passionate about a lot of things, Caleb," Kathryn said gently, smiling. "Even behind that tough exterior you once held, you were always sympathetic towards others, always caring about so many things."

"Yeah, myself mostly."

"Oh, Caleb, don't be so hard on yourself."

"It's true."

"But that's over, you know that. I think it's great what you've done for this girl. She probably feels a lot more secure now with you around."

"Really?" Caleb asked, never having comprehended that idea before. He knew he had extended a measure of grace toward Lindsey by allowing her to ride with him, but he never thought about the positive effects it might have on her. Could she really, actually feel more secure just by having a traveling companion beside her?

"Of course, honey," Kathryn confirmed. "She might never tell you it, but I bet she's incredibly thankful for your company. You'll never know how much you've really done for her."

"I haven't done anything for her, Mom."

"Sure you have, honey."

"I mean, we've had some conversations; I try to share my faith with her."

"She's not a Christian, then?"

"No, and that's really hard for me, because I know I just can't sit here and keep quiet." Caleb turned his back to check where Lindsey was. She was no longer parading in the parking lot, but had moved to the Ford and was sitting inside patiently, waiting for Caleb.

"Gosh, she's not a very happy person, I can tell. I mean, she's very energetic and really weird and silly at times, but when the serious stuff starts to fall into place, she gets so ... depressed. She seems to get like that a lot, and I can tell that the whole thing is doing a lot of damage in her life."

"Speaking from experience?"

"Oh yeah."

"See, you're good at reading people, Caleb," Kathryn said. "You know how Lindsey feels because you've been where she is. Maybe not in the same circumstances, but you know about being upset and depressed when life hits hard." Caleb nodded, and his mother went on. "That's why you've developed this compassion for her, Caleb, and I think it's wonderful that you want to help her."

"I do, Mom. You don't know how bad I want her to find Jesus."

"Oh, I think I do, Caleb."

"Yeah?"

"Well, of course, Caleb. That's the same feeling you had with your father and me and few months ago."

Caleb smiled, remembering how he had called up his parents the day he gave his life to Jesus to explain to them about his decision. They had been confused, not knowing what it meant to be a Christian. Kathryn knew that her sister, Elizabeth, and Elizabeth's husband, Chris, whom Caleb had been living with, were Christian, but she herself had never followed along in any religion.

That day on the phone was the first time Kathryn and Jon had spoken to Caleb in almost three years. They listened closely as Caleb rattled on excitedly to tell them about his faith in Jesus, and they were bewildered when he apologized for being such a difficult teenager to deal with and live with. Kathryn had cried that afternoon, overwhelmed and extremely elated that she was able to hear her son's voice so positive and gracious. She didn't know what his decision for Christ meant, but she could tell by his words and voice that it was something good, and she was thankful for it.

The next weekend Kathryn and Jon had flown to Bellingham to spend time with their son and witness his baptism. It was that weekend that changed the Lockwoods' lives forever, for by witnessing their son's change, they themselves became Christians not long afterward. If it hadn't been for Elizabeth's and Chris' strong encouragement and patience in their questions, Kathryn didn't know how she would have held up when they arrived back in North Carolina. The struggle was hard at first; Kathryn and Jon had no Christian friends, and neither had stepped foot into a church but a couple times in their lives. The phone bill rang up as they found themselves constantly calling their family in Washington for support and encouragement. After a week, they finally began attending a church, and things started to go more smoothly after that. When Caleb had called a couple of months later to announce that he wanted to move back home and start school in North Carolina to be near his parents, Kathryn and Jon were overjoyed. Now they were both waiting for him, anxiously anticipating his return.

"I remember, Mom," Caleb said, waving to Lindsey as she stepped out of the truck.

"God is good, Caleb, there's no doubt about that, and Jesus is definitely shining through you. There's no way Lindsey is going to miss it."

"I hope not," Caleb said. He watched as Lindsey climbed into the bed of the truck, and then attempted to climb onto the hood.

"Lindsey," Caleb yelled suddenly, pulling the receiver away from his mouth. "Don't do that, you'll scratch the hood!" Lindsey stopped and stood in the bed of the truck, painting a pout on her face.

"What's she doing?" Kathryn asked, amused.

"She's trying to climb onto the top of my Ford."

"And how old is this girl?"

"She's eighteen … and now she's dancing in the back of my truck."

Kathryn laughed. "She might be good for you, Caleb"

"What do you mean?"

"Well, when was the last time you danced or could let yourself go and act silly?"

"Church, last Sunday," Caleb smiled. "I like to dance."

"Well, Lindsey, from what I know so far, seems like a nice girl. Tell her hi for me."

"All right, Mom, I will. Tell Dad I say hi."

"Here, why don't you tell him yourself," she said, "I think he has a question for you." She handed the phone over to her husband.

"Hey, Caleb!"

"Hey Dad, what's going on?"

"Is she pretty?" Jon asked suddenly, cutting into Caleb's thoughts.

"What?"

"You heard me. What do you think about this girl besides her just being some girl that you're helping?

"What are you talking about, Dad?" Caleb argued, trying to avoid the subject.

"Don't act stupid with me! You know what I'm talking about!"

Caleb was silent, and stunned. He wasn't expecting a question like that, especially from his parents. What did his father mean, "Is she pretty?" and "What do you think about her?" Of course she wasn't pretty … she was … Lindsey. She was … well she was cute. Besides, he didn't feel anything romantic towards Lindsey, did he? "Dad, I haven't even known her a week."

"So what?"

Caleb wrinkled his nose in annoyance. "She … uh … has a pretty smile," he admitted hesitantly.

"Is that it?"

"Ah, Dad…." Caleb began uncomfortably. "Well … she's not like, model-type gorgeous or anything," he announced aversely.

"Most girls aren't, Caleb. According to society's standards, your mother wasn't one of the greatest looking girls in the world." Kathryn punched Jon in the arm, and he smiled at her before adding, "But she was always a knock-out to me."

Caleb watched as Lindsey jumped off the back of the truck and got inside the vehicle again. She sat patiently, waiting for Caleb to finish his phone conversation. Then her attention quickly became attuned to the radio as she switched through stations to find something to listen to in order to entertain herself. Settling on an oldies station, her face lit up and her eyes grew wide as she recognized a song. Instantly her body began to sway as she sang along to the words, making motions with her hands. Glancing over through the windowpane at Caleb, a sweet smile spread across her lips as she realized she was being watched. Caleb was amazed at how cute and silly she was, just like a small child. Even despite the struggle he knew was battling inside of her, she still managed to grasp a sincere, child-like demeanor that drew Caleb to her.

"Caleb, are you still there?" Jon asked, noting the pause filtering the phone lines.

Caleb was shaken awake as he flashed Lindsey a smile back. Then, speaking closely into the receiver he said softly, "She's just a friend, Dad. I don't … have feelings for her if that's what you're asking."

"Oh Caleb, you know I was just messing around, I didn't mean to get you upset or anything," Jon apologized, picking up the irked tone in Caleb's voice.

Caleb sighed, growing more upset, knowing that he had just turned the conversation sour with his attitude. "I know; I'm sorry, Dad. I wasn't trying to be rude, or anything, I just…."

"You don't have to explain. I'm embarrassing you, I know. I didn't mean to. I just wanted an honest answer, that's all. It was all out of fun."

Caleb was holding the phone lightly to his ear, and he sighed again at his father's apology, glimpsing back to his truck where Lindsey was inside. She had quit her singing and was leaning against the passenger's side door with her head turned downward and her face straight. Caleb didn't really believe she wasn't pretty. She was pretty, but it wasn't extremely obvious. Her attractiveness hadn't been a thought that crossed his mind when he'd first seen or met her, but he knew it was there, tucked away inside her features. It came out the most when she was smiling; or in her eyes when she was in fascination of something; or when she was engaged in conversation; or even now as she sat with those doleful eyes and slight frown that suggested boredom while waiting for Caleb, totally unaware that he was watching her. Indeed, Caleb suddenly realized that he had taken much more notice of Lindsey than he had intended, for every glint in her eyes or frown on her lips or flush in her cheeks made her appear, in his eyes, pretty.

"Caleb? Caleb, you're doing that silence thing again."

"She's pretty, Dad," he said slowly and quietly.

"Is she, now?"

"Yeah." He sighed a third time. "She is."

Mary sat at her kitchen table a couple of hours after the morning service feeling like a huge hole had been ripped out of her soul and was in desperate need of mending. The creased flap of paper on which rested Bryan's home phone number lay face-up on the small table, crying out to Mary to pick up the phone and call him. She didn't know why, but the church service had disturbed her whole afternoon, and for the past two hours, she hadn't been able to concentrate on any of her tasks. Her mind kept wandering back to the parts of speech about Jesus Christ that Mary couldn't comprehend, even though it sounded wonderful. With Andrea at her parents' house for the weekend, Mary had been especially lonely and empty-feeling, and she felt like company would do her good. Besides company, Mary had some things she wanted to get off her mind, and if Bryan's offer of help and encouragement was sincere, she felt she might as well take advantage of it. Grabbing up the phone, she stared at the paper for a moment before dialing Bryan's number nervously. *He probably isn't expecting me to call so soon. He's probably busy, or doing something that's more worthwhile than helping some sad, annoying 34-year-old woman.*

"Hello?"

"Uh hi, is this Bryan?"

"Yeah. Is this Mary?"

"You recognized my voice," Mary said surprisingly.

"Well, of course. It's only been a few hours since we last talked, right?"

Mary let out a nervous chuckle. "Yeah, pretty ridiculous, huh?"

"No, why's that so ridiculous?"

"Because you probably weren't expecting me to call so soon."

"I wasn't expecting you to call at all," Bryan admitted. Mary didn't respond, and immediately Bryan realized how that must have sounded. "Oh, I didn't mean that I didn't want you to call at all, Mary; I just meant that not many people like to take offers of help from perfect strangers. I'm glad you called, because I didn't know whether you had taken me seriously or not, and now I know that you did."

Mary let out a sigh of relief. "Oh, thank goodness. I didn't want to be annoying by calling or anything."

"Oh, of course not," Bryan responded. "It's actually convenient that you called today, because it's my only day off of work this week. I usually get Sundays off so that I can attend church and get other things done around the house that are too neglected during the weekdays."

"So do you live alone, then?" Mary asked curiously.

"Oh yeah, I'm not married or anything. I used to be, but ... it didn't work out I guess."

"Oh, that must've hurt. I've just been through a divorce myself," Mary responded sympathetically.

"I'm sorry, Mary," Bryan said slowly.

"No, don't worry about that. It just...."

"Didn't work out either?"

Mary chuckled. "Yeah. But I didn't call about that, of course."

"So what would you like to discuss, Mary?" Bryan quickly said, changing the subject.

Mary was reluctant in answering. "I was actually hoping that I could talk to you in person sometime this evening. I just have some thoughts and questions that keep swimming around my mind, and … it's all very weird for me."

"No problem," Bryan answered. "I can give you my address, and why don't you plan on coming over for dinner tonight? We could go out to eat somewhere, it will be fun."

"Oh, I can't," Mary said. "I have a daughter who is coming home tonight. She stayed with my parents this weekend so that I could work and get some things done; and because her father wouldn't take her like he promised." Bryan caught the negative emphasis in her voice as she spoke those last words. "So anyway, I have to stay home with her, you see."

"No problem," Bryan replied. "Bring her too. I'll cook something, and we can stay at my place and eat."

"Really?" Mary asked.

"Sure, why not?"

"Why not?" Mary agreed.

Lincoln was only a few hours away, and as the fading sun beneath the rusty clouds beckoned rain, Lindsey slumped in the passenger seat of the Ford and sighed. The weather always managed to determine her mood, and she could already feel her sunny disposition leave her. Along with that, she was anxious, determining when and how she should reveal to Caleb that her grandparents didn't know about him. She had contemplated not telling him, but she knew that would only pave the road for more lies, and she couldn't afford to lose Caleb's trust. She knew one way or another she would have to let Caleb know.

As the Ford sailed along the road, Caleb found himself smiling. He was relieved not only to be out of the mountains, but also to be one step closer to seeing his family. He had been ecstatic to talk to his parents on the phone, and equally excited that they had taken his news about Lindsey so well. He knew when he arrived in North Carolina he would be embraced and welcomed home with the greatest warmth he had ever felt in his life. Glancing over at Lindsey then, he regretfully wondered whether she would experience the same. His smile faded as he noticed her slumped posture as she gazed, distracted and bored, out the window. He noticed that she had looked that way a lot during the trip so far, and he knew that one of the reasons was probably fatigue. Driving six to seven hours a day was wearing them both out a great deal, although they had only been on the road together for a few days. Caleb decided that they needed to take a rest; make the trip more of a vacation than just a trek across country.

"Hey," he said quietly, watching as Lindsey turned her head to look at him.

"Yeah?" she replied tiredly.

"You know how I was saying that we could stop in Lincoln to do some fun stuff like see a movie or go to the mall?"

"Yeah. What? You don't want to do that anymore?"

"No, I do. I was just wondering if maybe you wanted to spend a few *days* there, just taking a rest from all this driving. What do you think?"

Caleb's own face lit when he saw the bright smile slowly cross Lindsey's face. "I hadn't even thought of that," she admitted. "That would be cool."

"Well, good," Caleb said. "And it wouldn't even have to be Lincoln. I mean, we could stay there for a couple days, but if there's anywhere else you want to go just to sightsee or rest or something, we could do that too."

The smile widened. "Oh, you are just too sweet, Caleb."

"Girls always say that."

"About you?"

"No, just about everything; about every guy."

Lindsey laughed. "That's true, but we mean it when we say it."

"I'll bet," Caleb replied.

"How come you're so nice?" Lindsey blurted.

"What? I'm nice? Nah, not me."

"Sure you are. You should compare yourself to other guys. You're definitely not like any guy I've ever known." Caleb frowned. Lindsey went on. "I mean, I've known lots of guys, and I'm not saying they've never been nice, or even sweet for that matter. Nick was always really sweet, but then he changed." Lindsey stalled, as if thinking. "No, it's not so much that he changed, it's just that he's a different person than you are, and there are things about him that don't always allow him to be the same kind of person all the time, you know what I mean?"

Caleb nodded. He knew exactly what she meant, and in seconds, images of his old life began to flash through his brain. He hated it when his past haunted him unaware. It happened often, and Caleb didn't know what to do. He was trying to forget it, but he couldn't, and he felt angered that he couldn't forgive himself, knowing that it was what God would want him to do. He was a different person now, because of Jesus, so why did he still feel so ashamed?

"Ah," Lindsey mumbled. "I don't know what I'm saying. I'm probably not making any sense. All I'm trying to say is that you're different."

"But how do you know I won't change?" Caleb asked suddenly.

Lindsey looked puzzled. "What do you mean?"

"I just mean that I'm really like any other person you've met. I mean … I'm nice, but they were all nice at one time too, right?"

"Well, yeah."

"So what makes me so different?" Caleb voiced, knowing that as a human being there was no difference between him and any other person. As the Bible said, all people are sinners and don't deserve God's kindness. Caleb often wondered why the Lord had bestowed his grace upon him.

"I don't know," Lindsey replied, confused. "I'm not saying it's bad that you're different…."

"Oh, I know, it's just that I hope you're not saying I'm any better than those other guys, because I'm not. I'm not any better than anybody. I used to be like Nick too, you know. I mean, I don't know Nick except what you've described to me. Besides him being a sweet guy, he broke your heart, and anybody is capable of breaking a heart."

Lindsey stared at him in disbelief. She was hurt that Caleb hadn't taken her compliment as such. Why did he feel the need to have to explain himself? "What are you trying to get at, Caleb?" she asked. He shook his head. "All I'm trying to say," Lindsey went on, "is that I think you're a great guy. I didn't say I thought you were any better than anybody else."

"I know."

Lindsey frowned as she stared at Caleb. He didn't look at her; he kept his eyes fixed to the road. What had just happened, she wondered. Why was Caleb so reluctant to accept her compliment? But she instantly knew that it went deeper than just a questionable compliment that was tugging at Caleb.

"Caleb, why are you so ashamed of yourself?"

"What do you mean?" he asked dryly.

"Why can't you just accept that you're a good person?" He didn't answer. Lindsey sighed and shook her head angrily. "I trust you, Caleb, whether you think I should or not. I do, and I truly think it's a miracle, or fate, or something, that made it possible for me to be here with you now. You're the only person I've ever known who has been so caring and sincere. I know I haven't known you long, and so maybe I'm just disillusioned or something. Maybe your sincerity will just turn out to be some façade or a mask. For all I know, you could be a murderer or rapist or something."

"Hey now," Caleb said forcefully, glancing at her.

"I don't think you're any of that," Lindsey replied, calming her voice. "I know I haven't known you long, but I truly know that you're a good person.

You've shared a little with me about your past – about how you used to drink and party and had bad relations with your parents – but I know there's nothing of that in you anymore. Even if there was a little of that, you're still different – in a good way. I can't explain it, but I know that there's something. There's something in you that I haven't seen in anybody else, Caleb...."

Lindsey continued talking, but her speech distanced itself from Caleb as that last comment rang in his ears. *There's something different in you that I haven't seen in anybody else....*

Maybe his mom and dad were right. Maybe Caleb was truly making a difference in Lindsey's life.

Thirteen

It is God who produces in you the desires
and actions that please him.
– Philippians 2:13

Lindsey wiped the back of her hand across her forehead, letting her head fall back while letting out a sigh. Her eyes would barely stay open as she fished through her deep suitcase for her pajamas that evening. She glanced over at Caleb and noticed him preoccupied with the television, trying to get it to work. All his baggage lay in a heap on top of his bed, and Lindsey contemplated whether it was a good time to tell Caleb about her lack of communication with her grandparents about her accident. Soon, the stir of voices echoed out of the television speakers as Caleb found an interesting talk show to watch. He walked over to his bed and began unpacking.

"I never … uh … talked to my grandparents about my accident," Lindsey blurted out without warning as she sat cross-legged on her bed, watching nervously as Caleb's head shot up from his unpacking to stare at her.

"What do you mean?" he asked.

"I mean just that, Caleb. I didn't call them after my accident. The last time I talked to them was a couple hours before the accident, but not afterward. They don't know I was in it, they don't know I gave away my Honda, and they don't know about you."

Caleb's mouth dropped open in shock and his neck perked forward. "What!" he exclaimed. "You never told them you were with me!"

Lindsey took her eyes away from Caleb's gaze and passively nodded to answer his question. "They have no idea."

"Are you serious?" Caleb nearly shouted that time, his voice hitting an usually high pitch. "You … you…." he stuttered. His hands flew to cover his face in bewilderment while thoughts and worries invaded his brain. Why hadn't she told them? Why didn't she feel like she could tell them? Caleb flung his hands down and shot an angry glare at Lindsey. "You told me that they knew. You lied?"

Lindsey nodded.

Caleb threw his head back in exasperation and turned his body around so that his back was facing Lindsey. His head, churning with many thoughts, worries, and concerns was pivoting left to right as he shook it with disapproval.

"I'm sorry," was all Lindsey could utter. Caleb was speechless. He knew this was going to cause a problem between Lindsey and her grandparents, as well as with him and her grandparents. He took a deep breath, determined not to let his anger and temper take their toll on him. He cursed Satan away, composed himself, and then turned to face Lindsey. Her head was lowered as she stared at the floor, and her hands were fidgeting as her fingers nervously played with her rings, readjusting and turning them.

"Why did you do that, Lindsey?" Caleb said, attempting to be gentle, his voice undeviating. "Why didn't you just tell them?"

"I don't know," she answered without looking up. "They would've been freaked out, especially my grandmother. She's so crazy about everything." Lindsey shook her head as she recalled her last phone call to her grandmother. "And they definitely wouldn't have agreed to me going off on the rest of my trip with some weird guy I hardly know, whom they've never met." She glanced up, and her big, sorrowful eyes bore into Caleb's small, confused ones. "C'mon, even you have to agree with that."

Caleb thought for a moment, not taking his eyes off of Lindsey's. He knew she was right. Her grandparents most likely would have been shaken up, and it made no sense that they would have let her continue her journey with someone she had just met. The idea had even seemed absurd to him when Lindsey first introduced it. Caleb sighed and sat down on the corner of his bed.

"Yeah, that's true," he finally voiced. "I suppose I should've realized that before, and double checked then to make sure you had definitely told them."

"Well, I did tell you that I had talked to them. I mean, you had no reason not to believe me."

"Yeah, but I took you at your word. I shouldn't have been so trusting." Caleb suddenly realized the offense in his words and quickly restated them. "I mean, even when you told me you had talked to your grandparents, I had some doubt that you were telling the truth, but I just left it at that. I guess I just didn't want to deal with anything that came from your grandparents. I wanted it to be that easy, I suppose." He stopped with his eyes lowered, studying some peculiar spot on the floor. Lindsey watched him. Her heart started to beat faster as a thought struck her mind. *He really did want me to come along*. She didn't voice it, however.

"Even if you had double-checked to make sure I had definitely told them," she said, "I still would've lied to you. So no matter how hard you drilled me, it wouldn't have done any good."

Those words eased Caleb's mind a little, and he nodded. "I think I just sort of, kind of, wanted you to come along," he finally admitted. Then he looked up.

Lindsey smiled. "You can trust me, you know," she said. "I won't lie like that again. I know it was deceiving. I'm sorry." Caleb just nodded again. Lindsey leaned forward and said in a silly English accent, "So can you ever find it in your heart to forgive me, Sir Caleb of Bellingham?"

Caleb laughed, his eyes glowing, and answered. "Of course. Where would this world be without forgiveness?"

"Oh yes, I do agree."

The same apprehension that Mary had been feeling that morning at church now clutched at her gut as she approached Bryan Tate's small home. Pulling into the driveway, Mary felt as if her lungs were constricting smaller and smaller. *What is wrong with me?!* She scolded herself. *Why do I always start worrying over nothing? Why am I even here? What am I doing here? Why do I always ask myself these stupid questions?* Before she could make herself any more nervous, she quickly jumped out of her compact Chevy and took quick strides up to the porch.

Upon hearing the doorbell, Bryan rushed from the kitchen out into the living room and to the front door. He opened it widely and greeted Mary with a soft, warm smile.

"Hey there, I'm glad you found the place all right."

Mary's heart leaped at the personable sight of Bryan's warm smile and welcoming eyes. Her voice caught in her throat, and for a moment, she couldn't speak. "Uh, yeah," she finally stumbled out. "I've been in this neighborhood quite a lot of times. I have a cousin who lives down this road actually."

"Oh, that's neat. Come on in."

Mary pulled the strap of her purse over her shoulder to keep it from slipping and stepped into the house. The warmth from the gas fireplace blazing nearby swirled around her body, and instantly her nerves began to ease. A pleasing aroma was wafting in from the kitchen, and suddenly Mary's mouth began to water. She hadn't realized just how hungry she was. Ever since the morning she hadn't been able to eat.

"So where's … I'm sorry, I don't remember your daughter's name."

"Andrea," Mary answered. "She's uh … I decided to keep her with my mom tonight. I thought it might make it easier to talk, you know, without having her running around and sitting restless and all that good stuff."

"Oh, all right. Whatever you say, you're the mom," Bryan said. Mary began to slip off her coat and Bryan quickly rushed to take it from her. "Oh, I can take that for you," he said, grabbing her coat and purse from her.

"Thanks," Mary laughed.

"Uh, have a seat," Bryan then offered, hurrying over to the couch to clear off some scattered books and newspapers that were covering it. "Sorry, I haven't had a chance to clean in here yet. I've been working on dinner."

"It smells wonderful," Mary admitted.

"Well, I'm glad. Cooking was always one of my strong points."

"Ugh, I hate to cook," Mary said as she lowered herself onto the couch. "I work at a restaurant, but you'll never find me behind the counter doing the cooking, no way."

Bryan followed suit and took a seat on a chair near the couch, facing Mary. "Where do you work?" he asked curiously.

Mary hesitated. "Oh, I work at the *Denny's* right off of the highway," she answered reluctantly, her face flushing.

"Oh yeah, yeah," Bryan said, nodding his head. "I've been there a few times." He noted the embarrassed look on her face as she had spoken and wondered whether she was ashamed to be a waitress. "So do you like working there," he asked, hoping to help her feel comfortable and open up with him.

"Well, it's a hard job to have when you're raising a child. It's not much of a career, that is."

"Yeah, that must be stressful at times."

"It really is."

"May I ask about Andrea's father?" Bryan asked sincerely.

"Sure. He uh … we just divorced a little while ago, and he helps with Andrea. He pays some child support and takes her on weekends. Yeah. There's really not much to say about him."

"I'm sorry," Bryan quickly apologized. "I don't mean to be prying or asking too personal of questions. Just let me know if I'm out of line or if there's something you don't want to talk about."

"Oh, no, it's okay," Mary assured him. "I guess I'm just still angry at him, you know. It's hard."

"Yeah, I've been through a divorce too. I think I told you that over the phone."

"Yeah, you did," Mary smiled, enjoying Bryan's comforting and warm presence. It was nice to know that this man had gone through a similar experience with divorce, and all at once Mary wanted to ask him about it. "So, may I ask you about what happened with your wife?"

Bryan sat up and glanced over at the wall before setting his gaze back on Mary. "My wife cheated on me," he answered slowly.

"Oh my gosh," Mary quietly gasped. "That's so terrible."

"Yeah, it was really hard; I loved her a lot. I wanted to work things out with her, I thought we could, but she was the one who actually wanted the divorce. She said she wasn't in love with me anymore. So I went along with her wishes."

"Well, I guess you wouldn't want to be married to someone who didn't love you and wasn't willing to make things right," offered Mary.

"Yeah," Bryan said quietly, nodding.

Mary's eyebrows came together in sympathy and compassion. She was speechless all of a sudden, wondering whether her question had possibly soured the night. Nevertheless, she knew she needed to say something else to keep the moment from becoming odd and uncomfortable.

"How long ago was that?"

"Oh, it was a while ago; about four or five years."

"Oh wow."

"Yeah, I've pretty much gotten over it. It's been hard, but thankfully I've had the Lord to help me through it. It was tough because I thought she was the one, you know?"

Mary nodded.

"We had known eachother since high school, and we started dating in college. I totally thought she was the one God put on this earth for me, so it was hard for me to accept at first that she would even think about doing such a terrible thing to me." Bryan kept speaking, and although his words reflected sadness and regret, Mary was stunned to find that Bryan's straight posture and direct eye contact were strong and unregretful. Indeed, his tone of voice was matter-of-factly, and Mary found that she liked how naturally he talked about God, as if God was a normal thing for everybody to believe and mention in their conversations. *Just like Granny and that boy, Caleb.* Mary had never personally considered the fact that two people were put on earth by God in order to find eachother and be partners. Although the idea was a new and odd one, she found it uniquely interesting and romantic.

"I suppose Ted wasn't who I was meant to be with, either," she mentioned.

"Mary, you had some questions about God, didn't you?" Bryan suddenly said, tactfully and successfully changing the subject. He was eager to hear about Mary's concern over church and determined to do what he could to introduce her to Christ.

"Oh yeah," Mary sighed. "I guess I'm just confused about everything. I really liked church this morning, but of course it was kind of out of my league, if you know what I mean."

"I think so."

"I don't know why I feel the way I do, but ever since this morning, I've been restless and curious and confused, and I just know that unless I get some things cleared up, this week is going to be hectic."

"So what do you want to know?" Bryan asked enthusiastically. "You can ask anything you want and I'll do my best to answer."

Mary took a deep breath. "I guess I just want to know about God, and about Christianity. Oh yeah! And Jesus … I can't say I'm very familiar with Him, either. I should be, coming from a Christian background, but I'm not. I liked what I heard about Jesus at church, so I was wondering if you could clear that up for me."

"Wow," Bryan exclaimed. He laughed. Mary sat on the edge of the couch with her back straight as if she was anxious about something. "Well, you might as well make yourself comfortable," Bryan invited.

Mary laughed and leaned back on the couch. "I love your house," she said honestly. "I felt comfortable the instant I stepped foot inside."

Bryan nodded as he wondered how he was going to go about explaining God and answering Mary's questions. "Will you excuse me for a moment while I go check the food?" he asked.

"Of course."

As Bryan made his way into the kitchen, he thanked God for putting such a desire and willingness in Mary to seek Him. Bryan also prayed and asked God for patience and the right words with which to speak to Mary. *Most of all, Lord, I just pray that You will speak through me, so that it is not I speaking, but You, Lord. Be with this woman, Lord God, and help her to see Your light. Help her to find You and realize how real You are.*

Entering the living room, Bryan walked over to the couch and sat next to Mary, looking her straight in the eye. He took a breath.

"I guess first of all I should tell you that Christianity is not just another one of the many religions out there that are being practiced. It is considered a religion, yes, but it goes beyond that. For me, and for many Christians, *being* a Christian is not just a hobby; it's not something that you *do*, it's something that you *live*, and at the center of it all is Jesus Christ. Basically, Christianity is about having a relationship with Christ…."

Monday, October 27, 1997

Well it's been exactly a week since I left home, and I'm about halfway to Virginia. Caleb and I made it to Lincoln late last night, and so here we are.

I can't believe how long we drove yesterday; we went practically the whole way across Nebraska. We were thinking about stopping in Omaha instead since it's only a little farther, but it's better this way because we can save time by taking highway 2 into Iowa instead of backtracking from Omaha. So, instead of setting out on the road today, we're just going to hang out for a couple days in this city for a little road-break. I didn't realize what a big city Lincoln is. I haven't seen it in the daytime yet, but last night, when we got here, I felt like I could shout for joy at all the city lights glowing. It was nice to see city lights after that trek through the Rockies and the Nebraska plains. I'm so glad we're out of them.

We're staying at the Savannah Suites Hotel. *It's pretty nice; it's one of the cheapest here. At first we were going to stay at yet another* Super 8, *but I talked Caleb out of it. I kinda wanted something a little nicer, especially to make this trip a little more of a vacation. I wanted to stay at the* Hampton *or the* Doubletree, *but those were just a tad bit more money for almost all the same stuff this place has. We get continental breakfast here, but we already missed it. We slept in (ahhhh!), and it was nice.*

After Caleb is out of the shower and ready to go (hopefully soon, I swear he takes longer in the bathroom than I do!), we're going to the mall to do some shopping (yay!), see a movie, eat a nice lunch, go roller skating (well that's what I want to do, but Caleb didn't seem too excited about it), and some other stuff. Caleb has been here before, a few years ago, when he first drove over to Washington and he stopped in Lincoln. He says there's a lot to do here. He mentioned a zoo and an aquarium, but I don't know about those. Somehow watching animals doesn't seem like the most stimulating thing to do. He says there's lots of cool museums and parks, and so I was thinking we should go on a picnic today or tomorrow. It will be fun.

Besides this, everything has been pretty good, so far. Caleb's absolutely cool, although yesterday, when I tried telling him that, he started telling me how he's not so wonderful. It was weird. I mean, I didn't expect him to say, "Yeah, I know how wonderful I am," but he didn't have to get all down on himself. I don't know what it is, but I know it has to do with before – when he used to drink a lot and party. I wonder why that bothers him so much. I mean, he has changed, but for some reason I get the idea that he's still ashamed of himself or something. I don't know, I still like him, and I still think he's cool. The coolest part about him is the whole fact that he's letting me tag along like this.

Well, he's finally out of the shower now, so I guess we're leaving soon. Bye now!

"Gateway Shopping Center!" Lindsey exclaimed incredulously as she and Caleb entered into the huge parking lot to scope out a spot amidst the myriad of cars. "Geez, how many malls are there in this city? I must've seen three already."

"There's a billion," Caleb replied. "I think about four or five."

"Four or five billion!?"

"Ha ha," Caleb said sarcastically as he shot Lindsey a glance. She stuck her tongue out at him. "This is the mall I went to before, so I'm most familiar with it." As Caleb found a spot, the two jumped out of the Ford and made their way to the entrance.

Lindsey ran ahead of Caleb a few feet, throwing her head back and thrusting her arms into the air at her sides. "Oh my gosh!" she yelled, spinning as she stared up at the sky with her arms outstretched. "You don't know how happy I am that we've come to civilization!"

"I think I have a pretty good idea," Caleb replied, right before he began running ahead of Lindsey, racing her to the entranceway.

Lindsey squealed as she attempted to keep up with Caleb. The two got to the doorway and Lindsey thrust the door open.

"Lindsey Milholland!" Caleb scolded sarcastically. "You almost knocked that old lady down when you went through the door! What have you got to say for yourself?"

Lindsey turned around to see an elderly woman slowly walking out the door and into the parking lot outside. She apparently was unharmed and un-offended by the two. Lindsey laughed. "Whatever, Caleb. I was miles away from her!"

Caleb and Lindsey strolled down the walkway and Caleb spotted the food court up on the second floor. Lindsey leaped onto the escalator and began running up like an excited child. Caleb challenged Lindsey, taking the other escalator, running up as it traveled downward. Lindsey made it to the top and turned to see Caleb dodging people as he ran up. She began laughing.

"Caleb Lockwood!" she scolded. "You nearly knocked down that old lady. What have you got to say for yourself?"

"Hey, hey," he defended. "She wasn't nearly as old as the woman you trampled over."

"I didn't *trample* her, geez."

As the two approached the food court, sweet smells of cinnamon flooded his nostrils. "Hey, we never had breakfast," he observed. "Let's get something to eat first."

"Okay, but let's hurry, because I'm really wanting to find an Old Navy or the Gap if this place has it."

Feet shuffled and registers beeped and buzzers went off, adding to the cacophony of mall sounds. Caleb and Lindsey waited in line patiently for cinnamon rolls and orange juice, but Lindsey began wavering back and forth in restlessness.

"You have to go to the bathroom or something?" Caleb asked, eyeing Lindsey strangely.

"No, I'm just so excited to be out of the car and walking about. At least, I want to be walking about. It's hard for me to stand in one spot for too long. Why is the mall so packed anyway? It's only a Monday."

"That's what I was wondering," Caleb agreed. "Hey, you know what else I thought of earlier?"

"Hmm?"

"Halloween is on Friday."

Lindsey's mouth opened in surprise. "Well, oh my goodness, you're right!" she said. "I hadn't even thought of that at all. So what shall we do, huh? You want to go trick-or-treating?"

Caleb grunted. "Ha. I don't even remember the last time I went trick-or-treating. I think I gave that up in my pre-adolescent years. You know, when I became too cool for it."

"Psh, you can never outgrow trick-or-treating," Lindsey commented. "I haven't gone since I was a kid, either, so I think it would be fun now. C'mon, just two big kids dressing up and scaring people, what could be funner?"

Caleb raised his eyebrows in uncertainty. "Uh, lots of things are funner ... and funner isn't even a word."

"Hey, you're no fun," Lindsey complained. "It would be cool, we could dress up as Frankenstein and his bride, or Beauty and the Beast, or Robin Hood and Maid Marian."

"Robin Hood ... I don't think so," Caleb said flatly. "But I'll consider Beauty and the Beast if I get to be Beauty."

"Whoa," Lindsey exclaimed. "Is there something about yourself you're not telling me?"

"Well, you tell me. You're the odd little person who's into Halloween in the first place."

"Hey now, no criticizing," Lindsey said.

"I'm kidding, Maid Marian."

"Well, we wouldn't have to go trick-or-treating," Lindsey insisted. "We could maybe just find a Halloween party somewhere, or…."

"I'll think about it, okay?" Caleb finally offered.

The two approached the counter and ordered their cinnamon rolls and orange juice, grabbing their small paper plates and heading for a large table in the center of the food court.

"I still think we should go to the zoo," Caleb said after they had sat down.

"Uh," Lindsey groaned. "All I remember about zoos is my dad taking me to one when I was really little, and I was scared of the gorillas. I just don't find it very exciting to watch animals."

"Oh, come on, Lindsey," Caleb argued. She said nothing, but continued eating her food. "You're no fun," he said in mock imitation of her. She set down her fork, tilted her head and stared at him.

"Okay, I'm listening. Say your peace."

"This zoo is so cool," Caleb began. "I'm telling you, you'll love it. And there's also a Planetarium somewhere around here too. We could go to that, you know, and watch some laser shows. I think it's in the University of Nebraska Museum."

Lindsey cocked her eyebrows, unconvinced. "You tell me I'm odd and immature for liking Halloween, and here you're begging me to go to zoos and planetariums? What's that about?"

Caleb smiled and laughed, nearly spitting his orange juice out of his mouth. "Okay, okay, you made your point. But will you at least consider it?"

Lindsey pursed her mouth and creased her eyebrows. "Uh … I still don't know. I'll think about it."

"Trust me, I know you'll like it. Besides, we're talking about animals. Who doesn't like animals?"

"I don't."

"Oh yeah, you do," Caleb asserted. "Maybe it's just those gorillas that have got you so disturbed."

"Ha ha."

Minutes passed quickly while Lindsey and Caleb enjoyed their sweet breakfast, occasionally interrupting their meal with small talk. The mall was loud, and Lindsey found it increasingly warm and stuffy. She leaned forward to slip off her jacket, and Caleb excused himself for a moment. She didn't pay attention at first, but when she turned to straighten her coat on the back of her chair, she noticed Caleb walking swiftly toward a middle-aged woman near the top of the escalator. A stroller with a crying child was sitting next to her, and a group of shopping bags were spilling all over the floor. Apparently the woman had tripped at the top on the escalator. From her stooped position on the floor with head lowered, Lindsey concluded that the woman, out of stress and exhaustion, hadn't tried to pick herself up. Lindsey watched as Caleb approached the woman and kneeled next to her, speaking gently to her. The woman's face went up, and Lindsey could then see the tears that had fallen out of the corners of her eyes. She instantly felt bad for the woman. Caleb offered his hand to the woman, and with his help she stood up. She was pregnant.

"Oh my gosh," Lindsey quietly whispered. "I can't believe it. What an angel." As she spoke the words, a loving smile crossed her face, and she couldn't take her eyes off of Caleb. A fleeting emotion rushed through her. Adoration? Admiration? Infatuation? Lindsey brushed it aside. Caleb helped pick up the woman's bags and belongings and handed them to her. With his free hands, he walked in back of the stroller and began pushing it while the woman walked alongside.

Lindsey shook her head in amazement and disbelief. Her head turned as her gaze followed Caleb and the woman to the nearest exit. She turned and leaned against the back of her chair. She didn't speak, she just thought. A few minutes later, she resumed her eating, and in a total of ten minutes, Caleb had returned.

"Why did you do that, Caleb?"

"Huh?" he asked as if nothing had happened.

"That was … really sweet."

"Oh, well, she needed help and nobody was doing anything."

Lindsey couldn't take her sights off of Caleb as she sat there, slowly shaking her head. "That was so nice, Caleb. I mean, I've never seen anybody do something like that. I don't think I would've helped her. I would've sat and felt bad, waiting for somebody else to help her, but I don't think I would've."

"Sure you would've," Caleb said, biting into his cinnamon roll.

"No," Lindsey said quietly. She bit into her cinnamon roll and peered around.

Caleb watched her face alter from amusement to quandary. The space between them had suddenly become very far, and Caleb felt like she was so distant from where he wanted her to be. A few more minutes passed while the two ate in silence, but to Caleb it felt like longer. "Lindsey."

Lindsey's head reflexively shot sideways at the sound of her name to peer at Caleb. "Uh huh?"

"Are you okay?" he asked. "You kinda seem to be staring off into nothing again."

"What do you mean, 'again'?"

"Well, you do it a lot," he answered slowly.

"I'm just thinking," Lindsey stated matter-of-factly, almost defensively.

"Can I ask what you're thinking?"

Lindsey giggled. "It's usually the girls who ask the guys that kind of stuff."

Caleb just shrugged.

"Well, I think different things," Lindsey answered.

"What were you thinking just now?'

"Oh, I don't know," Lindsey answered passively, gazing back at the throngs of people swarming the food court, the scrapes and squeals of chair legs as they slid across the floor ringing in her ears.

"Are you sure there's not something wrong?" Caleb asked again. He couldn't ignore the way her eyes would suddenly glaze over, and her mouth would droop. Lindsey didn't take her eyes off the mall scene, and when she did, she didn't look at Caleb.

"I was just thinking about being at my dad's," she said slowly, pausing before going on. "I don't know what I'm going to do when I get there. I mean, I had thought about starting college as soon as I was ready, whether it was in three months or three years, but right now, I don't feel like I could do that. I don't know what I'm going to do at all. If I don't go to college, then what? Am I supposed to get a job and just work for who knows how long? Then what's supposed to happen? I just start thinking about the future and I get all depressed because I feel like there's nothing to look forward to."

"Did you feel that way even when your mom was alive?"

"Yeah, sometimes," Lindsey admitted. "But not as bad. Before she died I was set to go to college. I wasn't sure what I was going to major in, but I had a couple ideas and careers in mind. But sometimes I would still wonder about what happens then. Is my whole life just going to be monotonous, just work and home, work and home? There's always these fun little vacation-things in between, and I'm really excited to be here, hanging out in Lincoln for a few days. I'm excited about riding go-carts, and possibly going to a zoo, but then it will all be over. We'll be back on the road with the fun in the past, and I'll be back to wondering, and feeling like I have nothing bright to look forward to. And everything I will have to look forward to is eventually going to pass anyway." Lindsey stopped and took a deep breath. It had been hard for her to speak, and Caleb could hear in her voice the attempts to keep down her emotion. Even now he could see the corners of her eyes shining from potential tears. She held them back, however. She sat up. "I guess it all comes down to the fact that sometimes life just seems so pointless, you know? Like, what's this life for, anyway?"

"Well, I definitely know what you're talking about," Caleb agreed, nodding his head. "I've felt like that lots of time, even after becoming a Christian."

Caleb halted, realizing that what he said could possibly add to Lindsey's confusion. How could he tell her that as a Christian, with Jesus in his life, he felt more complete than he ever had been? There were still times when he would gaze into the future, scared and worried at how it might turn out, but he ultimately knew that everything would stay in place with Jesus Christ, no matter what happened. He also knew that as a believer in Christ, he had an obligation to do the Lord's work, sharing Christ with others, and being a faithful follower. Caleb knew that God had a plan for his life, a blueprint, outlining the work He had for Caleb to do. Caleb didn't know what it was, or when it would come, but he knew it was something he could always look forward to. The prospects of his life in the future looked brighter than they ever had. Caleb knew there would be times in the future when that old feeling of depression would seep back up to haunt him, but Jesus Christ would remind him that there's something even greater coming to destroy the depression – Jesus himself. With all the little things in life Caleb had to look forward to, he knew the biggest one was eternity in Heaven with his Lord and Savior.

Caleb felt sorry for Lindsey that she seemed to have such a hopeless outlook on her future. But he didn't tell her that.

Fourteen

Don't be troubled. Believe in God, and believe in me.

– John 14:1

Slipping through her fingers unaware, the box that held the new table lamp that Chelsea had just purchased made a thump as it hit the pavement. Chelsea squealed in alarm at the thought of her new lamp cracking, or worse: breaking into pieces. She cursed in frustration, then bent over slowly and picked up the plastic *Target* shopping bag containing the box. Hurriedly she swirled around and began marching out of the parking lot and toward the front of the *Target* where two benches were parked just to the left of the entrance.

Taking a seat on one of the benches, the plastic bag crinkled in Chelsea's hands as she fished out her box, opened it, and began scrutinizing her lamp. Before she could notice the small chip on the base, a voice caused her to raise her head.

"Hey there, Mrs. Johns."

"Oh, hi there, Marianne. How are you doing?" Chelsea greeted, gazing up at the fatigued face of the redhead. She had always known Marianne to be an out-going and outspoken young character; something that seemed to Chelsea to be typical of most redheads. But today Marianne's head hung a little lower than normal, and even her attire – a black tank top covered with a gray wool V-neck sweater – belied her usual bright disposition, and her blue, green, and yellow wardrobe.

Marianne shrugged. "Okay, I guess. How about you?"

"Oh, I'm doing all right. I'm holding up better than I thought I would with Jillian gone and Lindsey away, you know?" Chelsea set her lamp down and leaned back in the bench, gazing up at Marianne who stood a few feet away.

"Yeah, I know. It's weird starting school again, because I'm not in high school anymore, you know? Everything's so different."

"I know, a lot of things have changed lately," Chelsea replied soberly, thinking of her own recent plight rather than referring to Marianne's new independence. "How is school going, anyway?" she asked, hoping to keep herself in as good a mood as possible. The day hadn't gone well for her. After a short disagreement with Dan about breakfast, she had rushed off to run errands, absent-mindedly forgetting her purse at home and having to drive back to town to retrieve it. After a few more bouts of plight, she wasn't surprised that she managed to drop her newly bought lamp on the ground by accident. Hopefully Marianne's company might help to bring a smile to her old, worn face for the first time that day.

"Oh, gosh, it really sucks," Marianne replied, instantly putting a hand to her mouth at Chelsea's aghast look. "Oh, I'm sorry, Mrs. Johns. I didn't mean to be so rude and say it like that...."

"Oh, don't worry about it, dear," Chelsea reassured, putting a hand up. "I've heard worse before. I was just surprised because I thought you might be liking the college life."

"Well," Marianne began, tipping her head to the side and staring above Chelsea, "it does provide more freedom than highschool, and it's not entirely all that challenging, at least not any more than highschool was for me, but...." She stopped, her eyes fixed directly in front of her, over Chelsea's graying head.

"But what?" Chelsea urged. "You don't like the teachers, or your classes?"

"Well, there's this one teacher I can't stand, but I don't think it's that." She stopped again, contemplating whether she should voice what was really the core of her problems – Lindsey's absence. She looked down into Chelsea's searching face. The woman was lost; she didn't look as nice and ready-for-the-day as she usually did. From the slight puffiness under her large, dark eyes, Marianne could tell she had endured a few nights of crying and worry. Poor Chelsea, she had always been so close to her daughter and granddaughter. But when Jillian had suddenly been in the accident, both Chelsea and Lindsey were torn, each seeking consolation within their own hearts rather than each other's. Once being so close, they had split apart as their support bridge – Jillian – was ripped apart from them. Marianne could feel Chelsea's hurt just by gazing into her dull eyes, because she had felt the same way. She missed her friend so much, more than she wanted anyone to know, and not just from the week Lindsey had been away. To Marianne, Lindsey's absence had been apparent for three months now – starting back in August when she lost Jillian. That's when Lindsey's world changed; she unknowingly isolated herself from the people she loved and cared for, constructing a fence around herself to keep out even the closest in her life. Yes, when Lindsey lost Jillian, Marianne lost Lindsey.

As she stood in front of Chelsea, who was eyeing her intently, Marianne knew she needed to make her feelings known, even to this woman who she feared might burst out in tears at the thought of Lindsey.

"I just really miss Lindsey, Mrs. Johns." As she said it, she noticed how Chelsea's back sagged a little and she leaned back in the bench, lowering her eyes to the ground. "Everything's too different without her. I mean, she was supposed to go to school with me, and now I just feel so betrayed and alone." Marianne attempted to laugh, remembering how excited she and Lindsey had been as they planned to schedule all their classes together and carpool every day to classes. "I just ... didn't think things would ... turn out this way. It's all too weird and odd and new."

Chelsea nodded, understanding Marianne's grief all too well, maybe even better. Losing Jillian and Lindsey within three months was taking a sharp toll on her usually strong spirit. "I hope Lindsey's doing all right," she said. "She didn't seem to be dealing with the changes very well, either, before she left."

Marianne nodded, and took a few steps closer to Chelsea, lowering her head. "Yeah, I know. I miss her so much. I think she's doing okay, though. I've talked to her on the phone a couple times already."

Chelsea's body straightened and she leaned forward a bit. "Oh, you have? When did she call you?"

"Oh, I don't know. I last heard from her a couple days ago. She was in Wyoming, I think."

"Oh, so she's still got a ways to go, then."

"Yeah, but she'll make it okay. Especially with that guy she's with."

The words didn't register at first, but when they did, they rang hard, like an alarm sounding in the distance. Chelsea's eyes narrowed in confusion and suspicion. "What? What *guy*?"

Marianne immediately noticed the profound expression on Mrs. John's face and instantly knew she had stepped into dangerous territory. "Uh, she didn't ... she didn't tell you?" Marianne stammered.

"Tell me what? What guy is she with?" Chelsea's once quiet and reserved inquiry now threatened to turn into hard-core interrogation.

"Well," Marianne swallowed, wondering how she could articulate herself well for Lindsey's sake. "Lindsey is traveling with someone now. His name is ... Caleb, I think. Apparently he's going to the East Coast, too, so they decided to travel together."

Chelsea leaned on the edge of the bench and shook her head. "I still don't understand. Did she pick this guy up before she left? Is he a school friend, or someone?"

"Oh, no," Marianne slowly and reluctantly answered. "She just met this guy on her trip. He helped her when she was in the accident." Right when

Marianne said it she knew she shouldn't have. Chelsea's face distorted again, and Marianne furrowed her brows in uncertainty. "She didn't tell you about the accident?" she asked, her voice hitting a higher pitch than usual.

"No, she didn't tell me about any accident. Dan and I haven't heard from her since last Tuesday."

Ouch, Marianne thought. From her view standing up, Chelsea's face almost looked brighter than Marianne's hair and her fiery eyes sparked with just a touch of hurt. Just a touch, though … she was ticked. "I'm sorry, Mrs. Johns. She called me right after it happened and told me about Caleb and everything. I had no idea she wasn't keeping in touch with you."

"It's not your fault, Marianne," but her voice wasn't calm and comforting. Chelsea stuffed the lamp back in the box and stood up. "No, this is just like Lindsey to do something like this. Who knows, she might've even planned to meet that boy and go with him…." Suddenly panic gripped her and she turned to stare Marianne right in the face. "Oh my gosh, who's to say she even went to Virginia? What if she…."

"Whoa, Mrs. Johns, no. I really don't think Lindsey would…."

"But how would you know, Marianne?" Chelsea argued. "Lindsey could've just lied to you. She could've lied to us all and we wouldn't know."

Anger shot itself through Marianne, and she crumpled her face in offense. How could Mrs. Johns talk about her own granddaughter that way? "You actually think Lindsey would do that to you?"

Chelsea shrugged. "Sure, why not? She hasn't called, she hasn't been keeping in touch with her *family*." Chelsea spit out the word as if it had a foul taste. "Sure, she'll call her friends, but not her family." That offended Marianne even more. "Besides, she's been acting so rude lately, as if she doesn't want anything to do with us. I wouldn't doubt if she just made up this whole story about going to her dad's just to get away."

Marianne's face heated with the surge of anger that once again crept upon her. "How dare you," she quietly, but angrily stated, almost whispering.

"What?" Chelsea's eyes widened in surprise.

"I'm sorry, Mrs. Johns, but how dare you? How dare you have such a low and worthless perception of your granddaughter? Yes, she has been acting differently, but she's been confused. For heaven's sake, she lost her *mother*." Marianne stepped back as Chelsea gasped and began walking out to the parking lot. She turned and watched Chelsea for a second before assuming a position right behind her. "I would think you would understand Lindsey's pain. I mean, you lost Jillian, too."

Chelsea stopped dead in her tracks and closed her eyes for a second, trying to restrain the emotions that were fighting their way outside. "I was so mad at Lindsey for leaving, Mrs. Johns," Marianne went on. "I felt like I wasn't important enough for her to stay, you know?"

Chelsea was holding her breath, and at Marianne's words she exhaled slowly, turning to face Marianne. "Yeah, I know," she agreed, crossing her arms, calming her emotions.

"Mrs. Johns, I'm sorry to upset you, but I trust Lindsey. She's never been a liar. Sure, she's had a twist of emotions, that's for sure … and a little negative surgery on her personality…."

Chelsea smiled.

"I'm convinced she would've told you somewhere along the line that she was in an accident."

Chelsea nodded her head but turned her face downward to hide the hurt that was displaying itself in her features.

Marianne sighed, wondering how the moment had suddenly turned so sour a couple of minutes ago. "She would've called, Mrs. Johns. She was probably just scared to."

Chelsea glanced up. "Scared to call me? Why would she be scared to call?" This time her voice reflected confusion and sadness rather than anger.

"Well, I don't … maybe…." Marianne stalled, worried that what she might say would upset Chelsea again.

Chelsea reached over and placed her hand on Marianne's arm. "No, what? I need to hear it."

Marianne lowered her head and sighed, then stared boldly into Chelsea's face. "Well, maybe she was worried she'd get the same kind of response from you that I got."

"Meaning…?"

"It's obvious, Mrs. Johns. She probably thought you would've been too upset about the car wreck and might've argued with her to come home. And *maybe* she thought that you wouldn't believe her about Caleb and start making accusations about why you think she *really* left, and then start calling her a liar."

"Why wouldn't I believe her about Caleb?"

"Mrs. Johns, *I* didn't even believe her when she first told me, and I'm her best friend."

Chelsea's head began to pound as a taunting voice inside mocked her. She suddenly saw herself; heard herself reproaching Lindsey; not trusting her. She lowered her head, mostly in shame. She had no reason not to trust Lindsey; Marianne was right. They'd all been through so much these past months, and Lindsey had her own life now. Chelsea knew she'd had so many head-on collisions with Lindsey that there was no reason Lindsey should approach Chelsea with anything. Chelsea suddenly realized that she had never sought to understand Lindsey. She was never willing to take Lindsey's rude comments as constructive criticism, and determine the areas of her own personality that were dour.

"You're right, Marianne," she said regretfully. Glancing down at the plastic bag hanging from her fingers, she took a breath and turned to find her car.

"Mrs. Johns?"

Chelsea turned.

"I'm … Lindsey cares about you, you know that, right? She's just … you know."

"Yeah, I know."

Dan was just sifting through the remaining bills scattered all over his desktop when the shrill cry of the phone on the lamp stand nearby caused him to jump in alarm. "Ugh," he mumbled, cursing the phone while making a mental note to buy a new one as soon as possible. "Hello," he answered in a quick, irked tone.

"Hi, Grandpa, it's me."

Dan's back straightened and his face lit up with excitement. "Lindsey, my girl. Oh, how are you doing, honey?"

"I'm okay," she replied in a nervous voice. *Well, he didn't sound mad, at least.* "I'm sorry I haven't called like I said I would," she quickly apologized before any debate could begin. "I don't have any excuse for it, so I'm not gonna try to play innocent."

Dan frowned. "Oh, Lindsey, I wasn't going to ask you about that. I know you've got things on your mind and stuff to do. I knew if there was anything at all that had gone wrong, then you would've called, or at least we would've heard about it somehow."

Dan noticed the hesitation and tension lingering between the lines as Lindsey's reply was delayed for a few moments. "Um, yeah, that's something I wanted to talk to you about."

"Oh?" Dan sat down, furrowing his eyebrows. He quickly peeked out the window to make sure Chelsea hadn't returned from shopping yet, and asked cautiously, "Lindsey, is there something wrong? Did something happen?"

Relieved at the understanding, benign note in her grandfather's voice, and suddenly awash with her flooding emotions that were threatening to seep through her well-blockaded exterior, Lindsey unexpectedly burst out in a waterfall of tears. She tried to speak, but choked on her words.

"Oh my gosh, Lindsey," Dan sat on the edge of his chair, worry beginning to filter through him. "What's wrong? Have you been in an accident, or something? Are you lost? Talk to me. I'll listen, I won't get angry."

"You promise?" she choked out in a small, shrill sob.

"Of course," Dan replied, confusion riding the edges of his words.

Lindsey took a deep breath and glanced out the hotel window to see Caleb lounging back in one of the folding chairs beside the large pool. "I, uh, have a lot to tell you. I'm all right now, I'm at a hotel in Lincoln, Nebraska."

"Oh, you're in Lincoln, Lindsey, that's great."

"Yeah, but uh," Lindsey forced a smile onto her face and awe into her words. "You'll never believe how I got here or what's been going on this past week."

Dan stayed silent, waiting for Lindsey to go on.

"Grandpa, I, know I should've told you this sooner, and you'll probably be a little shocked to learn about it, but...." She stopped and took another shaky breath. "I've been in an accident, back when I was in Wyoming. A guy named Caleb pulled me out of it and took me to the hospital. Don't worry, I wasn't in bad shape, it wasn't a big accident, I just swerved off the road to avoid hitting an animal and landed in a ditch. I was only in the hospital for a night."

Dan *was* shocked, and all of a sudden a little angry that Lindsey hadn't called him or Chelsea to tell them about her accident. "How long ago was this?" he asked firmly, working to keep a stable tone of voice so he wouldn't upset Lindsey. He could tell she was already under enough emotional stress.

"Uh, the day after I left. Last Tuesday night."

Dan closed his eyes and fell back in his seat, trying to calm his emotions. "Lindsey, why didn't you tell us?"

"I don't know," she answered in a sob, lowering her head. She fought to keep her tears back; otherwise she'd never be able to finish the conversation. "Like I said, I have no excuse. I was just scared, I guess. I didn't want Grandma to know, because she'd get all worried on me and would want me to come home. And I thought you guys would see how unfit I was to be taking this trip. It's like, I can't even take care of myself that I get into a wreck on the second day of my trip!" She started bawling then and set the phone down, flinging herself onto the bed like a small whimpering child. She could barely hear her grandfather calling for her through the receiver.

It was that moment that Caleb decided to come in from his nap outside. Not knowing why, he just felt an urge to check up on Lindsey, and sure enough, he stepped in the room right on time to find her face down on the bed crying, with the telephone receiver lying beside her on the floor.

"Lindsey!" he cried, rushing beside her. He knelt on the floor and put a hand on her shoulder, shaking her a little bit. "Lindsey, what's wrong? Are you okay," he asked in a soothing, paternal voice.

"Lindsey, Lindsey!" Dan cried.

Lindsey sat up, tears streaking her pink cheeks, and damp hair stuck to her forehead. "Can you please talk to my grandpa?" she asked in a nasal voice.

Caleb picked up the phone receiver. "Hello?"

Dan was taken aback by the unfamiliar, unexpected male voice on the other end. Where was Lindsey? "Hello? Who's this?" he asked gruffly.

"My name is Caleb Lockwood. I'm a friend's of Lindsey's."

"Oh my gosh, is she in the hospital? Are you a doctor?"

"No no," Caleb quickly reassured Dan. "Like I said, I'm just a friend of Lindsey's. We're at a hotel in Lincoln."

Dan immediately became worried and suspicious. *Caleb, the guy who pulled Lindsey out of her accident? What is she doing at a hotel in Lincoln with this guy?* He made no hesitation to voice his concerns.

"Did Lindsey tell you about the accident?" Caleb asked.

"Yes, she did, but she didn't get much further to explain to me about you."

"Sir, I don't know if Lindsey told you that I pulled her out of her wreck on my way to North Carolina. After learning we were both headed in the same direction, we talked and decided it would be best if we traveled together."

"Why? She doesn't even know you."

"Well, that's true, but we also didn't leave immediately following her wreck. I mean, I stuck around for a couple days to make sure she was all right, and I got her into a motel after she was released from the hospital."

"No offense, son, but I believe Lindsey was hardly in any state to make a decision and judgment on you, and whether or not she should be traveling with a stranger. I don't know how much she's told you about her, but she's been through a lot these past few months...."

"Losing her mother, I know," Caleb said quietly. "She's told me all about it. And no offense to you, sir, but Lindsey was also not in any state to drive all the way across the United States alone."

Dan's next statement halted in his throat. Caleb was right, and Dan knew it. "You know," he began, clearing his throat, "her grandmother and I, we tried to talk Lindsey out of this whole thing – driving across the country. It just seemed like such an unrealistic goal, especially for Lindsey at this time in her life."

Caleb nodded and glanced at Lindsey, who was watching him with red, swollen eyes that were filled with curiosity. Seeing her gazing at him so earnestly, as if he was her protector, trying to finish her conversation with her grandpa, he almost laughed. She seemed so much like a little child who was cowering beneath her big brother or her dad, not wanting to face any sort of conflict or deal with anything too emotional. She tried to hide so much, but he could see right through her. She wasn't as strong as she attempted to convey.

Even as her little-girl façade brought a smile to his heart, and a sense of pride at being her protector – her trustworthy friend, it also brought a feeling of sorrow and pity … and burden. Lindsey counted on him so much; and why not? Her whole world had crumbled after her mother's death until she felt she had no choice but to flee the state.

That's what she was doing, too. She was fleeing. This wasn't just a feeble attempt to locate her father for purposes of curiosity and longing. Caleb had a feeling Lindsey could care less about her father. She just needed a way out, and he had been it.

Poor Lindsey, who was so alone that he could see it in her eyes, and sense it in her voice, and outline it in her smile. Everything that seemed so positive to her held something negative within. Caleb frowned as he looked at her.

"Yeah, well," Caleb continued. "Lindsey can be a hard-headed girl, I think." Upon those words, Caleb winked at Lindsey, and she rolled her eyes, but smiled. She grabbed the phone away from him.

Sniffing and wiping her nose with the back of her hand, she spoke directly into the receiver. "Grandpa, it's me. I'm okay now, sorry about that. I just didn't want you to be upset with me."

Dan sighed, realizing that his prying of the situation hadn't helped. He had been reacting in just the way Chelsea would have. Still, he couldn't easily shake his concern over the fact that Lindsey was traveling with an almost complete stranger.

"Lindsey," Dan fumbled, choosing his words carefully, "do you really think it's necessary, or even *safe*, to be traveling with this Caleb guy whom you hardly know."

"Oh, Grandpa, believe me, I practically know his lifestory. You can learn a lot about someone by spending seven straight hours on the road with them."

"Yeah, and he sounds like a nice guy, but still…."

"Grandpa," Lindsey stopped him, making her voice firm. "I know I haven't been the most reliable granddaughter lately, or the most emotionally stable, but I'm not stupid. You might believe I'm a little screwed in the head because of Mom, but not so much that I'd carelessly throw myself in the passenger seat of some guy's truck. It wasn't like I was hitchhiking, you know."

"I know, Lindsey."

"Grandpa, I know you're still going to be concerned, even if I could have all these great things to tell you about Caleb to reassure you. But I honestly don't know what I can tell you right now. I trust Caleb, and there are a lot of reasons why. The best one is that we've known eachother for a week now, are halfway across the States, and still safe."

Dan nodded, knowing that there was absolutely nothing he could do to change the situation.

In her small neighborhood in Coeur d'Alene, Idaho, October 31st was drawing very near. All along Mary's neighborhood block, pumpkins scattered the walkways and porches of nearly every house, and some even sat atop the white, toppling fences. The yellow-orange vegetables, colorfully painted with haunted house scenes and carved in the shapes of ghosts and black cats, provided the perfect picture of the holiday and added the excitement that the season needed. Walking home after having just picked up Andrea after her morning shift at work, Mary wasn't oblivious to the damp smell of the dull afternoon, nor the odor of the rotting pumpkins next door, nor even the heavenly aroma of baked goods wafting through open windows. The sky was gray, but it was a bright day for Mary.

Today she and Andrea had decided to decorate for Halloween, and all afternoon after Mary's shift, they had been busily taping paper witches and ghosts around every unexpected corner of the tiny home, and spreading fake spider webs on the hall ceiling. This was Mary's favorite part of every holiday: the decorating. Keeping her mind occupied with the playful task had always helped to ease or rid her of any stress she felt from her monotonous life. Today, however, she was beaming; her dinner with Bryan last night was wonderful. She hadn't spent quality time with a nice man for a long time.

Bryan was so different from her ex-husband, Ted, and not only because of his gracious manner and friendly appeal, but also because of his *faith*. Ted had never been religious of any sort, and he and Mary weren't even married in a church. As Mary thought about it more, she realized that Bryan really had an attractive disposition, and he reminded her of that young man she met a week ago at work who had flared her curiosity in God in the first place … Caleb.

Yes, she began thinking about Caleb. At the time she met him, he seemed like an unusually *nice* boy; kind of quiet; even humble in a way. She thought that was odd, especially for his age, and she wondered if such men could ever exist. Then she met Bryan, and although he seemed a little more outspoken and confident than Caleb had, he convinced Mary that good men did exist.

Indeed, Bryan attracted Mary in more than one way. Not only did he have a selfless personality that any woman would desire, he was also physically good-looking. At 37, he was fit and trim, appearing to be closer to 30 years old than 40. And at five feet, eight inches, he wasn't that tall for a man, but at Mary's five feet, three inches, he seemed the perfect height. His dark, neatly trimmed hair and goatee outlining sharp facial features and a square chin were enough to melt Mary's heart. He was a good deal more handsome than Ted had ever been, although Ted had always seemed attractive to Mary. Bryan, then, was the sort of man that most women would drool over.

A faint smile spread over Mary's lips as she thought about the man. They were the same age. Mary was only a few years younger, but she sure felt as old as anyone could get. She caught a glimpse of herself in the window reflection; her thick, scraggly hair pulled up in a messy bun, the darkness under her eyes and the creases barely forming on the edges of her mouth. The smile fading, Mary's back slumped and she let out a sigh as she glanced away from her haggard appearance. *I do look old*, she confirmed, deciding that she was out of luck in the area of ever finding another man to be with, especially Bryan. He was too good-looking for her. Most likely he wouldn't desire her; he'd want someone who looked as good as him and....

Mary stopped herself. If there was one thing she had learned about Bryan last night, it was that he wasn't superficial or selfish. No, there was no reason he'd choose a woman because of her looks. That was teenager stuff, and Mary knew that's what she was acting like at that moment – a kid – a kid with a crush on that mysterious boy next door.

But Bryan was more than mysterious to her; she knew him. They had talked about so many things last night, and he had told her all about Jesus. She learned so much about the God who created the universe and all His children, and she learned that she was one of those children. Some of the stuff sounded vaguely familiar to her from her past years in church, but last night they had come to mean something. Bryan had cleared up so many things that had been fogged up in her mind, and she knew without a doubt that she wanted Jesus in her life. Too much in awe and wonder last night to sort through her brain and make any such decision, she wasn't sure how or when she should do it. Most likely she'd wait until church sometime when she could have a talk with one of the pastors.

With that thought, an unexpected and unstoppable smile suddenly flew across her face and she sat upright, continuing her work of painting the windows with Halloween stencils.

"Hey, Mom, you didn't put the big spider up in the spider webs on the ceiling."

Mary looked over at Andrea, who held the huge rubber spider in her hand while using the other to point toward the hall where fake webs were hung all over the ceiling. A frown was frozen on her face.

"Oh, honey, I know, I'm sorry. I was saving that job for you, though."

Andrea leaped in the air with excitement. "Oh good, lift me up then!"

Mary proceeded to obey her daughter's command, and as she did, Andrea asked her an unexpected question, with a sly grin twisted across her mouth. "So, did you have a good dinner with that man from church?"

Mary's face lit up. "Yes I did, honey. It was a very, very good night."

"Good, I'm glad to see you smiling, lately."

Bryan wasn't unfamiliar to the emotions that had encompassed him that morning and afternoon. They scared him in a way because he worried they might give Mary the wrong impression. They were feelings he felt before he and his wife had been married; when he'd first seen her in highschool; first asked her out on a date; and first kissed her. It was happiness, delight, exuberance, merriment … satisfaction. He felt … good. Good that he had enjoyed a fine evening with a fine lady, good that he had shared his faith, good that he had helped a person who was in need of Jesus, good that he cared about this woman….

He cared about this woman … he *did* care about Mary, in the most unexpected, undeniable way. It came on so suddenly last night when he had been sharing Jesus with her; but of course he had always been a somewhat sensitive and compassionate person. As he had spoken to Mary last night, she had watched him with such wanting, such longing. She had sucked in every word he said, and she did it openly and willingly. Yes, Mary was definitely not as skeptical as she seemed at first; she was open to the Lord, and Bryan smiled at the thought of her. She had small, pretty eyes, graced with short eyelashes, and her features were so soft and delicate-looking. He had noticed so much about her last night besides just her curiosity of Jesus.

Indeed, he had smiled a lot today at the thought of hèr. Or was it at the thought of her grasping Jesus, realizing she needed Him? Yes, that was it. That was what he felt good about; that he had helped a longing human being realize they needed Jesus. He felt good because he had done the Lord's work. He didn't feel good because he was developing feelings for this woman … no.

Honestly, he wasn't developing feelings, and Bryan had actually found himself alarmed last night after dinner when he had analyzed his proceedings with Mary. He was worried that perhaps *she* might be developing feelings for *him*. There was something behind her nervous laughter and flushed cheeks that set off a warning, and Bryan had done his best to scrutinize his behavior. He knew Mary's intentions were quite innocent; that she had originally come over to discuss God and clear up confusion, but nevertheless, Bryan knew he should be extra careful with the way he spoke to her and touched her, not wanting to give her any mixed signal. Yes, Bryan had a past with heartbroken women who took his excessive friendliness as a sign for something more. His behavior wasn't something he practiced intentionally, no; he had always just had a way with people and had always seemed to be better friends with women than men. In the long run, that had proven to be a disadvantage. In fact, his social personality, especially with women, had been one of the crumbling factors of his marriage. His wife could never trust him completely, although she had every reason to. His friendships with other women – his co-workers and his wife's friends – had always been innocent. He loved his wife fiercely. In the end, Bryan knew he had done nothing wrong to screw up the marriage, but she had just been too insecure of herself and of the relationship to stay with Bryan. He had been so hurt and had vowed to work on his behavior around women and abstain from dating for a very long time.

This Monday afternoon, he vowed to speak with Mary the next chance that arose about his feelings for her … those of a loving and caring friend.

Fifteen

I planted, and Apollos watered, but God made it grow.

So neither the one who plants nor the one who waters is important because only God makes it grow....

We are God's coworkers. You are God's field.

– 1 Corinthians 3:6-9

The loud but relieving laughter of Lindsey in response to the comedy show on TV brought Caleb out of the bathroom half-dressed to see what all the commotion was about.

Lindsey's mouth was half-open, as if she was readying herself for another attack of laughter, and her eyes shone as she sat engrossed in the program. At the flicker of movement she caught in her peripheral vision, she glanced over at Caleb quickly, back to the program, and in a double take shot her eyes back toward Caleb. Her big eyes widened and her head lowered at the sight of Caleb shirtless, clad in his plaid green boxer shorts with his khaki slacks riding his ankles. In one hand was a toothbrush stuffed in his mouth full of toothpaste.

"Whatcha watchin'?" he mumbled, gazing at the glowing screen, oblivious to Lindsey's amused stare.

She began to chuckle. "Nice legs, Caleb."

Caleb glanced at Lindsey, then to his legs before replying, "Thanks."

"What are you doing with no clothes on?"

"What? I have clothes on. Just a minute." Caleb turned and walked into the bathroom to rinse out his mouth. Lindsey continued talking to him from her spot on the bed in the hotel room.

"Are you getting ready for bed already? It's too early."

"Oh no," Caleb yelled over the running water. "I was gonna tell you in a minute."

"What?"

A couple of minutes passed, and Caleb finally came out of the bathroom wearing twill slacks, a blue cotton collar shirt, and his blond hair combed nicely out of his face.

"Whoa," Lindsey's eyes went wide again. "You look … nice. What's the occasion?"

A sly smile spread across Caleb's face. "You, me, dinner, and a movie," he replied in a mock-deep, gentlemanly tone.

"What?" Lindsey said slowly, smiling. "You mean like, a date?"

"A date … nah! Just something fun to do; go out tonight, you know." With skill and ease he quickly flipped his wallet out of his back pocket and whipped out a credit card. "I'm paying."

Lindsey's smile widened and she turned her head to hide it, eventually turning back to face Caleb. "That's so … cool."

Caleb motioned with his head for Lindsey to get up off the bed. "So come on," he urged. "Get ready, and we'll go soon."

Lindsey hesitated for a moment before swinging her legs over the side of the bed. "So where are we going?"

"That's … a surprise."

"What if I don't like the place?" she asked, grinning, crossing her arms.

"Oh, don't worry, we're not going to the zoo."

"That's not what I meant."

"I know. It's not the Planetarium, either."

"Caleb!"

Caleb snickered. "If you really don't like the restaurant, then we'll go wherever you like."

"Wow, works for me!" Lindsey sat up, walked toward her luggage lying atop the small round table near the window and fished out a nice skirt outfit. Then she swung it over her shoulders and marched past Caleb into the bathroom, eyeing him with guile the whole way.

Lindsey's confident extraneous appearance faded as she stood staring at her reflection in the large mirror. What was it that she didn't like about herself tonight? Sure, she liked to dress nice occasionally for fun nights out with her friends such as this, but all at once her excitement faded and a sense of despondency took over. Was it the way her chest didn't fill out the dress in the sexy way Marianne's did, or was it the way her belly seemed to abnormally bulge out slightly? Marianne had told her that a bulging, round belly was normal for most women, but then why had Marianne's always seemed to be so flat and thin?

Lindsey was a thin girl, but she wasn't *skinny.* She had a nice shape with full hips that she oftentimes didn't like, round, but small thighs, and slender arms. There was a time when she had been skinnier, when her face hadn't been so round. She knew there was more cheekbone to her than her skin exposed. Her weight had ebbed slightly up and down the past few years, and although Lindsey had always remained relatively thin through it all, it caused her self-image and self-confidence to ebb, also.

The slinky black skirt, embroidered with white flowers and butterflies on the edge, hung securely in place around her waist while a white tank and black cardigan complemented it nicely. Yet, Lindsey frowned at herself. Her heart began its beating parade. She felt so ... ugly. Maybe it was her hair. She needed to do something cute with her hair – but she didn't have time to curl it. She could put some pretty clips in it, but then she remembered she left her small bag with most of her hair supplies in the car outside. Lindsey settled for a beaded headband.

Lindsey touched up her face with powder and worked on her lips with lipliner. She began reminiscing to when she didn't care so much about the way she looked. Who was she trying to impress? When she had been going out with Nick, he never seemed to notice or bother with her imperfections. She knew them all, but he had seemed unaware of them, and that had helped raise Lindsey's confidence most of the time. But now she didn't have Nick; she didn't have a boyfriend to constantly compliment her and make her feel the beauty that she couldn't always see was there.

But how crappy to have to rely on a guy to be the source of your self-confidence. So what am I worrying about now? Who cares about how I look, Caleb's not gonna care.

All of a sudden it hit her. Why was she so concerned about what Caleb's reaction to her would be? She was trying to impress him, trying to look good for him, but why? It wasn't as if she liked him or anything.

Frustrated with herself she threw down the lipliner, smacked her lips together to rub the color in, took one more unsatisfied glimpse into the mirror and threw the door open.

"Are you ready?" Caleb asked, standing up from his seat at the table.

"Sure," Lindsey replied quietly.

She looked great. Caleb hadn't had the pleasure of seeing Lindsey dressed up and actually looking feminine. Most of the time she was in her jeans and sweatshirts, her hair tied up in a short ponytail on top of her head. Tonight it was down, framing her face perfectly, bringing out the appealing roundness of her cheeks. Caleb was amazed at how pretty Lindsey looked; but then again, it wasn't something he had been totally unaware of. He was sure Lindsey wasn't aware of it. That just made him all the more determined to treat her to a fun night.

"You look very nice, Lindsey," he admitted cordially.

Her smile was demure as she gazed away from his handsome semblance and gazed at the floor. "Thanks," she said honestly. She knew Caleb meant what he said, and she wouldn't be hardheaded. She would accept his compliment.

"So let's get going!" he said excitedly, rubbing his hands together. He grabbed his coat and waited for Lindsey to precede him out the door before following right behind her.

Lindsey's head spun and her body lurched sideways as Caleb rounded the corner a little too fast.

"Oops," he said, grinning. "Sorry, I didn't mean to go so fast."

"It's okay," Lindsey said weakly, shaking her head as if to clear up the dizziness. Caleb saw her motion and frowned with concern.

"Are you feeling okay?"

"Yeah, I just got a little dizzy when you rounded that corner. Too much time in the car, that's all. I'm just hungry, and I'm tired of sitting around in this truck all day, you know?"

"Yeah. It's probably best that we're spending a couple nights here to rest from the road."

"Tell me about it. I didn't think a cross-country trip could be so boring and tiring and lonely."

"Lonely? With me?"

"Ah, you know what I meant," Lindsey insisted.

Did he? Was Lindsey really still feeling lonely?

"I felt really stupid about crying so bad on the phone earlier while I was talking to my grandpa."

Caleb looked at Lindsey to find her staring at him with her eyebrows raised in uncertainty. "Oh, don't worry about it," he assured. "You don't have to worry about me or what I think. When I found you, I just got all worried, that's all."

Lindsey's eyes sparkled, but Caleb missed it. "You did?"

"Well yeah. I didn't know what was wrong, and I didn't want you to be sad."

Keeping a steadfast gaze on the road, he was again unaware of the smile slowly circling her heart and overcoming her face.

"Well, that makes me feel better."

"Good. Now I have a confession to make."

"Huh?"

Caleb signaled then and pulled the truck over to the side of the road. With the engine purring lowly, he turned to face Lindsey.

Whoa, she thought. *What's going on? Is he gonna tell me he loves me, or something?* she said jokingly to herself.

"I uh…." his head lowered and Lindsey could just make out the corners of his mouth raising. He looked at her to reveal laughing eyes. "I don't know where we are."

Lindsey just raised her eyebrows in question.

Caleb chuckled. "I'm lost and I can't seem to find the restaurant that I was going to take you to."

"Which was?"

"The Olive Garden."

"Are you sure they have one here?"

"Yeah. It's somewhere around here, I know it."

"Oh. Well, just to make you feel better," Lindsey started, fixing her gaze directly into Caleb's eyes, "I'm not very big with pasta."

"Really?"

"Really."

Caleb sat forward, seemingly satisfied. "So what do you say to a picnic?"

"A picnic? Caleb, it's kinda too dark to go eat outside anywhere."

"Hey, there are parks in this city. Well-lighted parks."

"Let's hope you can find one," Lindsey stated satirically.

Caleb couldn't explain the odd tension riding between himself and Lindsey at that moment, as the two sat across from each other on one of the park's many picnic benches. The park itself was mostly abandoned that night, save for a few strollers who passed by every now and then on evening walks. Their mumbling voices mixed with the whistle through the trees, the roar of nearby engines, and the occasional tweet of some type of bird, creating a dissonant chorus that added to the odd strain of the moment.

They had decided upon old-fashioned burgers and fries, taking their meals to this park to eat and talk, enjoying the night. But so far small talk had been the majority of their forced conversation, and silence mingled in between. They chomped on their burgers and sipped their sodas, glancing around uncomfortably. At least, *Caleb* was uncomfortable. To his knowing, Lindsey seemed fine and relaxed, engaged in the consumption of her meal. She didn't seem to mind the disconversation between them.

Caleb, on the other hand, was beginning to feel a little foolish as to why he couldn't think of much to talk about. What did it matter? It wasn't as if this was a date. Yet, that's what he was acting like it was – and he was the nervous, lovesick boy who wanted too much to impress his date.

Impress *Lindsey*? What for? It's not like he had ever tried before. They had already spent almost a whole week together and he hadn't yet felt this ... nervous. He couldn't possibly be developing feelings for Lindsey, could he? No, that couldn't happen; he hadn't even known her for that long. He shook his head of the thought. There was never a problem before with developing conversation between them. There had never even been a problem with silence, which at times could last for a couple hours on end. No tension, no nervousness, no insecurity around this girl.

Insecurity.

"I am not insecure."

Lindsey glanced up. "What?"

"Huh?" Caleb shot his head up and found Lindsey's eyes on his.

Lindsey began to smile. "You just said you weren't insecure."

"Oh. Did I say that out loud?"

Lindsey nodded with an air of satisfaction in her smile. Caleb was embarrassed. Yep, she could tell he was feeling a little absurd at that moment. And it caused her great satisfaction. "So what's going on in that mind of yours, huh?" she asked curiously, leaning forward, resting her arms up on the tabletop.

Caleb's eyebrows raised and he leaned back, folding his arms. "Nothing of interest to you," he answered complacently with a touch of a smile on his lips.

What a cutie. The thought darted through her mind so unexpectedly that it caught Lindsey unaware. Sure, Caleb was pretty good-looking, so why shouldn't she be thinking it?

Because she meant it so much more than she would have him know. She couldn't deny that she had been developing feelings for him since almost their first encounter after her car accident. She had meant what she said that first night – that Caleb was her hero. Yes, when she had first laid eyes on him in his truck while he drove her to the hospital, she thought she was staring into the face of an angel – which was a leap of faith to say, since she didn't know whether she even believed in angels or not. But even through her fuzzy vision that night, she couldn't deny that soft face which spoke with such a soothing voice.

And now, staring at Caleb from across the wooden picnic table, she noted his handsomeness even more. His narrow face graced with such chiseled features – surely, Lindsey thought, she must have a larger, rounder face than his – and his soft skin, delicate, thick lips...

Lindsey's heart fluttered suddenly, and she realized that yes, indeed, she really liked Caleb. He was attractive, and not only physically. Although he held personal views and beliefs that Lindsey did not share at the moment, she found that they only added to his warmth and caring personality, and to her affinity for him. He was also humorous and entertaining, especially that short time ago when he had obliviously walked out of the bathroom with his pants down, acting as if he hadn't a care that Lindsey was gaping at him incredulously. He sure wasn't shy.

And he *was* her saving grace; he had caused this trek across country to be so much more than it could have been. Caleb had truly helped lighten her moods and brighten her spirits, whether he was aware of it or not.

What was that smirk across Lindsey's face supposed to mean? After eyeing him for a few moments, she resumed eating her dinner, and Caleb was left to wonder what was actually going on in *her* head. There had been quite a few times when he had caught a certain twinkle in Lindsey's eyes as she gazed at Caleb, but he had never questioned if it meant anything. There had also been seemingly numerous times when the twinkle would be non-existent and instead her eyes would be glazed over, and unwavering; unnerving. Poor Lindsey, her mood and her spirits were always so unstable. One minute she'd seem silly and excited, and the next she'd be depressed. It bothered and concerned Caleb and only deepened his feelings of guardianship. For some reason, one which he was convinced to be coming from the Lord, he felt the need to protect Lindsey, to make her feel happier, and to fill her heart.

But wasn't that the Lord's job? Caleb reminded himself that he was only a tool for the Lord's workings. He mustn't get into the habit of thinking it was all up to him, because if it was, it would only end up in disappointment. Caleb had to keep on trusting God, and believe that He would ultimately end up fulfilling Lindsey's life. Sure, there was nothing wrong with caring about Lindsey and wanting to be a significant part of her life, but he had to remember that God's will for Lindsey was the most important, not his.

He watched as Lindsey stood up and began walking away from the picnic table, aching for a short walk in the cool breeze. Her hair played on the tips of the wind, and she brought up a hand to swipe it out of her face.

Caleb didn't say a word as she left, didn't even ask where she was going. He just sat there, staring at her as she stopped in the middle of the concrete sidewalk and inhaled the fresh air. Even now as he watched her, he knew his caring for her went deeper than friendship. But he was scared of it. Lindsey wasn't, after all, a Christian like he was. He knew it would be dangerous to get too seriously involved with her because of their conflicting beliefs. Jesus Christ was the most important person in Caleb's life – He had saved Caleb and changed his life dramatically – and Caleb knew that if he was to be in a serious relationship with a woman, it should be someone who loved the Lord as much as he did. That way, there was no faith to compromise, and what could be better than two people sharing their faith in Jesus together, always loving Him and loving each other? Yes, although still a "baby" Christian, Caleb realized the importance of putting Jesus at the center of any relationship. He couldn't fully surrender himself to the Lord if his girlfriend didn't feel the same way. He'd feel too much that he'd have to choose between the two, and that sort of relationship would certainly be conflicting.

How could he have felt this strongly for Lindsey all of a sudden, out of nowhere? But even as he thought it, he knew his feelings hadn't come on suddenly. They had been growing steadily since almost that first day in the hospital, when he'd felt the need to stick by the hospital until he knew she was going to be all right. He didn't forget the way she deemed him her "hero," or the pleased look on her face during their first conversation in her hospital room, or the way she ran up and hugged him that next morning when she found out he hadn't left her. All those small things had manifested themselves in his heart, and kept on growing larger and larger, and continued to grow even at that moment.

Caleb was baffled as to how it was that he could come to care for someone so much in such a short time. And the trip across country was only half over. How would he survive the next few days without revealing himself to Lindsey? More importantly, how would he get by once it was all over and she was gone? Well, she wouldn't be living too far, just a state away. They could visit as often as was possible.

Oh, what was he thinking? He shouldn't even be thinking about starting a relationship with Lindsey. The most important thing now should be her relationship with Jesus! Or her non-existent one, to be more accurate.

Confused and muddled all at once over his swirling emotions, Caleb decided it was a good time to pray. In fact, it was the *right* time to pray.

Inhaling the clean, cool air filled Lindsey's lungs with an invigoration that was needed at the moment. She wasn't oblivious to the odd quietness of the evening, or even the slight tension that laced itself through her and Caleb. How weird that was, considering that the beginning of the evening had been just fine.

Feeling a sudden burst of energy that she hoped would compensate for the oddness of the evening, she started quickly back toward Caleb to convince him to take a walk with her. As she neared him, she found his head bowed slightly and his folded hands up on the table. Her eyes narrowed in confusion, but she knew at once what he was doing. He was praying.

Lindsey found it quite intriguing, for she hadn't come upon Caleb like this before. She wondered what he was he saying. Obviously he was speaking to God, because that's what praying was. The whole notion of it all was actually kind of … neat. She smiled in the soft glow of the moonlight, watching Caleb as he humbly poured out his thoughts to the Lord.

Lindsey discovered herself wondering what it must be like to pray; how it must feel. She had never prayed before, obviously, she wasn't even quite sure about God's existence. But Caleb made it so real. He made God so real, just by these small things he did, and of course by his whole testimony of the way God had incredibly changed his life. How could she doubt that? How could she doubt Caleb's sincerity and his warmth, his selflessness and his protection over her? She liked Caleb so much, and she admired him for his leap of faith in believing in a Lord that had never seemed anything more to Lindsey but fantasy.

Caleb glanced up to find Lindsey watching him. He suddenly felt his face heat with a small bit of embarrassment that she had caught him praying, but it just as quickly faded when he noted the small smile polishing her lips.

Crinkling the food wrappers in his hands, he stood up, tossed the garbage in a nearby wastebasket, and said, "So, what should we do now?"

"I was just thinking about taking a walk. What do you think?"

"I think … that's a good idea."

"It'll be fun. I used to take walks along the beach with my mom all the time when I was little."

"Lead the way," Caleb smiled.

Lindsey smiled wider and stood resolutely for a moment, taking in Caleb's appearance and his whole … presence. She was glad that she was there with him, spending time with him, having him look after her. He was, undoubtedly, a good friend. A best friend. She wondered if maybe he could even be more – if he felt the same about her that she did about him.

Caleb noted Lindsey's stalling, and for the smallest moment he had the urge to reach out and grab her hand, leading her on a romantic stroll across the park. But he decided against it, once again appealing God to interfere on the moment and keep Caleb's thoughts focused more realistically, and less dramatically.

"C'mon," Lindsey finally urged. She turned and began running across the green lawn, which was lighted dimly from both the glow of the moon low in the sky, and the park streetlamps lining the walkways and poking out of the lawn. Caleb followed after, and in a matter of minutes, he caught up and the two were enjoying an easy-going walk, unable to suppress their laughter, or their buoyant spirits.

Sixteen

Jesus said to him, "As far as possibilities go, everything is possible for the person who believes."

– Mark 9:23

That Tuesday morning, Mary Jenkins awoke to a new, unaccustomed feeling: contentment. That was the only way to explain it. Yesterday, decorating the house with Andrea, had been fun and exhilarating beyond understanding. She decided it must have been the holiday anticipation, the excitement about her new knowledge of Christ, and of course, her wonderful dinner with Bryan.

She had awakened with the handsome man's face in her mind yesterday night but had quickly shaken it off in an attempt to make it to work on time. This morning, however, she had the day off, and so she lay relinquishing her time and focusing a bit of it on Bryan.

On Sunday night during their dinner, Bryan had prayed with Mary two times. Once, after their conversation about God, when Bryan had asked for the Lord to reveal Himself to Mary, and for her to keep open eyes and an open mind for his evidence in her life; and then again right before they ate when Bryan thanked the Lord for the meal. Mary had thought it was wonderful. He was so articulate in his prayers, with the words just flowing out naturally, almost as if they'd been rehearsed. Whether they had been rehearsed or not, Mary only knew that Bryan spoke them with an honest, earnest heart.

Suddenly overwhelmed with the need to pray, Mary sat up in bed, thinking. She had never really prayed before, but all at once she felt compelled to try it out. Why not? What could she lose? There were a few things on her mind and burdens on her heart that she felt she needed to get off her chest.

"Dear Lord, uh," she spoke aloud somewhat clumsily. Gripping her hands together even more tightly, she sat up straighter. "I just felt like I needed to do this. I believe that You're real. Growing up, I've questioned Your existence. I wasn't around many Christians who knew You the way Bryan does. And so now this morning, I come to You with a believing heart, and

I'm a little confused as to what to do next. This is all so new to me, and I hope it won't fade away."

Mary opened her eyes, glancing around at her surroundings. Indeed, everything good in her life had seemed to eventually fade, leaving space for only the familiar, insipid drone of life. Her eyes played around the bedroom scene; yes, everything looked normal, as it did most mornings. Her tiny square bedroom with bare walls and one short dresser next to the door were hardly the sight that would make one wake up and exclaim, "This is going to be a great day!" What was it exactly about believing in Christ that made people's lives so different? Maybe it was this feeling, this strangely happy feeling. But it wasn't as if Mary hadn't felt it before, when she hadn't known about God. There were times in her life when that strange feeling would sweep over her and cause her heart to smile. Those were usually at the highpoints in her life – when she was a child and on her way to the carnival for a day of excitement; when she graduated from high school and spent the next week with all her friends on the most extreme vacation of her life; when she met Ted for the first time; when they married, and when Andrea was born. Yes, those times were filled with inexplicable joy and contentment.

But all those times had eventually come to and end. Mary had grown up in a large family with little money. She hadn't just been a rebellious teenager; she had been pretty self-sufficient and responsible in most cases. She had spent all of her teenage years working and trying to support *herself*, even when living with her family. Looking back now, Mary realized that her childhood and early adulthood had been filled with mostly disappointment, confusion, heartache, and occasionally a little depression here and there. Just as there were times when a slice of joy would creep up on her, there were numerous times a bolt of melancholy would hit her. Her life had been filled with many ups and downs, like a wild ride on an unstable rollercoaster.

This morning was another one of those good feelings, which Mary was grateful for, because she'd take whatever bouts of happiness came her way. So often, even in her busy adulthood, she was forgetful of the world of contentment, being so preoccupied in the confinement of just trying to live and survive. She welcomed the days when she had work off and something fun planned in its place. Today would be one of those days.

Something was different about today, though. Something accompanied the gleeful feeling, something other than knowing she could be stress-free today. It almost seemed to come on for no particular reason. Even yesterday when she knew she had to work, she didn't find herself sighing with disappointment and dragging herself to work. She spent the whole day busily servicing customers with a genuine smile and positive attitude. Then, after work, with the anticipation of picking up Andrea and heading home for some holiday decorating, she had felt even better. There hadn't seemed to be any special reason why she had felt so good.

Just God. Just knowing she believed in Him.

She hoped that this morning God wouldn't turn out to be one of those temporary things. And so she prayed that He wouldn't.

"You know what I was just thinking?" Lindsey commented Tuesday morning as she stood in front of the full-length mirror in the hotel room, combing her wet hair.

"What's that?" Caleb asked, unwrapping the chocolate chip muffin as he sat cross-legged on his bed, disheveled in appearance from just waking up. His hair was half-sticking up from his head, his eyes dark and tired, and his prickly face an unshaven mess. Lindsey looked at him through the mirror. He looked even more tired this morning than he had other mornings. Probably because they hadn't gotten to bed last night until late, due to the fact that they knew they wouldn't be hitting the road early and could sleep in. It was almost 11:00 in the morning.

"I was just thinking that I should probably call my dad."

"Hmm?" Caleb caught her eye in the mirror. He quickly swallowed a piece of muffin. "Your dad?"

"Yeah. I mean, I called him before I left, you know, but I just got the answering machine." Lindsey put her brush down and turned to face Caleb. "I should probably try calling him again, just to make sure he got the message, you know?"

Caleb nodded. "Yeah, that might be smart."

Lindsey shook her head, a look of disgust on her face. "What was I thinking? Leaving a message that I was coming across the country to find him, and then going? I didn't even wait to make sure he got the message and called back."

Caleb raised his eyes, smiled widely, and shrugged his shoulders. "I just don't know what you were thinking."

"Me neither. I hope he's not gone on vacation or anything."

"Hey," Caleb sat up. "Don't worry about it. If for some reason you can't find your dad because he's gone, or whatever, you can just come home with me, and we'll figure something out there."

Lindsey was suddenly struck with a new sense of worry. "What if he doesn't even want me there, huh?" She gazed at Caleb with a fearful look invading her eyes. "I haven't even talked to him or acknowledged him in ten years. This really doesn't make any sense at all, Caleb! What am I doing?"

Sensing that she might topple over any moment from her panicky emotions, Caleb flung himself off the bed and walked toward Lindsey. Facing her, he put his hands on both of her arms at her side, staring directly in her eyes. “Lindsey, it’s going to be okay. I’ll be here to help you if there’s anything that comes up.”

“But what if he doesn’t *want* me, Caleb?”

“Why wouldn’t he? You’re his own daughter.”

“But I’ve ignored him, Caleb.”

“But he’s done the same to you, Lindsey. Don’t feel bad....”

“No he hasn’t!” Lindsey blurted out. Caleb stepped back. “He hasn’t ignored me. Not entirely, anyway. He tried keeping in touch with me, and he always did with my mom in keeping up with the child support payments and everything....”

Caleb raised his eyebrows, urging Lindsey to go on.

“He sent me cards and gifts on holidays and my birthdays, but after a few years they gradually stopped because *I* wouldn’t acknowledge them, or him. I didn’t want anything to do with him because of what he did to us. Mom pretty much felt the same way I had. My poor dad probably felt so helpless.”

“You’re talking about your ‘poor dad,’ but you don’t deny that he wasn’t nice to you or your mom, right? I mean, he hurt you guys, and then he left you.”

“Yeah, but he left for a good reason. By leaving, we weren’t ever hurt again.”

“Well, sure you were. You didn’t have a dad anymore.”

Lindsey’s eyes looked as if they were about to spill over. “But that was because of my own doing!”

“But it still hurt you, didn’t it?”

Lindsey stopped, gazing helplessly at the floor. She had so many mixed feelings when it came to her dad. She didn’t know who to blame for their lack of communication. It was true, she hated the fact that he had left her and her mom so many years ago, but hadn’t it been for their own good? As much as it hurt to have her father gone, it had relieved her also. And she was never blind to how much it relieved her mother. She had become a different woman, more independent, strong-willed, and loving. Jillian and Lindsey had grown so close after Terry’s escape. Terry and Jillian had met only a couple times after he left – when they were going through their divorce, and then once when Terry had come across the country to see Lindsey. She wanted nothing to do with him, though. Jillian hadn’t even urged Lindsey to see him; she felt the same way about him as Lindsey did. They were both still angry, and slightly scared. So Jillian had explained to him that it might be best if he stayed away, and he did. After years of unresponded phone calls and unacknowledged letters and cards, he had abandoned all forms of communication, besides the monthly child support payment, which came in the mail.

Lindsey walked over to her bed and sat down. "When I was little, I was so angry at him that I didn't realize how much I was probably hurting him by not keeping in touch. I was too concerned with my own feelings of anger and hurt. Now I realize that my dad was as innocent in this whole affair as my mother and I were. We were all victims of some sort, you know?" She glanced up at Caleb, and he took a seat on his bed across from hers.

"Still, you shouldn't blame yourself, totally."

"I know, but I can't seem to help it."

"You know what I think?"

"What?" Lindsey asked.

"I think that it's good that you're feeling this way, because it means you're forgiving your father; being selfless, thinking about his feelings. A lot of people in your position would probably hold on to their grudges. They wouldn't even try to get back in touch."

"But if my mom hadn't died, and if things hadn't changed back home, I don't know if I would even be thinking about my dad. I'm kind of going on this whole trek for myself, really."

"So what?" Caleb assured her. "Regardless of your circumstances, or even your motives, you're here, doing this, aren't you? You're trying to find your dad, and in the process you've come to realize that he needs your forgiveness and love. That realization would've come sooner or later, you know."

Lindsey nodded, still watching the floor. Caleb continued. "I can't even imagine how hard this must be for you, Lindsey. I would be really nervous if I was in your position. I mean, you really did grow up without a father, and so it's got to be difficult to try and regain him in your life all of a sudden."

Lindsey looked up at him then, gazing at him with her sad eyes and downcast lips, and for just a moment Caleb wanted to reach out and kiss those lips. He wanted to hug her and make her feel better, and help her to forget about all this "father stuff" plaguing her. Before he was able to act on his unexpected urgings, though, Lindsey's frown turned up, her eyes shone, and she let out a fit of laughter. Caleb leaned back, frowning.

"What's so funny?" he asked.

Lindsey just shook her head, unable to answer.

"No, what?" Caleb prompted.

"It's just … just … you look so … terrible!" Lindsey burst out.

Caleb crossed his arms. "Thank you very much. I'm glad to know you're smiling again at *my* expense."

"No, it's just that...." Lindsey began, unable to stop her giggling now because of the offended look on Caleb's face. "I just feel bad because you must be so much more tired than I had thought, with all that driving and everything."

"You could say that."

"How 'bout I take you out today, huh? We'll do whatever you want."

Caleb tipped his head to the side and cast his eyes toward the ceiling, acting as if he was thinking. Then, looking back at Lindsey, he began nodding his head with an insidious half-smile forming on his mouth. "Okay then," he huffed. "We're going to the zoo!"

"Oh!" Lindsey moaned, throwing herself back onto the bed.

"That's what you get for saying I look terrible!" Caleb feigned insult and bolted up off the bed, making for the bathroom door. Lindsey watched him, smiling the whole way. When he was finally inside with the door locked, and the shower running, Lindsey sighed and spoke quietly to herself.

"Well, Caleb, you're not *that* terrible-looking. In fact, most of the times you're actually quite ... good-looking." She stood up, walked over to the mirror, and resumed brushing her hair. "So much so that I can't stand it sometimes."

Caleb stepped out of the bathroom with a towel wrapped around his waist, and hair soaking and spread madly over his head. As he walked past Lindsey, he shook his head, causing water drops to fly in all directions. Lindsey shrieked and crawled backward on the bed to escape the flying water droplets. Lindsey watched as Caleb made his way to the other side of the room to retrieve some jeans and a faded blue sweatshirt from his luggage.

"I called my dad," she said.

"Already?"

"Yeah, while you were in the shower. He wasn't home though."

Caleb turned to her, a look of condolence on his face. "Got the answering machine again, huh?"

"Yeah," Lindsey breathed, disappointed. "Most likely he's working. He's a businessman, I know that much."

"What does he do?"

"Ah, I'm not sure. He works with some big company; I think he sells stuff; or comes up with product slogans, or something like that."

Caleb raised one eyebrow in question.

"Well, I never cared enough to pay attention to his life."

"Okay," Caleb answered, unimpressed. "So did you leave a message?"

"Oh yeah. I just said a little about you, and that we were getting close to Virginia. I gave him our hotel name and room number so that he can call back." Caleb noticed the grave expression crossing Lindsey's paling face.

"What's wrong?" he asked, expecting he knew the answer.

"Oh, I don't know. I'm just nervous about talking to him again. To tell you the truth, I was kind of glad I got the answering machine just now."

As Caleb walked back toward the bathroom, he patted Lindsey on the shoulder. "Ah, it'll be all right, you'll see." Lindsey just wrinkled her nose. "Oh, hey," Caleb began as a thought hit him. "When you talked to your grandpa yesterday, did he say anything about whether he might have talked to your dad or not?"

Lindsey shot her eyes at Caleb and sat up straight. The thought had never crossed her mind before. She knew her father knew Dan Johns' phone number. "No, he didn't say anything," she replied. "That's probably not a good thing, huh?"

"Well, why don't you call him really quick and see?"

The ringing phone in Dan and Chelsea's large bedroom echoed down the hall, and before Dan could make it up the stairs to answer it, Chelsea reached over from her position on the bed and grabbed it. "Hello," she answered in a low, weary voice.

"Hi, Grandma, it's Lindsey."

"Oh Lindsey," she cried, sitting up in bed, relief pouring from her voice. "It's so good to hear from you. Dan said you called yesterday."

"Yeah, I did. I'm sorry I didn't call sooner."

"No, no, honey, don't apologize. Dan told me everything. I'm so sorry you were in that car accident. It must've been scary."

Stunned by her grandmother's gentle and understanding tone, Lindsey was suddenly at a loss for words. "Well, it wasn't that bad."

"Well, I'm just glad you're all right." She paused for a moment, choosing her next words carefully. "Lindsey, I'm also sorry that … that I gave you such a hard time before you left. I was just … well … I don't really have any excuse for my behavior."

Lindsey's eyes grew wide in astonishment. Was her stubborn grandmother actually apologizing to her? Lindsey felt as if she was the one who needed to be doing the apologizing. "Oh, well, don't worry about it," she replied awkwardly.

Chelsea looked up to find her husband standing in the doorway, watching the conversation with growing amusement. Chelsea smiled at him and continued talking. "I saw Marianne yesterday while I was shopping, and she sort of helped me realize that I wasn't being very understanding to you."

"She did?" Lindsey frowned.

"Yeah, we started talking about you and she told me about Caleb and the wreck and everything."

"Was that before or after Grandpa told you I called?"

"Before."

Suddenly ashamed that her grandmother had to hear about her story from another source beside herself, Lindsey winced. "Oh, I'm sorry you didn't hear that from me."

"Well, I have to admit I was angry at first. I was probably a little rude to Marianne, but she actually started following me through the parking lot and sticking up for you."

Lindsey smiled. "Really?"

"Yeah, she's got quite a determined personality."

"Yes, she does. She's kind of stubborn, like you," Lindsey laughed.

"Yeah, I have to say she kind of reminds me of me when I was her age. But anyway, when I arrived home, Dan had news that you had called just a few moments before. He told me everything, and you can't imagine how relieved I was."

"Oh, I think I can."

"I'm sorry that I didn't trust you, Lindsey. I mean, when I heard from Marianne, I began thinking all these terrible things, like maybe you had lied to us, or were trying to deceive us. I guess I was just worried about you with this Caleb fellow."

"Yeah, Grandpa gave me the whole lecture."

"Well, even if he didn't, I'm not going to say anything. I trust you, and to tell you the truth, I kind of feel a little at ease to know that you have someone traveling with you now. Caleb sounds like a nice guy, from what Dan's told me."

Chelsea exchanged a glance with her husband. He was smiling widely, proudly.

"Thanks, Grandma. That really means a lot to me. And I owe you an apology too because of my behavior."

Chelsea was just as stunned at Lindsey's apology as Lindsey had been at hers. "Oh, well, it's all over now, okay? No hard feelings. You're my family, and I'll love you no matter what."

Lindsey lowered her head, her heart suddenly full of emotion. It was so good to finally hear such understanding from her grandmother. She felt as if a gap in her heart had been filled with that love that she had always wanted from her family. Although she had always known Chelsea loved her, she had never quite felt it.

"You know what? It was actually Caleb who got me to realize what cool grandparents I have."

"Well, I think I like that Caleb boy," Chelsea admitted. She knew at once that there had been a change in Lindsey during the course of her trip that Chelsea had feared she would never witness again; she was more inviting and pleasant. Chelsea couldn't deny that the boy must have had something to do with it. In short, he seemed to be a good influence in Lindsey's life, but Chelsea didn't voice her thoughts on that.

"I'm glad you do. I like him too," Lindsey replied honestly.

"Well, I just hope the rest of your trip goes well, Lindsey."

"Yeah. Hey, there was actually something important that I called to ask about."

"What's that?"

"I just called my dad again to make sure that he got my message before I left, but he wasn't there. I was wondering if maybe you guys had heard from him."

Chelsea's face lit up with excitement. "Oh, Lindsey, actually we did! He called sometime last week. Dan talked to him."

"Oh, can I talk to grandpa about it, then?"

"Sure, honey." Chelsea motioned Dan into the room, and handed him the receiver.

"Hey there."

"Hi, Grandpa. Grandma said that Dad called?"

"Yes, he did."

"What did he say, how did he sound?"

Catching the uncertain tone in her voice, Dan quickly spoke in a reassuring note. "He sounded just fine. In fact, he's looking forward to your arrival."

"Really?" Lindsey's eyes teared up.

"Yes, really."

Marianne had to shut her eyes to keep the tears from rolling out. After her encounter with Chelsea yesterday, she had all she could to keep her mind off of Lindsey, but to no avail. And now, she sat in her bedroom this Tuesday afternoon after classes, gazing at old photographs of herself and Lindsey on a school trip to Mexico two years ago.

Even among her growing tears, Marianne couldn't help but laugh at one particular picture. In it, against a backdrop of a city park, Lindsey was lying on her stomach in the bright green grass with Marianne, an absurd expression painted across her face. Marianne, on the other hand, had been laughing too hard while the picture was being taken to look up at the camera and smile. Recalling back now, she couldn't remember what it was that she had been laughing about.

It didn't matter. It could have been anything. Lindsey and Marianne had always been the type of girls who would laugh over the smallest thing; it often made them the most obnoxious and annoying of everyone involved. During that particular trip, Lindsey and Marianne had been warned several times to "keep it quiet," to "act your own age," or even to "behave!" Such juvenile warnings had never failed to encourage more laughter and "misbehavior" from them.

Marianne smiled now as she recalled one instant where, during one of the nights at the hotel, she and Lindsey, far too excited and hyper to go to sleep, had decided to play tag around the hotel. They tramped down hallways, sped up staircases, and rode the elevators until the early hours of morning. It was only when one of their adult leaders caught them stomping around in the lobby that they were forced back to their rooms. The night didn't end there, however. Lindsey and Marianne, of course, had requested a bedroom together and so had stayed up almost the whole rest of the night talking and laughing about anything and everything in the world.

That trip to Mexico, along with just being with Lindsey and sharing their usual fun together, had been one of the greatest experiences of Marianne's life.

So what had happened to all that fun? Where had all those unforgettable times gone? Why had they just stopped?

A wave of heartache and sorrow crashed upon Marianne like a giant wave hitting shore and causing the sand to ripple and part. Lindsey wasn't just away; she was *gone*. She had actually taken her stuff and moved, without a second thought as to what it might do to Marianne; as to what it had *already* done to her.

Seventeen

Don't pay people back with evil for the evil they do to you, or ridicule those who ridicule you. Instead, bless them, because you were called to inherit a blessing.
– 1 Peter 3:9

The October sun was high in the sky, just beginning to descend in the west as a thick patch of dark clouds began blanketing it, dulling its brightness. Lindsey shivered in the passenger's side seat of the Ford from the thin breeze that was wafting in through Caleb's open door. She reached over to the driver's side just enough to grab the door handle and pull it closed. After a few seconds, though, Caleb opened it right back up and jumped into the truck.

"So, is it closed, or what?"

A look of disappointment was spread across his face as he nodded his head.

"Yeah. I should've known the zoo wouldn't be open in October."

"Well, it wasn't something I had thought about either, if it makes you feel any better," Lindsey replied sympathetically.

Caleb just raised his eyebrows at her and started his truck. As the vehicle began gliding through the city streets aimlessly with Caleb silent at the wheel, Lindsey suddenly felt an overwhelming impulse to make him smile. It was clear from his straight-laced expression and quiet demeanor that he was obviously upset.

"I'm … I'm really sorry that you didn't get to go to the zoo like you wanted."

Caleb shrugged. "Uh, it's okay. It's not like you really wanted to go anyway, so it probably wouldn't have been very fun."

A pang of guilt stabbed Lindsey from the back, right through her heart and out the other side. He was right. She had made it no mystery that she was not the kind to get excited in the least about seeing a bunch of animals. She had been complaining the whole way to the zoo about it, trying to convince Caleb to reconsider. There were, of course, so many other, more stimulating things to do in a large city. So now, when she should be smiling with a touch of pride at her wish being granted, she found herself feeling overwhelmed by this thing she could only define as … guilt and … selfishness?

She cringed a little at the thought. "I … I'm sorry. I know I wasn't being very fair," she mumbled, forcing a smile. "I know you really wanted to go and I was kind of being a party-pooper about it."

"It's okay, really," Caleb assured her, although his tone was dubious.

"No, it's not. I mean, you would probably sit through anything I wanted to do, and at least pretend to enjoy it, but I don't even try to be tolerant when I'm faced with going along with something I don't want to do."

"Lindsey, it's really okay. I mean, the zoo's closed, and there's nothing we can do about it. Besides, I honestly don't want to do anything that you don't want to do; not only because it wouldn't be fun for me, but because I wouldn't want to put you through something that you couldn't stand."

Lindsey almost clenched her fists at Caleb's flat tone of voice. She couldn't tell whether he was being serious or speaking in a fit of sarcasm because he was truly upset.

"Ugh! We are talking about a *zoo*, aren't we?"

"Well, sure."

"Caleb," Lindsey whined. "I hope you're not really mad at me about it. I really am sorry, I am. I mean, I could've survived through a zoo, it's not that big of a deal."

"I know."

"You're making me feel guilty, you know!" Lindsey rambled on. "Somehow, in your own little way, you're making me feel guilty, and I really hate that feeling."

A thin smile spread across Caleb's lips. He glanced over at Lindsey. "Well, good. If I can't go to the zoo and see my animals, at least I can get some satisfaction out of knowing that you actually feel bad for giving me such a hard time."

"*And* I feel bad because you don't get to see your animals, not just because I gave you a hard time. I really do."

"Well, good. You should feel bad."

"Thank you, that makes me feel a lot BETTER!"

"It makes me feel better," Caleb exclaimed behind sparkling eyes.

"I know I've said it before, and I'll say it again. What *is* the big deal between you and animals, anyway? And I'm not trying to be rude or anything; I really want to know. I mean, you're like a little kid or something; all giddy about going to the zoo, and then totally dejected when you find out it's closed."

"Dejected, huh?"

Lindsey frowned.

"I'm not *dejected*," Caleb said light-heartedly. "I just like giving you a hard time."

"Okay, okay," Lindsey said, putting her hands up in the air as to silence any further conversation. "Let's just forget about all this silly zoo business and find something else to do so that we can stop wandering aimlessly around Lincoln."

"So what do you want to do?"

"It's your day to pick, remember? You couldn't do your animal thing, so pick something else, anything else. I won't complain."

Caleb lowered his eyes at her.

"I promise!" Lindsey said.

"Okay, okay," Caleb replied. "I just want to make sure that I don't choose anything that's not to your liking," he said jokingly.

"Shut up!" Lindsey screamed, hitting him in the arm. "Stop trying to make me feel bad!"

"I don't have to *try*, you're too easy," Caleb laughed.

"Ugh! Just drive!"

"Okay, okay, seriously," Caleb announced. "Why don't we see if the go-kart place is open, and then go back to the mall. There was a CD I saw yesterday that I think I want to buy."

"Sounds good to me," Lindsey complied.

A few days away from Lincoln, in a large house in a small city in Virginia, Terry Milholland sat on the porch swing outside staring at the orange sun, which was high in the cloudy October sky. The air on his neck was cool, and after being outside for almost a half-hour, Terry shivered from it. Yet, he ignored it. He wasn't in the mind-set to worry about the weather. He had come out here not long ago with the intention of thinking some stuff over, but so far, there were too many things cluttering his brain to make order of any of it; therefore, his mind was still a blank pallet, void of any reason or inference or results.

And so he had been slumping lonesomely on the porch swing that Tuesday afternoon staring; wanting to think and sort things through, but without success. What could he possibly come up with that might alleviate his feelings, his confusion, his desperate sense of being trapped in a dead-end alley with no way out?

And trapped he was. There was Lindsey, whom he hadn't seen or spoken with in nearly ten years. He wanted to, he had tried to be as much a father to her as he could, but living across the country had made it hard. All he could do was send cards and gifts, all of which were unreceived or just unacknowledged. Terry had never blamed Lindsey for disowning him and never wanting to speak to him. He had, after all, put her and her mother through many years of physical and emotional hurt, heartache, and fear. Even before Lindsey was born, Terry hadn't been the loving husband that Jillian deserved. He was an irritable, impatient, easily distracted man. His family was only the second half of his life; his work was the first. Indeed, his career was his most important asset. When either work or his wife called for his precious time, it was usually work that won over his heart.

Not to get him wrong, he did love Jillian, had loved her when he married her. But that didn't change the kind of man he was. Work was his livelihood, his living, the way he supported himself and his family. He couldn't afford to lose his job, but he could afford to lose … his wife?

No, he never intended for things to turn out the way they had with Jillian. He had loved her, and he had loved the way his life changed after he married her. Married life was sweet; indeed, Jillian was his first marriage, and he had been young – not even out of college. After they married, Jillian had received so much of his positive attention. After finishing college and earning his business degree, he had made sure he found the perfect job that would support them and a prospective family. It was a high-paying, well-respected occupation. But it was also one that required a great deal of his time.

After a while, when marriage wasn't as new and exciting, Terry's career tipped up the balance scale, leaving Jillian on the empty, weightless end. Terry started devoting too much time to his work and his social life; which usually consisted of late nights out with the guys drinking and visiting strip bars. And Jillian became one among the many statistics of neglected and abused wives who felt helpless, lonely, and depressed.

Terry wasn't physically abusive at first, and hadn't been until after Lindsey was born. The abuse he burdened Jillian with was verbal and emotional. If the house wasn't picked up when he got home from work, Terry complained; if anything was out of order in her appearance or demeanor, he complained; basically if anything wasn't to his liking, he would spare no time in reminding Jillian of what a lazy, inconsiderate wife she was. He was mostly ill-natured when she would cry. For most of their marriage she had been on her own, trying to fight and survive a life in which she felt trapped.

When Lindsey was conceived a few years after they had married, Jillian and Terry had sat down and engaged themselves in many late-night conversations on how they needed to better their lives for Lindsey. They agreed that things were more or less out of hand, and that it wasn't fair for the baby to grow up in such a hostile environment. With a little persuasion from Chelsea and Dan, Terry and Jillian even agreed to some family counseling.

With Lindsey's appearance into the world, a new life began in Jillian Milholland. She loved her baby to death; Lindsey had been her salvation to her old, sad life. She had been a light in the darkness; a new person to love and care for who would definitely receive that love and offer it back. Lindsey had made life worth living, and when times between Jillian and Terry would turn sour again, Lindsey would be the recompense for which Jillian could endure her trials.

Every morning, Jillian looked forward to seeing her baby and taking care of her. Her heart swelled uncontrollably with love every time Lindsey smiled that dimpled baby grin, and Jillian couldn't get over those sweet baby eyes that always gazed longingly at her, nor those cute chubby hands and feet that she just adored. Yes, she knew Lindsey needed her, so much more than Terry ever had, and likewise, Jillian had needed Lindsey.

The counseling was short-lived, and so was Terry's commitment to change his negative habits. He still spent a great deal of time with his job and his "other life," the important one that didn't consist of Jillian. She had to give him credit, however, for his adoration for his little daughter. He did love her; he had been truly ecstatic when she had been born. He gave her his time, but not enough. In the long run, he spent his hours elsewhere besides home, even at those times when he could have been home. When he was with Lindsey, he was a good father, but looking back now, he realized that his constant absence from her had indeed made him an incompetent father.

No matter what kind of father he had been, he was never a good husband to Jillian. Never. He treated her unfair. He claimed he had loved her, but love doesn't degrade or abuse. There were many times when he was just frustrated and bored with her, and it had given way to abuse. During his marriage, he had questioned why he had married her. Of course, he had loved her … then. So what had happened? Maybe they were just too young; maybe their marriage had been too superficial.

When Lindsey wasn't even four years old, Terry's self-control became less and less, to the point where he began physically abusing Jillian. It started with infrequent shoves or face-slaps and escalated to the point where Jillian was actually sent to the hospital three times. During those times, Terry would often realize how monstrous he was becoming and apologize to Jillian. A week or two would go by where he actually looked out for her needs and took the care that a husband should. But his behavior changes were always temporary.

After four years of the same routine, and almost twelve years of marriage, when Lindsey was eight and a half years old, Terry finally made the best decision concerning their lives that he ever had before; he ran away. Knowing that if he stayed he wouldn't be strong enough to better himself for his wife and child, he fled their lives, honestly realizing the pain he had put Jillian through and not wanting it to continue. He didn't know any other way but to leave it all and try to get himself some help and a fresh new start.

The only thing he was proud of within that whole marriage had been Lindsey, and the fact that he hadn't touched her once. His abuse was always aimed at Jillian, although deep down he knew that the negativities he displaced on her would ultimately affect Lindsey. He knew they already had when Lindsey got to the age where she recognized the abuse and would cry for her mom, or would run and hide during an argument, or would be hesitant in showing affection for her father. Yes, Terry knew that even though Lindsey was still young when he left, the damage had already been done to her, and of that, he wasn't proud.

And that was also why he never blamed Lindsey for not wanting anything to do with him. Jillian got out of the marriage and, as far as he knew after that, was living a decent life with her daughter. She and Lindsey had lived with Chelsea and Dan for a year and a half after the divorce, giving Jillian time to seek out a decent job and earn herself and Lindsey enough money to rent a place of their own.

A tear rolled down Terry's cheek. His heart ached badly. Oh, how sorry he was for all the wrong he had committed! If only he could have spoken with Jillian before she died and let her know how much he had loved her and how sorry he was. If only Lindsey could have known the changed man that he had come to be.

When he moved across the country with the intent in mind to be as far away as possible from harming his family again, he had indeed begun a new life. It had been hard, so terribly hard. The toughest part was, without denial, trying to give up the drinking. It took him almost two years, but during it all, there were good people backing him up; the same people who had kept him accountable to his drinking and watched his back afterward. One of those people had been Jenna, his present wife. She had struggled with alcoholism a few years before and was working as a volunteer at the rehab center where Terry met her. From the first day he met her, he knew she was special. They had quickly become friends, and when Terry finally became sober and got his life back on track, their friendship grew more personal and intimate, until the day when Terry finally asked Jenna to marry him.

He had been nervous about it because he was still afraid of himself. What if his old self should show up one unexpected day? But he was in love with Jenna, this wonderful dark-haired beauty who was so outgoing and outspoken and independent. He knew right off that she was a woman who could take care of herself in any situation, who went her own way. She was the total opposite of Jillian, which eliminated his uneasiness and solidified his confidence about proposing to her. She wasn't young and vulnerable like Jillian had been, so there would be no outlet for him to hurt her. Also, Terry knew without a doubt that he was a changed man. He wanted to be, and he was striving for it. He wanted a better life, he wanted so much that he knew his foolishness back in Washington had forced him to miss out on.

So he waited until he knew he was secure financially, emotionally, and physically. He had truly changed, and he loved Jenna to death. She had been his savior, his long-lost love. They had married, and shortly after, Jenna joined with Terry in his business, which made their marriage grow and solidify. Unlike his former marriage where he had a stay-home wife whom he barely saw or acknowledged, now he had a wife who joined him in his career. He would never again have an excuse to neglect her. And he never did.

He had been a great man and husband to Jenna. The only stipulation was that he never told her about Jillian or Lindsey. He gave her the basic facts about his childhood and growing up in Washington; old girlfriends; going to college; becoming an out-of-control drunk; and he might have even mentioned something about being in a former marriage that didn't work out. But that was it; there was no mention of a twelve-year abusive relationship in which a child was involved.

Terry put his head down in shame as he recalled everything in his past. He had lied to Jenna when there really was no justification for it. He was scared to tell her who he had really been, but would that have really mattered? She would have understood. Instead, he had been silent, deceiving, lying in order to save himself. In truth, he was hoping to wipe clean those past memories, but in the end they were always there, still trapped in the back of his mind, never to disintegrate.

And where was Jenna now? She had gone to her parents' house a couple of hours away in another city. Upset and betrayed, she had, in a fit of confusion, packed up a few things and left for a week … or however long it might take her to think things over.

Terry leaned forward on the swing and set his elbows on his knees, burying his face in his hands. His heart sank deeply. *Oh, what have I done?* He didn't want to drive his wife away. She was all that he had in this world. If she left him, what would he do? How could he ever start over again with such stains and blemishes in his past?

Resolving to call Jenna and talk to her, he stood up quickly and made his way into the house and toward the phone in the kitchen. He plopped himself down onto one of the kitchen stools and reached over to pick up the receiver. Before he had touched it, though, he noticed the small red light flashing on the answering machine, which indicated that there was a message. He pushed the play button. His lonely heart and downcast soul lit up a bit when he heard the voice of Lindsey on the tape. She said:

Hi Dad, it's me Lindsey. Gosh, I hate it that I have to talk to you again through this answering machine ... well, anyway, I guess you're busy right now and there's nothing I can do about it. So I am just calling to let you know that I'm in Lincoln, Nebraska, and so I should be there shortly. I guess I just mainly wanted to let you know that I'm still coming, and I was actually hoping to talk to you in person so that we could discuss some stuff. First off, I'm not alone; I am traveling with a friend who is also going across the country. There's more to the story, but I guess you'll have to learn about it later. Also, I just wanted to let you know that ... well ... I just ... am sorry ... I mean I know that....

There was a long pause on the line. Terry could only assume that she had upset herself and needed to take a moment to compose.

Dad, I know you're my dad and I love you for that. It's hard to just snap my fingers and make everything okay, and I'll be honest with you and say that it's not. I'm confused still, and I don't even know why I am making this trip. I want to meet you, Dad, and start over with you, but I'm afraid. I'm afraid you won't want me, or maybe you've forgotten me or something ... but mostly I'm afraid I might still be angry at you, when I know I probably shouldn't be. Anyway ... we'll be in Lincoln all day today, and then we're leaving tomorrow morning. If there's any chance you'll get this message before tomorrow, I'll give you the number to our hotel room. I can't guarantee that we'll be here at all because we've got plans for the day. Either way, I just wanted to ease your mind, I guess, and let you know I'm still coming.

I hope I'm welcome. I know I just kind of sprang this on you, and I'm sorry for that. My life's been so crazy since Mom died, I hope you understand.

Terry listened as Lindsey left the name of the hotel and her room number. After a few short words of good-bye, the answering machine clicked and buzzed. The message was over.

Terry felt a smile creep to his face as he uncontrollably let the tears cascade down his cheeks. She was coming, and she actually sounded ...

okay. She wasn't angry; she was just in the middle of some of life's hardest moments.

"Of course I understand," he whispered to himself, gazing at the machine.

He played the message back, wrote down the phone number, and after a few shaky breaths, he picked up the receiver and began dialing.

Lindsey practically shrieked as her eyes fell on the costume shop on the second floor of the mall. Startled, Caleb jumped at her side. "Whoa, what's your problem?"

Without answering, Lindsey shot towards the store, dodging shoppers as she went. Caleb threw his head back and followed her.

"Caleb, look!" Lindsey yelled excitedly as he entered the store. He found her perched near the wall fingering all sorts of Halloween junk.

"Now here's the part where *I* get to complain. What is it with you and Halloween, anyway?"

"It's just such a fun holiday. I mean, when else do you get to just dress up and act out of the ordinary, and it's okay?"

"And I suppose the trick-or-treating doesn't excite you?"

Lindsey laughed. "I have to admit that I didn't give that up until a couple years ago." She stood up and faced Caleb. "The last time I trick-or-treated was when I was sixteen. I got the hint when some of the houses my friends and I went to refused to give us candy because we were too old. One couple even gave us a whole lecture on how we were taking away from the little kids' opportunity to get candy and la di da. We thought it was pretty funny, so we kept going from house to house just to see what kinds of responses and reactions we would get."

Caleb responded with a questioning look etched on his face, as if he was silently expressing to Lindsey what a dork she was. "Gosh Lindsey, your story actually makes me feel embarrassed for you."

"Oh, shut up," she yelled, spinning around. "It's not like we went just for the candy. We were just messing around. You know, stupid teenager stuff."

"Stupid is right...."

Lindsey spun around again to face him. "Gosh you're *mean*!"

Caleb laughed. "I know just where to push your buttons, don't I?"

"Hey, don't forget that I know your weaknesses too, zoo boy!"

"Whoa, that was harsh," Caleb said, throwing his hands up in front of him as if to back off. "Okay, okay, I surrender. Just don't be thinking that you're going to get me to go on one of your weird trick-or-treating excursions."

"Ah, you're no fun!"

"Haven't I heard that before," Caleb replied, picking up a demented-looking mask, complete with warts and a large, round nose.

Lindsey proceeded to slowly make her way through the store, picking up items, trying on masks and wigs, and demonstrating an odd variety of Halloween knick-knacks. Caleb followed close behind her, growing more impatient by the second. "Can we go, please?" he whined.

"So now who's doing the complaining?"

"I know, I know. I am!"

Ignoring him, Lindsey gazed at a gorgeous pink gown, with white ribbon at the waist and neck. She stared at it longingly and sighed. "I can't believe Halloween is on Friday and I'm going to miss it this year. I mean, we won't even be able to find some party somewhere and hang out there. We're just gonna be on the road while Halloween passes us by."

"Hey, it's just one Halloween in many more to come."

"I always loved it, though. My mom and I always make a big deal about it. We get fancy, expensive costumes and decorate the house up really neat. Speaking of that, my mom would love this gown. I should tell her to go as a...."

Lindsey stopped mid-sentence, suddenly realizing what she had been doing. She didn't have her mother anymore. There would be no more Halloweens with fancy gowns and extravagant decor all around the house.

Caleb's sympathetic but considerate gaze was fixed on Lindsey's bewildered stare. She met Caleb's eyes with her wide ones but didn't say a word. It was Caleb who broke the silence.

"Do you still do that a lot? Forget, I mean, that she's gone?"

Lindsey just nodded.

"You know," Caleb said slowly, reluctantly, grasping for the right words, "we could find something to do Friday night. Whichever town we stop in for the night, there should be something going on there for Halloween that we can join in on."

"No," Lindsey mumbled quietly as she began walking out of the store. "I think I'd ... rather not, this year. It would probably be better, you know?"

"Yeah, okay."

Lindsey couldn't concentrate the next few minutes after that. Embarrassed by what she'd said, and suddenly hit with another bout of grief from the reality of her mother being dead, she found herself mechanically following Caleb throughout the mall. He spoke to her from her side as they walked together, from store to store, but the conversation was more or less one-sided. Caleb caught on to her change of mood and decided not to ask any questions based on the situation. Between small talk, he managed to say a little prayer for her.

Lord, this has got to be so hard for her. Please, help her to know that You're there for her, and that You love her. She needs a really positive note in her life right now, but I'm sure You know that even more than I do. I just pray that she lets that positive note be You, and can soon recognize Your love and faithfulness. People come and go; mothers die, but You are the same always; neverchanging; never leaving us.

Once again, even in the midst of his prayer to bring Lindsey to lean on the Lord, Caleb found himself wishing he could do something to take her sadness and pain away. He supposed it was that abrupt pang of overprotectiveness that led him to react the way he did a couple minutes later when Lindsey accidentally knocked into a young man, causing him to nearly topple over and drop all of his purchases onto the floor.

"Oh, I'm really sorry...." she began, her face flushing with embarrassment.

The man, who looked to be about Lindsey's age, was clad in baggy jeans, an oversized T-shirt and a baseball cap nearly covering his eyes. He bent over to retrieve his spillings. Lindsey did the same. As he did, he defensively let spill from his mouth a string of obscenities aimed at Lindsey. "Why don't you watch where you're going?" he finished off.

Lindsey stood up and stared unbelievingly at the boy. Stunned and hurt by his offensive remark, she could do nothing but watch him with her mouth dropped open in offense.

Caleb whirled around in anger and disbelief at the same moment he heard the boy curse Lindsey. A fierce animosity grew inside him as he watched the young man attend to his business without a care as to what he had just said. How dare he call Lindsey what he just had? She was so much better than that! Caleb was suddenly determined to stick up for Lindsey.

"What did you say?" he asked harshly.

"Excuse me?" Lindsey stumbled out at the same moment.

"You heard me!" the boy said again as he stood up and faced them, his eyes hard and cruel.

In a blaze of rage, Caleb took three steps to where the boy was standing, dropped his bags, and brought his arm up. Before Lindsey could figure out what was going on, the young man let out a yelp as Caleb's fist met his face.

The boy stumbled backwards and tripped over his baggy pants, his hand held over his face the whole time. Caleb, fire in his eyes, and rubbing his sore hand, stepped back to where the aghast Lindsey was standing, her mouth dropped even wider than it had been before. She grabbed his arm and stepped closer to him, as if shielding herself to what might come next.

"What did you do that for!?" the boy asked, slowly and awkwardly rising to his feet. His hand was covering his nose and mouth, but Caleb could still see the trickle of blood that had escaped and was running down his chin.

Caleb stayed silent, standing fixed as if readying himself for another attack. The boy, however, backed off a little. It was clear that he knew he would be no match for this brawny, older man, who obviously outweighed him. Besides, the force of that blow told him enough: Caleb wasn't someone to resume a fight with.

The boy began spitting out curse words and threats, all the while retreating backwards a bit as if he was just about to turn and leave. His face was getting messy now, with the blood smearing and making his appearance more hideous.

"C'mon, Caleb," Lindsey urged, pulling Caleb back by the arm and glancing around to her sides. A crowd was forming as curious shoppers stopped and stared, leaning in to find out what all the commotion was about. "Let's just get out of here, okay?"

After another few seconds, Caleb finally just shook his head at the boy, indicating that he wasn't worth it, swung around, and began marching toward the nearest exit to the mall.

Lindsey had to speed-walk to keep up with Caleb's quick, determined pace. She followed behind in silence, but after a minute or two, she couldn't contain herself much longer.

"Whoa, Caleb," she exclaimed as a smile penetrated her face. "I can't believe you just did that!" He didn't look at her but kept walking away toward the mall entrance to leave, as if in an attempt to escape his infidelity.

"You stuck up for me, Caleb," Lindsey continued, her face shining. "That was so … awesome!"

"No it wasn't," Caleb replied flatly, forcefully shoving open the large entrance doors.

"Why not?" Lindsey asked, exiting through the adjacent door. "I can't believe you actually punched that guy! It freaked me out a little because it was so un-Caleb-like, but you actually stuck up for me. It was cool!"

"It wasn't right, Lindsey," Caleb replied, attempting to keep his voice firm, but gentle.

"Says who?" Lindsey argued, her voice turning defensive. "God?!"

Caleb halted abruptly in the middle of the parking lot and turned toward Lindsey. His eyes were still on fire, and it struck a sudden fear and confusion in Lindsey to witness him so unusually angry.

"Well, yeah, as a matter of fact, God does say punching that guy out was wrong, and so do I!" He turned and began walking again, but at a slower, more controlled pace. Lindsey stood still for a moment, unable to bring herself to follow him. Forcing herself to move, she continued in stride right next to him. She knew beyond a doubt that he was upset; but it seemed to go deeper than just outside anger.

"Okay then," Lindsey began. "So is God just gonna let you or me be beaten down at any time without having rights to defend ourselves?" she asked boldly.

"Yes, He is." Caleb replied resolutely. "And you know what else, Lindsey?"

"What's that?"

"God actually asks us to love other people, no matter who they are, even if they're our enemies!"

"Oh really?" Lindsey stated rudely, with a hint of self-righteousness. Her and Caleb approached the truck and stood behind it. "Why's that so? What's so wrong about not loving a few people? I mean, it's kind of hard to love everybody, especially if they've done terrible things to you."

"Yes, it is, Lindsey, but what would you rather have in this world? Love or hate? What personally makes you happier?" Caleb asked, his hard tone of voice continuing. Lindsey thought she could detect a sliver of annoyance behind it, also.

"Okay," Lindsey finally agreed, but not before picking up the argument again before giving in. "So what does that all have to do with you hitting that guy?"

"Because it wasn't a very good example of love, was it? How are others going to see God's love in me if I'm punching and hitting other people?"

"But you were only sticking up for me!"

"It doesn't matter," Caleb yelled. "That's no justification. It's all fine and good that I was trying to help you, but I didn't have to punch the guy to do it!"

"Then why did you?"

The question hit Caleb right in the gut and weakened him. A short silence radiated as he racked his brain for an answer, but he could only shake his head regretfully. "I don't know," he breathed as his glassy eyes stared blankly at Lindsey. Walking around to the driver's side, he slowly entered the truck and rested his head on the steering wheel. Lindsey's heart slowed its rapid, nervous pace and began to swell with heartache and compassion for Caleb. She entered the passenger side and sat silently, glancing at Caleb every few moments. In the time they'd spend together so far on the trip, Lindsey hadn't witnessed Caleb so angry, nor had she seen him so broken and confused; he had always been her comforter and caretaker in her moments of confusion and grief. Suddenly she felt the roles being reversed.

"You've done that before, huh?" she voiced quietly.

"What?" Caleb mumbled without lifting his head.

"Hit people."

He cocked his head to the side to peer at her. "Yeah, I loved to pick a fight whenever I could, but I don't really want to talk about it."

She nodded. "Caleb," she said pleadingly, desperately wanting to change him back to the Caleb she was used to, "so you made a mistake. Nobody's perfect."

"You got that right," he mumbled again.

"Maybe *you're* trying to be a little too perfect … for God? Never wanting to mess up?" Lindsey suggested. "And so maybe you did mess up. Big deal! What, are you afraid God's gonna whack you on the back of the head with a big ruler, or something?"

Caleb sat up and looked at Lindsey. "No," he admitted. "God doesn't work that way."

"So how does He work?" she asked honestly, curiously.

Caleb sighed. "He would forgive me and love me just the same."

"So what are you worrying about then?" Lindsey asked. Caleb could do nothing but stare at her. She was right. She was so right. He had made a mistake, and he was sorry for it. It was as simple as that. He knew God's love was unconditional, and that just as there was nothing he could do to earn God's approval, there was nothing he could do to lose it.

Lindsey continued talking. "I don't know much about Christians besides you, but I do know that they're human too and can't be perfect either."

"God doesn't expect me to be perfect," Caleb said.

"Well, that's a relief," Lindsey exclaimed. Caleb nodded without taking his gaze off of Lindsey. Once again he found himself curious as to what was going on in that labyrinth of a brain of hers.

"So are you gonna start the car?" Lindsey asked.

"Can I ask you a personal question?" Caleb said unexpectedly.

"I never stopped you before."

"When you said that thing about it being hard to love everybody, especially if they've done bad things to you, were you … talking about anyone in particular?"

Lindsey just shrugged.

"Like your dad, maybe?"

"I don't know," Lindsey said softly, lowering her eyes. Caleb could see the uneasiness riding in those eyes.

"He hurt you and your mom pretty bad, didn't he?"

"Well, sure, Caleb. But we've already talked about this, this morning, remember? Besides, I'm ahead of you, because I've already forgiven him and am trying to make things right between us."

Caleb just lifted his eyebrows.

"But, to answer your question before … I guess there weren't always times when I felt love for him because of what he did to us…."

"Lindsey, you don't have to talk about it if you don't want to. I didn't mean to bring it up or make you feel bad or anything. I think you've been through enough just in the past ten minutes."

Lindsey smiled weakly. "Why don't we go see a movie or something?" she suggested. "Maybe we could even scout out the Olive Garden since we couldn't find it last night."

"I thought you didn't like Italian very well."

"Well, it's your day today, remember? And heaven knows, *you've* been through enough in the past ten minutes, not to mention the whole day with me pestering you."

"Well, I can't argue with that." Caleb smiled. He straightened himself in the seat and started the engine, pulling his seatbelt on.

"Good. I don't want us to argue again. I don't like knowing that you're upset at me."

"I don't think I could get truly upset at you, Lindsey. You're too sweet … too much like a little kid. Maybe I could get annoyed, but…."

"That's enough!"

Eighteen

Christ also suffered. He died once for the sins of all us guilty sinners although he himself was innocent of any sin at any time, that he might bring us safely home to God.
– 1 Peter 3:18 (The Living Bible)

"Well, Caleb, I just want to let you know that in spite of the zoo being closed, and that little situation at the mall, I really had fun today, especially at the movies. The movie was good."

Caleb, seated on his bed with one leg folded under him and the other straight out, glanced up from his reading and threw a smile at Lindsey. "Yeah, I did too. It was a nice two days off the road, huh?"

"Yeah, it was," Lindsey sighed. She almost didn't want to be leaving in the morning. It would be back to long, seven-hour stretches of country road ahead. She cringed at the thought, one particularly that was the least appealing. *We're not far,* she told herself. *It should only be a few more days, maybe three or four.* Lindsey's face crumpled again. Three or four days *were* a lot, more than she thought she wanted to handle. Oh well, there was nothing she could do about it. She was stuck in the middle of the U.S. and there were only two places she could go, backward or forward. The thought of driving back home and making things right with her grandparents and her friends actually seemed inviting. Going forward meant facing some unexpected, undecided future with a man she barely knew; that scared her to death.

Every hour of the trip had made Lindsey closer to the realization of what she was doing. The long hours of driving and thinking had cleared her mind and made her wonder exactly what it was back in Washington that had tempted her to leave. Back then it had made sense. To a foggy and confused mind, anything that attempted to escape reality had made sense. But now, as she and Caleb drew nearer to the East Coast, she knew she had little time left before her life would be suddenly altered again. All those old rationalities of meeting her dad and living with him and fixing out her life had diminished, sending new ones to pound her brain. She was thinking realistically now, and it didn't look promising.

And then there was Caleb, silent, calm, totally at ease with what lay ahead of him. He would be welcomed home to a familiar place and familiar people, the people who had actually raised him. Sure, there had been tough times between them, but with the way Caleb was now, and the loving way he spoke about his parents, Lindsey knew it would all turn out great for him. There he was, hunched over his Bible, seemingly unaware to the quick-hearted nervousness that was currently plaguing Lindsey.

Lindsey grabbed the TV remote and switched off the television. Aside from the dim table lamp and the light glow of the moon from outside seeping in through the curtained windows, the room was cast into almost total darkness. Lindsey slumped under her covers and closed her eyes to sleep. Caleb continued reading with the small table lamp between the beds serving as his light source. After a couple minutes of restless thought, Lindsey turned over in bed and opened her eyes. She was facing Caleb, and he was still reading.

His Bible. Gosh, Lindsey noticed that he read that thing every night. The Bible? How interesting could that be?

Lindsey silently scolded herself. It wasn't her place to question Caleb's reading preferences. He was a religious guy, a Christian, and they read the Bible, right? She personally had never read the Bible, so how could she even begin to judge whether it was interesting or not? Besides, as far as she had decided, Caleb was a pretty cool guy, so if reading the Bible was his thing, then the Bible must be pretty cool.

In fact, the whole idea intrigued Lindsey so much that she actually spoke up. "So, you like reading the Bible, huh?"

"Uh huh," Caleb mumbled in reply, ceasing to look up from his reading.

"Do you read that thing every night?"

"Well, I'm trying to get in the habit of it."

"Why?"

It was then that Caleb looked up and met her questioning gaze. "Well, it's important to me. I mean, it's a tool for Christians to use, in order to grow in their faith and knowledge of Jesus."

"Oh."

"And personally," Caleb went on, "I read it to make sure I'm keeping Jesus my number one priority."

Lindsey nodded. "Oh," she replied quietly, "well, is he?"

Caleb tilted his head slightly as he began to search for an honest answer. "I hope so. Yeah … I believe He is. I'm trying my best to keep Him in control of my life. It's hard sometimes, though."

Lindsey's face grew curious. "Why is it hard?"

Caleb shifted so that he was facing Lindsey. "Because if I was in control, I wouldn't be who I am now. I'm sometimes tempted to go back to my old way of life."

"Believing in Jesus is like believing in God, right?" Lindsey questioned. She knew Caleb believed in God, but his constant mentioning of Jesus was beginning to make her wonder if Jesus was a whole different thing.

"Well, yeah," Caleb answered. "God and Jesus are basically one and the same, just in different forms."

"What forms?"

"Well, I guess God is the deity form, you know, the unseen, powerful force that kinds of seems untouchable. And Jesus was God in human form. Emmanuel: God with us."

"God became a human?"

"Yeah, Lindsey, that's who Jesus was," Caleb answered, growing more excited and pleased by Lindsey's curiosity and questioning. He had to work to conceal his delight.

"Oh, okay," Lindsey said again, furrowing her eyebrows as if she was thinking about it. "So why did God become a human?"

"I guess … to show us that He's not as distant and impersonal as we sometimes perceive Him; to show us how much He loves us."

"Hmm."

"Well, and He also did it to offer us an alternative to the old way of receiving forgiveness."

"How's that?"

"Well, back before Jesus was born, way, *way* back, people used to offer animal sacrifices to God so that He would forgive their sins. When Jesus came and then died, all of that changed, because Jesus acted as the final sacrifice to God. You could say that He took on the world's sin so that we can all be forgiven any time we just ask for it."

"I don't get it," Lindsey said, creasing her forehead.

"Well," Caleb began, wondering how he could clear up her confusion. He quickly asked Jesus to intercede for him so that he could say the right words. "Sin is disobedience to God. When you disobey your parents, for example, you can't expect to go unpunished, right?"

Lindsey nodded.

"Well, God kind of works the same way. If you sin, you deserve punishment. The Bible says the penalty for sin is death."

Lindsey squirmed as her eyes went wide.

"Well, when Jesus came to earth and then died, He changed that system.

He was saying, 'They don't have to die anymore for their sins, because I have died in their place.'"

Lindsey nodded in understanding but then said, "Well, people still die, you know."

"Well, of course they do," Caleb agreed, "because many people don't know about Jesus' sacrifice for them, or they don't understand it and don't accept it. They still sin. Even Christians still stumble in sin. Jesus' death didn't mean we were never gonna sin anymore."

Lindsey was suddenly confused again. "So what good did it do then, if people are still the same? What's the catch?"

"The catch is that if we believe in what Jesus did for us by dying for our sins, then we really *don't* die. We will be forgiven by God and get to spend eternity in Heaven with Him."

"So, people who believe in Jesus and believe that he died to take away their sins will *still* sin...."

"...But are offered forgiveness by God...."

"...So when they do die, they go to Heaven."

"Right," said Caleb. "You can also look at it this way: there are two types of deaths, physical and spiritual. Christians only have to die once – physically."

"Hmm," Lindsey said again, her forehead still creased. "That's interesting. And what about all the other people who don't believe in all this?"

"Well, Jesus' death was for everyone; God's forgiveness is available to anyone, but it only applies to those who choose to believe it."

"Interesting," Lindsey said again.

"Yeah, I think so, too. But it's also pretty cool."

"So is that why it is so important to keep Jesus as a top priority?"

"Well, yeah," Caleb fumbled and took a few moments to consider his answer. Once again he uttered a silent prayer in his head for Jesus to speak the right words through him. "It's important because Jesus is the source of our faith, and He's the one who has ultimately changed our lives. I don't know how much you know about Jesus besides what I've mentioned, but like I said, He was actually a real person who lived on earth about 2000 years ago. He was sent by God; well, He was basically God in the flesh. He ministered to people and taught them about God and His love for us, and all these other cool things. He was killed after only a few years of his ministry, though, because the religious leaders of that time didn't all believe that he was who He said He was: God's son; a king of Heaven. Some people took that as blasphemy toward God, and some people just didn't like the fact that

He was stirring up new ideas, things that the Pharisees and religious leaders didn't like. I guess you could say that the religious leaders were pretty conservative in their beliefs, and when Jesus came, claiming to be from God and preaching all these new things, He seemed pretty radical. He did all this stuff that the religious leaders couldn't believe, like hanging out with the poor, dirty, sick, and unreligious folks. They didn't like that. And they didn't like how He didn't seem to go along with creeds and rules.

"So Jesus kind of walked in and stirred up a whole mess. But He wasn't really a rebel, or anything. He didn't try to break rules or be the center of attention. He only did what God commanded Him. He spent most of His time loving everybody and teaching them the same. He taught them about God, and all these other things. He had a lot of admirers. People followed Him everywhere to hear Him preach, and He even performed miracles."

"Miracles?"

"Yeah, through God, He was able to perform miracles, like healing the sick and causing blind people to see and all that good stuff. So a lot of people believed in Him because of these miracles. But they weren't solely for the purpose of getting people to believe in Him or to show off or anything. He wanted to demonstrate the power of God.

"Anyway, I guess the religious leaders got tired of it all and decided to have Him killed. Personally, I think they kind of knew that Jesus was the real thing, but they were too tired of having their own authority challenged and overlooked. It was actually one of Jesus' closest friends who ended up helping with His execution."

Lindsey let out a small gasp, totally engrossed in the story, as if she was a young girl again, listening intently as her mother read her a fairy tale. "What? Why's that?"

"I don't know, maybe he really didn't believe that Jesus was who He said He was. Anyway, Jesus was crucified on a cross, which I think I've mentioned to you before."

"Yeah, and you told me he was resurrected, too."

"Yeah, a couple days after He was buried, He came back to life."

"And tell me again why he did that."

"Well, because if Jesus had just died and stayed dead, then what would be the whole point of it all? He would've been just like any other person. But Jesus wasn't just another radical religious guy or prophet. There are many people like that in history who have made big impacts in the world, but we know Jesus was different because of His resurrection. God brought Him back to life, and so ultimately, He never died. That hasn't happened with any other person in history. After He resurrected, He spent 40 more days on Earth walking and talking among His followers, continuing to teach them."

"Weird," was all Lindsey could utter.

"Yeah, well," Caleb leaned back, relaxing against the headboard, "God is powerful and awesome and can do amazing things. If you want to learn a little bit more about Jesus and His life on Earth just to relieve some curiosity or confusion, His story is recorded in the Bible. I like the book of John, it's a good place to start to learn about Jesus."

"Do you really believe all that, Caleb?"

"About Jesus?"

"Yeah."

"Well, sure I do."

Lindsey nodded and turned around again in bed so that she was facing away from Caleb. It was a nice, exciting story. Maybe this Jesus fellow really had lived on Earth and had been this big, influential guy, but the whole dying and coming back to life thing – personally it was a little eerie and confusing.

With her back still to Caleb, Lindsey spoke over her shoulder.

"So Jesus was so important because he was like, God."

"Yeah, and because of the whole dying for the world's sins thing. There's a famous verse in the book of John, that says, 'God loved the world this way: He gave his only Son so that everyone who believes in him will not die but will have eternal life."

"Hmmm," Lindsey mumbled. She stayed silent, attempting to make sense of it all. *God loved the world this way* ... God loved the world? God loved humans so much that he allowed Jesus to die so that they could have their sins forgiven? It seemed pretty straightforward, but something just wasn't right. What was Christianity about anyway, the constant forgiving of sins, and trying to be a good person?

Although the thought kept her restless for the next few minutes, she was too tired to speak up and question any further. For now, she would tuck the nagging thought in a corner of her brain. It would have to wait until later.

The digital clock in Nick Pruitt's shiny red '97 Mustang read 11:53 p.m., and Marianne quickly reminded him of her midnight curfew as she urged him to "hurry up."

Her grinning face and chuckling eyes belied her urgent request, however, as the two had spent the whole night in a parade of laughter. Marianne wasn't afraid of returning home a little late; nothing could spoil the enjoyable day she had just spent with Nick.

Nick pressed his foot harder on the accelerator to speed up, and as he rounded a corner, he neglected to reduce his speed, thus sending Marianne flinging to his side of the car. The action brought her into another fit of laughter, but as she sat up straight again and pulled on her seatbelt, she reminded Nick to "hurry up, but be careful."

"I don't know how to do that," he said jokingly.

"I think you're right," Marianne agreed. She glanced over at her blond-haired driver and smiled. Nick really was a cool guy to hang out with. Marianne was beginning to understand why Lindsey had loved being with him. Not only was he agreeably good-looking with that baby-face and those deep blue eyes, but he was humorous and a good conversationalist.

Before Nick and Lindsey's break-up, Marianne had spent little time with or around Nick. She barely knew him before Lindsey had started dating him two years ago, only recognizing him as a school peer who shared some of her classes. After a while he began sharing her friendship with Lindsey too, and not long after that, he had asked Lindsey to go out with him. Through most of it, Marianne had been a side-spectator, never really having been part of the whole thing. She never spent time with Lindsey and Nick together; if Lindsey was with Marianne, she wouldn't be with Nick, and if she was with Nick, then she wouldn't be with Marianne. Marianne knew it wasn't deliberately planned that way, but it had still saddened her, even angered her at times. She felt neglected. Only when she finally approached Lindsey with the subject did things change. More group excursions were planned together, and soon Marianne and Nick began knowing eachother and became friends.

Now with Lindsey out of the picture, they had been spending more time together. Marianne knew that aside from Lindsey, she was probably the closest female friend Nick had. And she knew his need to change; to try and swerve away from his partying and old habits. For the last week, Nick had confided in Marianne about how Lindsey's leaving had been such a blow on him, a reality check. He finally realized and understood just how bad he had hurt Lindsey when he cheated on her, then dumped her. He also finally realized just how much he had cared for her, had *come* to care for her during her absence. It was true, he had told Marianne, how they say, "absence makes the heart grow fonder," or that "you don't know what you've got until it's gone." Marianne had only shrugged and acted indifferent to the comment, but she silently agreed. She didn't want Nick to know how much *she* missed her best friend. Yes, she had been the friend on whom Nick could lean, yet she did not trust herself to confide in him, to face the idea that she felt lonely and helpless without Lindsey. Where would that leave the two of them: wallowing in a deep muddy pool of their own regret and self-pity?

"Just move on," Marianne had told herself so many times lately. "Just forget about Lindsey and move on." The only good thing that Marianne had decided came out of the whole mess was that she and Nick came to be closer buds, and that he had been making a truly remarkable effort to change himself. He was making less and less contact with his other friends, instead spending more time with Marianne. This, of course, had produced a few rumors about the two of them, but Nick and Marianne didn't mind. Who cared what anybody thought? Nick had come to feel that his friendship with Marianne was of more quality than his other friends had ever been able to measure up to. Marianne was a strong-willed character, never failing him whenever he needed some will power to stay away from that party, or at least stay away from that beer. Whenever he did associate himself with a party, Marianne was sure to escort him and watch his back.

Tonight, however, the two of them had decided not to hang out with their fellow peers and instead spent the whole day watching cheesy horror flicks and action films at Nick's house.

The screeching brakes of the mustang squeaked as Nick pulled up to the curb in front of Marianne's house. He glanced at the clock: 12:02 am.

"Oh no, you're late. I hope I don't get you in trouble."

"No, no, I'll be fine. I have cool parents."

"Yeah, I know, you're always talking to me about how cool they are. I should meet them sometime."

Marianne frowned, and turned to put her hand on the door handle. "Uh, I don't think so, Nick. That might seem a little odd to people and add to some of the rumors that are going around, if you know what I mean."

"Oh yeah, that's right," Nick agreed with a childish expression across his face. "We're not going out, so we don't need to meet each other's parents."

"That's right. Well, I'd better go now." As Marianne moved to open the door, she felt Nick's hand lightly touch her arm.

"Marianne."

She turned to face him. His eyes were no longer bright and laughing, reflecting the carefree day of fun and laziness, but instead were gleaned with a sudden seriousness.

"Before you go I just wanted to make sure that I let you know how much I appreciate your friendship and your help with everything."

Marianne's straight-faced expression broke into a smile at the compliment. She nodded her head. "Me too. I mean, I've had a lot of fun hanging out with you. You're a really cool guy, Nick. I can see why Lindsey loved you so much."

At the mention of Lindsey, Nick's eyes went more slack, more regretful. He lowered his head and took his gaze off Marianne. "She did, didn't she?"

"She did what?"

"She loved me."

"Well, she did really care about you, Nick. You know that."

"Yeah, I do." He sighed longingly. "I just, wish that I had … known that…." Marianne watched with concern as Nick struggled to get the right words out. "I just want to beat myself up every day for what I did to her."

"Nick," Marianne cooed, leaning in closer to him. She hated that look on his face that she encountered almost every day, the expression of total self-destruction. She knew it well, for she had seen it in herself too. It broke her heart. "Nick, please don't do this to yourself. We've talked about this before. You need to stop getting mad at yourself. It's done and over with, and there's nothing you can do to change what happened. You've already apologized to Lindsey for what you did, right?" Nick nodded, glancing up and meeting Marianne's gaze. "I mean, at least you got the chance to talk with her and apologize."

"I just hope she knows how much I really meant it."

"I'm sure she does, Nick. She was probably blown away just by the fact that you called to talk to her. She probably didn't expect to ever hear from you again."

"I'd like to talk to her again. I would love it, actually. Do you have her dad's phone number?"

"No, but I'm sure I could get it from her grandparents."

Nick nodded and straightened himself in the driver's seat. "I hope she'll want to keep in touch. I really miss her."

Marianne lowered her own head in sadness and longing, and uttered a quiet, "I do too."

"Hmph," Nick suddenly groaned, smiling in retrospect of all the times in the past week he had poured out his feelings so freely to this trustworthy girl sitting next to him. Never before had he allowed himself to be opened up before any one person, save for Lindsey. Aside from her, Marianne had been the only other person he had ever really trusted enough to share himself. At first he had been reluctant to share his feelings about Lindsey, but Marianne had coaxed him on, encouraging him to talk to her and guaranteeing him that it would make him feel a lot better. It had. It had been good for him to open up to Marianne, and easy because he knew that Marianne had been close to Lindsey too. She understood what it was like to lose someone you deeply cared for, and thus, she was a safe candidate for Nick to lean on.

"I must seem like such a sap to you," Nick said suddenly, turning a questioning gaze on Marianne.

She chuckled. "I think you're one of the coolest guys I know, especially because you're a sap."

Nick grunted. "Gee, thanks."

"Seriously, Nick," Marianne assured him, giving him a reassuring pat on the arm. "I really like you and admire you. I have to admit that I haven't always, but now that I've gotten to know you, I'm almost sorry that you're still stuck on Lindsey. Otherwise I might go for you myself."

Nick smiled, shoving Marianne playfully in the arm. "Ha, ha, yeah right."

"Yeah ... right," Marianne replied. Then, opening the car door and climbing outside, she turned and leaned down to speak one more time to Nick before closing the door. "Thanks for letting me hang out at your house. It was really fun."

"No problem. And thanks for being a cool friend, Marianne."

"No problem." She shut the door, and within a few moments, the red Mustang was screeching down the street and around the corner until it was out of sight.

Marianne sighed, standing on the curb for an indeterminable amount of time. Nick had thought she was joking when she made the comment about going for him; but she had been dead serious.

She turned finally and began making her way up the concrete walk toward her front door. Nick was a sensitive guy, whether he was aware of it or not. Nevertheless, he was still clueless, as most guys in Marianne's experience were. Or maybe Marianne was just too abstract and unclear. Maybe that's why she just couldn't get a boyfriend, because guys couldn't read her. Even she had to admit that she was a confusing creature, and oftentimes she didn't understand her own feelings. With guys, she had always made better friends than romantic partners. But how would she necessarily know that if she had never experienced a real romance yet?

Well, obviously Nick wouldn't play a part in her romance life. Perhaps it was best that he didn't. Maybe it was best that he hadn't dug up the true meaning in her words. He was, after all, still so hooked on Lindsey, and Marianne was unsure that that might change anytime soon.

Nick slowed down as he reached another stop sign. His forehead was creased in thought and question.

I'm almost sorry that you're still stuck on Lindsey, otherwise I might go for you myself.

Nick had laughed it off, immediately taking it as just another one of Marianne's numerous off-the-wall remarks. But now, as he drove home silently with the wind whistling outside and beating at his car, he studied the comment more thoroughly.

What if Marianne was being serious and had meant what she said? Could she honestly have a crush on him? It was nearly inconceivable; Marianne was just too precious a friend right now. And besides, she was … *Marianne.* Funny, silly, playful, strong-willed Marianne.

And she was right, Nick was still stuck on Lindsey, so much that it was becoming a menace to him. He wondered if he would ever get another chance to show Lindsey how much he cared for her and wanted her back.

But what was he thinking? It was impossible now. She was gone, way across the country with some *Caleb* fellow whom she was probably sweet on. Oh well, things like that happened, life went on, people moved on. That's just what Nick needed to do: forget about Lindsey and move on.

* * *

Eight-year-old Lindsey stood outside the front-doorway as her dad rushed past her on the porch and down the steps to his awaiting car. The sky was a deep gray, the personality of an approaching storm. As Lindsey's waist-long hair flew wildly in the wind, she stretched out her arms to the departing man in her vision.

He was only a dark silhouette, nothing more, but she still knew that he was wearing a light blue jacket and gray slacks – the colors of defeat and depression, as well as the oncoming storm.

"Daddy," she yelled, her arms still high in midair while her small fingers moved about, attempting to grab onto the distant silhouette of her father. She bounded down the stairs and across the yard, desperately wishing to stop his abandonment. She knew he was leaving for good, but she didn't know where, and she wasn't sure why. He was a good daddy, in spite of everything that had happened between him and Mom; he was still a good daddy to her.

So why did he have to leave her? Would she ever see him again? Would she ever want to see him again? Did he even care about her?

Questions invaded her brain and desperation permeated her willpower, tearing apart all that was left of her sanity. A scream ripped from her throat as she flung herself through the open gate and onto her father's foot, holding fiercely to his leg.

"Don't go, Daddy, don't go!" she bellowed, tears spilling out from her eyes.

But he didn't respond. As if she was nothing but a pesky house cat, he shook her off his foot in one easy shake and began walking around the car to the driver's side.

Lindsey attempted to move but she was stuck to the curb, glued there by some unwanted force. She kept screaming. "Don't leave me, pleeeeease!" she pleaded. "I need you, I need you! Whatever I did, I'm sorry! I'm sorry!" The small eight-year-old body began rocking back and forth, despondent, utterly spent.

The next sound was the car engine choking and sputtering, then running with full force. As the man drove away without a word of recourse or a final farewell, Lindsey leaned forward on the sidewalk and sobbed, resting her head on the cold pavement while the wind tore at her backside and the rain threatened to drown her in her own sorrow.

In the next instant, she was suddenly back on the porch – only it wasn't the porch at her house. It was another, unfamiliar porch, sitting in front of an unfamiliar house. But somehow she knew it belonged to her grandmother. And she wasn't eight years old anymore, either. She was a teenager now, years later, having survived the torment of living without her father.

The sky was sunny this time, and Lindsey could feel herself breathing in the warm air, feel it cascading down her throat and into her lungs. She felt calm all of a sudden. Peace, contentment. The weather was fine, and so was her mood. The gentle lapping of water on shore began to fill her ears, and it sounded like music to her. She smiled.

In a minute, that all faded away, though. A distant buzz broke the monotony of the waves on shore, creating a discord to her music. Her smile disappeared, and as she watched the cloudless blue sky above her, a form appeared out of nowhere, accompanied by the annoying buzz. Growing louder and coming closer, Lindsey realized that the object in the sky was a small, private airplane. Intuitively, she knew her mother was in it, although she wasn't sure how she knew. She also knew that something bad was going to happen, and her mother would be the victim.

Gazing up at the airplane as it cascaded through the sky, Lindsey squinted from the bright sun, and could actually make out her mother's face staring back from one of the windows in the plane. Jillian waved down to her daughter.

Lindsey screamed. "Noooooo!" She jumped off the porch and began running toward the beach, hoping somehow to stop her mother's deadly fate.

All at once the airplane plunged downward as it's engine ceased, twisting and colliding through the open air toward a group of hills just off of the beach. Lindsey watched in horror as mysterious flames suddenly engulfed the aircraft, leaving a trail of fiery residue across the sky.

Although the plane didn't have a long way to fall, it seemed to fall for an infinite period of time. Lindsey was screaming the whole time, jumping up and down on the beach in panic and dismay. At the very last moment before the plane crashed into the hills, as if in slow-motion, Lindsey thrust her body onto the beach, closed her eyes tightly and covered her ears to block out the terrifying scene. She screamed the whole time.

* * *

She screamed the whole time.

Lindsey twisted around in her bed, finally waking up before the plane had a chance to crash. As her eyes flew open and began taking in the scene around her – that of a hotel room – she suddenly realized that she had been dreaming, and remembered that she was safely in Lincoln with Caleb.

Relieved beyond measure that she was back in the real world, she inhaled a shaky, nervous breath and sat herself up in bed. Her heart was pounding furiously inside her chest, and her forehead was saturated with perspiration, as was her pillow and bed sheets.

She took another deep breath and flung the hot, damp covers onto the floor. For a while, she sat on the edge of the bed, recalling her dream.

What a terrible dream it had been. Without warning or invitation, she had been forced to recollect the most horrible moments of her life – those of losing both her parents.

Only, in real life, neither incident had happened the way it had in her dream. She had never even observed her dad running out on her, nor had she witnessed her mother's death in the airplane crash. And as far as she knew, the plane had not crashed right outside of her grandmother's house on the beach.

She also knew that her father hadn't run out that way, so determined and resolute and … careless, leaving a helpless eight-year-old daughter sobbing on the curb as he rushed away in his car without a final turn of the head or mindfulness to his nagging conscience. No, when her father left, Lindsey had been gone somewhere, never having seen him leave, nor attempting to stop him from leaving. The only thing Lindsey could relate to in her dream was the emotion; the terrible feelings of emptiness and brokenness, depression and helplessness, horror and pain that had overtaken her whole being and had left her screaming and crying profusely.

That part was real. Okay, so she had never outwardly broken down and sobbed uncontrollably, or screamed out of pain till her throat hurt, but inside her mostly-controlled exterior, there was another story playing. And it just played itself out in her dream.

Lindsey's hands suddenly flew to her face as she began sobbing. The images in her head now – of her mother plunging helplessly to her death in a fiery plane and her father carelessly walking away – were just too much for

Lindsey to handle. Never before had she wondered about the way her mother died. Never before had she been curious to know the details of the plane crash, but now she couldn't drive the dreadful image out of her mind, nor cease to wonder whether that was how it was for her mother in real life. How had Jillian felt when she knew the plane was going down? What did she feel? What panic-stricken emotions were playing themselves out in her horrified eyes as she realized that she was going to die?

Or did she even realize that she was going to die?

Lindsey began crying harder as she considered the thought.

"Oh, Mom," she cried, her shoulders heaving in fits of sobbing. "I miss you, I miss you. I want you back, please...."

Suddenly struck with the thought that she wasn't alone in the room, she sniffed loudly and poked her head up out of the confines of her hands. She glanced in front of her toward Caleb's bed. She sighed with relief when she saw that it was empty. The covers had been slung back, and a damp bathroom towel was tossed in the middle of the floor.

Caleb was up, and from the looks of it he was gone. So, thankfully, he hadn't witnessed her foolish outburst.

Nineteen

What great nation ever had their gods as near to them as the LORD our God is near to us whenever we pray to him?
– Deuteronomy 4:7

Lindsey turned her head toward the clock. It read 8:49 a.m. Checkout was at 10:00. Lindsey stood up and made her way into the bathroom. Hopefully a refreshing shower would ease her troubled mind a little, and the knowledge of the approaching six-hour day on the road would alter her thoughts. She and Caleb would be heading out of Lincoln, Nebraska, crossing the state border and the Missouri River into Iowa, then turn southward into Missouri and drive as near to St. Louis as they could.

Lindsey sighed with dismay at the thought of the coming day. They would be on the road a very long time, mostly non-stop, as they'd been doing. Lindsey doubted that they'd make it to St. Louis in one day. It would definitely take more than six or seven hours.

Not wanting to ponder over it any longer, Lindsey shut the bathroom door and jumped into the shower. She wondered where Caleb could be. Maybe he was just having continental breakfast in the hotel lobby. Well, wherever he was, Lindsey just hoped that he knew checkout time was in an hour.

The hot shower water helped to alleviate Lindsey's troubled emotions over her dream, just as she hoped it would. Yes, that was all she needed, to wake up and get into reality so that the dream could fade and eventually disintegrate into a distant, far-off memory.

Lindsey didn't realize that she had taken an extra-long shower, and by the time she was out, dressed, and had brushed her teeth and combed her hair, it was already almost 9:30. She didn't have much time to pack up and have everything out by 10:00.

The bathroom door creaked as it opened, and when Lindsey walked out to pack away her nightclothes and toiletries, she took notice of the fact that the room was still the way it had been a half-hour ago. The curtains were still closed, the television shut off, Caleb's bed empty, his shower towel still undisturbed in the middle of the floor, and his suitcase still flung open with shirts and pants and various other items spilling out of it. Lindsey frowned. Where the heck was Caleb? Why wasn't he back yet? They only had a half-hour to pack up and check out, so he had better hurry it up whatever he was doing.

Shaking off the uneasy feeling that began to settle on her from Caleb's mysterious absence, Lindsey took herself to the bathroom again to finish her morning routine. She took ten minutes to quickly put on her makeup, blow-dried her hair so that it was barely damp, and fixed it up in two barrettes that would keep it out of her face. Glancing at her wristwatch, she saw that it was already 9:50.

She stepped out of the bathroom again, half-expecting to see Caleb that time sitting on his bed, waiting for her. He still wasn't there. And everything was still the same.

That uneasy feeling settled over her again, and it caused Lindsey to crease her forehead in question and confusion. *Caleb, where are you?* She quickly packed the rest of her belongings away in her suitcase, doubled-checked to make sure she didn't leave anything in the room, and headed toward the door. It led right outside to the balcony, overlooking the parking lot. She scanned the whole lot thoroughly with her eyes – Caleb's truck was gone.

All at once, unexpectedly, her heart sped up in worry and anxiety. *Oh no, oh no!* Her mind whispered. *He's gone, he's gone. But where did he go? Is he coming back?*

"Of course he's coming back," Lindsey told herself strictly, attempting to convince herself that she was worried over nothing. Wherever Caleb went, he would be back soon. He wouldn't just up and leave her. He couldn't forget about her.

Could he?

No, she told herself. She was being irrational. Since he was obviously going to be late for checkout, Lindsey decided she should probably go pack up his things for him and get them down to the parking lot and wait for Caleb to return.

So that's what she did. It took her only five minutes to shove the rest of Caleb's belongings in his disordered suitcase and wheel it downstairs along with her own stuff. Setting the luggage to the side, she hastily ran around the building into the lobby to check out at the front desk. As she approached the front desk clerk she peeked into the small room where breakfast was served, but saw no sign of Caleb.

"Good morning," the polite receptionist at the desk greeted.

Lindsey forced a smile. "Hi. I'm checking out of room 304." Lindsey tossed her room keys onto the desktop, and before the receptionist could utter another word, Lindsey asked her about Caleb. "I was wondering … by any chance has my friend been down here at all this morning? He's that guy that I've been hanging out with for the past couple of days, remember? I think you talked to him yesterday morning – he's that blond fellow who's kinda tall and…."

"Oh yeah, I know who you're talking about. Yeah, he was down here early this morning for breakfast – probably around 7:30 – and then he left. I didn't see where he went. I just assumed he went back to his room."

"Oh, okay."

"Did you lose him, or something?" the girl asked with a warm smile on her face.

Lindsey tried to laugh, but all that came through was a clumsy smile – a disappointing reassurement on her part that she hadn't lost him. "No, I uh, just … can't seem to find him. He must've gone somewhere and lost track of the time, or something."

"Well, I'm sure he'll be back soon. Did he know checkout was at ten?"

Lindsey just nodded, then turned to walk away. Although she had told the receptionist that Caleb had probably just lost track of time, she couldn't bring herself to believe it. For some reason, there was a bad feeling tugging at her, urging her to start panicking. But she knew Caleb better than that, of course. There should be no need to worry or panic. He was Caleb, after all; caring, lovable Caleb who would never run out on Lindsey like her own father did.

And as that thought invaded her worried mind, she actually began to consider it.

Caleb glanced at his wristwatch and noticed that the time was later than he had realized it was. It was nearly 10:30. Caleb stepped on the gas pedal, and the truck went lurching forward. He hoped Lindsey wasn't wondering where he was. But why should she. Checkout time was at 11:00 after all. She had probably only woken up a half-hour ago and was just getting out of the shower or something.

As the Ford sped up even more, dodging other vehicles on the road, swerving back and forth between lanes, Caleb noticed a back up in traffic a few blocks ahead. Oh no, he probably wouldn't make it back to the hotel for another ten or fifteen minutes. Oh well, that would still give him time to pack up and get checked out.

Caleb turned up his music and leaned back in the driver's seat. It was going to be a long day.

Lindsey's dream began to refresh itself in her mind as she sat outside on the curb, resting her arms on her lap, staring out into the parking lot.

She had already received a few weird looks from the other departing guests who found it odd that a teenage girl was sitting alone on the curb with luggage at her side, staring worriedly out in front of her. One of the maids even walked up and asked her if she was all right. Lindsey convinced the lady that she was just fine and was only waiting for her friend who "must've lost track of the time, or had car trouble or something."

Lindsey's legs began to fidget with restlessness, and she began playing with the rings on her fingers in nervous anticipation. It was past 10:30. It was almost 10:40. Every minute that went by ticked loudly in Lindsey's head, mocking her, taunting her. Irrational thoughts crowded her brain, things she could not help but wonder about. *How could Caleb forget about me? He must've left. Maybe he got tired of me asking so many questions. Maybe he couldn't handle my emotional instability anymore. What if he just up and left really early? But then why would his luggage still be here?*

But then how could he have forgotten about me? Where could he have just up and gone for almost three hours, never leaving a note or calling or giving me any hint of where he might be! He must've known that checkout time was 10:00. He was the one who got the room, for heaven's sake!

And now, to the jumbled mess of her thoughts, she added another idea. One that helped refresh her dream of being a small girl, calling out to her dad on the curb as he drove away and left her.

Caleb left me just like my dad left me.

As that possibility hit her, she tried to dissuade it with more realistic and positive explanations, but all that she came back to was the small girl holding her arms out toward her father's dark silhouette.

Lindsey began to cry again, just like this morning when she had woken from the awful entrapment of her dream.

With her tear-stained face resting in her hands on her knees, Lindsey didn't even notice the blue Ford pull into the parking lot. It was only when it screeched to a halt right in front of Lindsey that she thrust her head up and saw Caleb.

The sight of him only made the tears stream out harder. She stood up, but didn't move.

Caleb panicked when he saw her face. She had been crying, and she was extremely upset. Not angry-upset, but frightened-upset, as if something terrible had just happened. Had it?

"Lindsey!" Caleb called as he jumped out of his truck and rushed to her still form. He stopped right in front of her, his concerned eyes scanning Lindsey's worried stare. He put his hand on her arm. "Are you okay? What's wrong, what happened?"

"What happened?" Lindsey replied, confused. So Caleb really didn't know what was wrong? He really had just lost track of time? "I … I didn't know where you went," she stammered. "I thought maybe you just left."

"I'm sorry, Lindsey. I woke up early and couldn't get back to sleep, so I went and had breakfast in the lobby. I decided to just let you keep sleeping, so instead of coming back to the room I went back over to the mall to buy this shirt that I saw yesterday. I got caught up talking with somebody and lost track of time."

"Did you know check-out time was at ten?" Lindsey asked quietly, not taking her eyes off of the pavement beneath her feet.

A strong surge of guilt swept over Caleb, and at once he took notice of the two suitcases sitting next to where Lindsey was on the curb. He glanced at his watch again. It was nearly 10:45. He had been forty-five minutes late. No wonder Lindsey had been panicking.

"Oh no, I'm so sorry," he apologized again. "I honestly didn't know that check-out was at ten. I was thinking it was eleven. I was thinking I'd get here with a little extra time to pack up and get outta here."

"I already packed for you," Lindsey said quietly, with just a hint of annoyance trailing her tone of voice.

"Yeah, I see that." Caleb managed a smile, but Lindsey was expressionless. Caleb could only wonder at the menagerie of emotions flooding through her right now. "I'm so sorry, Lindsey," he said once again. "Please, don't ever, ever think I would just leave you, okay? Why would I do that, Lindsey? I could never."

Lindsey stared at the ground, nodding her head.

"Why did you think that, Lindsey?" But before she answered, he suddenly knew. Of course, she had already been through an abandonment situation with her father when she was younger. The whole idea made Caleb sick to the stomach with guilt.

Lindsey just shook her head, then turned and picked up her suitcase, flung it in the back of the truck and climbed into the passenger seat. Caleb silently followed suit, and within minutes, they were out of the parking lot, headed eastward toward Iowa.

For the most part, Lindsey stayed silent that first fifteen minutes as Caleb took highway 2 out of Lincoln eastward toward Iowa. The only time Lindsey spoke up was to remind Caleb that once they hit Iowa they needed to get off on I-29.

Setting the road atlas onto the passenger's-side floor, Lindsey turned toward the window, kicked off her shoes, and lay back in her seat to take a nap. It had already been an exhausting morning, and Lindsey was not looking forward to the rest of the day. If they were determined enough to make it into St. Louis today, Lindsey already estimated that it would take nearly the whole day.

They should just stick to their six- and seven-hour days. Lindsey could at least handle six hours on the road, but just barely. The thought of driving for any longer made her want to pull out her hair in frustration and scream. Perhaps she should mention that to Caleb; let him know that they shouldn't bother to go all the way to St. Louis today. They weren't in any hurry, after all. They had all the time in the world. Besides, the closer they got to the East Coast, the larger Lindsey's anxiety grew. Already twice on this trip she had gotten that sick-to-the-stomach feeling that accompanies nervousness and anxiety. Now, as the thought of approaching Virginia crept into her mind, her stomach began to knot itself once again, forming a fist that twisted with determination.

Lindsey squirmed in her seat, trying to force the thought of Virginia out of her mind. Perhaps she *would* tell Caleb that maybe they should take it easy today.

But for now she was too upset and embarrassed to even face Caleb, let alone say a word to him. What a fool she must have seemed to him; a silly little scared child crying alone on the curb. How many times on this trip had Caleb seen Lindsey cry? Enough.

Lindsey pushed the thought out of her brain as she once again pursued sleep. She thought that as long as she could sleep most of the hours away, then the trip would at least be a little more bearable.

The sky was overcast today with the sun taking refuge behind the thick veil of gray clouds. It looked like it might rain, but Lindsey wasn't quite sure. She hoped it wouldn't. Rain had a way of putting her in depressed, hopeless moods.

As the Ford made its way further along the highway, the big-city sights of Lincoln disappeared into more fields and pastures. *Boring*, Lindsey thought. *Boring and depressing.* There was absolutely nothing to look at out here. All the more reason for Lindsey to close her eyes and attempt sleep.

But sleep was hard to come. Lindsey couldn't help but recognize how fast the time had gone by already. It was Wednesday. Lindsey and Caleb had already spent exactly a week together. Just last Wednesday Lindsey had been released from the hospital in Deer Lodge, Caleb had gotten her a hotel room, and the two had decided to travel together for the rest of their trips. Wow, she had only known Caleb for a week, but it seemed like so much longer. He had, after all, already shared with her openly so many things about his past, things about his family and his faith.

Yes, he had been very open about his faith, which had baffled Lindsey during this past week. Openness was just not a quality she thought guys were equipped with. Sure, she had known few other people who were "Christians," as they'd called themselves, but never had they been so open and honest about what that meant as Caleb had. Even though Lindsey was, for the most part, still confused as to what the big deal was about being a Christian and believing in God, she couldn't deny that it was very important to Caleb and had made a big impact in his life. She knew about his past, after all, and if what he mentioned about it had been accurate, then Lindsey could only conclude that Caleb was a wholly new person.

And, Lindsey couldn't deny, his faith had really made her think. She was curious about Christianity, about God. How was it that a person could be changed so dramatically by a religion, by a faith in something that seemed utterly unrealistic and childish?

But Caleb hadn't made it unrealistic and childish. For him it really was real, Lindsey could see that. She could already see just how important God was to Caleb, and how he worked so hard to keep it that way. Sure, it baffled Lindsey, but it also entranced her and caused her to admire and like Caleb all the more.

Even though she and Caleb seemed worlds apart right now, Lindsey knew she was going to miss him. In a few more days, as they hit Virginia, Caleb would drop off Lindsey, they might say a few departing words, and then it was good-bye. She might never see him or speak to him again. How would she deal with that? Just the thought of ending this trip and having Caleb leave her life was a violent crash on Lindsey's heart. She had grown so close to Caleb, so dependent on him, that she couldn't imagine not having him by her side any longer.

And all of a sudden it hit her; she *had* grown dependent on Caleb, more than she had expected or realized. He was, after all, her hero, like she had told him last Tuesday night at the hospital. Ever since that night, he had been looking out for her, caring for her, being her protector. Caleb had possessed qualities that seemed so distantly unique and admirable from any other guy she had known. And because of that, Lindsey had clung to him unknowingly. She wasn't ready to give him up, either.

She cared about Caleb, too, and she hoped that whatever happened after these last few days together, they could at least keep in touch once in a while.

Besides, they wouldn't be too far apart from each other, only a state away. He would be in North Carolina and she would be in Virginia....

She would be living in Virginia ... soon ... with her dad ... very soon.

As the anxiety once more stirred in her stomach, Lindsey shook her head and again repositioned herself on the reclined seat, trying to make herself comfortable, trying to make herself feel okay, trying to make herself fall asleep.

Caleb glanced over at Lindsey squirming in her seat, trying to get comfortable and fall asleep. She was restless, he could tell. It was probably his fault. She had a terrible morning all because of him, because he couldn't get the time straight.

Caleb mentally kicked himself, then decided that before he got any angrier with himself he should probably pray. So he quickly asked God to ease his guilt-ridden heart, to ease Lindsey's restless heart, and to guide them safely along the rest of their trip together.

Bryan Tate drove carefully down the street, glancing in his rearview mirror periodically, desperately wanting to slam on his brakes and show that vehicle behind him just what they deserved for following so closely behind him! *Ah, don't let Satan use little things like that to get to you, Bryan,* he told himself.

Checking his directions from Mary one more time, he turned right on the next road to find her house. Today they had agreed to share a lunch together at her house. She would be working the late shift at work, so she said she had all day to do nothing and would like to make him lunch to pay back for all his kindness to her. Bryan decided it was a wonderful idea. Indeed, he couldn't deny that he had been looking forward to seeing her again. She had been great company last time they were together. She was an interesting, amusing woman, and of course he was eager to meet Andrea.

Also, their meeting would be the perfect opportunity to share with Mary what he had been wanting to share with her since Monday...to let her know straight out, before anything else got underway between them, that he was only seeking a good friendship with her and that she shouldn't take his affectionate behavior to mean anything more.

Hopefully she would understand. Besides, maybe he was totally wrong about her; maybe she didn't feel anything for him.

Or maybe he was totally wrong about himself. He was, after all, looking forward to their lunch tremendously. He had been ever since they planned it yesterday afternoon, and it wasn't just for the opportunity to let her know his intentions for their friendship.

His heart racing a little faster and his smile spreading wider on his lips, Bryan finally pulled his vehicle into the small driveway that belonged to Mary Jenkins' tiny house.

It was a cute, quaint place, square in appearance. The yard was yellowing with grass that needed mowing, and the siding on the house was chipping off. But once Bryan was actually inside, it seemed befitting to Mary. It was decorated, not plainly, but simply, which Bryan found he liked. His former wife had always gone all out with extravagance, always wanting *things*, meaningless things to decorate with. Mary had all the essentials, but nothing more. Each room was rather small, but for only two people it seemed appropriate. The living room was furnished with a worn couch, an old television and VCR, a few bright green plants and framed pictures on the walls. Inside the kitchen, Bryan could see a kitchen table and chairs that looked twenty years old.

Bryan liked the way Mary seemed to live a simple life. She didn't have a large, immoderate career or a fancy house. She didn't even have a car to take her to and from work! Her small way of living made her appear more humble to Bryan. Indeed, she knew what her priorities were.

"This is my daughter, Andrea," Mary said once they were situated inside the house.

"Well hello, Andrea," Bryan smiled largely, outstretching his hand for Andrea to shake. She did so with a smile on her face. "I'm glad to meet you. Your mom has told me all about you."

"Likewise," she stated proudly. Mary and Bryan glanced at each other and exchanged amused smiles. Andrea was too cute in her purple and pink dress with her hair tied up in a ribbon. Mary later revealed to Bryan that she had wanted to dress up for this special occasion of meeting him. What a unique six-year-old.

"So, Bryan, you'll have to tell me all about your work. We really didn't get much of a chance to talk about you at our last meeting."

"Hey, no problem. I'm good at talking about myself." Mary laughed as she walked into the kitchen to set the table. Bryan followed behind her.

"Mama, I'm going to my room to play with Sunny, okay? Just call me when lunch is on!" Andrea raced to her room without waiting for a response.

"Okay, honey," Mary called behind her.

"Who's Sunny?" Bryan asked curiously.

"Oh, just one of her dolls."

"She's a very polite girl," Bryan commented, walking to Mary's side, quickly offering to help with the dishes. After she refused, she said, "Yeah, well, I guess she gets such gracious manners from her wonderfully gracious mother." *She certainly doesn't get them from her father!*

Bryan laughed. "That you are, I'm sure," he said.

"Oh hey!" Mary spun around quickly and faced him. "Before anything else, I wanted to tell you that I uh … was wondering if you'd help me … in becoming a Christian."

"Wow, really," Bryan questioned, amazed. He knew God was working strongly in Mary, but he hadn't expected that she'd respond so soon. It was wonderful, a true miracle from God. "Of course, Mary, I'd love to," he said. "Actually, I'd be honored."

"Oh good," she replied, excited. "I wasn't sure exactly what I was supposed to do or if there were any formal steps in becoming a Christian. I didn't know if I should wait and talk to a pastor or anything."

"Well, if you wanted, you could, if you had any questions or anything."

"No, I just…." she stopped, looking past him out the window. She was light on her feet, he could tell, obviously light-hearted and pleased with her commitment to follow Christ. As he gazed at her his heart melted. She was indeed going to be a very special woman to him.

"You just…?"

"I just knew I needed to do this, you know." Mary took a step closer to Bryan, and he motioned for her to take a seat in one of the kitchen chairs. She did, and he sat opposite her. "I prayed yesterday for the first time. I wasn't sure how or if I was doing it right, but I just told God that I believed in Him and in Jesus."

"That's the best way to start," Bryan said assuredly, nodding his head. "You start by inviting Jesus into your heart and your life."

"Yeah, that's what I did."

"Good, I'm glad you did. I prayed for you."

"Oh, you did?"

Bryan nodded. Mary noted the sharp way he was dressed today – nice slacks and light blue collared shirt for work. He was stunningly dashing. She tried not to focus on that.

Mary reached out and grabbed Bryan's hands in her own. "Thank you so much. I couldn't have done this without you. You are a good friend to me already."

Bryan was overwhelmed with emotion all of a sudden. Who would have known that God would use him in such a seemingly simple way to help bring someone to Him? It was an awesome feeling.

"Thank you, Mary. But I didn't really do anything. It was all God. He was seeking you."

"That's a scary thought."

"It's an awesome one, though."

"It sure is."

"So I take it you're definitely coming back to church next Sunday?"

"Oh, of course!" Mary burst out, jumping up from the chair and reaching to open the cupboards full of dishes.

"Good, because having a Christian family is essential to your faith."

Mary stopped at the mention of a "Christian family." She thought of her own Christian family back when she was a child and wondered if that's what Bryan was referring to. She slumped a little bit and turned a restless gaze on Bryan. He was instantly concerned.

"What's wrong, Mary?"

She shrugged her shoulders, wondering whether she should speak up or not. Did having a church family mean that she'd be constantly reminded of her mistakes, and when she was failing in God's eyes? Would her church family never let her forget that she was a sinner? Is that what a church family was about?

"Mary, if something's wrong, I'd like to see if I could help you with it."

Mary thought of Bryan. He hadn't mentioned her mistakes at all. While he was explaining about Jesus to her last Sunday, he had mentioned the importance of repenting and asking for forgiveness of sins so that she could seek an open and blameless relationship with God, but he hadn't condemned her personally for her own sins. She decided she might as well voice her concerns. After all, she knew she didn't want to get caught up in this Christianity thing if it was just going to end up the way it had been before.

She sat back down at the table and began to explain in detail about her "church past" and about her experience with Christians. She told Bryan of her rebellion as a teenager and how she despised the Christians she had known for always judging her and hurting her. She spent a great deal of time pouring out her past, about how she never gave a care to God all the way up to the part where she met Caleb at work last week and how his short remark to her about God was what convicted her to give church another chance.

Bryan sighed heavily and stared straight at Mary for a few moments before answering, "I'm sorry you've had to go through that, and to witness such behavior from Christians. But I can honestly tell you, Mary, that they were wrong when they judged you and condemned you for not believing in God."

A huge weight lifted off Mary at the sound of his words, and the conviction in his voice.

"God wants all of his children to know Him and seek a relationship with Him, but the way to go about that is not to condemn people. God always loves us, whether we know Him or not."

"Really?"

"Oh yeah. All those years during your rebellion and your defiance of God, He still loved you the same and kept after you. I know that for a fact, because here you are now, fully seeking to know Him."

Mary smiled. It was the truth.

"Sometimes it's hard for me to believe that God loves me no better than he loves that drug dealer in the street or that seemingly 'terrible' sinner who lives next door, but He does, because he made us all to have a relationship with Him."

Mary listened intently, soaking up the words.

"There are just some people who choose His offer of grace and some people who don't. But it doesn't make either person better than the other. We're believers because of our faith and our desire to follow Christ, but it doesn't make us more loved by Him. We are as loved as we have always been and always will be. If it weren't for God's unconditional love, we wouldn't be sitting here with each other as believers. He pursued us, and it's only because of Him that we're here as we are."

Mary nodded, her eyes wide.

"Your family and friends who said those things to you about being a sinner and being a disappointment to God were wrong in what they did, but it didn't make God love them any less. Hopefully they've realized their mistake by now. As Christians, we are called to love other people and to minister to non-believers in loving, gentle ways. We are not called to condemn and to judge others, no matter how bad they may seem or how far away from God they are. We love them no matter what, just like God loves us."

Mary straightened herself in her chair and decided to add to the conversation. "I think maybe the reason my parents and my friends seemed so harsh on me is *because* they loved me so much and were worried for my salvation. They didn't know how else to react."

"Sure, but that doesn't make what they did to you right."

"No, it doesn't, but it's something I never considered before. It kind of makes me feel bad that my so-called 'Christian' family didn't even know God well enough to know that they needed to be loving instead of judgmental. You know, I feel sorry for them in a way that they couldn't trust God in such a situation."

The afternoon wore on, and after Mary had finally set the table and served lunch, she, Bryan, and Andrea had shared a pleasant meal and conversation around the table. In that short hour, Bryan had learned so much about Mary and Andrea, about their past lives, about Andrea's school, about their hobbies and fun times together. It was indeed a wonderful lunch.

After Andrea left the table only twenty minutes after arriving, Bryan and Mary were left to themselves for more personal conversation. Bryan learned more of Mary's marriage to Ted. She seemed very cold and blunt about it, so Bryan didn't pry or ask too many questions. She was obviously not on good terms with this Ted and was still very angry about whatever it was that happened between them. So Bryan learned more about her work and the ladies she worked with.

It would have been the perfect opportunity to let Mary know about what had been on Bryan's mind since Monday – letting her know about his friendly intentions toward her and nothing more – but strangely the topic, which had been so heavy on his heart, hadn't even come up in conversation. It hadn't even come up in Bryan's mind.

After the hour was over, Bryan had to get back to work, so he cordially thanked Mary for the wonderful lunch, planned to see her again Friday night, and strolled out to his car to make his way back to work.

It was only when he was back at work that he noticed his light step, his frolicsome behavior and his … fluttering heart?

And all of sudden he realized that he had, in a haste of contentment and eagerness, made a date with Mary for Friday night!

A date?

Twenty

We don't look for things that can be seen but for things that can't be seen.
Things that can be seen are only temporary.
But things that can't be seen last forever.
– 2 Corinthians 4:18

Lindsey was only dimly aware of the soft hum of the engine, the quiet music playing out of the speakers, and the slight bumps in the freeway down which they were traveling. She was caught in that in-between state of sleep and wakefulness and had been for nearly the whole two hours since they got on the road. When the Ford hit a large rut in the road and bounced sharply, Lindsey was jarred into full consciousness. She gazed out the window for a minute or two, watching the gray sky and telephone poles whiz past against a background of yellow pastures and fields.

She yawned and sat herself up. Propping her elbow up right under the window she leaned her head against her hand and sighed. It was only 1:00, but they were already well into Missouri.

"Have a nice sleep?" Caleb asked tiredly.

Lindsey just shrugged and mumbled a short, "I guess."

"You know what I just thought of?"

"What?"

"We've lost two hours of our lives from this trip, because we've crossed two time zones."

"Wow," Lindsey replied, not enthused. "No wonder we're so tired."

Since Lindsey was awake, Caleb turned the radio up, leaned his head back until it was resting on the back of his seat, and continued driving silently. He still felt bad for the way the morning had turned out, but he didn't want to bring it up with Lindsey. He was sure she was still upset at him, but he didn't say anything about it. Nevertheless, he didn't want them to spend the rest of their day together with this tension riding between them. He wanted to talk to Lindsey; somehow make sure she was all right and wasn't angry with him or anything.

Putting his left hand on the wheel, he leaned sideways a little and used his right hand to reach behind his seat and grab the plastic bag that was sitting on the floor. Lindsey watched him curiously, wondering what he was doing. He swerved a little on the road and she reached out and grabbed the steering wheel.

"I'm fine," Caleb said, finally grabbing the plastic bag and leaning forward. He handed the bag to Lindsey. "Here. This is for you. I bought it this morning when I was at the mall, and I would've given it to you earlier except that you were too upset."

Lindsey's eyes widened in surprise. Caleb noticed how weary and worn out she appeared. "You got me a present?"

"Sure," Caleb responded, smiling vaguely. He watched her as she pulled out a small wrapped box out of the plastic bag and began opening the gift. As she did, she glanced up at Caleb with a smile on her face and shook her head slightly in disbelief. Wow, she couldn't believe he had actually bought her something. That was so nice!

"Oh my gosh," she exclaimed as she pulled out a miniature stuffed animal from the box. It was a chubby teddy bear dressed up in faded blue overalls with a straw hat on its head, holding a small rake. In its hat were stuck tiny leaves of different colors. Lindsey's smile broadened and she looked up at Caleb with sparkles in her eyes. "Thank you so much," she laughed. "It's so cute."

"Yeah, I just saw it and thought of you. And of course it's appropriate for the season."

"Thank you very much," Lindsey said again, tossing the garbage into the backseat. She laid the small bear gently on top of the dashboard where they both could admire it. "It's perfect."

Caleb smiled with pleasure that she had liked his gift and stared ahead. Hopefully that would ease the tension a small bit.

As if reading his thoughts, Lindsey suddenly said, "Look, I'm sorry for the way I acted this morning. I didn't mean to make you feel bad or anything."

"No, no, don't be sorry," Caleb insisted. "It's my fault if anything. I wasn't even paying attention to the time. You had every reason to be upset. I probably would've been freaking out too if my ride had been nearly an hour late coming to get me."

"It's just," Lindsey went on, feeling like she had to explain herself, "I had this terrible dream last night, about my dad walking out me and my mom getting in the plane crash and...." Her voice faltered, and she cleared her throat to go on. "It was weird because the way I lost my parents in my dream was different from how it happened in real life. It was worse, much worse, and I woke up pretty freaked out and I just...." she stopped, not knowing where she was trying to go, just feeling like she needed to tell Caleb about her experience.

He caught on to her uneasiness and quickly stepped in. "Hey, don't worry about it. It was just a dream, you know."

"Yeah, but it was so real. I can't remember the last time I had a dream that was so terrible and vivid."

Caleb's heart sank for Lindsey. All of a sudden he wished he had been there in the hotel room that morning when she had woken up to comfort Lindsey from her dream. Every time Caleb thought about Lindsey's life and her circumstances, he always felt a great burden weighing on him, a wave of compassion that crashed over him. His past life had been pretty terrible, too, but of course he had Jesus to pull him through, and it was still tough at times dealing with his past. He was so afraid for Lindsey, so concerned that she might never see God as anything more than fantasy or a therapy tool; as a result, she would never know what kind of better life she could be living wish Jesus in it. If only she would open herself up and respond somehow to Jesus. So far she had been asking questions, and she had listened to every word Caleb spoke about his faith, but she hadn't really *responded*. Caleb couldn't as yet tell whether she genuinely interested in Jesus or not.

Caleb suddenly realized that he was worrying again, worrying over Lindsey's salvation as if it was all up to him. Even if he never witnessed her responding to Jesus, at least he had the faith that God was pursuing her. Indeed He was, and He wouldn't stop until He had her. Caleb knew that much.

"Lindsey, I truly am sorry about this morning, I hope you know."

"Oh, I know, Caleb. Don't worry about it. It's over with." Silence followed for a few seconds, then Lindsey went on, "My life must seem like one big mess-up to you."

"No, not at all," Caleb answered honestly. "Until you've been a hard druggie and have been depressed to the point where you want to die, then I don't think your life is a mess-up at all. In fact, it seems very stable compared to what I've been through."

Lindsey smiled. He was probably right. Lindsey had actually had a good life growing up. Things had only seemed to fall apart in the last few months. She was curious to ask some more about Caleb's past, but she didn't want to bring up any ghosts to haunt him. She knew how bad he already felt about his past.

"Besides," Caleb continued, "for Jesus, a life can never be too messed up to put back straight."

"Hmm," Lindsey responded. It was obviously true since Caleb was a walking testimony to how this Jesus fellow could change lives. Could Jesus do for Lindsey what he did for Caleb? Probably, but Lindsey didn't think she had enough faith right now to believe in it all. It all sounded nice and promising, but other times it also sounded out of reach.

"Caleb," Lindsey began slowly, wondering how she should word her statement. "How was it … that you knew this whole God thing was real? I mean, with a guy like you and your past, what was it that made you believe?"

Caleb had to think about that one for a minute. "Well," he stumbled out. "I don't know exactly what it was that made me believe. I don't think it was any certain thing I heard or learned. I think for some people they get these big booms or revelations and just know that God is real, but for me it took a little while. I was pretty stubborn. When my Aunt and Uncle first started introducing me to Christ, I was hardheaded and close-minded. I never wanted to hear anything they had to say. I couldn't really comprehend a God at all."

"So what made you change your mind?" Lindsey asked.

Caleb shrugged. "I had no other way out, I guess. I felt like I was at a dead end in my life, like I wasn't going anywhere except down. God made sense to me, you know? I mean, He's a loving, merciful, forgiving, compassionate and personal God – all the qualities you would look for in someone, right?"

Lindsey didn't say anything but frowned in thought.

"So in the long run it wasn't really anything that my Aunt and Uncle had to say that made me believe. It was something I saw in them and in their lives, something I knew I wanted and needed. Slowly, I just felt Jesus start working in my heart, and eventually I became open to him and started seeking him." Caleb stopped for a moment, his brain churning and working as he recalled his struggle with Christ before he gave his life to Him. "So when you ask what it was that made me believe … I can't really say. I just knew it was real. I mean, when I first confessed my sins to Him, it was like a weight was being lifted off of me. I knew right then that my life was going to be radically changed because Jesus was in my life now. You see, other people can't get you to believe in Jesus, it's something Jesus does. He changes your heart."

"Hmm," Lindsey said, wondering what it all meant. It seemed pretty straightforward, but just in case, she wanted to clear it up of any loopholes that might be lingering. "Okay then," she said, "if Jesus can just change our hearts and make us believe in Him, why doesn't He just change mine right now?"

Caleb glanced over at Lindsey with incredulity. Was she actually saying that? *Oh Lord, help me now,* he pleaded. *Here we go....*

"Do you *want* to believe in Jesus, is that why you're asking that?"

"Not necessarily. I'm just trying to clear up a few things."

"Well, Jesus probably *could* snap His fingers and suddenly change your heart, but He doesn't force any of us to believe in Him."

"Why not?"

Caleb's eyes widened. He couldn't believe his ears. It was nice that Lindsey was trying to find answers, but she seemed to be challenging him, trying to get him stuck so that she could conclude that his belief in Jesus wasn't valid or something. "Lindsey," he retorted. "Why *would* Jesus want to force us into belief? He gives us free choice of will. He wants to know that His followers actually *want* to follow Him. God isn't just this great big mean guy who wants to order us around. He hopes that we will seek Him, and then He can work in us from there."

"Oh," Lindsey said. Maybe Caleb was right. *I mean, he'd know, wouldn't he?*

Lindsey took a deep breath and shook her head as if to rid her brain of all the questions and confusion cluttering it. She wasn't trying to fight with Caleb or challenge his beliefs, she just felt like she wanted to find answers to this whole Christianity thing. Then again, maybe she was making it more complicated than it was. "Look, Caleb, I'm sorry. I'm not trying to put down your faith or anything. I myself just find it hard to believe in something I can't see or experience."

Caleb's heart wrenched as if a huge hand was gripping and squeezing it. Lindsey was almost as stubborn as Caleb had been before he became a Christian. She almost seemed impossible to get through, but God could work miracles. He had done so in Caleb's life.

A few moments of silence ensued before Caleb spoke again. "Well, I see God all around me," he admitted quietly. "I see him in other Christians, I see him at work in my life, I see him in the world; in the environment."

Lindsey didn't look at Caleb this time. She just sat still with her hands in her lap gazing out the window. She remembered what Caleb had said earlier in their trip about how there's so much beauty and order in the world; most likely he was referring to the environment and how things work in nature.

Caleb went on. "I just say, why not believe and trust in something you supposedly can't see when everything else in the world that you can see is failing all around you."

To that remark Lindsey's churning thoughts halted as the words stung her ears.

She turned to face Caleb, her face reflecting anger. "Everything around me isn't *failing*," she spit out, although she wasn't sure that was altogether true.

"Is that right?" Caleb ventured, challenge in his voice. "You yourself said that I must think your life is a mess-up. I mean, your dad ran out on you and your mom, your grandparents obviously weren't important enough for you to stay with them, your ex-boyfriend broke your heart … and, well, your mom is gone, Lindsey."

Lindsey was stunned and hurt by Caleb's abruptness. Tears stung the corners of her eyes, and she felt ready to slap Caleb for his forwardness about her personal life. "So my life isn't peachy-keen," she shot back at him. "So what! Nobody's is!"

"I'm not saying that," Caleb explained, sighing in frustration. Now he had made Lindsey upset again. "I'm just trying to make a point as to how nothing in this world is worth trusting in or can bring you real peace or happiness."

"Hmph," Lindsey mumbled, grinning, "as if I didn't already know that."

Caleb looked over at her. She was slumped in her seat and had turned her face back toward the window. "I'm sorry if I made you feel bad, Lindsey. I got a little caught up and wasn't thinking about what I was saying."

Lindsey just shook her head. "Yeah, well, you were pretty much right. I have problems, I know."

"Everybody does, though, Lindsey. I don't think anybody's life is as smooth as they might think it is or want it to be."

"I know people with good lives, though; happy people. There are lots of happy people out there."

"Well, sure," Caleb agreed. "I'm happy most of the time, and I'm sure you're a happy person most of the time. But people can never be that way all of the time. Even with all those people whose lives seem so perfect and who seem to have everything going well for them and never seem to be sad … there's always something, you know, that keeps them from knowing real … joy."

Lindsey noticed that Caleb was speaking slowly, thoughtfully, from experience obviously. "So are you telling me that believing in God makes all the bad stuff go away then?"

Caleb eyebrows raised as his eyes widened. "Yeah, I wish," he exclaimed. "No, you still have problems and go through life like everyone else. Christ just somehow makes life manageable and livable … and more joyful, more worth living."

"How?"

"I have no idea. He just does." Caleb glanced over at Lindsey who was watching him with curious eyes, no longer challenging or angry. "It's kinda neat," he admitted, smiling.

"So," Lindsey began slowly, trying to piece it all together, "if I said that I believed in God, then my life would change like yours did?"

Caleb almost laughed. She must be so confused, he thought. She was just like a little kid, but at least he could tell now that she was somewhat serious. "Being a Christian isn't just about believing in God," he explained. "It's about having a *relationship* with Jesus Christ; believing in Him, trusting Him, living for Him, all that good stuff."

"Oh," Lindsey said slowly. Simple enough, right? She didn't quite know. She was still somewhat confused. At least she knew who Jesus was, anyway, from her conversation with Caleb the other night when he had told her all about Jesus' life on earth.

A long pause lingered between them for a few moments, and then Lindsey finally said, "Caleb, I'm glad you seem to have your life figured out and working for you. I still have yet to get to that point."

"You will," he said confidently, uttering a short prayer in his head that Jesus would continue to work in Lindsey's heart.

Chelsea stood on the beach outside her house and gazed at the water as the violent waves crashed on the shore. With her arms wrapped around her shivering body, she contemplated whether it was time for her to return to the house. It was almost 6:00 in the evening and the sun was already descending behind the dark water's edge, leaving the floating islands nothing more than dark silhouettes against a sharp orange sundown.

Chelsea smiled in pleasure. She had no cares pressing on her today. Lindsey was fine and wasn't angry with her anymore, Terry was welcoming her arrival, and because of those wonderful circumstances, Chelsea and Dan's marriage had seemed as happy and solid as ever. No longer had Chelsea been plagued with troublesome nights and fretful thoughts about Lindsey. She felt freed from all of that. Lindsey would be just fine, and she believed it. She didn't have to be concerned anymore.

Sighing in relief she dug her toes in the cold sand, realizing just how chilly it was outside. Turning quickly, she began retreating into the house to warm herself and start dinner for her and Dan.

At the edge of the backyard, a crash sounded from inside the house and startled Chelsea. She stopped in her tracks, stunned. Had Dan tripped and knocked over a lamp or vase? She crinkled her face in confusion and worry and broke into a run toward the back door. Flying inside, she gasped at the sight of Dan crumpled painfully across the living room floor. His body was limp and lying on its side, his face knotted in pain as his eyes flickered open and closed.

"Daniel!" Chelsea screamed rushing to his side. She dropped to her knees and rolled him over on his back. She knew at once that he had had a heart attack. His face was pale and his forehead was dotted with perspiration. Thankfully he was alive. He moaned and tried to reach up for Chelsea with his right hand. Tears fell down her face and landed on his cheeks. Fearing to move him in case of shock, she shot up from her position on the floor and ran to the phone, dialing an ambulance as fast as she was able to.

"Is he going to be okay?" Chelsea asked the doctor eagerly with tear-stained cheeks.

"It's hard to tell exactly right now, but he should be," was the reply.

Chelsea sank back to her chair in the waiting room. Her good friend Carrie Lindbergh was by her side and gripped her hand. "Don't worry, dear, everything will turn out just fine."

Chelsea was unconvinced. She shook her head back and forth. "No, it was really bad, Carrie. You should have seen him. He's had small heart attacks before, but this was worse. I don't know if he can hold up any longer."

"Try not to see the worst of things, Chelsea," Carrie insisted, continuing to pat Chelsea's hand. "I'm here for you, so is James. You know that."

Chelsea nodded her head, still not feeling any better. She continued to fret. How could this have happened? She had been feeling so wonderful today. Her life had finally seemed to take a turn for the better. In one instant, that was shattered. She couldn't take losing Dan. That would be too much for her. If she lost Dan, she knew her life would be over. In fact, she might even be the one to take her own life if she lost Dan.

No, no no! she screamed inside her head. How could she think such thoughts? Carrie was right; Dan would be fine. He was alive when she had found him, after all. But he didn't look good. She thought she had even overheard some of the paramedics saying something about him being paralyzed.

With that thought in her head, fresh tears began rolling down Chelsea's cheeks. "Oh Carrie," she pleaded in distress. "I couldn't handle losing Dan. I don't know how I'd live without him."

Carrie's heart almost burst in agony for her good friend. She continued to reassure her. "You'll live," she said confidently. "You'll live with the help of James and I. And you'll live with the help of Jesus."

Wednesday, October 29, 1997

Halloween is on Friday. Wow, this is going to be the first holiday without my mother. It's going to suck, especially since I'll spend it on the road. I would still like to stop early Friday night and try to catch a party or something with Caleb, but I can tell he's not into all this Halloween stuff. Besides, I already told him that he could forget about it. Oooooohhhh, I'm so upset. This trip isn't fun anymore, it's just plain tiring. Hanging out in Lincoln was fun; I wish we could do that again. I wish we could do anything to stall time. Every day, I grow more unsure about where I'm headed. I have a destination, but I still feel like I'm headed nowhere. Oh well, we'll see how my circumstances unravel themselves when I arrive in Virginia.

We're already across the state of Missouri and in St. Louis. Yes, we actually made it there from Lincoln in one day despite my doubts. It really didn't take as long as I had thought either, which stinks because now we're one step closer to Virginia. We go into Illinois tomorrow. We're gonna follow I-64 across southern Illinois and Indiana into Kentucky. Most likely we'll stay in Louisville. I've already calculated that it will only take about 5 and half hours with stops, so at least it will be a short day.

The day after that will be when we drive into Virginia. So we'll get there on Halloween. We'll probably stay somewhere for the night so that I don't show up at my dad's doorstep really late in the evening. But wouldn't that be funny – "Trick or Treat, Dad, it's your daughter!" I'll wait until Saturday morning to show up.

Lindsey stopped writing and lifted her hand from the page. She turned her head to look at Caleb who was already underneath the covers in his bed attempting sleep. She knew she couldn't stay up much longer or else she'd disturb him. It was only nine in the evening. Lindsey was tired of course, but she didn't feel like going to sleep so early.

I wish I didn't have to show up at all. Maybe I should keep on going with Caleb into North Carolina and start my own life there somehow. I could start college in the winter, maybe go to the same college Caleb is going to be attending. He's the only person I know right now who I trust, and I'm so afraid to let him go and venture out on my own. I've been thinking about it all day, and I don't know what I'll do without him.

The ivory-colored paper in her small journal dampened as Lindsey's tears cascaded down her cheeks and dropped onto the pages. She quickly wiped them away and scooted off the bed and toward the door to leave. She didn't want Caleb to discover her crying, and for some reason she felt stupid that she was. Her affection for Caleb didn't seem to make any sense.

She wondered about that as she glided across the room in a few big steps, pulled the door open and disappeared in the hallway. Hearing her leave, Caleb opened his eyes and lifted his head.

"Lindsey?" But she was already in the hallway.

Gripping her journal and her black-ink pen tightly to her chest, she stepped slowly and lightly in the hallway, wondering where she should go. Outside, she decided. She felt like some fresh air.

Indeed the air was cool and sweet as it drifted across her face and into her lungs and she inhaled it deeply. There was nobody outside in the pool, so Lindsey made her way to one of the reclining pool chairs and lay back in it, staring at the black, starry night. She couldn't stop thinking about Caleb.

She didn't know what she'd do without him. Already he had made such a big mark on her life, a positive one, and she was afraid to let that go. She cared so much about him, *so much* that at times she questioned her feelings. For most of the trip she had leaned on Caleb as a big-brother figure, a good, good friend. But now she wasn't quite so sure. Her heart fluttered as she thought about his handsome face and his sweet smile. She remembered how nice he had looked that night in Lincoln when he had taken her out on a picnic beneath the stars. They didn't say hardly a word to eachother that night, which had been really odd. All Lindsey knew was that she had spent most of that evening with Caleb on her mind, not being able to concentrate on much else. She was aware that he cared about her also, but she didn't know to what extent.

She laughed at herself and scolded her childish inclinations about Caleb. Of course he didn't have feelings for her. How could he? She had just been this annoying, nagging little tag-along who asked too many questions and must have appeared too unstable and juvenile. How could he care about *that?*

But she had seen the way he always looked on her with affection and compassion during those times she had been upset. He never acted like she was a burden or a tag-along. He had always put her first and considered her needs and feelings. *And* he had stuck up for her at the mall when that guy had been rude to her.

Lindsey smiled automatically as she imagined again how angry Caleb had appeared, how determined he had been to come to Lindsey's rescue. Even Lindsey knew it probably wasn't right to punch that guy, but she couldn't help smiling as she thought about it now.

Yes, she would miss Caleb terribly. But his leaving would just be another hole in her life among many. She could probably handle it.

Twenty-One

I have told you all this so that you will have peace of heart and mind. Here on earth you will have many trials and sorrows; but cheer up, for I have overcome the world.
– John 16:33 (The Living Bible)

Over two hours on the road Thursday morning had already taken Lindsey and Caleb across the southern tip of Illinois and into Indiana. Lindsey had been driving in an attempt to better her skills at the clutch and to give Caleb a rest from driving. For the first hour of the trip, Caleb had been too nervous with Lindsey at the wheel to even lean comfortably back on the seat. She caught on very well, however, and so far hadn't had a problem, so after much persuasion and argument from Lindsey, Caleb had finally backed off and shut his mouth. A few minutes after that, he had actually fallen asleep.

Now they were into Indiana, and Lindsey smiled to herself as she imagined what Caleb's reaction would be when he found out how far she'd driven without his help. Most likely he would be proud of her.

Lindsey checked her rearview mirror and blind spot to quickly change into the right lane. They hadn't stopped once yet, and Lindsey was squirming to get to a bathroom. The next rest stop was about ten miles.

Lindsey glanced over at Caleb. He seemed to be sleeping peacefully. He needed it. He was probably more exhausted than Lindsey was. Lindsey liked being with Caleb. She loved the fact that he was sitting next to her in the truck and that they had shared all this time together. She wondered what people thought when they saw them together. Did people think Lindsey and Caleb were a couple? She smiled at that thought. Or did they think they were brother and sister? They really didn't look much alike. Caleb's blond hair was lighter than Lindsey's, and their facial features didn't really resemble each other's at all. Lindsey had soft, round features, while Caleb's were more defined.

Lindsey rolled her eyes and bopped herself on the head despite her growing smile. She couldn't believe herself. Absolutely nothing was going to happen between them, and she knew it. She might as well stop thinking such ridiculous thoughts before she really got sucked in.

Or maybe it was too late.

Caleb made a noise and shifted in his seat. Lindsey glanced over at him again. He was still sleeping. Or maybe he was just resting his eyes. Maybe he hadn't been asleep at all for the last two hours....

Lindsey let out a startled scream as a loud popping sound shattered the silence and the truck suddenly jerked sideways. Caleb bolted up in his seat and steadied himself. He was in a daze. What had just happened? "Pull over," he yelled at Lindsey, not meaning to sound rude despite his harsh tone of voice.

Lindsey did just that, a little hurt by Caleb's remark. With her hands shaking, she nervously pulled over to the side of the freeway. *Oh no*, she thought to herself. *I wasn't paying attention and now I'm going to get it. Caleb's gonna be really mad at me.* But she wasn't even sure what it was that she did.

The minute she turned the truck off, Caleb jumped out the door and ran around the truck to find out the problem. Lindsey slowly opened her door and got out, hesitantly moving around the truck to where Caleb was standing.

He was kneeling down behind the truck groaning some kind of phrase, obviously upset. As Lindsey approached him, she noticed what it was he was studying. The back right tire had been blown out and was flattened. Some pieces of rubber that had flown off were trailing on the highway behind.

"Crap," Caleb muttered, standing up with his hands on his hips. Lindsey cringed. She hated to see Caleb so upset. She didn't know whether she should say sorry or not because she wasn't sure if popping the tire was her fault. Too scared to even say anything she decided to stay silent. Her face was a mask of emotions.

Caleb finally turned to her and started the conversation. "What happened?" he asked.

Lindsey shrugged and shook her head. "Uh, the tire blew out?"

"Well, obviously," Caleb retorted.

"It wasn't my fault!" Lindsey argued, although she wasn't quite sure that was true.

"Weren't you paying attention to the road?"

"No, I was sitting in the back playing road games! What do you think?"

"Well, I just want to find out what it was that you drove over that you declined to miss!"

Lindsey's mouth dropped open in shock. He was making it sound like she intentionally drove over something to pop the wheel.

"I didn't see anything in the road," she explained angrily. *At least I didn't see anything before I was looking at you.* "It could've been anything really small. A sharp rock or a nail that wouldn't have even been noticeable."

Caleb knew she was right. He also knew he probably shouldn't be so angry with her. It was only an accident, after all.

Before he could apologize though, Lindsey spoke again. "What are you so mad at me for anyway? It was an accident! If you had been driving, it probably would've happened too, but then you wouldn't have gotten mad at me. You sure have a temper, you know that, Caleb? You just gotta jump on someone, anyone, to relieve your frustration. Why don't you just calm down? It's not the end of the world!"

Lindsey turned on her heels and walked away. Caleb was shocked speechless. Yes, she was right. He knew she was. He lowered his head in shame. He hadn't realized that he still had his flighty temper.

Slowly, Caleb made his way to the front of the truck where Lindsey was leaning staring out at the passing traffic. "You're right, you know," he said. "Before you told me all of that about myself I *was* actually going to apologize."

Lindsey looked at him unconvinced, then turned her head back to the road, ignoring him.

"But I suppose I needed to hear it anyway," Caleb continued.

Lindsey didn't speak for a long while. Caleb just took a spot next to Lindsey and stood beside her as they both stared ahead at the vehicles passing by. Finally Lindsey sighed. "Well, I suppose it takes a big man to actually apologize for something like that. Most guys would probably just keep defending themselves."

"That's true."

"Sorry for yelling at you," she said.

"I'm sorry too," Caleb replied. After a while he added, "So now what are we gonna do?"

"Well, before this happened, I was about to stop at a rest area about 10 miles up the road."

"Good thinking, I really gotta go," Caleb commented.

Lindsey smiled at him. "Me too. I don't know how much longer I can wait."

"Well, just go over beside those bushes or behind the truck or something."

"No way!" Lindsey disputed. "I'm not a guy, I'm not just gonna go out in the middle of nowhere in plain sight!"

"Have it your way."

Lindsey rolled her eyes. "I'll hold it until we can find a way out of here." She walked to the passenger's side door, opened it and retrieved the road atlas. She flipped to the map of Indiana and spread it out on the front of the truck. Together Caleb and Lindsey leaned over it to discuss their plan.

"I take it you don't have a spare tire," Lindsey said flatly, raising her eyebrows at Caleb.

"Uh, no."

"Not smart."

"So where exactly are we?" Caleb asked.

"We just passed Posyville," she replied, pointing to it on the map. It was only twelve miles into Indiana. They were still near the border.

Caleb noticed that I-64 didn't actually run through any small towns until Lynnville, which was about 21 miles down the road. Even then he wasn't sure how big Lynnville was or if it would even have a place he could purchase a new tire.

"The next town from here is Stacer," Lindsey commented, "which is about 7 miles from here, but it's not on the freeway. It's off it a little bit."

"Hmm," Caleb pondered over the map. "How far back is Posyville? Should we go back there?"

"Well, I figure we're in between the two towns so it wouldn't matter either way. But Posyville didn't seem like it had much to it. It was kind of small and … well, small."

Caleb laughed. "There sure isn't much civilization out on this freeway. It doesn't even run through any major towns until New Albany, and that looks like it's on the Kentucky border."

"Ugh," Lindsey groaned. "Great. Now what?"

"Well, we could wait and see if someone will stop and help us out."

Lindsey frowned. That seemed unlikely. She looked sideways toward the road. There weren't many cars passing by as it was. "Well, I suppose we could do that, except we don't know how long it will be until someone does stop to help. Do we even want to wait? What if it ends up taking all day?"

Caleb noticed the few cars passing by on the road and agreed with Lindsey. She was probably right. Nevertheless, he thought they should at least wait a short time just in case someone was willing to stop.

At the *Denny's* in Coeur D'Alene, Mary Jenkins worked swiftly and cheerfully, barely keeping her mind off of Bryan. She was anxious about their date for tomorrow night. It was Halloween, and they had decided that after taking Andrea trick-or-treating, they would drop her off at Mary's parents' house and check out a really neat Halloween party that was going on at one of Bryan's colleagues' houses. Mary was so excited. She didn't remember the last time she had been to a Halloween party. Ted had never been into the holidays much.

Mary was just contemplating whether she and Bryan should go see the new scary movie out in theatres when she came upon a certain customer at work who instantly caused her to frown.

"Hey, Mary! Good to see you," came Ted's exaggerated-cheerful voice. Mary smiled in feigned surprise.

"I'm sure it is, Ted," she said non-enthusiastically. "Is it just coincidence that you happen to be sitting at one of my tables?"

"Not at all. I told the hostess to sit me where you could serve me so that I could speak with you."

"You could've spoken to me anytime, Ted, but instead you decided to come in and ruin my day."

"Hey now, calm down, babe," Ted said, smiling arrogantly.

"Don't call me 'babe'," Mary warned. "And don't expect good service from me."

"Well, you know I never did, Mary. You were never good at giving me what I needed."

Mary fought back tears as she shot an icy stare at him. "Did you come in here just to harass me, Ted, or do you actually want something to eat because I don't have time for your idiocy."

"All right, all right," Ted said as he told Mary what he wanted. She quickly jotted it down on her pad of paper and left the table without another word to Ted. She couldn't believe the nerve of him! How dare he come into her work like this! He had no right! Maybe she should do something to contaminate his food … or maybe she should purposely "forget" to bring his food or give him the wrong order … or maybe….

She stopped herself. It wasn't right of her to be vengeful with Ted. As much as she wanted to pound in his face, she knew that Jesus wouldn't be very pleased with her actions. In fact, Jesus wouldn't be pleased just with her thoughts. She knew that no matter how bad she wanted to hurt Ted, she wanted to please Jesus even more. She knew the importance of loving other people, even her enemies. Ooh, but it sure was hard with Ted.

"What's wrong, Mary?" asked a fellow waitress as she noticed the distraught look on Mary's face.

"Oh," she almost burst out crying, "it's my ex-husband Ted. He's here and he purposely sat at one of my tables to harass me today. I don't know what he wants."

"He probably just wants food."

"Oh, Karen, there are a million other places in town he could've gone for food. He said he wanted to talk to me."

"Do you want to switch tables with me? I can take his."

Mary smiled, grateful for Karen's thoughtfulness. She considered the idea. "No, I don't want him to think I can't face him. But I also don't want to start bawling right in front of him. That sure would please him, wouldn't it?"

"He sure seems like a cruel guy, Mary."

"He wasn't always like that. At least not outwardly."

Karen patted Mary's arm. "Well, whatever you do, don't give him what he wants. If he wants to harass you, don't let him know it bothers you. It shouldn't anyway. If he wants to act like a stupid little kid and say mean things to you, then just ignore him like a little kid. Show him you're stronger than that."

"I don't know if I am."

"You are, Mary," Karen said sharply, looking intently at Mary. "You are much stronger than you think, and you deserve better than Ted."

Mary smiled. She had better than Ted. She had Bryan. Even if Bryan turned out just to be a great friend, at least she had him, and she had God.

"Thanks," Mary said quietly. Karen smiled at returned to her work. Mary wasn't going to let Ted ruin her day. He would be in and out of the restaurant, and that would be that. Then she could continue the day as if he'd never been around. He couldn't hurt her. She was determined not to let him.

She thought of Bryan again and their soon-to-be date and a smile penetrated her face uncontrollably. Oh, she couldn't wait!

A half-hour later, Mary dropped Ted's plates to the table creating a large clang as the porcelain dishes hit the wooden top. She smiled at him. "There you are, Ted, enjoy your meal, I won't be back until you're ready to pay and get out of here."

He grabbed her arm suddenly and motioned for her to sit with him. She reluctantly agreed and slumped herself in the booth opposite Ted.

"Look," he said seriously, "I actually wanted to ask you if I could take Andrea tomorrow for the weekend."

Mary's eyes grew wide in astonishment. "No way!" she argued. "You had the chance to take her last weekend when it was your turn to take her. This weekend we have plans."

"I never ended up going on that trip last weekend, Mary," Ted explained, trying to reason with her. "Something happened and I couldn't make the trip, so I felt awful about missing Andrea. I wanted to make it up to you and her, so I thought I could see her this weekend."

"Well, as much as I don't want to *punish* you, Ted," she said calmly, not believing the words, "I can't let you take Andrea because, like I said, we have plans."

"Halloween plans, I take it."

"Yes, in fact we do," Mary replied. Should she tell Ted about Bryan? Sure, why not? "After I take Andrea trick-or-treating, I'm dropping her off at my mom's place and then I have date for the evening."

Ted didn't seem to notice Mary's mention of the date. "Why don't you drop Andrea off at my place instead of your mom's? That way you can still do your Halloween thing with her, and I'll still get her for the weekend."

"My mom's already made plans of her own with Andrea. It would be cruel to tell her to cancel them."

"Well, it's also cruel to deny Andrea to her own father," Ted bit out sharply.

"*And* it's cruel to choose a selfish vacation trip over your own daughter when she was really looking forward to seeing you!"

Bryan kept silent.

Before he could utter any words in his defense, Mary went on. "You had a chance to see Andrea last weekend when you were supposed to, Ted. But without any warning or reason, you broke that off at the last minute, which was not only cruel to Andrea but cruel to me! This weekend she's mine, and if you want to see her, you'll have to wait until next weekend! You get what you deserve, Ted, and this is what you deserve!" Without another word, Mary stood up and walked away without a backward glance. Ted ate his meal in silence, wondering how he could convince Mary to let him take Andrea, but knowing there was no use. Legally he could only see her every other weekend, so it wasn't a crime for Mary to be keeping Andrea from him this weekend.

After he was finished and had the bill, he wrote out a check, left Mary a small tip after much deliberation, and began walking out of the restaurant. He caught Mary right before he left. "So, did you say you had a date tomorrow night."

"Yes, I do," Mary said proudly with her head held high. "I met him at church Sunday night and he's a wonderful man who absolutely adores Andrea."

Ted just nodded. "So you've been going to church, huh?"

"Yes," Mary said, speculating whether Ted was about to make fun of her or not.

"Well, I'm happy you seem to be doing well. Have a good time tomorrow night, and tell Andrea I love her."

Mary was taken aback by the sudden kindness and abandon in his voice.

She was startled out of words for a second before she finally managed a small, "I will, thank you."

At one-thirty that afternoon, after waiting on the highway for help for over an hour, Caleb and Lindsey finally agreed that no one was going to stop and help them. They sighed and decided that they would have to take the seven-mile walk into Stacer. The wind was blowing slightly and the air was chilly. No sun shone to warm their backs against the cool breeze. Lindsey grabbed an extra sweatshirt from one of her suitcases in the bed of the truck and put it on under her coat. After Lindsey retrieved her purse and Caleb checked that he had his wallet, the two started their trek down Interstate 64.

"I still can't believe nobody was willing to stop for us," Lindsey said.

"Well, there isn't much around this area and people might be really suspicious of strangers."

Lindsey rolled her eyes. "Whatever. It's not like we were trying to hitchhike or anything."

The wind was blowing against their backs and it caused Lindsey's hair to fly in front of her face. She continually had to sweep it out of her eyes and her mouth. "Ugh," she finally yelled in frustration. "I should have brought a pony-tail holder or something."

"Well, this shouldn't take us too long."

"How long do you think?"

"Well," Caleb wondered, tipping his head slightly. "Seven miles ... probably a little over two hours."

"Two hours for seven miles!"

"Well yeah, seven miles is a long way."

Lindsey sighed. This was going to be a much longer day than she had anticipated. "So then what? Do you think if we find a tire place they'll give us a ride to the truck and stick it on for us?"

"Or we could call a tow-truck to bring it into town so that we wouldn't have to back-track."

"Oh yeah, that's probably smarter."

"Either way we're losing time."

"Oh, it doesn't matter," Lindsey said, suddenly enjoying her new adventure with Caleb. "It's not like we're on a tight time-limit or anything."

"Well I'm really anxious to get home and see my parents as soon as possible."

Lindsey's heart sank. He just wanted to dump her as soon as possible and get on with his life. "We'll only be behind a few hours," she said roughly. "It's not like we won't still make it to Louisville tonight."

"I know," Caleb said, noticing Lindsey's sudden disappointment. "What's wrong?"

"What do you mean 'what's wrong?' Nothing's wrong."

"Are you sure?"

"Of course I'm sure, why wouldn't I be?" she said defensively.

Caleb stalled. "Uh … because you suddenly just turned snappish on me."

Lindsey didn't say a word but quickened her stride and kept her eyes fastened to the road ahead.

"You're not looking forward to seeing your dad, are you?" Caleb guessed, positive that that was the reason she had seemed so down lately. "Lindsey, talk to me, will you?"

"Why should I?" Lindsey barked as she kept on walking. "It's not like any of this is going to matter once you dump me off and get along with your own life!"

"Dump you off?" Caleb was astounded. "What do you mean? Do you think I just … don't want you here or something?"

Lindsey finally stopped walking and turned to face Caleb. "Well, no, it's just…."

"Just what, Lindsey?" It was getting harder and harder to understand Lindsey and to put up with her. She was so complicated Caleb was never sure whether he wanted to hug her to take all her cares away or whether he wanted to slap her face and shake some sense into her. Even now he could see in her eyes how difficult it was to talk to him.

"You have your good life ahead of you and I'm glad for you, but I just…." She couldn't explain herself to Caleb, couldn't articulate herself. But how could she? How would she ever make Caleb understand her when *she* was even perplexed by her own roller-coaster feelings?

"Well, how do *you* know you don't have a good life ahead of you, Lindsey?" Caleb challenged her. She couldn't answer. She just shook her head and stared at her feet.

Caleb backed off, suddenly tired and frustrated with Lindsey's cynical feelings. "You know what," he said. "You are really being pessimistic, Lindsey. It's like you only see the worst in things."

"Well, I don't try to…."

"It's like you're all upset at me for having a family to return to, and you're feeling sorry for yourself that you won't have that. But you don't know that you won't!"

Lindsey immediately came to her defense. "You think I'm jealous of you, Caleb?" she spat out. "I don't care about your family, okay! I'm only upset because I don't want you to go and leave me, that's all!"

Caleb raised his eyebrows and took a step back. What was she talking about?

"I really don't want this to end," she went on sullenly, looking as though she was about to cry. "Yes, it's true, I am not looking forward to getting to Virginia, but it's not because I think I'll have a bad life. I'm just scared of what's ahead and I wish I didn't have to go through it. I wish we could just keep driving, you know? You don't know how bad I'm going to miss you when you're gone."

Caleb was touched, and also a little stunned at Lindsey's confession. "Well, it's not like we won't keep in touch," he assured.

"It won't be the same thing," Lindsey said, choking back tears. "I … really … like you, Caleb," she struggled out.

Caleb wasn't sure how to take the meaning of that phrase, so he said, "Well, I like you too, Lindsey. I mean, I care about you, that's why I wanted you to come along with me on this whole trip."

"How?" Lindsey asked.

"How what?"

"How do you care about me?"

Caleb shook his head. He didn't know. Suddenly his heart started beating faster and a heat crept up his face. Lindsey stared at him with her eyes wide and pleading as he struggled inside himself to determine just how he felt about Lindsey. "I…." he said slowly. "I care about you so much at times that I … I feel like I never want to leave you."

Lindsey nodded and turned around before he could see the tears run down her cheeks. He frowned in confusion. Just what was wrong with Lindsey? Was this all about her missing Caleb? Of course that was understandable, he would miss her too. He ran up to Lindsey and stepped in front of her, stopping her. She kept her head down.

"Lindsey," Caleb pleaded looking down at her, "why are you so sad?"

She sniffed and wiped at her eyes. "I wish that I had someone like you, but I don't. I don't feel like I have anybody." She looked up at him then, strengthening herself to say what she wanted to say next. "I wish I *could* have you, but I know that's impossible taken the circumstances. You'll be gone after tomorrow."

Wow, Caleb thought. She really liked him. He had to praise her boldness. At that moment as he stared down at her face he felt another urge to kiss her, but something held him back. She obviously had deep feelings for him, but could he say the same thing about himself? He cared about her, but was it the same thing that she was feeling?

"Well, Lindsey," he said, managing a smile. "We'll see what happens when we both get home. We're not gonna be that far away from each other, you know. We can still see each other."

Lindsey's heart fluttered for a moment when it looked as if Caleb was going to kiss her. When he didn't, she was upset but quickly changed that as he told her they could still see eachother. Maybe things wouldn't turn out so bad. She just nodded, suddenly feeling a little foolish about her confession. But obviously Caleb felt pretty much the same, or else he wouldn't have suggested that they keep seeing eachother.

Lindsey turned again and began walking. Caleb followed behind her. "Well, sorry about being all stupid like this," Lindsey said, wiping at her eyes again.

"Don't worry about it, Lindsey," Caleb said. "I don't want you to feel stupid, okay?"

"Got it," she replied.

It was almost three-o'clock in the afternoon by the time Lindsey and Caleb made it to Stacer and found an Auto Parts shop. They waited and had lunch at a nearby cafe while the tow-truck went and retrieved the Ford from the side of the freeway and brought it in for its new tire. By the time four thirty rolled around, the two were already back on the freeway and headed toward Louisville, Kentucky.

Twenty-Two

Because of his kindness, you have been saved through trusting Christ. And even trusting is not of yourselves; it too is a gift from God. Salvation is not a reward for the good we have done, so none of us can take any credit for it.

– Ephesians 2:8-9 (The Living Bible)

Lindsey glanced over from her television program and her head did a double take as she spotted Caleb's Bible lying across the room on the windowsill. She creased her forehead as her brows came together in speculation. For some reason, she suddenly felt drawn to the paperback Bible as if there was an aura of light shining around it, hypnotically drawing her interest in. What was it about that little book that took her curiosity and held it within its pages? It must have been the way Caleb poured over it every night. It obviously wasn't just any book. It didn't take a Christian to realize that. So what was the big deal, Lindsey thought.

Or maybe it was her growing curiosity in God and in Caleb's faith whether, Lindsey wanted to admit it to herself or not.

Scanning the room and quickly moving to the door to check outside in the hallway, Lindsey picked up the Bible when no sign of Caleb was found. She hesitantly brought it over to her bed where she sat cross-legged and spread the book out in front of her. She noticed right away how the Bible wasn't just an ordinary plain Bible, it was a study Bible. Not knowing where to look first, she flipped to the end of the book, which contained an index of many different topics and issues and their related Bible verses. The list of topics seemed myriad and ranged from such issues as abortion, appearance, complaining, drinking, gossip, homosexuality, and self-pity to contentment, faith, love, talents, trust, and the will of God. Lindsey was amazed at all the various issues the Bible had mention in. She particularly noted a few such topics as comfort, depression, healing, pain and death; things she was all too familiar with. There was so much and Lindsey suddenly wished she could look up some of the verses related to those topics, but she wasn't sure how.

Instead, she resolved to just flipping randomly to any page that she landed on. She found herself at the beginning of the book of Philippians.

The bright yellow shine of the highlighted text instantly grabbed Lindsey's attention. Unsure of where she should start reading she settled with the portion that had been highlighted by Caleb. It was Philippians 2: 3-11:

Don't act out of selfish ambition or be conceited. Instead, humbly think of others as being better than your selves. Don't be concerned only about your own interests, but also be concerned about the interests of others. Have the same attitude that Christ Jesus had.

Although he was in the form of God and equal with God, he did not take advantage of this equality. Instead, he emptied himself by taking on the form of a servant, by becoming like other humans, by having a human appearance. He humbled himself by becoming obedient to the point of death, death on a cross.

This is why God has given him an exceptional honor – the name honored above all other names – so that at the name of Jesus everyone in heaven, on earth, and in the world below will kneel and confess that Jesus Christ is Lord to the glory of God the Father.

Lindsey stopped as she came to the end of the highlighted section. She wondered what it was about that particular passage that stood out so much to Caleb that he had highlighted it. Lindsey continued to flip through the pages and found many more highlighted sections of text. It looked as if Caleb had read practically the whole book!

She thought of the words she had just read. Because of Caleb's explanation of Jesus Christ a few nights back, Lindsey wasn't too confused by the meaning of the words. In fact, they almost made sense to her. In it, the author had been telling the readers that they needed to have a selfless, humble attitude, because that was how Jesus Christ lived. He was humble to the point of servanthood as a human, but he was also equal to God and given the highest honor. *Wow*, Lindsey thought as she found the page again and studied over the words. *This Jesus guy was some character.*

She suddenly remembered Caleb telling her the other night that if she wanted to learn more about Jesus, then the book of John was a good placc to start. It didn't take her long to find it, and within minutes, Lindsey was engrossed in Scripture.

Lindsey was so involved in reading and thinking that she didn't hear Caleb open the door and walk slowly into the room. As his eyes flew onto the figure of Lindsey cross-legged on the bed, bent over, reading his Bible, he suddenly paused as his heart nearly leaped out of his chest. *Thank You, Lord,* he cried silently in his heart. *Keep her curiosity and her search for comfort strong because that way I know she'll find You.*

As if hearing his thoughts, Lindsey glanced up and saw Caleb. Feeling like she had just been caught with her hand in the cookie jar, she quickly slammed the Bible shut. "I'm sorry, I um … I was just," she stumbled out. Her face began to warm up as a soft red glow invaded her cheeks. "I shouldn't have been reading this. I should've asked you."

"No," Caleb remarked as he walked to the bed and stood in front of Lindsey. "Why should you be sorry? It's not like that's a private diary with a lock on it or anything."

"Well, yeah, but I was just…." Lindsey cleared her throat and cast her head down, suddenly too embarrassed to look at Caleb. *He's probably really satisfied with this,* she thought.

"You can read it any time you want, Lindsey," Caleb offered, sitting on the other bed next to Lindsey's.

Lindsey shook her head and glared at Caleb with a smile forming on her lips, "You probably love it that you caught me in here reading your Bible. Go ahead, say it."

Caleb just shrugged his shoulders.

She tipped her head up, threw the Bible onto Caleb's bed and declared proudly, "Yeah well, it's not like it means anything that I read it, you know … I was just…."

"Just what?"

Lindsey shook her head, thinking of how to reply.

"Just … curious?" Caleb offered.

Lindsey rolled her eyes and scooted off the bed, making her way toward the bathroom to change into her nightclothes. "Maybe," she replied, shutting the door hard behind her.

"You're weird, Lindsey."

"So, today's the day we make it into Virginia," Caleb announced as soon as the two were on the freeway after they had filled up the Ford's gas tank at a Texaco station.

Lindsey shrugged and moaned a little.

"So, it's Halloween."

Lindsey looked at Caleb and managed a small smile before her face retreated to a sullen expression.

So many words were building up inside Caleb, wanting to force themselves out, but in the end Caleb figured that he had said enough to Lindsey within the past week. After tomorrow, they would be separated from each other, and there was nothing more Caleb could do for her. Whatever was left weighing on her heart would be up to her to work out and up to Jesus if she would accept Him.

But tonight, he thought, tonight he could make special. Even though he didn't want to celebrate Halloween, Caleb could still take Lindsey out just like she had wanted.

After an indeterminable amount of time had passed, Caleb found Lindsey fast asleep on the seat next to him. Yes, tonight he would make Lindsey smile.

Terry embraced Jenna eagerly and lovingly and held her for as long as she allowed him. She had agreed to come home to meet Lindsey when she arrived, and also to try and work things out with Terry. They had talked a couple of times since Jenna had left, and without coming to a definite conclusion, Jenna had decided that she loved Terry enough to try and accept his daughter into their lives. But it had been tough; it was tough, and as she allowed herself to be held by her husband, she cried. She thought about the man he used to be, the man he had described to her. It was too hard to believe, yet she knew undoubtedly that it was true; Terry had once been a violent person with an uncontrollable anger. But now, as he held her gently and stroked her hair, she knew she would never have to fear him like his previous wife had. Jenna cried for that woman who was now gone from the world.

"I'm sorry, Jenna," Terry apologized whole-heartedly. "I don't ever want to lose you, I couldn't bear it. You mean so much to me. You've changed me, you have. Aside from Lindsey being born, you have been the single most positive happening in my life."

Jenna pulled herself away from Terry's embrace and stared up into his tear-streaked face. "I know," she said. "I love you too much to leave you. I'm willing to work things out. I believe that couples should find ways around their problems, not run away from them. But you can't understand how tough this is for me. I feel like I'm going to be sacrificing so much when your daughter arrives. I've never had children, and I…."

"I haven't, either, Jenna," Terry confessed, "not really. Even when Lindsey was growing up, I was never there for her. This is incredibly tough for me, too, especially considering my background."

"I know, Terry, and I'm sorry."

"We'll get through this, we will."

Jenna sniffed and put her arms around Terry's waist, pulling herself closer to him once again. She forced a smile onto her face. "So, when should we be expecting Lindsey's arrival?"

"Well, I was guessing either sometime today or tomorrow. But I can't be sure."

"So we're just gonna have to sit around and wait, huh?"

"Exactly. You don't have to, but I do. I need to be here when she arrives."

"Do you think she'll call again?"

Terry shook his head regretfully. "I wish she would. I wish I could've talked to her in person before she got here. I'm so nervous I can't stand it."

"Every time she called here she got an answering machine," Jenna added. "She must be terribly frightened, too, and terribly bold. I mean, she has no way of knowing that we'll actually be home. For all she knows, we could be gone on vacation, or something."

Terry chest lifted as he sighed deeply. "From what I've learned from her grandparents, she seems like a pretty bold and determined young lady."

Jenna smiled genuinely. "She sounds just like her father. You should be proud, Terry."

"Yeah, I guess I should be."

Friday, October 31st Halloween

After driving through the top of Kentucky all day, Caleb and I have finally made it into Virginia.... Finally we're here. It took us a little over a week to make the whole trip, and that was only because we stopped in Lincoln for those few days.

Ugh, I feel like crying. I can't handle this. Just thinking about how close I am to my father now makes me queasy and sick to my stomach. At least I know he's expecting me. Thank goodness he called my grandpa. We're not actually in Marion, yet. We're in Cliffield, but that's still too close. Caleb thought we should go all the way to Marion, but I strongly disagreed. I think he's getting annoyed at me. I suppose that's understandable. I haven't been the happiest little barrel of monkeys today. I don't think I've smiled once. I wouldn't doubt if Caleb takes off the second he drops me on my father's doorstep tomorrow morning.

Oh, listen to me. All I can do is complain and feel sorry for myself. Caleb was right, I am so negative and pessimistic. If he knew what I was writing down he would be so disappointed with me. I don't want to end our trip together being remembered as a big disappointment.

Anyway, the whole town is covered with Halloween stuff. I swear every house and yard we passed is decorated. It makes me kind of sad because I'm going to miss Halloween this year, and it's all my fault. Just because I can't share it with my mother anymore doesn't mean I can't still enjoy it. I could just walk up to Caleb and tell him I've changed my mind, and that we could go do something tonight, but after the way I've been acting I don't think that would be such a hot idea. Besides, I've learned by now that Caleb is not a Halloween kind of guy. At first I thought maybe he just felt too old for it, but now I think it has something to do with his faith. Well, that's cool, too. Either way, tonight is going to be just like any other night. But I guess that shouldn't matter. Why should it be any different? It's only a silly holiday, anyway.

Oh well, tomorrow is the important thing. My mind is so jumbled up. It's hard for me to come to terms with the circumstances of my life. So much has changed in so little time, and it's hard for me to grasp. How does anybody get by? I know some people have it worse than me, so how do they survive?

I know what Caleb would say to that. He'd say, "They survive with Jesus." Isn't that funny? I know Caleb so well now that I can predict the things he'd say.

Well, maybe he's right. I seem to have done okay so far. I mean, I haven't totally fallen apart or jumped into the depths of depression. I know it's because of Caleb, because of everything he's been to me....

...Or rather, it's because of ... Jesus?

It was early evening and the sun had just hidden itself under the horizon. The sky was dark blue, nearly black, and as Caleb pulled the Ford over on the top of a hillside and turned off the engine, Lindsey frowned in curiosity.

"What are we doing?" she asked.

"Stay here," he told Lindsey eagerly as he jumped out of the truck and ran over to her side to open the door for her.

"You know, if I get too used to all this gentlemanly, chivalrous behavior, I might have to use that to my advantage in the future."

"I know, I know," Caleb stated, feigning arrogance. "Women just love me and my gentlemanly wiles."

"Yeah, right," Lindsey laughed

"C'mon, Lindsey, you even admitted yesterday how much you love and adore me and can't live without me," Caleb teased.

Lindsey stopped and frowned, suddenly embarrassed. "Oh, I did not!" she argued. "I only said that I ... just forget what I said!"

"I was only messing around, Lindsey," Caleb replied seriously. Then, "I know what you said ... you want me, admit it!"

"Shut up!" Lindsey laughed, punching Caleb in the arm. "You wish!"

Caleb laughed as he took Lindsey's hand and helped her out of the truck. Then he ran to the bed of the Ford and lifted out a blanket and a paper grocery bag.

Lindsey followed Caleb as he led her to a small grassy spot on the hillside. There was no light save for the moon and the dim of the Ford's headlights.

Spreading out the blanket, Caleb sat and took two flashlights out of the bag and set them up on the blanket so that they could see easier. Lindsey sat also. Then Caleb pulled two small paper boxes and two forks out of the bag.

"Ooh, what is it?" Lindsey asked excitedly as she opened the top of the box.

"It's apple pie. I hope you like it."

Lindsey was ecstatic. "Oh my gosh, you are so thoughtful, Caleb," she exclaimed. "I love apple pie. This is so awesome, thank you."

"Just a little picnic to begin the evening. And you're welcome."

"So what are we doing afterward?"

"Well, I thought we could get dinner somewhere and then, well, play the evening by ear, I guess."

Lindsey nodded silently.

"Sorry it's not the traditional kind of Halloween thing, but you've probably guessed by now that I'm not really into all that."

"That's okay," Lindsey assured him. "I'm not crying about it."

Caleb and Lindsey sat quietly as they ate their desserts. Lindsey was surprised by the way her evening was turning out so positively because of Caleb's thoughtfulness. He truly was a rare friend, one whom she would desperately miss after tomorrow.

Finishing up the last bite, Lindsey pushed aside her fork and the paper box, and brought her knees up, wrapping her arms around her legs. "Are those the Appalachians?" she asked, staring at the mountain chain silhouetted against the moonlight.

"Yep," Caleb answered.

"They don't look like the Cascade Mountains. They seem more soft."

"Yeah, it's pretty, huh?"

"Yeah. Look how bright the moon is, it's amazing." Caleb just nodded as he put away his box and fork and turned to stare at the mountains. Neither said a word for a few minutes.

Caleb broke the silence. "Yeah, God made that. It's awesome."

Lindsey shivered as a cold breeze drifted across her back. She instinctively stuck her arms inside her sweatshirt under her coat and hugged herself as tight as she could to keep warm.

"Caleb?"

"Yeah?"

"I … I just want you to know that I don't doubt there is a God, or heaven or anything like that," Lindsey explained, her voice quivering slightly from the cold. "I just don't know if, right now at this point in my life, I can have that much faith."

Caleb was surprised by the sudden change in subject, but he nodded in understanding and support. "Well, God will always wait for you, and He'd want you to seek him no matter how big or little your faith is."

"For me, I just … well, I guess I'd need something else to know for sure. You know, like proof, or some more questions cleared up and all that."

"Well, that's okay, too," Caleb assured Lindsey, noting how desperately she was trying to find answers. "But believing in God and living for Jesus doesn't mean that you have to know all the answers first. God doesn't want our relationship with Him to be based on facts. You shouldn't have to say, 'I believe in God because scientific evidence has proved this and this and this about His existence,' you know?"

Lindsey lowered her head and rubbed her hands to keep them warm. "I know," she replied, suddenly feeling foolish. Caleb had a point. Maybe Lindsey had just been trying too hard with this whole God thing. Why not reach out and have some faith? She knew she wanted it. She wanted Jesus in her life like He was in Caleb's life; she wanted her life to change.

"Look up at the moon, Lindsey. See the mountains?"

Lindsey looked up and nodded and a small smile stretched across her face as she realized how eerie and beautiful it looked. "It's pretty."

"I look at that kind of stuff – sunsets, rainbows, winter mornings when the sky is light blue and there's frost all over the ground – and it's all the evidence I need to know that there is a God. This world was created by a hand of power and beauty."

Lindsey crinkled her nose and stared at Caleb, almost laughing, but smiling as she realized how wonderful his words sounded to her. She glanced back at the dark mountains, their soft hilly curves barely touching the bright moon sitting on top of them. How great to believe and know that those were created by God, by the God of the universe, by the personal God of humanity.

"You look at that stuff a lot differently after you're a believer, after your heart's been changed." Caleb leaned over and shoved Lindsey with his outstretched hand, wondering what she was thinking. She was completely amazed at Caleb's words. All at once she found herself siding with Caleb's views and seriously considering them. Everything that came out of his mouth had so much validation to her. She wondered how it was that he would know so much, and think so much. And suddenly, she knew she believed. There was a God, and she was finally accepting that fact. But it wasn't because of anything Caleb had argued or convinced her of, it was this unexplainable, overwhelming sense of just knowing, as if God himself was trying to talk to her at that moment.

"So this is how you know God is real?" Lindsey said quietly, not taking her eyes off the mountains.

Caleb turned his head to watch her. The cool wind was blowing wisps of her blond hair around her face, and without meaning to he raised his hand to swipe the hair out of her eyes. She turned her head to look at him and he instantly brought his hand down.

"Not only that, Lindsey, but God loves you – Jesus loves you and wants you to know Him. He wants to have a relationship with you."

The force of those words crashed in Lindsey's heart and she suddenly understood it all. This is what it was about, this was the big mystery that she had been trying to uncover. Jesus loved *her* and wanted her.

"So that was why God allowed Jesus to die for us," Lindsey breathed. "Because He loved us."

"Yeah, because He *loves* us and wants us to know Him. We can't know God without Jesus. Jesus is like the mediator between God and humans, a bridge, kind of. Because God is so perfect and holy and we're not, we can't have a relationship with Him without knowing Jesus and accepting His sacrifice on the cross. Jesus has already died for our sins, Lindsey, so that now when we do sin we can be forgiven by God when we ask Him."

Caleb's words rang true in Lindsey's ears as everything fell into place. Her eyes began to grow moist with fresh tears and she leaned her head back slightly to keep them from running out. Unexpectedly, an image of her mother flashed in her brain. "Caleb?"

"Yeah?"

"Why did she die?"

"Your mom?"

"Yeah."

Caleb took a deep breath and shifted, lifting his hand to rub his neck. He sighed, waiting a moment. "I don't know, Lindsey. I can't tell you that. Part of the journey of being a follower of Christ and living with faith includes not knowing all the answers. I still question God myself sometimes, despite my strong belief and trust in Him." Caleb stopped when he noticed his voice was quivering, suddenly realizing how cold he was. Glancing at Lindsey in the darkness, with limited sources for light, Caleb could make out the dark, sorrowful circles under her eyes from constant crying, stress, and fatigue that had plagued her during the last two weeks. "All I can say for certain is that God wanted it like this for a certain reason."

"What reason? What kind of reason would He have to make my mother die?"

"God didn't kill your mom, Lindsey. Please don't ever think that." Lindsey stayed silent as a hard look transformed her subtle features. "This is life, Lindsey. This is the life humans live, and it's hard to understand sometimes. But God wants us to keep on trusting Him no matter what. It's all about having that faith that God is ultimately in control and He has plans and purposes for every part of our lives." Caleb stopped, contemplating his next words, praying for the right ones. He went on slowly and cautiously. "I believe all that has happened was in order to provide an opportunity for you. Like God knew your mom's death would bring you to this point in your life where you're questioning and seeking Him."

Lindsey lowered her head to hide the downpour of tears. Caleb put his hand on her back reassuringly and continued talking.

"If your mom hadn't died, then maybe you wouldn't be here with me; you would still be the same person that you were before."

"Well, what was wrong with me, then?"

"You were … depressed … dying."

"But God would've still found another time to change my heart, wouldn't he?"

"Maybe, Lindsey, I can't say for sure, all I know is that we have to grab up those opportunities that God throws at us, no matter what circumstances are surrounding them. Just whatever you do, please don't blame God for your mother's death. Don't let this ruin your chance to get to know Him. Too many people pass up opportunities to know Jesus because of bad things in life."

It was true, Lindsey had questioned so many times, although not sure to whom, why her mother had died. It had felt so cruel and unjust, and even with Caleb's words about God, she still wondered why God didn't just stop it.

"Lindsey, it's so easy for people to focus on the bad things in life, and then blame God, instead of looking at the good things, and thanking Him."

Lindsey sniffed, allowing herself to cry before she was ready to speak again. She felt Caleb scoot closer to her and put his arm around her back to comfort her. The gesture somehow made her feel safer, stronger. Finally she lifted her head and in a small voice said, "I want to know Jesus."

Caleb's heart almost leaped out of his chest, and immediately he began thanking and praising Jesus for changing Lindsey's heart. "Then you can," he said in reply. Taking Lindsey's hands in his he said, "We're going to pray."

"Really," Lindsey replied with a smirk on her face and a glimmer in her eye. "I've never prayed before."

"Well, there's a first for everything," Caleb smiled back. "I'm gonna give you an invitation to invite Jesus to be a part of your life, okay?"

Lindsey nodded eagerly.

"All you have to do is repeat what I say; just talk to God, okay?"

"Okay."

Caleb closed his eyes and Lindsey followed suit. "Dear Lord, I believe in You and in what You did for me by dying on the cross."

Lindsey repeated the words from her heart.

Caleb went on. "I ask now that You take away my sins, Lord, and help me to start off new."

Lindsey choked the words out. Caleb could barely keep his own emotion out of his voice.

"I don't want to live without You anymore. Please enter my heart, and be a part of my life."

Lindsey repeated it with all of her heart.

"In Jesus' name I pray, Amen."

"In Jesus' name I pray, Amen."

Lindsey opened her eyes. Caleb had an elfish grin spread over his lips. He was ecstatic. "So that's it?" Lindsey asked.

"That's what I first said when my Aunt and Uncle prayed with me."

Lindsey couldn't stop the smile from penetrating her lips. "So how did you feel afterward?"

"Better, like I knew my decision was going to change everything. Just think about it, Lindsey, you belong to God now. He has so many promises for you, and no matter what happens from here on out, He'll be right there with you through it all."

"You should be a pastor, Caleb," she replied, grinning widely.

"So how are *you* feeling?" Caleb asked curiously.

"I feel, like my heart is expanding so much it's going to explode."

"And is that a good thing?"

"Oh yeah."

Lindsey leaned over and hugged Caleb, silently thanking him for his care and concern for her the past week. After pulling away, Lindsey said cheerfully, "So, what're we going to do now?"

"Well," Caleb started slowly, "I was asking around earlier and I think there's this church thing going on really soon somewhere downtown."

"Really? What kind of church thing?"

"I don't know, just a fun church thing."

Lindsey thought about it a moment, a little unsure. "Or we could just see a movie," Caleb offered.

Lindsey smiled before replying, "Why don't we do both?

Twenty-Three

Jesus answered him, "I am the way, the truth, and the life. No one goes to the Father except through me."

– John 14:6

The sharp blade of sunlight that was drifting in through the bottom of the curtains rebounded off the mirror and came to rest on Lindsey's sleeping features. Before the brightness could penetrate her eyelids and wake her up, however, the alarm clock that was sitting on the nightstand between the two queen-sized motel beds buzzed irritatingly, throttling Lindsey into consciousness.

She groaned as she lifted her arm out from beneath the covers and slapped the alarm with her hand to turn it off. Caleb rustled in his bed but remained asleep. Lindsey didn't budge from her position in bed until reason slithered its way in to her brain – it was Saturday. Today she would meet her father.

Lindsey jerked awake and pushed herself off of her stomach-position on the large bed. Her heart began thumping wildly as she jumped up and raced to the bathroom, yelling, "Caleb, get up, we have to leave in an hour!"

Caleb barely heard Lindsey's shriek as he rolled over, nearly falling out of bed.

Lindsey popped her head out of the bathroom door. "Caleb!" she hollered, hurling a towel at him. It barely made it to the foot of the bed. Lindsey picked up his toothbrush case that was sitting on the countertop and tossed it at Caleb. It hit the back of his head.

"Ouch," Caleb moaned, turning over again.

"Wake up!" Lindsey screamed.

"What's your problem, woman!"

"Don't call me that! It's the day, remember? We have to get going so we're not late!"

"Oh yeah," Caleb replied exhaustingly, finally sitting up in bed, "it's *the* day."

The shower turned on just then as Lindsey got in, and Caleb took his time to get out of bed. His mind was still foggy with sleep and it wasn't until his eyes came to rest on Lindsey's open suitcase that he registered to full extent what was happening. Lindsey was leaving him today. After sharing the countryside for over a week, they would finally have to be separated and to go on with their individual lives.

As that thought clicked in his brain, Caleb's heart fell to his knees, and he sank onto the nearby chair. He *would* miss Lindsey, terribly. He understood that now, and he knew she would feel the same way because she had told him so the other day. She had confessed how much she cared about him and how awful it would be after he was no longer in her life.

They were such strong words, but Caleb hadn't fully understood them before. Sure, Lindsey had a crush on him, but that's all it was ... wasn't it? Or was there something deeper, as sense of companionship and meaning that Lindsey had found in Caleb that she hadn't found with anybody else?

It couldn't be, Caleb told himself. *How can you develop feelings like that for someone after only a week or so?*

Suddenly confused and downhearted, Caleb lowered his head into the palms of his hands and let it rest there as he gazed at the floor. He and Lindsey had spent every waking moment together for the past week, so perhaps it was plausible that something deeper between them could exist. So many experiences had been shared between them in that small amount of time. Even Caleb couldn't deny that it had all meant something. He cared about Lindsey too, but was it that strong?

Oh Lord, he whispered, *suddenly I'm having all these mixed feelings for Lindsey. I should be satisfied that she's in Your care now, one of Your children, and that I can leave her with that peace of mind; but all I can think about is the fact that she's gonna be gone. Oh God, help me to figure out what this all means.*

Caleb didn't know how long he sat there gazing at the floor as his mind churned and his emotions were cast out to sea, left sloshing in the waves.

The sound of spraying water stopped, and Caleb realized that Lindsey was finished with her shower. He had to get focused and concentrate on the day ahead; he mustn't waste all his efforts on what might have been, or could be. For now his task was to drive Lindsey home to Marion, Virginia. After that, well, he would cross that bridge when he came to it.

The morning wore on in a rush as Lindsey swiftly went about finishing her morning routine, all the while reminding Caleb to "hurry up" or "get moving." Her adamant demeanor annoyed Caleb, especially since Lindsey was supposed to be frightened about seeing her father, not insistent. He almost made a comment to Lindsey to "cool it," but in the end he decided against it. He knew Lindsey must be terrified inside and she was only trying to be courageous. Caleb didn't want to upset her any more than she had already been during the past week and a half.

By 9:57 that Saturday morning, on the first day of November 1997, Caleb and Lindsey were all packed and ready to hit the road.

Lindsey's heart skipped a beat as the Ford pulled into the curb in front of Terry Milholland's house. Lindsey only glanced quickly at the house before flinging her head around to set pleading eyes on Caleb. "I can't do this," she uttered desperately, and Caleb could see her eyes becoming teary.

"Of course you can, Lindsey," Caleb tried to assure her. "We've come all this way, and you haven't backed out yet. So I *know* you can do this."

From inside the house Terry pulled back the curtains in the kitchen window and noticed the small blue truck parked outside his house. His heart suddenly began beating rapidly as he noticed the back of a girl's head. Obviously she was talking to the driver. Terry's breath caught in his throat, and he suddenly felt as if he had been running up and down flights of stairs and was suffering from fatigue. He was weak and nervous. *I can't do this,* he thought to himself. *She's right there, outside my house. That's Lindsey. That's my daughter.* His eyes became moist and suddenly a hand was at his shoulder: Jenna.

"Is that her out there?" she asked quietly, almost in a whisper.

Terry stalled for a moment to compose him self before answering. "Yeah," he barely replied.

Lindsey shook her head back and forth, and Caleb grabbed her hands to calm her.

"I'll go with you," he offered, squeezing Lindsey's hands between his own in a gesture of sympathy and support.

"Okay," Lindsey replied somberly. For a few more minutes, they sat in the truck unmoving. From Lindsey's uneven breathing, Caleb could tell she was a nervous wreck. Reaching out his hand, he pushed a wisp of Lindsey's hair back behind her ear, and Lindsey stared up at him in surprise.

"You won't leave me?" she asked quietly.

"No," Caleb whispered back. "I'll stay here tonight just to make sure you'll be okay the first night. I'll call you later today and tomorrow morning before I go, okay?" Lindsey nodded, and without another word he opened his door and walked around to Lindsey's door. She finally turned her head back toward the house and noticed the blue and green plaid curtains in the small kitchen window swaying as if they had just been moved.

Caleb opened her door, and slowly Lindsey slid out of the truck. As she stood staring at the house in front of her, Caleb ran to the bed of the truck to retrieve her luggage. Then, coming back to Lindsey's side, he gently took her hand in his own and began advancing up the driveway, pulling Lindsey along. She reluctantly but willingly forced her self to budge, thoughts and pleads and recollections of the past plundering her brain.

The front door opened before Lindsey and Caleb could make it to the porch steps, and Lindsey saw her father for the first time in years. He stood in the doorway, his face etched with emotions Lindsey understood right away. He looked unfamiliar to her, and she almost wondered whether they were at the right house. But from the silence on his lips to the painful joy reflected in his eyes, Lindsey knew this was him; this was her father.

"Lindsey?" he barely said.

She swallowed, attempting the force down the knot that was stuck in her throat. "Yeah," she whispered, and the tears came.

"I'm so sorry about Jillian," Terry said.

Lindsey couldn't respond. Her chin quivered as she tried to control the emotion that was itching to be released. Caleb didn't say a word as Lindsey let go of his hand and began walking up the steps toward her father. Terry came down to meet her, and when he did, he hesitated a few moments before flinging his arms around her and hugging her for the first time in ten years. Lindsey stood there, feeling slightly uncomfortable, but after a short moment, she brought her arms up and hugged her father back.

Through muffled cries, Terry told Lindsey how sorry he was for the past years, and Lindsey couldn't respond except with tears. Caleb backed away to return to his truck and give Lindsey and Terry their space. Before he could turn around, though, he noticed the small woman standing at the doorway smiling at him, silently thanking him.

The gray sky was thick with clouds, and as they moved along, hiding the sun in their folds, Caleb drove away without glancing back in his rearview mirror.

"So Lindsey, what kind of career aspirations do you have for your future?" It was a simple, typical type of question to ask a teenager, so Jenna didn't think twice before asking it, yet she couldn't deny the tension building around her from the awkwardness of the moment. Somehow she thought meeting Lindsey would be easier than it was.

Lindsey picked up her cup filled with Diet Coke and took a sip. She turned her head to stare out the restaurant window at the pedestrians and vehicles passing by. Marion was a nice, cute little town. She liked how trees and bushes lined most of the roads and sidewalks, especially at this time of year. Although it was a dark, bleak autumn day the colors of fall were brightly evident in the environment. Lindsey sighed and folded her hands in her lap. She wondered how she would answer Jenna's question.

"Well," she began, still gazing out the window. "I haven't really thought much about that. I mean, there are things that I've thought I'd like to do, but then I always find something about it that I don't like and so I keep searching. Nothing really seems to appeal to me."

"Well, what kinds of things do you like to do? That should give you an idea of a career choice."

"Yeah, well I like to write, I guess. I'm kind of an artsy person, but artistic careers seem hard to come by – you know, like being an actor, or a dancer, or a painter or writer."

"Have you done any freelance work?" Terry asked, savoring every word his daughter had to say about her life. He was so intrigued, especially because a lot of the things she had described about herself reminded him of himself when he had been her age.

"Well, not really. I mean, I wrote short stories and poems for the school newspaper, and I write in my journal a lot, but I haven't done anything really serious."

"You should think about writing, Lindsey. It sounds like you'd be great at it," Jenna praised. Lindsey just shrugged her shoulders. What was eating her? She couldn't figure out why she wasn't happier or more elated than she was at that moment. Jenna continued on. "You could do children's books, or work in the publishing or editing industry. Or have you ever thought about journalism?"

"I don't like research," Lindsey admitted flatly. She picked up her fork and poked at the mashed potatoes on her plate. Suddenly she had lost her appetite. Terry began speaking, but Lindsey was too busy checking her watch that she didn't notice what he was saying. It was almost 8:30 p.m. Lindsey had spent all day with Terry and Jenna. At first it had been awkward. It was as if Lindsey had just showed up at these strange people's house for some weird reason she had forgotten about. There had been so much to learn and so much to see and so much to cry about throughout the day. But Lindsey hadn't wanted to think about any of the bad times, and she was sure her father felt the same, so nothing controversial had really come up between them yet.

By the afternoon, Lindsey had become more comfortable with Terry, and she had finally remembered his face. Being able to recognize him put her more at ease, yet she had still questioned herself all day as to why she was there. Now, as she sat in a booth in a restaurant with her father and step-mother sitting across from her, she told herself it was just gonna take some time getting used to, that's all. In a week or so, she'd feel she belonged here. Yeah, that was all she needed, time.

"Lindsey?"

Lindsey thrust her head up and realized Terry had been speaking to her. "I'm sorry," she apologized. "My mind is somewhere else."

Terry nodded, wondering what it was that was swimming through Lindsey's head. He figured she must have so many questions, so much emotion inside that was just bursting to get out, yet he didn't know where to begin to make it all up to her. He had to say something, though. "Lindsey," he began slowly, hesitantly, "I know you probably have a lot of questions about what happened between your mom and me."

Lindsey looked down again and shook her head. "Not really. I mean, it doesn't really matter anymore, does it?"

"Don't you want to know what happened? I feel like I should explain."

For a long while, Lindsey couldn't say anything. The waiter came and offered the three more coffee. After he filled Jenna's cup and left, Lindsey spoke. "Me and Mom didn't talk about it much, but I know what happened. You don't have to explain anything. It doesn't matter now because I know you're different. I can tell just by looking at you that you're not the same person. In a way that's kind of odd because it's like I don't know you. But I'd rather know you as you are now than as you were."

"I *am* different, Lindsey. I've grown up a lot in the past ten years."

Lindsey nodded and a smile stretched across her face as she thought about her past week with Caleb. "I've grown up a lot, too, just in the past two weeks."

"Why did you come here, Lindsey?" Jenna asked curiously. "I don't mean that in a sarcastic way, but I'm just curious as to why you suddenly decided to mend ties with your father after all these years."

"I," Lindsey began, fixing her eyes on Jenna. Although she seemed to be looking straight at her, her eyes glazed over in thought as her gaze went right through the woman sitting across from her. "I didn't know what else to do," she answered quietly.

Caleb paced the small motel room back and forth from the window over to the door. He had just spoken to his parents on the phone, so they were expecting him tomorrow morning. He was so restless, so excited to leave and see his parents that he felt as if he could jump right out of his skin at any moment and just take off! But he couldn't leave Lindsey. She was expecting a call from him.

He checked the clock on the bed stand. It read 9:06 p.m. He had tried calling half an hour ago, but nobody at Lindsey's father's house had answered. They must be out doing some family-type thing, Caleb had figured. *She should be back by now,* he told himself.

Picking up the phone receiver and dialing the number, he waited anxiously for an answer on the other end of the line. After five rings, Caleb was just about to hang up when a woman answered.

"Hello, this is the Milholland residence."

"Hi, this is Caleb Lockwood. I'm calling for Lindsey."

"Caleb? Oh you're the young man that brought her here."

"Yeah, I told her I'd stick around town for the night just to make sure she was getting along fine."

Jenna smiled. "That's very thoughtful, Caleb. We're just walking in from dinner, so I'll go get Lindsey for you."

"Thank you very much." Caleb waited as Jenna set down the receiver and called Lindsey.

"Lindsey, you have a phone call from Caleb."

Lindsey's smile widened and her heart raced at the news. Trying not to appear too thrilled, she politely asked where she could find the phone and Jenna directed her to it.

"Hi, Caleb," she said as normally as possible when she picked up the receiver.

"Hey there, how's it all going?" he asked quietly and considerately.

Lindsey wanted to cry at the sound of his voice, so thoughtful and protective. "I already miss you," she admitted, trying to hold back the tears. "This is all really, really, well, weird. I don't know if I can get used to this."

"Just give it some time," Caleb assured her, "and don't forget to pray."

"Yeah, that's what I told myself." She sighed. "So, did you talk to your parents?"

"Yeah, I did, and they're expecting me tomorrow. I can't wait. I feel like it's been forever since I've seen them."

So tomorrow you're gonna be gone for good. "Well, I'm glad you're excited. It will be good seeing them again."

"Was it good seeing your father again?"

Lindsey's eyes dimmed. "I don't know. I didn't remember him at first, so it was a little odd." She sighed again, blowing her bangs up from her forehead. "Don't forget to call me when you make it home tomorrow," she finally said.

"I won't."

"And be a safe driver."

"I will. Hey, do you want me to stop by tomorrow morning before I head out of town? It would be kinda early, but...."

"No," Lindsey stated, not so positively. "It probably would be best if you didn't." The words came out slowly, choppy, uncertain.

"All right," Caleb said slowly. After a long moment of silence, Lindsey knew that it was time to say good-bye. If she hung on any longer, she'd lose her head and start bawling all over the place.

"Caleb, I gotta go now," she whispered.

"All right."

"I'll talk to you later."

"We'll get together soon, okay?"

"Okay."

"Bye, Lindsey. Take care."

"You too." Those last words barely escaped Lindsey's lips, and as she heard Caleb hang up and the line go dead, the tears began falling out of her eyes uncontrollably. Again she was stuck in the unfamiliar with nobody and nothing to give her comfort.

No, wait. That wasn't true. She knew that wasn't true anymore. She had Jesus, of course. She had her newfound Lord and Savior.

Suddenly she wondered about her father and Jenna. Were they Christians? Did they know about God? If they did, she thought, it would make things a whole lot easier.

"Did you say good-bye to him?" Jenna asked as she walked into the kitchen and found Lindsey wiping her eyes.

Lindsey nodded. Jenna walked up to Lindsey wondering whether she should hug her or try to say some comforting words to her. In the end she just stood there and spoke. "I know this is incredibly difficult for you, Lindsey," she said. "It is for us, too. I mean, Terry's elated that you're here. You don't know how much he was looking forward to you coming here after you called." Lindsey looked up at her but stayed silent. Jenna went on. "I myself was a tad bit indecisive about it all. I mean, Terry never told me about his past life. I never knew about you. This was all just a big whack on the back of my head, you know?"

Lindsey's eyes widened. "You didn't know about me?"

"I didn't know about you or Jillian. I mean, I guess I knew about Jillian; I knew that Terry had a previous wife, but that's about it." She stopped and thought a moment before pulling out a chair and sitting down. Lindsey followed suit. "I guess it's partly my fault, though, that I didn't know about Terry's former life because I never bothered to really ask or find details, you know? I just trusted him and figured that everything he told me was enough, and I didn't need to know anything else. I loved him. People do crazy things for love, sometimes. That's why I'm still here, Lindsey. This is gonna be a big change for us all, especially me because all of a sudden I have a step-daughter thrust at me, but I'm willing because I love Terry."

Lindsey was wiping her eyes some more. Jenna hadn't known about her? It was all so complicated and confusing, and Lindsey's head began to spin once more. She started to feel dizzy. She had a father, and she had a stepmother, too, but she didn't feel like it. Not yet, anyway.

"I don't feel good," she said, standing up and putting one hand on her throbbing head.

"Oh, you must be exhausted," Jenna exclaimed, helping Lindsey up. "We'd better put you to bed."

For the next few moments as Jenna was at her side, Lindsey almost felt normal again, but not quite. *It'll just take time,* she told her self again for the hundredth time that day.

Sleep was hard to come by, even as exhausted as Lindsey was. After lying in bed for almost two hours with churning anxieties and thoughts creeping in and out of her head, sleep finally found her, and she drifted off restlessly.

Twenty-Four

You will know Christ's love, which goes far beyond any knowledge.
– Ephesians 3:19

Two weeks later: Saturday, November 15, 1997

"Mommy, I can't find my shoes," Andrea wailed down the hallway as she poked her head out of her bedroom door. "Mom?"

Mary hurried from the kitchen, checking the silver watch on her wrist and swiping her hair behind her shoulders. She had been watching out of the kitchen window for Bryan.

"I'm here," she called as she walked down the hall past Andrea and into her own bedroom to check her image in the mirror.

"MOM! Where's my shoes?"

"Andrea, I don't know, honey," Mary called from her room. "Did you check under your bed and in your closet?"

"Well, yeah," Andrea stated matter-of-factly, putting her hands on her hips as she stood resolutely in the middle of the hallway.

"Well," Mary mumbled, "find another pair, and hurry, or we're gonna be late."

Andrea rolled her eyes, sighed in dismay and entered her tiny square bedroom to seek out another acceptable pair of shoes. It was Saturday afternoon and Bryan was going to take them both out to lunch and then to the zoo. After the zoo, Andrea was going to be dropped off at her grandparents house so that her mother and Bryan could go out that night.

Andrea flung the doors to her closet open and peered inside. She slumped to the floor and started putting an old, tattered pair of tennis shoes on. She had wanted to wear her nice dress shoes since they were going out to lunch, but those she couldn't find. So she had to settle with the musty, dirt caked old tennis shoes that were wearing out at the toes. Well, she thought, perhaps Bryan could remedy that. If she mentioned something about her shoes at the zoo, then he'd probably offer to buy her a new pair. He'd been doing that a lot lately – coming to see her mom, eating at their house with them, taking Andrea to special places and buying her neat things – personally Andrea rather liked it. It reminded her of when her father and mother still lived together. Her father still took her every other weekend to stay with him, and they had fun together, but it just wasn't the same anymore. She didn't understand why her mommy and daddy had to live apart from each other, but having Bryan around made it easier. He cheered her mommy up a lot. Mary had started going to church with him every Sunday. Last Sunday Andrea had gone with them. She didn't go to the big service that her mom and Bryan went to, but a fun room for the kids where they played games and did fun activities and learned about God. Andrea liked church and was excited about going tomorrow.

Picking herself up off the floor, she heard a knock at the front door suddenly and gasped in excitement. "It's Bryan!" she yelled, dashing out of her room and down the hall to the door. Mary followed behind her.

"Hey there!" Bryan greeted gleefully. "Are you all ready to go?"

"Yeah," Andrea answered proudly, turning to fetch her coat from the closet. "I couldn't find the shoes I wanted to wear so I had to wear *these* old ones." She held a foot out and made a face as she said it for effect.

"Well, would you like help looking for the other shoes?" Bryan asked, smiling up at Mary. She smiled back. Andrea frowned. That was not the response she was hoping to get.

"No," she stated flatly.

Bryan walked over to Mary and leaned in to kiss her cheek. "It's good to see you," he said, although he had seen her the night before. Things between them were getting pretty serious, but Bryan was unlike any man she'd ever known or been with. He was different: respectful, cautious, and godly. Mary hadn't seen any of it coming at first, but she had realized that from the first day she met Bryan she liked him. He had been so thoughtful and caring. For a moment, Mary thought about the young man she had met at work almost a month ago, the young man who had been traveling across the country to North Carolina; Caleb. It was him whom had introduced her to Christ. He was the one who spoke a caring word when she needed to hear one and who had ignited her interest in God because of how he had appeared – so … so, loving and humble. One young man with a tender disposition and a few thoughtful words had changed her world. She would be forever grateful to that boy. She wondered how he was doing and whether he was back home safe where he wanted to be. She figured he was as she thanked God for him.

"So are you ready?" Bryan asked, wrapping his arm around her waist.

"I feel like I've been ready forever," Mary said with laughter in her eyes. "I was waiting for you. You've got me feeling like I'm back in high school again for heaven's sake!"

"Oh, I'm sorry," Bryan apologized jokingly. "So what you're saying is that I make you feel extremely young and attractive and desirable?"

Mary laughed and shook her head. "Uh, something like that," she chuckled.

"Can we go now?" Andrea looked slightly annoyed, not only from the shoe incident but also because of the current hold up between her mother and Bryan.

"Let's head out!" Bryan exclaimed, leading Mary and Andrea to the front door before him.

"Thanks for doing this, Bryan," Mary said once they were out the door. "Andrea loves the zoo and I don't always have time to take her to do anything. I feel so neglectful. She spends most of her time at my parents' house."

"Don't worry about it," Bryan assured Mary. "You know I love spoiling you guys."

"I know," Mary smiled. What a wonderful turn her world had taken; a strange and unexpected turn, but wonderful nevertheless. Climbing into the passenger side seat of Bryan's car, Mary thanked God for his work in her life.

Lindsey arrived at the airport fifteen minutes after Caleb did, and after checking in her luggage and making sure of her departure time, she strode to the waiting area where she would eagerly anticipate the flight for Seattle, Washington.

The waiting area was crowed with people reading newspapers and chatting with one another as they waited for the plane, and Lindsey lifted her eyebrows in amazement. She hadn't expected so many people, and now she didn't have a spot in which to sit. Every seat was taken. And where was Caleb?

Before she could answer that question she noticed Caleb striding toward her. Immediately her frown grew into a bright smile and she dropped her backpack and flew into Caleb's hug. Instantly she teared up.

"Oh my gosh, Caleb, I missed you so much!"

"Me too," Caleb admitted. It had been unexpectedly hard to not be able to see Lindsey during the past two weeks. It had been wonderful seeing his parents again and starting a new life with them, but a day hadn't gone by that he hadn't thought about Lindsey. He had called her a few times and she had sometimes been good, sometimes not. Concerned and worried that Lindsey wasn't adjusting well, Caleb was actually relieved to hear the news that she had decided to go home to Washington. Lindsey had called him up last

Thursday to tell him about it. She was grateful that God had given her the opportunity to see her father again and mend the broken ties between them, yet she wasn't comfortable there in Virginia, even after almost two weeks. There was still an empty, heavy place in her heart, and Lindsey missed her grandparents and friends back at home so much. She knew she needed to go back because that was where her home was. She told Caleb how much she loved her father and how happy she was to have met him and brought him back into her life, but living with him was not the way it was supposed to be. She could always visit him any time she wanted to or needed to, she had told Caleb. And now they would always keep in touch. He had a separate life from her and she had a separate life from him, and it was just too difficult to try and work their lives into each other's.

Lindsey had asked Caleb if he could meet her here at the airport so that they could say their good-byes to each other.

"I think you're making the right choice, Lindsey," Caleb said. Then, "Where's your dad and Jenna?"

"They had to work today," she explained. "And I told them not to come. I thought it might be harder for them, and I wanted to be able to see you and talk to you privately."

Caleb nodded his head. There could have been so many things to say to Lindsey, but he was void of everything except a single nod and the smile he managed to stretch across his face.

Lindsey noticed his loss of words and realized she felt the same way, too. She began to laugh. "Well, so much for that! We don't even have anything to say to each other."

"There's a lot I want to say. I just don't know what it is, yet."

"Well, first of all I want to apologize to you," Lindsey said.

"For?"

"Well, for giving you such a hard time during our trip," Lindsey went on. Caleb's eyes widened.

"No, you didn't give me a hard time, Lindsey."

"Well, I was kind of stubborn, you know? But I just want to let you know how much you really do stand out, Caleb, whether you see it or not. I have never met or known anyone like you. I … I can't even explain how much you stand out as one of God's children. I just hope I can be as strong as you are some day.

"I'm not strong," Caleb insisted. "I just did what I thought God would have me do. And I prayed a whole lot, so that helped, too."

"You know, Caleb, out of all the crazy decisions I've made in the past month, I think asking Jesus into my heart was the smartest one."

"I think you're right," Caleb smiled.

Lindsey glanced behind her and noticed a few vacant seats where people had left, so she grabbed Caleb's arm and they sat down.

"Want to know what the other two best decisions I've made were?" she asked Caleb, smiling slyly.

"What's that?"

"Coming on this trip and meeting you. I mean, if it weren't for those, I wouldn't have come to know Christ."

Caleb put his head down for a moment to hide the emotion that was building up inside him. "It would've happened somewhere along the way, Lindsey. God was going after you and He wouldn't have given up no matter what."

"I know, but I'm glad it happened this way."

"Me too, although you did present a big challenge for me."

Lindsey laughed. So Caleb did agree that she had been stubborn and a challenge. "It's amazing to think about how my life has changed so much in such a short time," Lindsey said, astouded, shaking her head at the thought.

"I know. It's overwhelming, huh?"

"Yeah. I mean, besides not being in high school anymore and just starting out in the real world, I've lost my mother, met my dad, made up with my grandparents, gone through so much emotional strife, and I met Jesus."

"Well, I'm sure things won't stop there. Once you get home, there'll be a lot more changes. That's the one thing God promises in our lives, changes. Changes for the better."

"You got that right," Lindsey agreed wholeheartedly. She looked away from Caleb and seemed to be staring at a spot on the floor in front of her. "It's almost scary to think about all the changes that'll take place when I get home. I mean, I'm a different person now, and I definitely want to share with my family and friends what has happened to me. I wonder how they'll react to me."

Caleb shrugged. "They'll love you no matter what. And most likely they'll welcome your changes because they're such positive ones."

Lindsey nodded. She was nervous about going home and seeing her grandparents. Most of all she was nervous about seeing Marianne and, especially, Nick. Would they snicker behind her back as to how crazy she had been to travel across the country only to come right back home? Would they shoot little I-told-you-so glances in her direction? Probably not, but Lindsey couldn't help feeling a tad bit foolish about her previous behaviors and personality. They all must have thought she was a nut! But now things would be different, and although Lindsey was still shaken up and grieved by her mother's death, her family and friends would see how much more stable she was with Jesus in her life.

Lindsey and Caleb shared a moment of silence, observing the swarms of people coming in and out of waiting areas and doors and lobbies, and listening to the shuffle of their feet as they glided down the smooth floors or stomped to and from chairs. It had been a while before Lindsey finally spoke up again.

"I also wanted to thank you, Caleb."

Caleb looked at Lindsey. She was watching him with wide, serious eyes. "What for?" he asked.

"Well, you know; for getting me here. For taking me to the hospital and letting me ride with you on our trip, and for taking care of me and teaching me about God."

Lindsey thought she noticed Caleb's cheeks redden slightly.

"You don't know how much it meant to have you with me during this time in my life. There were so many times I felt like I wouldn't be able to survive without you. I depended on you a lot, you know?"

Caleb just nodded as he drank in Lindsey's words. She went on.

"I think I depended on you so much because you were so protective of me, you know? You looked after me during the whole car accident, and you looked after me spiritually; not to mention you punched that guy out for me at the mall."

Caleb shook his head and chuckled at the remembrance. "Yeah, yeah, that."

Lindsey scanned over Caleb with her eyes, the laughter in them suddenly replaced with profoundness. "I think that's when I really fell for you," she admitted. "I realized then how much you cared for me. I would've loved to stay with you and for our little adventure to keep going, but … I understand now that it can't be that way because I would depend on you too much.

"All my life I've depended on people, and in one way or another, they've let me down. Now … now I finally realize that I can depend on Jesus, and you've taught me that He's more reliable than any person could ever be. *You* taught me that, Caleb. I needed you for that … to open my heart to Jesus, but now … now I don't need you anymore." Lindsey stopped as her words caught in her throat, the words that were coming out slowly but carefully. She was on the verge of tears. She swallowed and looked away from Caleb. "And to say that I just *want* you … well, that would be selfish. I need to get to know my Lord."

Caleb's head lowered again as the tears poured out from the corners of his eyes. He was embarrassed to let Lindsey see them. Lindsey looked at Caleb and noticed his slumped posture as he stared at the floor. She also noticed his hands rubbing his eyes as he tried to swipe away the tears.

"Hey," she said very quietly, leaning down in order to get Caleb's attention. He tipped his head slightly in her direction and just peeked at her.

At that moment all the sights and sounds around the two had faded into a hazy, blurry mass. Lindsey was only aware of the moment. The sight of Caleb with tears running down his cheeks hit a nerve in her and she knew she would start bawling at any second.

"Please don't cry," she whispered. "I don't think I could handle it." She swiped a hand across his cheek.

Caleb turned his face away and once more stared at the ground between his feet. "You don't know how much it means to me to know that I've been used by God in such an awesome way."

"I think I can guess," Lindsey replied, and Caleb smiled.

All at once, Lindsey's flight was announced, and she and Caleb scrambled to their feet. Lindsey picked up her backpack and threw it around her shoulder. She stared up at Caleb. "I guess this is it."

"Yeah. Take care, okay?"

"I will." She forced a weak smile and brought her face up to kiss Caleb's cheek. He smiled as she backed away.

"Thank you, Caleb, for everything." She laughed nervously. "I know that sounds hoaky, but I totally mean it."

"I know," Caleb replied.

Lindsey nodded, and after a reluctant moment, she swung around and started following the herd of people moving toward the doorway to get onto the plane. Lindsey couldn't stop the flow of tears the whole way onto the plane. She forced herself not to look back at the doorway, but even if she had, she wouldn't have seen Caleb. He had already turned around and was heading out of the airport.

Chelsea and Daniel Johns were already at the Seatac Airport in Seattle by the time the plane arrived and eagerly awaiting their granddaughter's return. Having urged her husband to show up early at the airport, Daniel had finally given in and for nearly an hour and a half now, Chelsea had been leafing through nearly eight different magazines as the couple sat in the waiting area.

When people started piling off the plane and walking through the doors that led into the waiting area, Chelsea and Dan both stood up – Chelsea rather quickly while Dan sighed heavily from fatigue and had to push himself up from his hard seat. His weariness didn't keep the elation from mounting inside him, though, when he saw Lindsey stroll through the doors with her hands clutching her backpack straps.

Before she had a chance to glance around thoroughly and spot her grandparents, Lindsey heard the excited squeal of an all too familiar yet painfully relieving voice.

"Lindsey!" Chelsea shouted, jumping up and squeezing through people in order to get to Lindsey. Lindsey's eyes widened with surprise and laughter as she saw her grandmother bounding across the waiting area toward her. She dropped the backpack from her shoulders and walked quickly to meet her grandmother, with Dan close behind her.

"Hey," Lindsey greeted as she came upon her family. Chelsea stopped right in front of her as she noticed the uncertain look twinkling in Lindsey's eyes. Was that excitement or disappointment? Her eyes were sort of glazed over and hard to read, yet her lips were smiling slightly. Was she unsure of something?

For a few moments, the two women stood gazing into each other's faces. Dan noticed the hesitation and quickly moved in to intercede.

"Lindsey," he said quietly. She focused her gaze on him. He noticed the moisture forming in the corners of her eyes. "Is this what you want?" he asked boldly. "To be here with your grandmother and me ... is this what you really want?"

Lindsey thought about it for a moment. She already missed Caleb terribly, and surprisingly, she missed her dad and Jenna, too. Maybe she should have spent some more time with them. Maybe she hadn't given herself enough time to rationally think through an explanation of where to go next....

No! She scolded herself. She wasn't taking herself anywhere! God was in control! He would work things out no matter what, and she knew that the right thing was to go home and fix the situation with her family and friends. There had been too much left behind there, too many unspoken feelings and words and thoughts. She was a different person now, and they needed to know that, also. The past was gone, and she needed to focus on the moment. Jesus was with her now.

Yet, she was confused still, especially so as she faced these two adults who had been so caring and loving toward her throughout her life and were her only real family. Was this what she wanted? The realization that she was home hit hard and seemed to shatter all reason, sending the pieces flying in all directions. Doubt began creeping up in its place. She was scared to step forward, to walk through the entrance of another huge change in her life. Although she knew in her heart that it was the right thing to do, she couldn't help feeling as though she wanted to turn and run away again. Wouldn't that be the easiest thing? To just drop it all and go? To try to erase all the bad stuff, to forget about all the uncertain stuff, to ignore all the frightening and life-changing moments? Questions began swirling in Lindsey's mind, and for a moment, she felt that the doubt and uncertainty would overwhelm her, yet a deeper prodding pushed her onward.

Finally, Lindsey tilted her chin upward slowly and began nodding. The emotion inside of her hindered her from speaking, lest she break down and cry once again as she had so many times within the last month. Yes, she told Jesus silently, this is what I need to do. Thank you for bringing me home.

Tears flooded out of Chelsea's eyes and she grabbed Lindsey in a hug. Dan joined in on the hug, and by the time most of the people in the waiting area had drained out and gotten on their ways, Lindsey, Dan and Chelsea were left behind, filling each other in on the latest news.

Twenty-Five
Epilogue

Who is a God like you? You forgive sin and overlook the rebellion of your faithful people. You will not be angry forever because you would rather show mercy.
– Micah 7:18

"I can't believe it's just a week 'till Christmas!" Lindsey exclaimed as she helped her grandfather dig in the attic for the Christmas tree decorations. It was the eighteenth of December already, and they were just putting a tree up. The rest of the household decorations, including the outdoor house lights, had been put up near the beginning of the month, but Lindsey had felt that they should wait for the tree. They didn't want it to grow dry and brown after all by the time the twenty-fifth arrived.

"It snowed again last night. Did you notice?" Dan asked as he shuffled through the contents of a worn out box, waving his hand in front of him to disperse the dust in the air. He put a fist up to his mouth as he coughed.

"Yeah," Lindsey replied excitedly. "I'm glad, too, because now me, Marianne, and Nick can go sledding on Saturday like we had planned. I love the snow."

"So what are your plans later tonight?"

"Well, what day is it again?"

"Thursday."

"Hmmm," Lindsey wondered, furrowing her brows in thought. "Oh! Well there's college group tonight at church."

"Are you gonna go?"

"Yeah. I invited Marianne and Nick, but they haven't really given me a straight answer yet."

"Didn't Nick go with you last week?"

"Yeah, actually he's been coming with me the last few times. I think he's still a little uncertain about it, though."

"What do you mean?"

Lindsey chin lifted and her eyes narrowed as a sneeze crept upon her.

"Bless you," Dan said.

"Thanks," Lindsey sniffed. "Anyway, what I mean is that I think he's still not used to me, you know, being a Christian and all. It was like, I just suddenly came home one day and I was almost a whole different person. So suddenly Nick and I, and Marianne and I, have all these little conflicting beliefs and principles, and it's just hard for them to adjust to me."

"Nick seems to be interested in church, though, if he still keeps on going," Dan offered. "There must be something there that he's liking."

Lindsey grunted. "Nick's not interested in church, Grandpa, he's interested in me. I'm pretty sure he's only going to please me, because he knows I want him there."

"Guys will do almost anything for the object of their affection." Dan said cheerfully, recollecting the numerous times in his past where he had sacrificed his reputation and made a fool of himself just to impress Chelsea. He smiled.

Lindsey spoke again. "I suppose," she mumbled, lifting her eyebrows and rolling her eyes in irritation.

"Honey, if you know Nick cares for you so much, which he obviously does, and that he's seriously sorry for what happened between you two, which is obviously is, then why don't you consider giving him a second chance?"

Lindsey knew the question had been coming. She was aware that her grandparents weren't oblivious to Nick's feelings for her. Yet they had always held back, kept out of what wasn't their business. Now Dan had found the perfect opportunity to question what had been in his mind for the past month since Lindsey had been home.

"It isn't so much a question of second chances in general," Lindsey explained, stopping from her work and sitting on her knees on the dusty attic floor. She swiped some long blond strands from her eyes. "I would give him a second chance any day if he just…."

She stalled. If he just what? Loved Jesus? She knew it wouldn't be wise to get into a relationship with Nick unless he could understand and share her faith. Jesus needed to remain first, and she knew it.

Over the last month, she had found herself questioning God so many times, and her commitment to him. Without Caleb with her to provide the comfort and the answers she sought, Lindsey had felt lost at first. She hadn't known what to do next. Thankfully, Caleb's phone calls had helped a lot and had aided in sustaining her faith. Yet she knew she couldn't depend on Caleb forever. She needed to make her faith her own. Being involved in church had helped a lot, and Lindsey looked forward to going twice a week as she had been for the last month.

After a few moments of silence, Dan spoke up. “If he just what?” he asked.

Lindsey shook her head and began studying a crystal candle vase, overturning it in her hands as she replied. “If he could just … be willing to understand me more, and my faith; my new self. It’s like he just wants to jump right in and begin where we left off, but I’m not the same Lindsey as before, you know? I mean, I have forgiven him for what happened, and I trust him. I can see that he’s changed a lot too. But until he wants to get serious with God, I can’t get serious with him because I don’t want to be dragged down. I have to learn to trust God, not men, you know?”

Dan wasn’t sure he knew, but he nodded anyway because they were wise words.

Chelsea and Dan used to attend church, but for many years they hadn’t, due to life’s busy schedules, and due to their own lack of interest in the church. Dan had never really known whether he truly believed in God, and now, with Lindsey’s sudden confession of faith, he had been challenged to question his own beliefs. She had him and Chelsea both seriously curious, and they had actually agreed to attend church with her this coming Sunday. Dan was a little nervous, but excited also. The change that had been made in Lindsey was alarming but wonderful, and when they had first heard her story Dan had been amazed. A little skeptical, but amazed. He wanted to check this God thing out for himself.

“Well,” Dan continued, “whatever reason lies behind Nick’s interest in church, the important thing is that he’s going, right?”

“Yeah, I suppose,” Lindsey replied.

“Perhaps he’s only been coming because of you, but maybe soon it won’t be like that anymore. Just give him a chance, okay?”

Lindsey nodded in reply. She sniffed again, rubbed her cheek where it was itching, and continued to sort through boxes to find the Christmas decorations.

After a few minutes, Lindsey walked over to the small attic window to investigate some more boxes. She once again blew some hair out of her face as she kneeled down. The small light peering in through the window caught her attention and she focused her eyes outside to the crystal blue water, the white-capped islands, and the frosty beach. It was still early in the afternoon, but the sky was a light gray color, sort of morose. Lindsey smiled in spite of it, though. Normally this kind of dull weather had a negative effect on her, but not today. It was nearly Christmas.

It would, of course, be her first Christmas without her mother.

Lindsey stared out the window for a long time thinking on that. She could hear the distant call of seagulls and the waves splashing on the beach. Hidden somewhere behind the veil of clouds she could see the dull light of the sun attempting to break through, but it couldn't. It was okay, though.

Lindsey knew this Christmas would be a good one, and that she would be okay.

Nick arrived early to pick up Lindsey for college group, and surprisingly Marianne was in the Mustang with him. Lindsey peeked out the window of her second-floor bedroom and smiled thankfully. So Marianne decided to come after all, she thought. That was good. It would be her first time, and today was supposed to be especially fun because it was a pre-Christmas sort of thing. The group was going to have a movie night and go out for pizza after doing the usual worship and a message.

Marianne's wavy hair bobbed and bounced as she and Nick strolled down the driveway to Lindsey's front door, trudging through the snow that hadn't been cleared away yet. Lindsey remembered when she had first seen Marianne the day after she had returned home on the plane. How she had missed her friend with the beautiful, lively hair that seemed to complement her shining personality! Despite the girls' excitement at seeing each other again, however, a small chasm had quickly built between them as Lindsey had professed her newfound faith. Marianne hadn't embraced the new change well. Lindsey figured it was probably because she was unfamiliar with it, and only knew the stereotypes behind Christians. Also, Lindsey was sure Marianne just felt that Lindsey was in another crazy "stage" of her life that the death of her mother had driven her to. It was sad that Marianne didn't seem to trust Lindsey or her choices. To Marianne, Lindsey was still "unstable," as Lindsey had overheard her tell Nick, once. It hadn't bothered her as much as she thought it should, though. She knew that she wasn't unstable, that the new change in her life was something that would last. It was permanent. It made her who she was, now. She prayed that Marianne as well as Nick would be able to understand that one day.

Lindsey rushed down the staircase, skipping the last few steps and just jumping over them, landing hard on the floor. She had the door pulled open before Nick or Marianne could even ring the doorbell.

Nick's face immediately lit up. "Hey!" he greeted buoyantly. "Someone's in a good mood today."

"That's because me and Gramps finally got the Christmas tree today and decorated it."

"Well let's see it," Nick requested, stepping in through the front door.

Marianne smiled at Lindsey as she followed behind him.

"Hey there," she said a little uneasily. Lindsey smiled back, but her heart silently began to break. She and Marianne hadn't spoken much at all lately, and it saddened Lindsey. She wondered if things would ever be the same between them again. Maybe one day Marianne would understand her and be able to see past their differences. For now, she was just happy that God was bringing her to church tonight. She quickly prayed that He would work in Marianne's heart.

Nick walked into the living room ahead of the two girls and was greeted by Dan and Chelsea, who were just coming in from a walk on the beach outside."

"Hey there, Nick," Dan greeted loudly. "Picking Lindsey up for church?"

"Yep," Nick said. Then, "Lindsey told us you got your tree so we had to see it."

Dan and Chelsea greeted Marianne as she appeared behind Nick, followed by Lindsey. For a few minutes the five people stood there sharing brief conversation, but Lindsey reminded them that they needed to be off unless they wanted to be late. In a matter of seconds, the three teenagers were piled into Nick's mustang and headed for church.

"Lindsey, Caleb called you tonight while you were gone."

Lindsey had just walked through the front door and was slipping off her jacket when she heard her grandmother speak.

"What was that?"

"Caleb called, dear."

"Oh yeah," Lindsey bopped herself on the forehead for forgetting. "I was supposed to be expecting his phone call today after church, but the whole group ended up going out for pizza and stuff."

Lindsey dashed upstairs to her room to call Caleb. She couldn't believe she had forgotten. For the first couple of weeks Lindsey had been back home, she and Caleb had called each other three or four times a week, if not more. But lately they had limited their phone time together, for no real known purposes. Lindsey couldn't believe she had actually forgotten, though.

She jumped on her bed and leaned against the headboard while picking up her phone receiver and dialing Caleb's number.

"Hello," came a quiet, groggy voice.

"Hey, Caleb, it's me. Sorry I'm calling so late, but I just got back."

"Hey, Lindsey," he said in barely more than a hoarse whisper. She had obviously woken him up. She had forgotten that he was three hours ahead of her in the time zone. "I called you earlier."

"Yeah, I know. I'm sorry I missed it. I totally forgot."

Caleb feigned insult and gasped. "Oh my gosh, you forgot about me? That sure makes me feel special."

Lindsey could tell he was smiling. She laughed. "Hey now, don't go making me feel bad!"

"You don't feel bad," Caleb commented. "Besides, it's probably a good sign that you forgot about me because it means that you're not relying on me so much, and that you can get to the other things in your life."

Lindsey frowned. What did that mean? She was about to tell Caleb how she didn't rely on him, but then changed her mind. She knew she did, she had, anyway. Maybe he was right. Her forgetting about him was probably a good sign.

"Well," Lindsey continued. "Guess what?"

"What's that?"

"I finally got Marianne to come to church with me tonight."

"That's great," Caleb replied, not sounding too enthused. Lindsey knew that he was just tired.

"Yeah, I thought so."

"Are you guys getting along any better?"

"Well, not really. We still haven't been speaking much. I feel bad sort of, because I don't take the initiative to call her when the opportunity arises. I end up doing something else, and I wonder if maybe it's my fault that we're not keeping in touch too well."

"Hey, friendship is a two-way street, okay? Don't blame yourself. You can only do so much, you know."

"I know," Lindsey sighed. I'll call her tomorrow and see if she wants to do something. It will be Friday night, after all."

"How's what's-his-name? Nick?"

Lindsey chuckled. "He's fine, too. He's still been coming to church with me." Her voice trailed off disappointedly and Caleb noticed it.

"What?" he asked. "Is that a bad thing?"

"Well, no, it's just," she sighed. "We had a little talk tonight and he definitely wants to get back together with me. I swear, he was nearly begging me, Caleb."

Caleb's heart flinched at those words, and suddenly he felt a little discontented. He quickly shook it away, though. "Really?" he mustered out. "What do you think?"

"I don't know," Lindsey admitted. "I guess I'd like to. Being around him the last month has made me realize how much I still care for him, but I want to be smart, you know? I can't just go and make hasty decisions, especially when God is involved, you know?"

"Well I'm glad you're thinking that way," Caleb assured her. "It seems you already know what you need to do or don't need to do."

"Yeah, I guess you're right," she replied. She was confused about Nick, but she knew for now what she needed to do, and she didn't want anything hindering her relationship with God.

"Have you talked to Nick about what he believes?" Caleb asked unexpectedly.

Lindsey frowned. "Well, no, not really. I've really only talked about my own faith, but I have been a little … indecisive, I guess, about asking him about his."

"So talk to him more about him," Caleb offered, "and find out where he stands. I'm sure he knows by now how important your faith is to you, and he's obviously not gonna sabotage that. He doesn't want to. He just wants to get to know you again. Just keep praying about it, okay? And talk to him some more. Maybe you guys could work things out."

Lindsey couldn't believe her ears. Caleb was actually trying to give her guy advice! She smiled. "Thanks, Caleb," she whispered. Then, "So is there any special girl in your life, yet?"

Caleb laughed. "Nah, not really. I'm not really looking, though. Hey, I told you that I applied to Campbell University, right?" he went on, changing the subject.

"Of course," Lindsey said.

"Well, I already got my acceptance letter."

"Caleb, that's great!"

"Thanks. I'm starting in the spring. I'm gonna keep working 'till then to make a little extra cash."

"That's so awesome. I get to start school real soon here."

"That's right, you're going to that community college with Marianne, right?"

"Yep. I start in less than a month, at the beginning of January."

"Are you excited?"

Lindsey sighed as she thought about it. "Yeah," she finally mustered out. "Yeah, it will definitely be new, but it will be nice, too. I signed up for some pretty interesting classes."

"That's good. I'm glad for you, Lindsey."

"Me too. God is truly wonderful."

"I agree."

After a few more minutes of short conversation, Caleb and Lindsey bid their farewells and their goodnights. As Caleb lowered the phone receiver down, he suddenly had a strange feeling. It had been a good conversation, but somehow a little upsetting. Caleb could already tell that they were beginning to drift away from each other pretty quickly. Their phone calls to each other were less and less frequent, and the conversations themselves became shorter every time. It wasn't that they were bored of each other, it was just the circumstances of life. They had lives apart from each other, on opposite ends of the country. Caleb knew it would be impossible to keep in touch forever. Once day they would probably lose all contact with each other whatsoever. But that didn't have to be bad thing, Caleb convinced himself. It was like Lindsey had told him at the airport the day she left him for good – she just didn't need him anymore.

Caleb lay awake for nearly a half an hour staring at the dark ceiling and thinking and praying. Somehow he knew for certain that he wouldn't hear from Lindsey again in a long time, nor would he see her again in a long time, if ever.

Lindsey sat on her bed staring directly in front of her across the room at the wall. Their conversation had seemed a bit odd. Clearly they were already drifting apart. There wasn't much more to tell each other about their lives than they already had, and once school started for both of them, it would be harder to keep in touch.

Lindsey hadn't thought about Caleb very often lately, and although she knew that it was most likely a good sign, it left her dispirited. Things between her and Caleb hadn't turned out the way she had wanted them at first, and now they couldn't. She had to be realistic. They were at opposite ends of the country and probably wouldn't see each other again in a long time. It just wasn't plausible. She had to get on with her life. Although she knew that she could call Caleb any time, or take the time and effort to actually visit him, she knew realistically that that would probably never happen, at least not any time soon. She would get too caught up in life. Maybe one day in the distant future, though....

Lindsey shook her head and slid underneath the covers. She didn't want to think about any of it. It was too trying, too confusing, too emotionally draining. There were people in her life she needed to focus on now, and that was her friends and family.

Lindsey slowly fell into sleep with thoughts of Caleb and Nick and Marianne and Grandma and Grandpa swimming in her brain. She dreamed about Caleb. She dreamed that the two of them were on a road trip together and stopped at a park for a picnic. They enjoyed a nice lunch and sat underneath the shady trees to protect themselves from the sun. They talked and laughed, and discussed many things. And then, for some reason, Caleb said good-bye and was suddenly gone. Lindsey wasn't worried, though, or sad. She knew somehow that things were going to be just fine.

February, 1998

It's been a while since I've talked to Caleb. I talked to him only twice last month, but not yet this month. Oh well, it's kind of sad, but I suppose I knew we couldn't stay buddy-buddy forever. Last time I heard he had a romantic interest, so that's probably good. She sounded like a neat girl; goes to church with him.

That means I will have to talk to Caleb soon and tell him that me and Nick are back together. Ahhh! Who would've guessed? Not me. I didn't see it coming at all! What can I say? I'm a sap, and on Valentine's Day Nick did this super-cute-romantic thing for me where we went out for dinner and dancing and all that great stuff. Then he got down on his knees like he was gonna propose and asked if I would be his girlfriend. It was so funny, but it was sweet, also.

Nick became a Christian at the beginning of this month. I was a little unsure at first about his motives – whether he just wanted to win me over, or whether he truly felt convicted by God. I know it was the latter. I'm a walking testimony to how Jesus saves and changes lives. I also know that Nick is genuine in his faith because I was there when he broke down in front of God, knowing that he needed to be changed. I felt so bad for him. I don't think I've ever seen Nick cry before. I think he realized for the first time how seriously he betrayed me when he cheated on me and how sinful that was. He wanted forgiveness. He admitted that he needed it. And I told him he could have it and I helped him pray. He's been in love with Jesus ever since.

Before all that, though, he was always really curious about Jesus and asked me loads of questions. I think I know what Caleb felt like when I was always pestering him, but Nick wasn't as bad as I was. I just kept praying for him – that he would be able to see his need for God. Talk about answering prayers! I'm still working on Marianne, though. I have no doubt that she will be changed in time. She's already growing curious, even more so now that Nick's found Jesus. She comes to church with us very often, now, almost every Thursday and Sunday. Thank You, Lord!

As for my grandparents – their time will come too. They have attended church with me a lot, but I don't think they're too serious about it yet, or about God. I will keep praying for them. I asked Caleb to, also. I don't know why, but since I've been home I can just feel the power of God working around me, in my family and friends. It's so awesome; it's so overwhelming;

it's the coolest thing in the world!

Oh! I think Nick just knocked on the front door! We're going out tonight with a group of people. School's been going great and I've met a lot of cool people and made some new friends. Welcome, Lindsey Milholland, to your new life. It's not a perfect life, it won't ever be, but it's going to be exciting and hopeful! I think for the first time I feel like I have something to look forward to. I'm not sure what that is, but I know it's there waiting for me and I'm looking forward to it. Thank You, Lord!

Oh! I just heard Grandma open the door to let Nick in. He's gonna be at my bedroom door soon, so I should probably go.

Mmmm, I'm suddenly in the mood for a cinnamon roll ... isn't that weird?

*

Printed in the United States
6066

9 781591 294177